Tell Me

This book is a work of fiction. Names, characters, places and incidents are the product of the author's imagination or are used fictitiously. Any resemblance to actual events, locales or persons, living or dead, is coincidental.

For Mercy
I love being on this journey with you

PART I

Chapter 1

1998 -

She was watching me again. The Purple Cauldron coffeehouse was filled with the Thursday night crowd and the blond poet with the emerald eyes and the black Doc Martens was sitting at the next table with a petite brunette, and she was watching me, Meagan Summers.

I turned my head and focused my attention back to the stage and the man up there who was boring the crowd with the monotonous way he recited his words. He wasn't very good. The blond was good. She was the star poet around here. She drew in the crowds and she knew how to keep them captivated. It had as much to do with her beauty as it did her poetry.

Jenna Bradshaw sat across from me drinking a mocha cappuccino and flipping my cigarette pack end over end on the table. Jenna didn't smoke. She was an aromatherapist and yoga instructor at the healing center next door. We shared the tenth floor of the building across the street and were closer than sisters.

"So have you heard from Basil yet?" she asked, referring to Basil Waite, the drummer/songwriter I had lived with for three years and had thrown out two months earlier when I'd returned home early from a business trip to find him in bed with a stoned nineteen-year-old. I was the publicity director for a national magazine called *Natural Beauty* and my job often required absences. Not a good thing when you shared an apartment with a sexy dark-haired drummer who had a perpetual hard-on. Basil was often my undoing. I worked while he got stoned and played video games. I remained monogamous, he did not.

"Once," I said. "He called yesterday to ask if I've forgiven him yet."

"Don't tell me you have," Jenna groaned.

"Please! If I'm in therapy for any reason, it's to stay away from him."

"Good."

Jenna adjusted the beads around her neck and kicked off her tan Birkenstocks. She was an earthy girl. Twenty-four years old and the most spiritual person I'd ever met. We'd lived across the hall from each other for five years, becoming friends when I was twenty-one and fairly new to the magazine game, and she was nineteen, living off a trust fund and deciding her destiny. We'd clicked instantly and had been best friends ever since. Jenna had studied to get her degree in aromatherapy and I had spent the next five years buying shares in the magazine --until I owned thirty-five percent-- and amassing a quiet little fortune playing the stock market and falling into a few good investments. People knew I had money; it just wasn't obvious how much. I tried to live fashionably but modestly. So far I'd been doing a good job.

Even Basil hadn't known how wealthy I really was. He accepted the black Saab I drove and the expensive clothes I wore as possessions that could fall within the salary I earned at the magazine. Anything more elaborate would have tipped him off and that was the last thing I needed. Who knew what the man would become if he thought I had money? It was a potential headache I was never interested in having.

The frosted doors at the back of the coffeehouse swung open and in bounced my sister Danielle, wearing khaki pants and a black rib knit sweater that clung to her breasts. Danielle was nineteen; a university student who lived at home with our parents and often came to me pleading the use of my couch after one of her many spats with our mother. Her wavy brown hair was pulled back in a floppy ponytail and she wore little makeup on her fresh, round face. We looked nothing alike. Danielle had a medium build with large breasts, a long upper torso, and short legs, while I had long legs, was slight of build, and had medium-sized breasts. She looked like our father and I looked more like our mother. Her nose was upturned and bulbous; mine was straight and narrow. We both stood at an even 5'7, both fair complexioned; only Danielle had a few light freckles scattered across her nose and cheeks that always crinkled adorably when she was annoyed. They were crinkling now, which meant she'd had another fight with our mother and was coming to me for support and a place to sleep.

"Let me guess," I said when she approached the table. "Mom's pissing you off."

"What else is new?" she whined, sinking into a chair beside me. "When is she going to accept that I'm an adult now?"

"When you start acting like one."

"Oh, great. Now you're against me too."

"I'm not against you, Danielle," I said, dragging on my cigarette. "You're welcome to stay with me as long as you want but things at home are never going to change until you either confront Mom like the adult you claim to be or move out."

For me the answer was simple. I'd made my escape at eighteen, but for Danielle it was impossible. I may as well have been telling her she could fly. Asserting that our mother mind her own business was a skill only I seemed to possess. Even our brother Josh, who was three years older than me, had lived at home until he was twenty-four because he'd been too afraid to tell our overbearing mother he needed his freedom.

"I tell Dad," Danielle groaned.

"Do you even know our parents?" I asked, laughing. "Telling Dad that Mom is giving you a hard time is a lot like telling a chiropractor there's a comet hurdling toward earth—what the hell is he going to do about it?"

Jenna laughed, reminding me that she was in fact still at the table, and Danielle cried, *"Meagan."*

I shook my head. "Be realistic, Danny. Dad is the sweetest man on the planet and that's why Mom's had him by his balls his whole life. Aside from offering a sympathetic ear, there's not much he can do. You have a better chance of getting through to Mom on your own."

Satisfied, I settled back in my chair and my ear was suddenly bent by a metallic scraping noise that sent a prickly tingle up my spine. The tingle subsided and the scrape came again.

"What *is* that?" I asked Jenna, cringing as another small shudder of displeasure crawled its way up my back.

She glanced around the room. "What's what?"

Scrape!

The hairs on my arm stood at attention. *"That."*

"Don't know."

"It's her," Danielle whispered.

My eyes followed the pointed finger on her lap and fell upon the source of my discomfort. It was the stunning blond poet with the trendy uneven layers in her hair and the full pouty mouth. She was eating a piece of blueberry pie and every time the fork reached her mouth, her teeth clamped down on the metal utensil and scratched up the length of it and that horrible scraping noise twisted my ear.

"Jesus Christ!" The sound was driving me insane.

The poet's eye caught mine and she smiled, causing her coffee companion to glance at me with interest.

"That's Amber Reed," Jenna said, giving a small wave in the poet's direction. "She went to Lilith Fair with Rachel, Becky, and me. You'd have been there too if you didn't stay home whining over Basil."

"I wasn't whining," I said. "And who would have watched Bacon?"

Bacon was Jenna's pet pig. She'd rescued him from some old farmer's ax ten months earlier and had convinced the building's superintendent to let her keep it. Jenna was a most peculiar woman.

"I would have found someone."

Amber waved back at Jenna and pushed the last mouthful of pie between her lips, forgoing the nerve-bending scrape and giving my ears a break. I crushed my cigarette in the ashtray and reached for my espresso. I had a list of pet peeves an arm's length long and fork-scraping was at the very top.

Danielle left to head back to my apartment while Jenna and I remained in the Cauldron for one last cup of coffee. The coffeehouse was nearly empty now and as I stood at the counter waiting for Mitch, the owner, to fill my order, I felt something brush against my bare arm. This had been happening a lot lately and I didn't have to turn to know what it was.

"Here's my plate, Mitch," Amber said, pushing a black dish across the counter. She stood so close I couldn't move my arm without touching hers and I decided I wanted to know how she'd react if I did. I moved. Amber didn't flinch.

"And my fork." She slid the dreaded utensil across the granite countertop, apparently unaware of the pressure of my arm against hers. Suddenly, she turned and smiled at me. "Hey, Meagan."

She knew my name. The greeting caught me off guard and I quickly drew back my arm and managed an uncomfortable, "Umm…hi," as Mitch placed two steaming cups in front of me.

Amber pulled a cigarette from the pack concealed in her hand and, frowning as if she'd forgotten something, asked, "You wouldn't happen to have a light, would you?"

I smelled a setup but swallowed back my suspicion. "Sure," I said, grabbing the cups. "At the table."

Amber followed me to where Jenna still sat and I could feel her eyes on my back as we walked. Placing the cups on the table, I handed her my silver Zippo.

She lit her smoke. "Hey Jenna."

Jenna took a sip of cappuccino. "What are you up to tonight?"

"Not much," Amber said, shrugging and blowing a long gray plume above my head. "Rachel and I were thinking of going out for Chinese. You guys wanna come?"

Her body seemed surprisingly thin for someone who chowed down on blueberry pie and Chinese food after ten in the evening.

"I don't know," Jenna responded, looking at me for verification.

"I can't. Danielle, remember? I have to go home and see what her problem is."

Amber gave me a meaningful look. "Too bad."

I shrugged off the discomfort of her stare. "You guys go ahead."

It wasn't until I was in my apartment that I realized Amber had failed to return my lighter. I went back across the street but the gang had already left.

"Hey you!" Mitch called, as I turned to leave.

"Me?" I looked around.

"Yeah, you. Highlights girl."

I sighed. Everyone assumed the auburn streaks in my brown hair weren't natural. They were.

"Meagan," I corrected, walking toward him. "Meagan Summers." I thought he should know that by now. Jenna and I had been frequenting the Cauldron for two years.

"Meagan, right. Amber left this for you." He stretched his arm across the counter and handed me my lighter. There was a yellow post-it note attached that read, *I O U one inconvenience, Amber.*

I laughed at the bubbly script and Mitch said, "She's nutty, that one, but one of the best people you'll ever meet. You'll see."

I thought them peculiar words but only shrugged my indifference and headed home to make Danielle a cup of tea and get her to talk about what was bothering her. Within an hour she was asleep and I found myself wishing I'd gone to the restaurant with the others. Then I remembered I had an early morning meeting and it seemed a good thing I hadn't gone after all. I was so responsible sometimes I sickened myself.

Chapter 2

"You look great," Amber said. She was standing in my living room, a guest Jenna had invited weeks earlier when we'd decided to throw a retro party for no better reason than to get people together and have a good time. Several of the guests were people I didn't know. The invitations had stipulated that 1980s attire was required and each guest was encouraged to bring one or two guests of their own. We'd ended up with thirty-seven people that, fortunately, my apartment was large enough to accommodate.

Amber adjusted the blue and white headband on her forehead and smiled. Her hair was dyed black for the occasion and she wore a long, off-the-shoulder striped blouse paired with spandex pants and high-heeled boots. I'd decided against going retro, even though it was my party, and wore black leather hip-huggers with a glittery silver tank top. My hair fell in loose tangles around my shoulders and my skin sparkled with a touch of glitter that I'd carefully spritzed around my throat, shoulders, and chest. The glitter was the only thing even remotely eighties about me.

"I couldn't do it," I said, laughing. "Living the eighties once was enough for me. But I'm glittery so we'll say I was going for glam-rock. And you? Pat Benetar, right?"

She gave an embarrassed chuckle. "People keep guessing Joan Jett."

"No way," I said, shaking my head. "See that hard-looking woman by the window with the spiked leather bracelet?"

"Joan Jett?"

"Mm-hmm. I don't think you could abandon your femininity long enough to pull that off."

She laughed again, a throaty little chuckle, and I suddenly found myself embarrassed by my own comment. If my suspicions about her sexuality were correct, I probably shouldn't be making jokes about her femininity. What if I offended her?

"Have you seen Jenna around?" I asked uncomfortably. Those emerald eyes were boring through me again and I felt the need to extricate myself from the conversation before I said something *really* stupid.

"She went across the hall to grab a few things."

"I better help. Excuse me."

I turned on my heel just as Jenna strode through the door, looking like Cyndi Lauper, her arms filled with bags of chips, plastic glasses, and napkins emblazoned with the long-forgotten question, "Where's the beef?"

"We need more peach schnapps for the fuzzy navel fountain," she said. We were using her apartment for the party supplies and mine for the actual party.

"I'll grab it."

"Wait," Jenna called over the sound of the B-52's *Love Shack*. Our DJ had it cranked to full volume and some of the guests formed a conga line and happily bounced around the room. "We also need paper plates, orange juice, another bottle of wine, and that second tray of hors d'oeuvres in the fridge."

"Jesus, I better grow a few more hands."

"I'll help," Amber said, suddenly beside me again. We went across the hall to the quieter apartment and tried to recall everything Jenna had listed.

"Did she say wine?" I asked, poking around the fridge.

Amber grabbed the paper plates and the orange juice I stacked on the counter. "Wine, schnapps, and hors d'oeuvres."

"Got it."

We returned to the party just in time to hear someone yell, "I told you to get your fucking hands off her!" It was a gruff male voice that boomed over the music, startling several guests.

"Shit." I placed the things I'd been carrying on the coffee table and grabbed the two biggest men in the room, Paul, an ex-linebacker, and Jeff, an avid bodybuilder, and they strode with me like celebrity bodyguards toward the sound of the yell. Two men were shoving each other in the center of a small circle that had formed around them while a worried female looked on through splayed fingers.

Paul and Jeff followed me into the circle while Jenna did the same from the other side with two large men of her own.

"Excuse me," I shouted over the commotion. The two men glanced in my direction but continued shoving each other. "Hey! The two of you are going to have to leave."

One of the men backed off while the other, more intoxicated one, snarled, "Who's gonna make me?"

I indicated the two men behind me and the two behind Jenna. "They are."

"Just take it outside," Jeff said, folding his massive arms across his chest like an angry bouncer in a biker bar.

The drunk man stared up at him. "All right, take it easy there, Schwarzenegger." He marched toward the door, followed by the man he'd been fighting with and the woman they'd been fighting over.

The door slammed behind them and the party kicked back into action. Another conga line formed. People resumed their conversations. Jenna went across the hall to grab more supplies and returned pushing several people through the door in front of her.

"I had to lock up," she said. "They were in there playing with Bacon."

"Hey guys." A voice came from behind Jenna's head and I grinned.

"Josh, I'm surprised you came," I said, turning to face my brother. "And so *late.*" It was almost midnight and my accountant brother was not known for his ability to party.

"Great costume, Jenna." Jenna blushed and Josh indicated the paper-thin model on his arm. "This is Melody. She just got back from a show in New York."

I sighed. Josh and his predilection for waifish airheads.

"Alexander McQueen," Melody said in a bored tone as her pretty blue eyes surveyed the scene. I thought she was lying. "Why does everyone look like this?" She spoke as if she had an accent. She didn't. And I found myself disliking her already.

"It's a retro party," Josh explained.

"Thrilling."

Jenna and I exchanged a look. "Can I speak to you for a moment, Josh?" I said.

Melody sniffed the air and walked over to the first guy she spotted smoking a joint. The man's eyes lit up when he realized the model was coming to him.

"What's up?" Josh asked, his eyes following his latest conquest across the room.

"Get rid of her."

He laughed. "Why?"

"Why? Because she's a stuck-up bitch. Worse even than Marianna, the uber-model from Milan. What do you do, hang around outside of modeling agencies waiting to pick one up?"

Melody appeared beside us. "I'm bored, Josh," she complained. I shot him a look and an hour later I had the pleasure of watching one of our "bouncers" forcibly remove Melody from the party for being caught shooting up in the bedroom with some slick-haired junkie no one recalled inviting.

"So that's how she stays so thin," Josh joked after his initial shock wore off. He turned his attention to Jenna and from then on whenever I looked for either of them they were huddled away in a corner somewhere, deep in conversation.

"Excuse me," a sandy-headed man said, tapping my shoulder. He had something concealed in his hand. "You're Meagan, right?"

"Yes." I sipped my wine. He was cute, in a preppy sort of way. Big brown eyes. Boyish face. Not my usual type but he was definitely attractive. He opened his hand and my eyes fell upon four evenly broken pieces of ceramic. He had broken one of the fairy statues I collected and it was my favorite one! I felt the frown crease my forehead.

"I'm so sorry," he said, shyly. "Someone bumped into me and I knocked it off the shelf. If you tell me where you bought it I'll buy you a new one."

He couldn't buy me a new one. Not from the same place I'd gotten that one. The broken pieces slid into my hand and I managed a weak smile.

"Ireland."

His eyes widened. "Did you just say *Ireland?*" He looked so cute I couldn't help laughing.

"My uncle lives there. It's okay," I said. "Really. It was an accident. I'm just glad you told me about it."

"There must be some way I can make it up to you."

"Maybe you already have. You've given me an excuse to go back to Ireland and that will make my uncle very happy."

The man smiled engagingly. "Can I buy you a drink at the

fountain before your flight?"

I laughed. "Sure, but you do realize it's *my* fountain, right? Rented, of course."

"I realize that."

"I like a big spender."

"Well, then, wait till you get a look at the trays of food I also had prepared for you. I like to be extravagant on a first date."

We were grinning at each other when Amber suddenly appeared before us. "I don't mean to interrupt," she said, her eyes expressing that she meant it entirely. "Rachel and I are taking off now and I just wanted to tell you what a great party it was."

"I'm glad you had a good time," I said sincerely.

"I'll meet you at the fountain," the man said. Smiling, he strolled away from us.

"Did you see the uber-model get tossed out of here?" I was very proud of that.

"Was she a model?"

"The poster girl for bulimia," I said. Amber laughed. "What I'd really like to know is who brought the junkie. No one will admit to it. Anyway, I should probably check out the alcohol situation and see who needs what."

"So I'll see you around the Cauldron?" she asked.

"Probably. God knows Jenna and I are in there enough."

Amber squeezed my arm. "Okay, bye." And I watched her walk away, forgetting all about the man who was waiting for me by the fountain.

The party went on until five in the morning, with the last of the diehards noisily stumbling out the door as they tried to find the elevator. I shut out the commotion and turned to survey my surroundings. The apartment was a disaster. Nothing had been destroyed or soiled but I couldn't have been left a bigger mess to clean. Jenna was passed out on the couch. She'd fallen asleep hours earlier and I began tidying the area around her. I filled two large garbage bags before realizing I'd had enough and wanted to go to bed.

Staggering into the bedroom, I pulled off my clothes and threw on one of Basil's old shirts that I had taken to sleeping in and crawled into bed. My head hit the pillow and I slept soundly until hours later the earthquake struck. First the bed started bouncing, as if someone was jumping up and down beside my head. Then the shaking began, like two giant hands gripping my biceps and violently shoving me back and forth. Someone was laughing, a bubbly girlish giggle, and I wondered why it sounded so close, why the person wasn't running for cover. My eyes refused to open.

"Get out," I mumbled. But the shaking and giggling continued.

Someone was calling my name. I peered out through half-opened lids to find Jenna sitting beside me, smiling and bouncing up and down. A hammer pounded behind my forehead.

"What are you doing?" I groaned. My tongue felt like a dirty piece of shag carpeting and as the room made its orbit around my head I realized I'd done far more drinking and smoking the night before than I'd thought.

"Can I borrow your car?" she asked chipperly, rolling a left-over lollipop around her tongue and looking like she'd slept on a cloud all night. "I have to take the champagne fountain back to the rental place." She grinned. "Unless of course, *you* want to do it."

Pulling a pillow over my head, I breathed in the cool material that immediately turned to a suffocating heat. "Keys are in the kitchen."

"I know." Jenna jangled the keys by my ear and the sound was amplified by a thousand. She lifted the corner of my pillow and the morning sun burned my retinas. "I'll bring you back some tea."

The pillow flopped against my face again and I listened to Jenna's footsteps getting quieter as she left the bedroom and passed through the living room. The hammer struck again.

"And Tylenol," I called after her.

"And Tylenol," she confirmed, and I pictured the words coming at me from over her left shoulder, grateful she'd decided to forgo the obligatory lecture on herbal versus conventional remedies and was just going to get me the pills.

Slowly, I rose from the bed and made my way into the living room where I resumed the cleaning I'd begun earlier that morning. Jenna returned thirty-five minutes later and helped me finish the job. Then I went back to bed.

The next morning as I was leaving for work I found a small package sticking out of my mailbox in the lobby. The mailman never arrived until after nine so I figured the super must have unlocked the box for whoever had shoved the package inside. Tearing open the plain brown wrap, I found an anonymous note that said, *sorry again*, and a beautiful statue of a tiny fairy sitting cross-legged in front of an oak tree that had a keyhole opening at the base of the trunk. The statue sat on a small wooden plaque inscribed with the words, *The Keeper of the Gateway to Fairyland*. I loved it. It was twice as expensive as the one that had been broken and came with its own memory: that of a friendly but mysterious man who had made a sudden impression on my life then disappeared. There was no way to thank him and it was the sweetest, most romantic thing anyone had ever done for me.

My obsession with fairies began with my grandmother Mary O'Reilly (whom my siblings and I affectionately called "Gran") and followed me well into adulthood. Gran was senile by the time I'd really gotten to know her but she could still spin a tale in the thickest Irish brogue that would have me spellbound for hours. She loved to talk about fairies. When I was ten years old my mother dragged me to Gran's house three times a week after school and she cleaned while Gran and I talked.

Gran's knuckles were large. They cracked when she flexed her hands and the popping sound always terrified me, making me think the fingers would one day pull away from the first gnarled knuckles and fall to the floor in front of me. Gran's fingers held two rings, on her left hand her gold wedding band, and on the right hand a silver band with Celtic knot work twisting around an oval moonstone in the center. This too looked like a wedding band, only this ring was far more important to Gran and came with a peculiar meaning, one Gran shared with me alone. The ring would someday belong to me, she'd said.

Someday came eleven months later when Gran suddenly died of a stroke. The ring had been given to me after the funeral and I had always known what I was meant to do with it.

"When the time is right," Gran used to tell me. "Keep it safe, Meagan. And when the time is right you'll feel it in your heart and you'll know what you must do."

But the time had never been right and at twenty-six years old I still wore the ring my grandmother had cherished for over thirty-five years. I still believed in fairies and I still wore the symbol of my gran's secret heart.

Chapter 3

"I know the meeting is at three, Ted," I said into the receiver. Ted Markham was the publisher of *Natural Beauty* magazine. He was thirty-seven years old with a slightly receding hairline and John Lennon style wire-rimmed glasses. He'd discovered me when I was a twenty-year-old bar manager running a part-time advertising business on the side and had made me his publicity director. Together we'd gone on to make the magazine a national success. "Have I ever missed a meeting, Ted?"

"No," he chuckled.

"Then why are you bugging me? I'm on my way out the door."

I looked at Jenna, who sat on the couch waiting for me to get off the phone so we could go across the street to watch the Thursday night poets. Amber would be there. Amber was always there. With one published book behind her, she was the star poet at the Cauldron and her name scribbled across the chalkboard outside always drew in the crowds. "Go ahead," I mouthed to Jenna. She shook her head.

"Where are you going?" Ted asked. He was notorious for his mind-numbing chitchat and the last person you wanted to get on the phone with if you were in a hurry. Ted was my employer but he was also a friend.

"Out. Look, I'm in a bit of a rush so I'll talk to you tomorrow, okay?"

"*Earthstuff*'s being a pain in the ass again. They're bitching about their advertising space."

"I know," I said. *Earthstuff* was a cosmetics company whose owner, Tye Barker, always wanted more for his dollar. "I'm on it. I talked to Tye yesterday. He's not pleased with the price increase but we're working it out. It should be settled soon."

Ted and I hung up and Jenna and I headed out the door. By the time we took our seats at our regular table near the stage and ordered a couple of French vanilla cappuccinos, Amber was approaching the microphone. She looked great in her casual attire of faded blue jeans with a rip in the knee, her hair dyed back to its usual platinum blond, and a black silk skirt that cut inward at the waist, revealing delicate curves that might not appear to be there otherwise. From a purple spiral notebook, she read, her left hand rising every few seconds to brush away the softly razored bangs that repeatedly fell into her left eye. She was stunning to watch. She flirted with the crowd, teased them, kept them on the edge of their seats, dying to know what she'd say next.

I sipped my French vanilla and watched this as if really seeing it for the first time. She had some sort of power over these people, I noticed. They stared up at her with expressions of fascination, as she leaned into the microphone as seductively as if she were having sex with it, and recited her words as if she'd created them herself rather than merely arranged them in a pleasing composition.

"Isn't she good?" Jenna whispered, as Amber finished reciting her second poem.

"Mm-hmm." I nodded, but I hadn't heard a word Amber had said until she placed the notebook on the small table beside her, pulled a brown leather stool up to the microphone, sat on it, and hooked the thick heels of her boots around the bottom rung.

Her hands gripped the seat between her legs and, casually leaning back, she said, "This is something new I've been working on." Her eyes met mine and I looked away. Hated when she looked at me like that.

When I looked up again her eyes were still locked on my face and I wished she would reach for her notebook again. Anything to break the uncomfortable stare.

"Why does she do that?" I complained, reaching for a cigarette. Other eyes in the room followed Amber's to land squarely on me.

"Do what?"

I thought Jenna knew what because she was smirking. And if the stares didn't stop soon I was going to leave the table until Amber finished her set. Suddenly her eyes looked away and the other eyes did the same. I remained in my seat.

Cautiously, she began reciting her third poem. It was a slow seduction, her voice whispering through the room like a gentle breath of air, caressing each audience member in turn. And the poem itself was so descriptively racy I blushed at the sound of it and shifted uncomfortably in my seat. The emerald stare met mine again, daring me to make a move, and I could feel her eyes go through me as the coffeehouse became charged with the heat of her words.

At last it was done. She thanked the crowd for their attention and gathered her notebook and cigarettes from the table. My heart pounded beneath my chest as she skipped down the stage steps and headed toward us. Dumbly, I realized I couldn't take my eyes off of her.

"Sit with us," Jenna said, her foot pushing out the chair opposite us. Amber sat.

"So what did you think?" she asked Jenna, pulling a cigarette from the pack on her notebook and reaching across the table for my lighter.

I O U one inconvenience flashed before my eyes and I smiled. Amber pulled the orange-blue flame to the end of her cigarette, snapped closed the metal lid, and smiled back at me. She handed me the lighter and as our fingers brushed a small charge ran up the length of my arm, startling me, and I pulled away quickly. From the look of surprise on Amber's face I knew I wasn't the only one who'd felt the strange energy. Our eyes locked and something silent passed between us.

"Great," Jenna said, suddenly. We looked at her slowly. "The poem," she explained, arching an eyebrow in my direction. "It was great."

"Oh." Amber smiled appreciatively.

"Did you see the people in this place? You got everyone horny."

My cheeks flushed and Amber laughed, stealing a sideways glance at me. Quickly, I brought my cup to my lips in an effort to hide the embarrassment I knew was revealing itself on my face. I had the disturbing sensation that Jenna was gossiping about me, and right in front of my face! She was wrong too. Amber had most certainly *not* gotten me horny.

Oh really? questioned a voice in my head.
Shut up.

"Did you like it?" Amber asked me. There was an uncertainty in her tone that immediately put me at ease.

"Very much," I confirmed. "I have a habit of missing the point sometimes, so correct me if I'm wrong, but to me the poem seemed more about a desperation to touch someone rather than the reality of actually doing so."

Amber smiled reassuringly but there was a bittersweet curl to her lips. "No, you have it right. I was afraid the point would get lost somewhere in the telling, considering the poem's graphic content."

Graphic was putting it mildly. What Amber had done up there was nothing short of porn. She said things you were always told you shouldn't say in mixed company, and she did it in a manner that suggested she was secretly getting off on her own words. She sat up there and she spilled her tale and all the while she looked…*orgasmic.* No wonder people fell all over themselves just to talk to her. The woman *was* sex.

Amber ordered a double espresso and I found myself becoming increasingly aware of her presence. I noticed her eyes— seemed I was always noticing those—so big and impossibly green, the slope of her long neck and the chain that dangled from around it, weighted by some invisible pendant that dipped down between the small breasts beneath her silk shirt. Then there was the flawless white skin, the even white teeth concealed behind perfectly pouty heart-shaped lips that all but begged to be kissed, and—

My mind suddenly locked onto a terror and turned it to ice.

"Oh my God. Shut up!"

Jenna and Amber swung their heads to face me. Had I actually just said that out loud? My cheeks flamed.

"Are you telling *me* to shut up?" Jenna's eyes locked onto mine.

"No…I…" I couldn't come up with words. "I have to go," I said, springing to my feet. "I have to prepare my notes for that meeting tomorrow." Jenna nodded but I knew she wasn't buying it. No one was buying it. "I'll see you guys later," I said, and darted out the door like an escaped convict.

At home I paced, wondering what the hell was wrong with me. I didn't fully believe in sexuality as a concept. I was spiritual enough to believe that souls could fall in love with other souls regardless of things like race and gender; it had just never happened to me. Then with a genuine horror, I realized that with Amber I sensed it was possible. I *could* fall for her. Hadn't I spent an awful lot of time thinking about her lately? Wasn't I flattered when she looked at me *that way*? How many times did I find myself smiling, just looking at her? And the man from the party, I'd forgotten all about him the minute Amber had sauntered up to us. Oh Christ! Was it possible I was *attracted* to her? My mind wrapped around the word and I knew at once it was true. I was actually attracted to a *woman*.

I paced some more. I paced and I smoked and I listed all the reasons it didn't matter and all the reasons I shouldn't be attracted to her nonetheless. I knew it wasn't *wrong*, but I also didn't need any further complications in my life. I had just gotten over Basil. The last thing I needed was to discover I was a lesbian.

"Just make it go away," I pleaded. "I really don't want this."

I didn't know who I was pleading with but I was frightened enough to give it a shot. The worry exhausted me and by the time Jenna strolled through the door an hour later, I was spent.

"Why did you rush out like that?" she asked, never one to beat around the bush. I told her I wasn't feeling well.

"Oh." Jenna plucked a bottle of Evian from the fridge and tossed herself on the couch. "Amber thought it had something to do with her."

"She did?" Perceptive poet.

"You know she's gay, right?" Jenna was watching me, gauging my reaction.

"I kind of figured that."

"Well, the thing is, she's really attracted to you. Cute as you are and all that." I smiled. "So she thought you picked up on that tonight and got spooked."

Tossing myself on the couch beside her, I sighed. "That's pretty much what happened," I agreed, omitting for the moment my own confused attraction. "Apologize for me, okay? I don't want her thinking I'm homophobic or something."

"Homophobic." Jenna threw back her head and laughed. "That sounds like such a guy thing. Wanna come over for some tea?"

"Sounds good."

What Jenna failed to mention was that Amber was across the hall sitting in her apartment. We stepped through the door and my breath drew up short as I was met with the sight of her, sitting cross-legged on the end of Jenna's couch, smoking a cigarette. Amber was just as startled to see me and an eerie silence floated above the room as in one horrible instant I realized Jenna had set us up.

"Chamomile?" she asked, the amusement thick in her voice.

"What?"

"Chamomile tea?"

I glared at her. "Raspberry," I said out loud, and secretly mouthed the words, *you're dead.*

She shrugged. "Raspberry it is," she sang out joyfully, and disappeared behind the small kitchen wall.

My feet refused to move from the ground they held by the door but I forced them forward and sat in the overstuffed chair across from Amber. I didn't know what to say, how to explain my strange behavior earlier and my presence there now.

"Maybe I should leave," Amber said, staring at her feet.

"W-Why?" I stammered. The thought of her leaving on such terms disturbed me. "Listen, if it's about earlier, I'm sorry. It was rude of me to walk out like that."

She shook her head. "That's not it. I just think I make you uncomfortable."

I sighed at the impossible situation before me, the one I was forced to confront thanks to Jenna and her mischievous nature. "You do," I responded honestly. "But probably not in the way you're thinking."

Her eyes met mine. "In what way then?"

She was staring at me and I couldn't lie to those eyes. Again, I wondered what was wrong with me as the truth erupted like an inflammation in my throat. It poured out of me and I told her it was possible I was attracted to her.

"I've never been attracted to a woman before," I said. "It freaked me out."

Amber smiled. "I noticed."

"I was telling myself to shut up." *God,* why didn't I just *stop speaking*?

"I know."

She leaned forward to crush her cigarette out in the ashtray and arched an eyebrow when she caught me peering into the kitchen in search of Jenna.

"I don't think she's coming back," I said. And again I realized I wanted to kiss this woman. I wanted to feel her mouth on mine and touch that soft blond hair. If only I could build up the nerve to do it.

But I hadn't had to. Hadn't had to even dwell on the thought a moment longer because Amber suddenly said, "I'm sorry, Meagan, but I'm going to kiss you." And before I could respond it was happening. Her lips met mine, coaxing them apart, and my tongue made a gentle exploration of her mouth. She tasted sweet. Cotton candy, I thought, and my body drew into an energy I had never felt before, an intensity that called me into her and made me want more. Her tongue met mine and I took it in, allowed it to search my mouth as her hands slipped into my hair and she breathed softly against my lips. I couldn't believe what I was doing but it didn't matter. I only wanted to be kissing her, feeling her warm body pressed to mine and her fingers in my hair. When it was done I was left with the realization that I had never experienced a more sensual, all-consuming kiss in my life.

We stared at each other, speechless. Then there was Jenna. Jenna standing at the threshold between the living room and the kitchen, holding three steaming mugs and grinning from ear to ear like she had been there the whole time.

The next morning, Jenna showed up in my bathroom with two Irish cream coffees. It wasn't like her to be up before seven and I was immediately suspicious. She closed the toilet seat and sat down, sipping her coffee and watching me attempt to apply my makeup in front of the bathroom mirror. She was holding something back, something that amused her. Finally, she could contain herself no longer.

"Amber wants to know if we'll be in the Cauldron tonight," she said, smirking.

The eyeliner pencil slipped from my fingers and fell in the sink, circling the porcelain once before landing in the drain.

I plucked it out and turned to face Jenna. "How much do you know?"

"All of it."

"I see." I turned away from her again and shyly glanced at her reflection in the mirror. "And your reaction is?"

"Unimportant."

"Jenna."

"But supportive nonetheless."

Why I worried it might have been anything else was beyond me. Jenna was the most accepting person I'd ever known.

"So what should I tell her?" she pressed, as I again attempted lining my eyes with the pencil. My hand shook and I dropped it to my side.

"I don't know. This whole thing scares the hell out of me. What do you think?"

She laughed. "I think you probably didn't spend a moment's thought on Basil last night."

"Who?" I asked, catching the humor in the air and giggling. Getting over Basil wasn't a simple process but it was happening.

"Eight o'clock then?"

My stomach gave a nervous flutter. "Sure."

Chapter 4

"What the hell is this?" Ted demanded, tossing the offending galleys on the conference table. Friday morning meetings usually went smoothly but today Ted was pissed. *"Ten ways to get him to say "I do"*?" He glared accusingly at his staff. "Last month we ran an article on how to make a man feel guilty and I told you people *then* that type of article was unacceptable."

"This is a women's magazine, Ted," said Elaine Hill, our reluctant-to-hear-any-opinion-other-than-her-own editor-in-chief. "And like it or not *this*," she picked up the galleys and waved them in the air, "is exactly the kind of article women want to read."

The two assistant editors joined in with nods of agreement and murmurs of "she's right" as Elaine settled back in her chair, a satisfied smirk cracking the corners of her smoke-ravaged face. Too much sun and too much smoking had taken its toll and often just looking at her made me think I should quit smoking. She was a cynical woman with hard eyes and lips set in a permanent sneer.

"What do you think, Meagan?" Ted asked, peering at me from behind his steepled fingers. It was common knowledge around the office that Ted considered me his protégé and valued my opinion. He kept me involved in every decision made concerning the magazine and the two of us worked as a team.

Clicking my pen in and out, a habit I knew drove Elaine crazy, I said, "I think our advertisers won't like it. They buy space in our magazine because we speak to a demographic separate from the man-obsessed, fashion-crazed sect other women's magazines focus on. Our slant has always been part naturopathic/part feminist, celebrating a woman's intelligence as well as her beauty. If we start going the 'wrap yourself in a fur while seducing him into bed' way we might lose some of our bigger advertisers whose products speak to a less fashion-conscious more socially aware group of buyers."

"Ha," Elaine scoffed. "This from the woman in Armani. Is that a *Gucci* watch, Meagan?"

"*My* fashion sense is irrelevant. It's our readers we should concern ourselves with, Elaine, not each other. They are the ones who buy the magazine after all, not us."

"No, we just write it."

"I don't write it. Do you?"

"No," she barked. "*I* decide what goes in it, and if I want to accept articles on revenge, manipulation, or how to give a good hand job it's up to *you* to go out there and get me the goddamn advertisers who are willing to put up with it and keep their mouths shut."

My temper flared. Elaine and I had always had problems, a constant battle of wills. "Excuse me? When did you become the fucking publisher around here? The last time I checked Ted was still in charge."

"I am, ladies," Ted interrupted. He was accustomed to the volatile working relationship Elaine and I shared and ignored the way we often cursed at each other. So did the nine other people at the table.

"Stop bickering and listen up. From now on you are to stick to the regular format until *I* tell you differently. Do you hear me, Elaine? The *regular format*. If that's such a problem for you I'm sure you can always find a job as an assistant editor at one of those high-end glossies you're so obsessed with turning *Natural Beauty* into."

He was hitting her where it hurt, her love of power, and reminding her she could have some or none.

"We are an alternative woman's magazine and it is by that standard that we will continue to meet our circulation goals. We will not imitate the dozens of other big name magazines that are constantly imitating each other."

The room broke into grins and applause. The staff admired Ted for his integrity. He had a vision for his magazine and come hell or high water, he'd stick to it. I was around to make sure that happened.

"On to other business," he said, waving his hand for silence. "This morning Rick, Meagan and I met with a new distributor we will be using starting November first. We will also be expanding our number of pages and taking on some new advertisers. Meagan." He turned to me, indicating I now had the floor.

Reaching into my briefcase, I pulled out a handful of contracts I'd spent the last month securing. "Okay. *Fresh Air* wants to up their ad from a half-page to a full-page, again, starting November first. We have three new companies who want half-page ads and I've secured a deal with *Jamieson Vitamins* for a full page ad to be run every month for the next six months, effective immediately. If their sales numbers increase during that time we'll hammer out a new deal at the end of the sixth month. *Gold Moon Clothing* is sticking to their quarter page but they want to change the ad itself. They have a new logo so we'll have to update. We also have a fourth company that wants a full page advertorial."

"We don't do that," Elaine interrupted.

"We do now," Ted said. "Full page with small print at the top that says *Advertisement.* You know what I'm talking about. We've all seen these."

Elaine glared at me and I gave her an unaffected shrug.

"Each of you will be given a detailed list," I continued, "but here's a quick rundown to give you an idea of what we're looking at. *Fresh Air* – full page. *Earthstuff,* full page but with smaller print so they can add to their product list. *Underground Hydroponics,* up from a quarter to a half page. In total we'll have about fifteen changes to make but be prepared for more in the coming months. I've been talking to the people at *Clairol* about their *Herbal Essences* line and *Neutrogena* seems interested in advertising their skin care products with us."

"That's it then?" Ted questioned, approving my progress.

I scanned my list. "For now."

"Good, onto content. Elaine, I'm not impressed with what we've been printing lately. Check the slush pile. There has to be at least some worthwhile material in there. If not, commission some. Get our regular freelancers on the job. I'm also thinking a feature each month on one particular herb and its uses—cosmetic, culinary and medicinal. Can our food editor handle that?"

"Susan has a degree in herbology," Elaine said stiffly.

"Good. And tell her I don't want her missing anymore meetings. This is twice now."

"How would you feel about an 'Ask the Aromatherapist'

column?" I asked Ted, thinking Jenna would be perfect for the job.

Elaine crumpled a sheet of clean yellow paper. "Doesn't anyone stick to working within their own department anymore?"

Ted ignored her sarcasm. "I think that sounds like an interesting idea." I shot Elaine a triumphant glare, which she sneered at. "Did you have anyone in mind?"

"Sure she does," Elaine muttered to one of her assistant editors. "Probably a boyfriend." The three editors glared.

"As a matter of fact I do have someone in mind. I'll have to see if *she's* interested—"

Ted nodded. "Get me the details and re-submit the idea to me next week. Meeting adjourned." He rose from the table. "Rick, Meagan, please don't forget our meeting tomorrow with Peter Gregory and John McIntyre from the Gregory Investment group. They'll be here at nine, and I know it's a Saturday, but please be here by eight-thirty."

People filed out of the room after Ted. Rick, the magazine's financial manager groaned, "I hate getting up early on weekends."

"It's just this one time," I said sympathetically. Elaine made kissy noises through her aging, puckered lips.

"Her mouth is glued to Ted's ass," she told her assistant, and the woman laughed.

"By the way, Elaine," Rick said sweetly, "your raise request has been denied. It's just not in the budget right now, you understand."

I lowered my head to hide my amusement and Elaine stalked from the room, her assistant scurrying behind her like a battered puppy.

"Hard-ass bitch," Rick grumbled.

"She is good at her job though," I admitted.

"Not good enough for a raise." Grinning, he threw an arm across my shoulders. "Let's go get some lunch. We'll take the money out of what should have been Elaine's salary increase."

"She's so generous."

"No one nicer."

At home I showered and hoped to grab a quick bite to eat before joining Jenna and Amber at the coffeehouse but found that when I thought of food my stomach gave a nervous flop and I managed to choke down no more than three bites of a toasted bagel.

The shower was cold --hot water problems again-- and I wanted to call the super but realized I didn't have time to wait for him to get the job done. It always took him hours to finish a job, as he loved to sit around gossiping while sipping a cup of black coffee I'd been stupid enough to hand him the very first time. It was a habit impressed upon me in childhood when I would watch my mother busily preparing snacks and beverages for whatever repairman happened to be in the house.

7:45p.m. My stomach gave a hungry gurgle and another nervous flop. How was I to approach this new situation? Amber and I had kissed; now what? Did I walk into the Cauldron as aloof as if nothing had happened between us the night before? Or was I now obliged to show some sort of acknowledgement or interest? I didn't know, and nothing put a knot in my stomach like uncertainty.

7:58p.m. Jenna and Amber were already on their second cups of whatever when I walked through the door. I bought a bottle of water at the counter and approached the table with a small wave in the way of a greeting. There was an empty chair beside Jenna and an empty chair beside Amber and I felt a lot depended upon which one I chose. I chose the one beside Jenna, thinking it might seem presumptuous somehow to walk in and plop myself beside Amber, and yet, by the look on her face I got the impression I'd made the wrong choice.

"No coffee tonight?" Jenna asked as I cracked open the bottle of water.

I shook my head. They didn't really need to know how caffeine affected my stomach in the most unpleasant way when I was nervous. I got through those first awkward moments by telling Jenna about my column idea and asking if she'd like to be the resident expert.

"Are you serious?" she squealed.

"Yep. All we have to do is submit a sample column, a question from a fictitious person that you will answer. We print it, hand it in to Ted, and that's it. Elaine will pitch a fit but Ted'll eat it right up. What do you think?"

"I think I'm about to embark on a third career. *Ask Jenna.* I absolutely love it. You are my best friend in the whole world". She crushed me in a hug and Amber laughed.

"You should have seen Elaine's face. First Ted goes for the idea, and then Rick tells her she's not getting a raise—I was absolutely dying!"

"Elaine's the editor-in-chief," Jenna explained.

"And the two of you don't like each other?" Amber asked.

"Not really."

"The woman gets mad because Meagan has some sort of power over Ted."

"No, Ted's my boss," I said, laughing.

"Yeah, and not once has he ever shot down one of your suggestions. He's gonna pull you in, watch. He's gonna make you his co-publisher."

"I'm working on that already," I admitted, thinking of the stocks I was continuing to buy. They would serve me well in the coming months.

Jenna gave me a disapproving look. "You're doing something sneaky, aren't you? To your own friend. Meagan, I don't like when you get like this."

She was making me sound like a horrible person and I didn't like it.

"You're not my mother, Jenna. I already have one of those and believe me, she's enough. And as for doing something sneaky, well, maybe I am. But I'm not doing anything to Ted that he won't thank me for later."

"Your ambition is gonna choke you."

"Can we talk about something else? My ambition is just fine. Your problem is you have none."

"I have two jobs!" Jenna protested. "And now you've pulled me into a third."

I shrugged. "So back out. I'll find someone else."

"No, I want it." She laughed. "You just freak me out sometimes."

Amber sipped her coffee and smiled. "I don't know you *that* well, Jenna, but I get the feeling you get freaked out easily."

"She does." I rose from the table, deciding I'd like a cup of coffee after all. "Ask her about the time aliens abducted her uncle Steve."

Jenna burst out laughing. "I never said I believed that!"

"Please." I turned to Amber. "Her uncle Steve is as loopy

as my grandmother was, only my grandmother was an old woman and Steve was thirty-three at the time. I'd just moved into the building and I find this blond hippie sitting in the hallway crying. So I put down the box I'm carrying and go over to ask her if she's all right. And she's got the whole look, right? She's got the long straight hair, which eventually got chopped off, the sandals, the love beads… Anyway, she's *sobbing*. So, I approach her, a complete stranger, and she just throws her arms around me, bawling her face off and babbling about how her uncle Steve was abducted by aliens the night before and told her they were coming back for her."

Amber couldn't hide her amusement. "What did you do?"

"I didn't know what to do. I'm just holding her and she's sobbing into my neck and I'm thinking, "Please don't let this crazy girl be my neighbor.""

Jenna continued to giggle. "You were not. You liked me."

"I felt *sorry* for you. I thought you were completely insane. I was *afraid* of you."

"Is that why you followed me into my apartment, made me tea, and stayed with me all night to prove there weren't any aliens coming?"

"So you admit you believed it!" I was victorious.

"You stayed with her all night?" Amber's eyes softened on my face.

"Had to. Then once she calmed down I realized she wasn't really insane. Her uncle Steve signed himself into a mental hospital shortly after. How is Old Lobotomy Joe, anyway?"

"I told you not to call him that. And he's fine. He's been sane for five years. You know that."

"Okay, I'm gonna grab an espresso. Who wants one?"

"I'll have one," Amber said.

"Make mine a latte," Jenna chimed in.

"Always have to be different , don't you?" I teased.

"You know it."

Laughing, I went to grab our beverages. When I returned Jenna was running a few "column ideas" by Amber. I found her zeal endearing. Give her a plan and she'll run with it, I thought. Can't help but love that Jenna.

Time passed quickly and we kept each other well entertained --Jenna with her tales of colonic irrigations gone awry in the back room of the health center; Amber with her predilection for dirty limericks, tickling the Irish in me; and me with my stories of Basil's stoned out antics, like the time he thought my mother was coming onto him because she kept offering him a piece of "her" pie and he coolly informed her that he wasn't "into older chicks".

We were laughing so hard I didn't see or hear Danielle approaching from behind.

"Meagan." Her hand gripped my shoulder and I jumped, narrowly missing Jenna's cheek with my elbow.

"Jesus. You sound like Mom."

"Shut up."

I chuckled. "What are you doing here?"

"Hi, Danielle," Jenna said.

"Hey Jen."

Jenna cringed at the shortening of her name and I smirked. Then I remembered Amber sitting across from me and felt my amusement dissipate and my nervousness come flooding back. I felt as if Danielle had caught me in a compromising position, hand in the cookie jar, which was ridiculous because we weren't doing anything but talking.

"This is Amber," I said, after long seconds of thought. "Amber this is my sister, Danielle." The two exchanged hellos. "So what's the problem this time, Danny?" I asked, knowing Danielle had come home drunk as our mother had called me a few days earlier to complain.

Danielle plopped herself in the chair beside Amber.

"Mom's being a bitch," she said, shrugging. The freckles crinkled.

I sighed my all-knowing big sister sigh. "The couch is yours. Maybe I should invest in a pull-out."

Danielle stretched luxuriously, a lazy mannerism I'd often admired. "That would be heaven. Or you could just get a two-bedroom apartment."

"Yeah, or *you* could just learn how to stand up to Mom."

She swiped my keys off the table, twisting the one she needed off the silver hoop. "And risk losing a sisterly bond such as this? Never."

"Smart ass."

"I'll leave the door open for you."

"Yes, you will."

Rising from the table, she took one last look at Amber, and I watched the recognition dawn on her face. "I know you," she said, easily. "You're the fork-scraper. Big sister's pet peeve. You drove her nuts." In a whiff of Tommy Girl perfume she was gone. The silence she left behind was nerve-breaking.

Embarrassment flooded my body and I scrambled to my feet. "I need another bottle of water," I said, and bolted for the counter leaving Jenna behind to deal with Amber's surprised reaction.

I could have killed Danielle. Why would she say something like that? My sister was smart enough to maintain a spot on the honor roll but too dumb to know there were certain things you just didn't say. Amber got up to go to the bathroom and the minute I saw the door close behind her I rushed over to Jenna.

"Oh my God!"

"It's okay," Jenna interrupted, before I had the chance to go off. "I told her what Danny was talking about and she laughed and said she was doing it on purpose to annoy Rachel—the girl she was sitting with."

"I know who Rachel is," I said, slumping down in the chair Amber had vacated. "Thank God she has a sense of humor. I was so embarrassed."

'You should be," Jenna giggled. "I've never seen you make such a horrible impression."

My back stiffened and my mind went on red alert. I couldn't stand the idea that someone might not like me. "What do you mean, horrible impression?"

"Think about it," Jenna said casually. "First you refuse a dinner invitation without so much as a thank you for being invited in the first place—"

I cringed. Had I really done that?

"—Then you pretty much ignore her at our party."

"I didn't know the purpose of the party was so I could entertain Amber all evening," I said sarcastically. "Besides, I talked to her."

"Okay, you talked to her. Then *last* night you bolt out of here because one of her poems makes you uncomfortable and you end up looking like a homophobe."

"You said I didn't."

"I lied. You looked like you were racing off to join the anti-gay militia. But that's okay because you remedied that and proved you weren't when you kissed her."

"She—"

"Kissed you, whatever." Jenna waved her hand impatiently. "And just when you were starting to look like a half-way decent human being your sister marches in here and announces your neurotic—"

"I prefer 'idiosyncratic'."

"—inclination toward pickiness, which truthfully, borders on obsessive-compulsive disorder if you ask me."

"I didn't ask you, and what's your point?" The problem with the truth was that it was true.

"My *point* is she's still interested. You've done nothing but offend her since the day you met and yet, somehow, she sees some redeemable quality in you."

Amber returned from the bathroom and I wondered if she found me as objectionable as Jenna so obviously did. Sometimes the intimacy in our friendship was too much to bear. Not for Jenna, the little white lie. If she told one she couldn't live with herself until she took it back.

Amber took the chair beside me and said BeBe's, a club around the corner, was having live music. We decided to go check it out and Jenna's words haunted me on the short walk over. She knew I was mad. She nudged me, playfully flicked my hair, and when none of her efforts paid off and we were standing in front of the pink and black building with the neon lights she threw her long arms around my neck and smacked my cheek with one of her trademark, "I'm still your buddy" kisses.

"Don't be mad," she said, ignoring my discomfort at her public display of affection. "I was just bugging you."

I felt very childish suddenly. So what if I didn't like what Jenna had to say? At least with her I did know I would always get the truth—eventually.

"Are we going in?" Amber asked. She looked like she wasn't sure what was going on between Jenna and me.

I messed the back of Jenna's hair, a sign that all was forgiven, and nodded. Once inside the club we were met and successively hit on by Noel Ford, Basil's lead singer and new roommate.

"Basil's not here," Noel offered, answering a question no one had asked.

"So?"

"So—I don't know." He staggered away, another rock-n-roll beanpole, but his words stuck in my head and I found myself wondering what Basil was doing. Damn Noel.

"I'm gonna get us some drinks," Jenna said, nodding at Amber. She headed off to the bar and Amber and I grabbed a table in the corner, silence between us. We never seemed to know what to say to each other.

"My friend Zeppo is having his first exhibit at an art gallery uptown tomorrow night," Amber said, the first to break the silence. "Wanna go?"

Thoughts of Basil fled my mind as I digested this new invitation.

"The only thing," she continued, "is that Zeppo's a bit eccentric and demands that everyone attending be barefoot."

Was she serious? She was. The thought of my sensitive feet being pressed against the cold marble floor I imagined did little for my enthusiasm but I smiled sweetly and said, "Sounds like fun." Amber looked pleased.

Lack of sleep made me late for my meeting with Ted and the investors the next morning. Ted was furious. He pulled me aside and demanded to know why while Rick occupied the men from Gregory Investments in the next room.

"I'm sorry," I lied. "I was up all night with a family emergency."

Ted's tone softened and I immediately felt guilty. "Is everything all right?" he asked.

"It will be." The three men sat around a glass table in the conference room waiting. "We better get in there." I said, nodding at the room.

Ted pressed the small of my back as we stepped through the door. "Gentlemen, this is Meagan Summers, our publicity director." The men rose from their seats.

"I apologize for my tardiness," I said, shaking their hands.

"She was busy on the phone with a new advertiser," Ted said quickly, crafting a lie of his own. "Meagan's our workaholic of the group."

The men nodded their approval and I flushed, ashamed of

the praise that, today, I didn't deserve.

"Shall we get down to business then?" John McIntyre asked. We sat and the meeting began.

"Here's the deal," Peter Gregory said, wiping the lenses of his glasses with a white handkerchief. He pushed them back up his nose. "Gregory Investments is looking for an up-and-coming enterprise to throw some money into, preferably, but not limited to, a monthly publication. We are a multi-million dollar organization—" Ted's eyes lit up. "—with an interest in the ever-expanding fields of alternative health care, beauty, and new age awareness. Dilbert Gregory, our founder and my grandfather, started this firm with the intention of using his resources to back consciousness-raising, personal-empowering businesses and organizations while turning a nice profit at the same time. One could say he was ahead of his time. He would have loved the changes we've seen as the millennium approaches."

Peter sighed wistfully and I admired his obvious pride in his grandfather's vision.

"Anyway," he said, pulling himself from the thoughts that briefly encumbered him. "What I'd like now is for you to explain to me why we should invest in *Natural Beauty* and why a magazine that promotes itself as a leading publication in the alternative women's market last month ran an article detailing how to make a man feel guilty." He peered at his notes. "And I quote, "Everything from forgetting to take out the trash to failing to help you reach orgasm, we'll show you how to riddle him with guilt and have him begging your forgiveness.'"

I cringed. Damn Elaine!

"It's funny you should bring that up," Ted said. "I was just discussing that particular article with my staff yesterday and I can assure you, nothing like it will ever appear in our pages again. It was an oversight on my part, I'm afraid and the work of a sometimes overzealous editor-in-chief." That was putting it mildly.

"I see."

Ted nudged me under the table, something he often did when wanting me to add to a conversation.

"Mr. Gregory," I began.

"Peter." He smiled at me.

"Peter. Let me allay any concerns you might have regarding the content and/or goal of this publication. When I came to work for Ted six years ago it was because he convinced me he was starting a publication that would make a difference in how people viewed their surroundings themselves, and in the end, often each other. He wanted a magazine that spoke to a demographic not often spoken to. It was a risky idea, *then*. Today it's quite commonplace. People are more open to new ways of thinking. They are interested in alternative ways of caring for themselves and that is what *Natural Beauty* is about. It's about finding one's inner beauty as well as one's external beauty and we are always on the cutting edge of what's new in the alternative women's market. We keep ourselves on top of the trends but we also introduce our reader's to topics that may seem new to them but which are really hundreds, sometimes thousands of years old. *New Age* is a term that can be deceptive. Often it describes only things that have been forgotten but are new again once we are reminded of them. Did you happen to see our August issue?"

Peter nodded. "An interesting article on feng shui."

"That's exactly where I was going with this," I said, smiling. "feng shui has existed for thousands of years but from the letters we got in response to that one article, you'd never know it. That's what *Natural Beauty* is about, opening people to ideas that can in one way or another improve their lives. *Natural Beauty* and Gregory Investments would go well together because they have the same ultimate goal: to push the limits of convention and support a new way of thought as we enter the Aquarian Age."

"Aquarian Age," Peter agreed. "Grandfather was so looking forward to that. He predicted an age of enlightenment and inner growth. A lot of people thought he was crazy" --Crazy grandparents I could relate to-- "But look around us. He was right."

"I think I would have liked Dilbert Gregory," I said.

"Without question. He was the strangest, kindest, millionaire around."

Until now John McIntyre had remained silent. "Could we see this year's financial reports?" He asked, directing the conversation back to business.

Didn't matter. I could tell Peter and I had made an important connection.

Rick pulled a stack of papers from his briefcase. "I've made copies for each of you," he said, distributing the pages around the table. "As you can see, *Natural Beauty*'s stock has continued to rise each year and we continuously turn a healthy profit."

Peter and John studied the reports and exchanged a look. "You don't seem to need us at all," Peter said, almost sadly.

Ted was quick on the draw. "We do if we want to go international."

"Ah, so the goal is to spread the word the world over. Interesting."

"We think so. There's a lot of potential here. We just need the financing."

"That's our job," Peter said happily, glancing at me.

John shot him a look. "Of course we'll need to have our accountant look over these reports and we'll have to talk to our associates, but it looks good." He tapped the pages on the table top and placed them in his attaché. "We decide things fairly quickly. Peter here shoots from the gut so give us a call in two weeks and we should have an answer for you."

John and Peter rose simultaneously. "It's been interesting gentle—er, people."

Peter reached for my hand and I gave him the engaging deal-closer smile Ted had taught me years ago. "It was a pleasure meeting you."

The two men left the room and Ted swept me up in his arms. "You're incredible," he gushed, spinning me once and depositing me back on my feet. "All that stuff about wishing you'd known his grandfather—he ate it right up."

"Ted, I meant it," I said, laughing.

"I know. And believe me; your sincerity in that one comment probably won us the money."

"It's true," Rick chimed in. "I was watching Peter while you were doing your sales number and I could see it on his face. He wants to give us the money. He wants to give *you* the money because you pulled his heart-strings talking the way his grandfather would have with all that 'let's make the world a better place' stuff."

"That's why I gave her this job," Ted enthused. "Brains, beauty. There's not a man around who can resist Meagan's charms once she's on a roll."

I laughed. "Stop it, Ted. You're making me sound like

your little corporate whore."

"No, you're not my whore, you're *Natural Beauty*'s whore and we both know it."

"I'm not sure I like that comment."

"I think it's a compliment," Rick said.

"Oh, it's a compliment. It may be backhanded, Meagan, but it's yours."

Later that evening I was dressing for Zeppo's show when Jenna bounced through the door wearing boxer shorts and a baggy sweatshirt. Her hair was pulled back in a short, messy ponytail.

"What are you wearing?" I asked, amused. "You can't go to the gallery like that."

Jenna was confused. "Why would *I* be going on *your* date?"

I laughed. "It's not a—" The words caught in my throat. Amber hadn't invited Jenna along. In fact, she'd waited until Jenna had gone for drinks before inviting me. "Oh God," I groaned. "It is a date, isn't it?"

"Yep."

"I can't do this, Jenna. How can I go on a date with a woman?"

Jenna pulled a short black dress with spaghetti straps from my closet. It was backless and made of a thin, almost transparent, fabric. "Easy. You just go. Wear this one. It's sexy."

"Yeah, but how sexy do I want to be?"

She giggled. "You tell me. Besides, I have my own plans for the evening." Her eyebrows moved up and down really fast and I knew she was in the mood to be mysterious. I'd learned long ago not to question Jenna when she was being mysterious. Whatever she was doing she would tell me after she'd done it and no amount of probing was going to get it out of her any sooner.

"Big date?"

"Something like that."

"Is he cute?"

"I think he's adorable. Brown hair, big brown eyes. Totally sexy grin. But that's all you're getting out of me, Meagan. For now."

"Okay."

"Hey, you better hurry. You're gonna be late."

Jenna left so I could finish getting ready. I wore the dress she'd chosen. When I got to the gallery I was amused to find Amber had chosen a similar dress, only in green, which went well with her eyes.

"I wondered what was taking you so long," she said, greeting me at the door with a warm hug. I stiffened, hoping no one was watching, and handed my shoes and jewelry to the attendant who promised them safekeeping until I returned. Amber led me through the crowds of people, my feet already becoming cold against the hardwood floors.

"I want you to meet Zeppo," she said, leading me past canvas after canvas of ridiculous paintings that were nothing more than splashes of color against a black backdrop. I stared at the art while secretly thinking I'd seen the fuzzy-headed stoned man on PBS make better art of a tree.

My eye caught an oddity across the way, a man dressed in black Converse sneakers with no socks, wearing a yellow and orange floral-patterned baby doll dress with a string of pearls around his neck. Added to this monstrosity was a silver spike pierced through his lower lip and big fake lashes a la Carol Channing.

I smirked, thinking up some smart ass quip to share with Amber when I realized, to my horror, that he was exactly the man she was pulling me toward.

Oh God, I thought, *don't laugh. Meagan, don't you dare laugh at him!* I coughed instead and only nodded when Amber asked me if I was all right.

"Zeppo," she said, dragging me before the weird man. "This is Meagan."

"Hello, I—"

"Where have you been?" Zeppo whined, ignoring my extended hand.

The amusement was gone. I hated him.

"Zeppo!" Amber reprimanded. "I'm trying to introduce you to someone."

His eyes flitted over my face impatiently. "Meagan, yes I heard you. Why weren't you here? That fat woman over there was staring at one of my paintings for like fifteen minutes. She just kept *staring!* Then she walked over to the next one and stared at that!" He shoved a fist in his mouth. "I can't take it. Go tell her to leave."

"No. Did you ever think she was wondering which one she wanted to buy?"

"She wasn't," he cried. "She's fat and she's ugly and she hates me!" Zeppo kicked an invisible stone and I had the feeling I was in the presence of a five-year-old.

"I'm sure she was just admiring them," I encouraged. Amber smiled at my effort.

"Why are you wearing that ring?" Zeppo suddenly demanded, grabbing my wrist and yanking my hand to his face for a closer inspection. "I said *no* jewelry. Didn't that glorified waiter tell you?"

"He told me."

"Then why are you wearing it?"

Several people turned at the sound of his shrieking and I wanted to crawl into a hole and die.

"Are you trying to jinx me? She's trying to jinx me! She wants my show to fail!"

I was stunned. Speechless. I hadn't taken the ring off because it was Gran's ring and I never took it off. Not for anyone or anything. I wanted to explain but Zeppo twisted my wrist, bending it backward, and I almost cried out in pain.

"Jesus Christ," Amber hissed, releasing my wrist from Zeppo's snake hold. Four long finger marks left their imprint across my veins.

"Shit." I shook off the pain and moved to hide Zeppo's destruction behind my back but Amber grabbed my arm and turned my wrist to the light. Her eyes widened in surprise and she pressed my wrist under Zeppo's nose.

"Look what you did. You better get a fucking grip and apologize right now or I'm leaving."

"I'm sorry," Zeppo said meekly. "I didn't mean it. I'm just really nervous."

I shook my head but said nothing. What could I say? It's okay? It wasn't okay. He was a rude, artificial little man and no amount of apologizing could make up for what were obviously flaws in his character. He'd behave that way again. Perhaps not to me, but to someone.

Amber placed my hand back at my side and Zeppo burst into tears. "I want to go home," he cried, bending down to bury his face in Amber's neck. She rolled her eyes at me.

"I want to go home!"

Again people turned to gawk and, pretending to see something interesting across the room, I walked away. I couldn't handle being a public spectacle and Zeppo was making sure all three of us became one. He composed himself and I came back.

"You're rude," he said, giving me a disgusted look.

That was it. My temper flared and I took a menacing step toward him. "Listen, you freaky fuc—" My eye caught Amber's and my words fell short. For her sake, I shut up. I counted to five, feeling the blood boil beneath my skin, and told myself to take deep breaths. It was what Jenna would suggest.

Zeppo looked at me. "I don't like you."

"That's it," Amber said, throwing up her arms. "Goodbye, Zeppo." She took my hand and Zeppo latched onto hers.

"No, Amber. Wait. I like her, I do. Look, she's so cute in her little black dress and I've been a jerk. I'm sorry. I'm sorry!"

Amber looked at me and I shrugged. It wasn't the sort of behavior I was used to but it *was* kind of amusing.

Zeppo became the perfect host after that. He led me around his paintings, explained their various meanings, and tried to be a gentleman. It was an exhausting evening. Zeppo was exhausting. And when Amber suggested we leave a few hours later it was all I could do to keep from skipping to the door with shouts of, "Hooray! Hooray!"

"Do you want to go for a drink?" I asked excitedly, when we were out on the curb and I was happily breathing in the fresh night air. "Or we could go for coffee, or grab a late dinner. I don't care. Whatever you want." I was talking fast. So fast it showed my obvious glee.

"You couldn't wait to get out of there, could you?" Amber asked, smiling.

"I'm sorry. Believe me, I'm doing my best to hide how overjoyed I am."

"I'm the one who's sorry. For the most part Zeppo acted like a jerk and aside from calling him a freaky fuck," she grinned, "I think you handled your temper pretty well. Thank you." She squeezed my hand. "I'm sorry if you hated him."

"I didn't—" I began, but Amber arched a disbelieving eyebrow and I smirked. "Okay, I hated him. I would have liked nothing better than to tell him off."

"What stopped you?"

I shrugged. "Jenna told me this was a date so I was on date behavior."

Amber threw back her head and laughed so hard it startled me. "Oh, *Jenna* told you this was a date."

"Yes."

"You didn't think so?"

"I didn't know. I still don't know but I'd be really happy if we could just drop this and go for a drink or something. What do you say? I'll make it up to you."

"How, Meagan?" Her eyes flirted with me.

My throat locked. "I…umm…what?"

She smiled. "I think a drink sounds pretty good after dealing with Zeppo. He can really deplete my energy sometimes."

"I can imagine." She seemed depleted and I found myself admiring her even more for her ability to sustain such a friendship. There was something special about Amber. Sometimes I would catch myself in her, or her in me, and I barely knew her. That was the crazy part of it all. Something told me I knew her when I didn't really *know* her at all. I was just drawn to her. When I was with her I didn't think about Basil. She made me forget him entirely. She made me forget everyone.

Chapter 5

Days passed into weeks and I grew to know Amber as more than just the poet with the eyes. She was funny and intense. Then humorless and laid-back. Each day I found myself unraveling another clue to her mysterious nature and becoming increasingly comfortable in her presence as time pressed forward, moving us past the uncomfortable place we'd started and into a friendship that was both easy and filled with an unnamed energy neither of us was capable of describing. There hadn't been anything physical between us since that first kiss and I sensed it was because Amber was handling me with kid gloves. She didn't want to scare me off, and I was becoming increasingly infatuated with her.

I found myself wanting to spend every minute with her but eventually business called and I was yanked back down to earth. *Earthstuff* was threatening to pull their ad and since that fell within my duties, I was asked to fly to Montreal to meet with Tye Barker to smooth things over. Tye was an old friend. We'd done business several times over the years and I knew the meeting would be a breeze. Gregory Investments had come through and *Natural Beauty* was on the verge of going international. There was no way Tye was going to want to miss out on that. I just had to get to Montreal and speak with him face to face. I was leaving on Friday, I told Amber. She looked sad and a thought popped into my head.

"Do you want to come?" I asked, somewhat surprising myself.

She smiled. "For the weekend?"

Dumbly, I nodded.

That was the weekend I realized I was in love with her. We stood in the hotel lobby where the desk clerk informed us that the magazine had booked a room with only one bed because they assumed I'd be traveling alone, and there weren't any other rooms available. I hadn't planned ahead and now felt like the whole incident reeked of a calculated attempt to get Amber into bed.

"The room *is* large enough for two," the desk clerk offered helpfully.

Amber and I exchanged a glance. "It's fine by me," she said, shrugging.

The man raised an eyebrow in my direction and cast a fervent glance at the small line forming behind us. "It is settled then?" he asked, his charming French accent becoming slightly irritated as the line behind us slowly grew longer.

I nodded. "I guess it's settled."

"*Tres bien.*" He scrambled for one of the dangling keys on the corkboard behind him. This was an old world hotel. No keycards. No computers. Everything was still done on paper. "If you will just sign these forms," he beckoned, shoving a wad of paperwork in front of me with a put-upon sigh that brought out my inner prankster.

"So many," I stalled.

"*Oui.*" He snapped.

The line behind us continued to grow and the man's breath turned to an impatient hiss as I shot Amber a secret grin and went about signing the documents *very slowly*. Rudeness, I felt, deserved its own reward.

Page by page I slowly and painstakingly signed my name like one who had never used a pen before. "And where do I sign this one?" I asked, tapping the point of my pen directly on top of the giant red "X" he'd made earlier, the same red "X" I'd signed my name beside on three other forms. Amber glanced from the page to the man and smirked.

"*Ici,*" he said eagerly, shoving the tip of my pen with his finger and sniffing the air like he smelled something foul. "Here. Where your *pen* is."

"*Oh here?*" I pointed with my finger and giggled like I couldn't believe I was such an idiot. The line behind us shifted uncomfortably and the man tapped the gray and white marble countertop with a perfectly manicured finger. He began pulling the forms away before I finished the "s" on my last name and I fought him a little, pressing my palm against the bottom of the page and securing it to the counter. "Wait! Did I sign them all?"

Amber looked like she was going to burst as "Pierre" yanked the pages out from under my hand and huffed, "*Oui Mademoiselle*, you have signed every last one!"

"Good… now about the room." There was a collective groan behind us and the man shoved a key at me.

"You are in room four-oh-three," he said, haughtily. "And I wish you a very pleasant stay." We were dismissed.

Amber and I fell into the elevator roaring with laughter. *"Oh here?"* she mocked, jabbing her finger at the air in front of us. Swiftly, she shifted into a pompous French accent, screwing up her face. "*You have signed every last one*! Oh my God, you had him so pissed I thought I was going to die laughing right there."

The doors glided open and we stepped out into the fourth floor hallway and found our room. The clerk had been right about the room. It was spacious and pretty, with a view from the window a mile long. Two chairs and a small coffee table sat in front of a stone fireplace. To the left was a large bathroom, complete with floor to ceiling mirrors, a shower and a Jacuzzi tub. A long blue couch stretched along one wall in the bedroom area, and across from that, situated in the center of the room was a bed so big Amber and I could both sleep in it and still have three feet of space between us. That was an unlikely scenario but the thought still occurred to me.

"Mind if I take a shower?" Amber asked, strolling into the luxurious bathroom.

I glanced at my watch. "That's fine. I have to take off now anyway."

There was the sound of a tap being turned on. "Great."

I gathered my purse and briefcase from where I'd dropped them on the bed and called out to Amber. "I'll be back around five, okay?" No answer. "Amber?"

"Did you call me?" Amber yelled over the din of the shower.

"Yes, I –"

"You have to come in here. I can't hear you."

Nervously, I approached the bathroom. "I'll be back by five," I repeated, avoiding eye contact with the crystalline shower curtain.

Amber poked her head around the transparent drape and smiled. "You're so cute."

"Why?" I knew she didn't mean cute as in *attractive*-- she meant silly.

"You're just so –" She searched for the right word. "Shy."

Shy. It wasn't a word often used to describe me but I supposed in that situation it was precisely the right one. I couldn't shake the idea that Amber was naked behind that curtain and it was making me uncomfortably curious. I wanted to see her, and that struck me as a perversity I wasn't willing to deal with just then. The last thing I wanted was to discover I was a peeper thirty minutes before a business meeting.

The water went off and a long golden leg stretched to the bathroom floor. I turned my head.

"I gotta go," I said quickly, and high-tailed it out of there, jumping into a cab downstairs and rattling off *Earthstuff*'s address to the disinterested driver.

The meeting went as planned and when I returned Amber was sitting in front of the empty fireplace reading a book and eating strawberries off a silver room service tray.

"I hope you don't mind," she said, dropping the book in her lap. "I got hungry."

"No problem." I tossed my purse and briefcase on the floor by the bed and sat in the chair across from her, plucking a strawberry off the tray and savoring its sweet taste.

"How'd the meeting go?"

I shrugged. "Piece of cake."

"Supreme confidence, huh?"

"Where business is concerned, yes."

A room service menu sat on the table and I picked it up, absentmindedly reading down the list of entrees. Amber moved to the window.

"Looks like rain," she said, sliding her hands into the back pockets of her cut-off shorts. Her legs seemed more tanned than the rest of her.

My eyes glanced down at the menu again. "I hate rain."

"You do?" She turned to face me. "Why?"

Because the first time I ever saw a dead body was in the rain. It was the year Gran died and I had come across it while playing with a boy in the woods behind our neighborhood park. Sometimes the image still haunted me. The open eyes. The rain spilling into the agape mouth and dripping over the decomposing lips and down the chin.

I shook my head. "It's stupid, really. Just something that happened when I was a kid."

"And it made you afraid of the rain?"

"Something like that. Nightmares sometimes. But it only gets to me when I'm alone."

Her eyes met mine. "You're not alone now."

My heart gave a nervous flutter. "No."

The rain started up quickly, falling in glistening noiseless sheets outside the window behind her back. I stood. Amber moved toward me and the room grew dim, yielding to the darkness outside and wrapping us in its silent embrace as evening waxed around us. The sky was a purple-gray and the world ground to a halt as I felt the breath leave Amber's body in a long slow stream and saw the smile curl the end of her lips.

I smiled back. "I'm sorry, Amber," I said, "but I'm going to kiss you."

She laughed and then my lips met hers, initiating the kiss like she had the first. Then the intensity again. The fervor I assumed only I noticed, but I was wrong because when we broke our embrace Amber said, "Do you feel that when we kiss, Meagan? That energy? I felt it the first time and thought I'd imagined it. Now I know I hadn't because it was just there again a second ago."

I nodded. "I think it's the oral equivalent of an orgasm."

She raised an eyebrow and grinned.

"You know what I mean," I added quickly.

"I know. Did you want to order something?" She pointed at the room service menu still clutched in my hand. We seemed to have made an unspoken agreement to stay in and decided on stuffed mushrooms, baked lobster tails, and a bottle of champagne. It was going on the company expense account. We could have ordered the whole menu for all I cared.

By the time we finished eating we were already calling down for our second bottle of bubbly. Amber sat in the center of the large bed and raised her glass at the bellboy as he handed me a fresh bottle of champagne and carted away the servicing tray. She patted the space next to her. I sat down and refilled her glass.

"I have a confession to make," she said.

I poured a glass for myself and set the bottle on the floor

by the bed. "Go for it."

She grinned mysteriously. "I wasn't exactly bothered when we found out there was only one bed."

I laughed. "Me either."

"Really?"

"I didn't do it on purpose."

"I know."

"But I'm glad it worked out the way it did."

She looked at me meaningfully. "Are you scared?"

"Are you?" I countered. The champagne was loosening my tongue.

"Why should I be?"

"Why should I?"

She laughed. "Do you always do that?"

"Do I always do what?"

"Answer a question with a question."

"Do you want the truth?"

"Yes."

I sipped my champagne. "I'm terrified. And what scares me even more than wanting to make love to you is that I've come to realize I feel compelled to tell you the absolute truth every time you ask me a question."

She took the cigarette I'd been smoking from my hand and took a drag. "Are you saying you're usually a liar?"

I took the cigarette back. "No. But I can do it if I have to."

"And you can't with me?"

I dragged on the cigarette one last time before crushing it in the ashtray. "I don't think I can. You'd look at me with those big green eyes and the truth would come pouring out. It's been happening since the day we met. That makes me vulnerable and *that* scares me."

"I'm scared too," she admitted, leaning back against the pillows.

I stretched out beside her, rested my head on my folded arms, and stared up at her, awed. "Why?"

"Because it's you," she said, easily. "Because I knew you were straight from the first second I saw you but I couldn't help wanting you. And I do want you, Meagan, more than you could know."

I didn't know how to respond to that. "Wanna see my

tattoo?" I asked.

"You have a tattoo?" She thought that was funny. I didn't look like the type who would have an ink blot under my Donna Karan business suit and violet Victoria's Secret matching bra and panties.

Of course, she hadn't seen those either. The suit had come off and I'd changed into loose fitting jeans and a button-down shirt when I'd closed myself off in the bathroom earlier to take a shower.

"It was a mistake," I said, lifting the back of my shirt. The tattoo was at the base of my spine, in that small crease at the bottom of the back, and rarely did I allow anyone to see it. "I was young, drunk, and stupid."

Amber leaned in to inspect the damage. "A butterfly," she said. "I think it's sexy."

I laughed. "I think you're full of shit."

"I have a tattoo."

"You do?"

She grinned. "No. I just want to get naked with you."

"Is that lesbian foreplay?" I joked.

"No, this is." She pressed forward and kissed me, then slowly started unbuttoning my shirt. She kissed my neck and my throat and playfully tugged on my hair.

"Don't be afraid, okay?" she whispered.

I shivered at her breath on my ear. "I'm not."

"Good, because I really want you. You're so beautiful."

"I want you too." I touched her face, kissed her, and we undressed each other. Slowly at first, and then passionately, tearing away each other's clothes and falling on the bed together.

Amber turned out to be the most incredible lover I had ever encountered. She made me gasp, and I wasn't a gasper. A talker, maybe. A moaner, a whisperer, even a screamer at times, but no one had ever made me gasp for breath or awakened as many sensations within me as she did. I touched every inch of her that I could, with my hands, my mouth, my tongue. I thought of all the things I would want someone to do to me and then did those things to her. When it was done we lay wrapped up on the bed together, spent.

"Jesus, Meagan," she said. "You have so been with a woman before."

I laughed. "Swear to God, I haven't. Nice flattery, though."

"I am *not* flattering you. That was –"

"Amazing," I whispered.

"Fucking right it was. I thought you were scared."

"I was, at first."

"But?"

I lit a cigarette. "I don't know, suddenly being with you felt like the most natural thing in the world. I don't know when it first happened, Amber, but somewhere between that first kiss and now you've crept into me and I feel utterly consumed by you. Is that the way it works?"

Laughing, she stole my cigarette again. "You mean does lesbianism creep into your bloodstream like a virus?"

"Not lesbianism-- *you*."

She gave back the cigarette. "I don't know, Meagan. I know what you're saying because I feel it happening too but I don't have an answer for you because this has never happened to me before either. I feel like we're connected in a way I've never known and nothing has ever felt more right."

I smiled. "So you do feel it."

"Yes, I definitely feel it." Then her eyes met mine and there was a sudden sadness about them. "But don't hurt me, okay?"

Her words startled me. Filled me with guilt for something I hadn't even done. "Why would I hurt you?"

Lovingly, she touched my face. "I don't know, but I feel you have the potential to break my heart."

I didn't want to believe that. Couldn't believe it. "I won't hurt you, Amber," I said. "Because the truth is, I'm in love with you."

It was so easy to get lost in Amber. There was something about her eyes and the way they seemed to peer into my very soul. She didn't look at me so much as through me. Capable of saying everything and nothing with a mere look, throughout the weekend I would discover that although we did talk --a lot-- ultimately, words were unimportant between us. We were connecting on a level that surpassed the need for incessant conversation and this new realm was both intimidating and enlightening. Being in Amber's presence was like being in the center of a healing light and I found myself becoming liberated from the stereotypes and biases that were more a part of the person I was than I'd ever truly believed. When we made love I did not feel as if we were two women coming together --only two people-- and the wonderment of it all was that I'd never known I could be so unencumbered.

By Sunday there wasn't an inhibition left between us. We had examined every inch of each other, body and soul. We talked, made love, basked in the lapses of comfortable silence, and talked some more, leaving the room only once during the entire weekend to do some shopping, and then returning to continue the cycle we'd begun.

Amber slept on the flight home, her head resting gently against my shoulder. I stared down at her sleeping form and I knew I was infatuated. I felt like I'd always known her, like there was some strange, ethereal connection that pulled us together. I knew her soul, it seemed, while at the same time only just discovering who she was as a person. I was discovering a new world, and doing so was always a challenge, but there I was, about to embark on a journey and already curious to know the outcome. I never was good at waiting.

The next three weeks passed quickly. Three weeks of falling more deeply in love with Amber. We had settled into a relationship quickly and hadn't spent a night apart since returning home from Montreal. We took turns sleeping at each other's apartments and all around basked in the euphoria we felt when we were together.

One Friday morning Amber left my apartment with promises of returning later and, happily, I went about cleaning, stopping only when my nose was met with the lemony-fresh scent that indicated a job well done. Spotless. I put away my cleaning supplies and allowed myself a smile as someone knocked on the big metal door. Jenna screwing around, I knew, because anyone else would have to buzz up from the lobby. I swung open the door and the grin froze on my face. Basil! Basil Waite. Ex-boyfriend and killjoy.

"What do you want?" I asked coldly, sizing him up with a glare.

His thick black hair fell in bouncy curls around his shoulders, his body as long and lean as ever, and his eyes dark and seductive. They slid over my body, pausing on my breasts, and leaving me feeling naked in my frayed cut-off shorts and white ribbed tank. He grinned at my bra-less chest and I cringed.

"You're looking good," he said, biting his lower lip. "Gonna let me in?"

I didn't move. "Why?"

"So we can talk."

My arms dropped to my sides and Basil brushed past me into the living room.

"We have nothing to talk about," I said as he plopped himself on my couch and sparked up a joint.

The skunky odor overpowered the fresh scent of my living room and I gave a disgusted sniff. Basil inhaled the offending smoke and offered me the joint. I couldn't help thinking him stupid. Had he even noticed that I hadn't smoked a joint with him in over three years?

"Well?" I asked impatiently. My foot tapped the floor.

Basil shrugged. "I miss you." He flicked the ash off the end of the joint into his hand and tilted it away from him. The ash fluttered silently to the floor. Frowning, I moved to pick it up.

"So?"

"So don't you miss me?"

"No."

"I don't believe you."

"I don't care."

I placed an ashtray on the table in front of him and his hand suddenly slid up the back of my shirt. I felt a small jolt. Nothing terribly thrilling, but enough to make me consider what it would be like to sleep with him again. Would it be as good as it had been in the beginning? As good as it was with Amber? No, that was impossible.

An image of Amber lying beside me flashed before my eyes and I almost laughed out loud at the perplexity of my situation. Basil was staring at me through hooded lids, all loose-limbed and raring to go. I felt nothing.

I peered at him more thoughtfully. Nothing. I tried to imagine his hands on my body and couldn't. It was finally gone. I was free. I didn't want Basil at all.

"I think you should leave," I said.

He merely looked at me. "Come on baby," he said, rubbing his stomach. "Fix me a steak like you used to?"

"You must be kidding."

"Please," he whined, and slipped into playing Mr. Needy, his most dreaded alter ego. "I haven't had a decent meal since we broke up."

"Yeah?"

"Why the hell did we break up anyway? We were great together." His filthy boots slammed against the top of my coffee table and I cringed. It hadn't been great between us since we passed the one-year mark.

"Remember that time we went to the zoo and that monkey got a hold of your hair and was trying to kiss you through the bars?" He laughed. "We had a lot of good times. Remember?"

I knew what he was doing. He was trying to get me to remember the chemistry we'd had in the beginning. Bringing up the zoo incident was a thinly-veiled attempt at reminding me of the amazing sex we'd had in the reptile house.

"I'll show you a snake," Basil had groaned that day. Then he'd pressed me up against the glass while a hundred beady-eyed reptiles slithered behind my head. It was the creepiest thing I'd ever done, and now Basil was trying to get me to bring it up. I wouldn't.

"I remember the good times, Basil," I said in a bored tone. "I also remember how you couldn't keep your dick in your pants."

"History, baby. We can move past that."

"I don't want to. I don't even want you sitting on my couch. And stop calling me baby. There's nothing between us anymore and there hasn't been for a long time. Deal with it."

Basil did not take the news well. "You fucking dyke!" he yelled, springing to his feet.

The words reverberated in my head and I nearly fell over. *"What?"*

"You heard me," he hissed, strolling toward the door. He waved a bony finger at me. "Oh, I know all about you. The whole fucking city's talking about how you're dyking around with some little blond bitch."

Words failed me. I felt like throwing up. Staggering to the door, I swung it open and steadied myself against the handle. "Get out." My voice was ice.

"Gladly." But instead of stalking into the hallway Basil pressed his face into mine and stared at me with cold black eyes.

"Into pussy all along," he hushed. "I should have known. It explains why you were such a lousy fuck."

Tears welled behind my eyes. "I hate you," I whispered.

"Yeah? The feeling is mutual. *Cunt*." He slammed the door behind him and I was left to choke on the sickness that crept up in my throat.

I hadn't planned on anyone knowing yet. Somehow Basil had found out and it wouldn't be long before others did too. I knew Basil didn't really mean the hurtful things he'd said-- it was just his way of expressing the pain of rejection; but I also feared his words could be true. Was I a dyke now? I studied my face in the mirror by the door.

Dyke.

Somehow it still didn't ring true. My cheeks were flushed and wet with tears but it was the same face I'd had last week, the same one I'd had last year. Nothing about the image in the glass had changed but I knew, without a doubt, that I was not the same person. Amber had come along and she'd screwed with who I was. She'd changed my most basic nature. I struggled to imagine myself with any woman other than her and couldn't. I still wasn't gay. I didn't even think I was bisexual. The face in the mirror stared back as the realization dawned on me. It had nothing to do with sexuality! I gasped. It was the thing! The thing Gran said I would know when the time came along, and now it was here. The ring…and the purpose…and I knew what I had to do. I darted for the phone.

It was dark by the time Amber arrived. The street below was eerily quiet and I fantasized that the universe had banished all life from the area in reverence to us. The time had finally come and I wanted it to be perfect.

Amber entered the candlelit apartment and followed me into the bedroom, filled with more candles, vases of fresh flowers, and a bottle of white wine on ice. I didn't know if this was her idea of romance, but it was mine. She said she thought it was beautiful and my anxieties dissipated.

She sat on the bed and I poured two glasses of wine and sat down beside her. Then I proceeded to tell her everything that had happened with Basil. Throughout my tale she didn't say a word, only listened, but I could sense her fear. That she thought I might go back to him was clearly marked in her eyes.

She turned away from me, bent her head, and stared at the floor. I crouched in front of her, so she was forced to look at me. The emerald gaze met mine and she managed a weak smile.

"My honesty hurts you?" I asked.

"A little."

"I can't lie to you." I sat down beside her again.

"Why do you insist that?" She wanted to believe me but she was afraid.

"Because you're my soul mate. My grandmother always told me that the one person I would never be able to lie to was my soul mate."

She smiled. "I thought you said your grandmother was crazy."

"Not always." Twisting the ring on my finger I felt myself filled with an emotion I had never felt before, a *rightness*. "My gran gave me this ring," I said quietly. "It's not worth much monetarily but it was never meant to be. It has one purpose, which not another living soul knows other than me."

"And you're going to tell me?" she whispered.

"I have to. Truthfully, I'm obligated to."

"I don't understand."

"You will." I took a breath. "My grandmother had a secret lover when she was a young girl in Ireland, a woman. Her name was Rosalie and my gran was desperately in love with her. But my grandmother was also afraid. She carried on an affair with this woman-- or girl I should probably say-- for four years, until she married my grandfather at the age of nineteen and eventually left Ireland."

"What happened to Rosalie?" Amber asked.

"She eventually married too. Her family followed my grandmother's over from Ireland and anyone else who might have known this story is now dead. My grandmother drifted in and out of lucidity but her story never changed when it came to Rosalie. That was very clear in her head. Sometimes as she talked I thought perhaps she wasn't really there with me at all and was actually off somewhere with Rosalie. Gran swore me to secrecy."

"How old were you?"

I laughed. "Ten."

"Wow, I'm not sure *I* even knew what a lesbian was at ten."

"Did you know you thought other girls were pretty?"

Amber thought about the question. "Yes," she said slowly.

I nodded. "See, I didn't. My grandmother would be telling me this beautiful tale of love and betrayal and sometimes I'd just look up at her wrinkled face and think, *God Gran, you're really gross*. But I could never hold the thought because what my grandmother was talking about was so much more than love. She believed Rosalie was her soul mate and that there was a bond between them that would last through time. The ring is a symbol of that bond."

Amber sat back against the headboard, fascinated. "Did Rosalie give her the ring?"

I pressed back beside her and couldn't help smiling. "You relate to Rosalie, don't you?"

"I think maybe I do. The impression I'm getting from your story is that Rosalie wasn't as afraid as your grandmother. It's sort of like us. Would she have gotten married if your grandmother hadn't?"

"No," I said, quietly. "She wanted to be with my grandmother but my grandmother didn't see how that was realistically possible, considering the era.

"She loved Rosalie, I'm sure, much more than she ever loved my grandfather, but *he* made sense. Being with him made her normal. It was hard for the two women to accept they would never be together again, not in that capacity anyway, but they worked on it and instead became friends. Rosalie had the ring specially designed for my grandmother and she created the symbolism. She chose a moonstone because it's the stone of silence and dreams. That was their bond, to always dream together and to always keep silent about the love they shared. They *were* soul mates. The physical part of their relationship ended when each of them married but nothing could truly pry them apart. Rosalie gave my gran the ring and told her that as long as she wore it they would always be connected. My grandmother never took it off. It was her way of never truly abandoning Rosalie and she continued to wear it long after Rosalie died and until the day of her own death."

Amber sipped her champagne. "And that's why you wouldn't take it off at Zeppo's show."

I twisted the ring on my finger. It was going to feel strange being without it. "I've never taken it off. For six years I wore it on a chain around my neck, and when I was sixteen it finally fit my finger. It's been there ever since. But there's more. See, I always knew the ring wouldn't be mine forever. I was its temporary guardian, so to speak. Eventually, I would find the right person, the one who matched *my* soul, and the ring would serve as *my* bond to him." I smiled, slipping the ring off my finger. "Or her, as it turns out. It's you, Amber. You're the one who fits me and I want you to have the ring. But know that if you accept it, we will be bonded until the day you remove it or until the day we die."

"I—I don't know what to say," she stammered, her eyes misting. "Are you sure?"

"After sixteen years of knowing when it was wrong, yes I'm sure. It couldn't belong to anyone else; I know that in my heart. I know you're my soul mate --although you may be too pragmatic to believe that-- and I know it's right."

Lovingly, she touched my cheek. "I'm so in love with you," she whispered. "I've been in love with you since the first time I ever heard you say my name. And I don't fall in love easily, that's the scary part. I can love someone, but not like this. I've never felt what I feel for you. I would love to wear your grandmother's ring and accept whatever symbolism it locks us into."

"I don't take this lightly, Amber," I warned. "This is very important to me."

"I can see that. And the fact that you're giving it to me makes it even more special. I know what's between us is unusual. Your ring is a symbol of that and I would never betray it."

Satisfied with her response, I slipped the ring on her finger, and smiled as her eyes misted over.

"You're a peculiar woman, aren't you Meagan?" She was grinning.

"Yes." I never shied away from my oddities.

"And so utterly honest."

"With you."

"Always?"

"Yes."

Chapter 6

The coming weeks were definitely those of discovery. Amber wore the ring and she knew what it meant but that didn't stop her from teaching me a few lessons along the way.

The first lesson came one evening while we were in the Cauldron with Jenna. It was a Wednesday evening, open mic for musicians and singers. Sarah, an acoustic guitar wielding songwriter, was at the mike murdering her latest musical rip-off, a song that sounded peculiarly like Jewel's "You Were Meant for Me," and I wondered if I was the only one who noticed how similar her "original" songs were to those that got massive radio play.

Amber sat beside me, her leg pressed against mine under the table, her hand casually resting beside my thigh. She didn't have a problem with public affection, especially not in the Cauldron where everyone knew she was gay, but she knew it made me uncomfortable so she was going easy on me --for now.

A familiar figure came through the door and Jenna turned and smiled.

"Isn't that your brother?" Amber asked, recognizing him from the pictures in my apartment. She hadn't met him at the party.

Josh crossed the room, took the seat beside Jenna, and I felt my suspicions mount. Josh, Mr. Yuppie Accountant, in a coffeehouse? Jenna giggling like a schoolgirl? Was it possible...?

"Oh my God!" I gasped.

"What?" Josh asked, innocently. He squeezed Jenna's hand and she grinned.

"You know what! *Josh* is the mystery man? *Jenna* is the reason you've stopped dating those vacant-headed models? Why didn't you *tell* me?" But I couldn't hide my own grin. It was crazy but they actually looked good together!

Jenna giggled and glanced at Amber. "You've been so busy lately. Besides, it wasn't all that serious at first."

"And now?"

They looked at each other like a couple of honeymooners. "It's serious."

"I can't believe you didn't tell me," I scolded, jumping to my feet and crushing them in a hug. "But I think it's great."

"It was *killing* me not to tell you," Jenna admitted. "You're not upset?"

"Why would I be upset?" My eyes turned to Josh and I suddenly gave him a hard look. He was known for being a playboy. "And you better not fuck with her either, Josh. I'm warning you right now."

"For Christ's sake, Meagan. Why do you always have to get like that? I'm not gonna hurt her. Quit being everyone's guard dog and relax."

"I'm just saying –"

"I know what you're saying. That's in the past, all right? I don't need to nail every pretty girl I see anymore. I'm crazy about Jenna."

I broke out laughing. "Well, crazy is always a fitting word where Jenna's concerned."

"Hey!" Jenna joined in my laughter. "Is that a spot of dust on the table, Meagan? You better wipe it up." Everyone enjoyed making fun of the fact that I was a clean freak.

Amber laughed and I turned to face her. "You've met Amber, right?" I asked my brother, knowing full well he hadn't.

"I don't think I have." Josh extended his hand across the table and I saw his eyes make note of the ring on her finger. He didn't react.

The two exchanged hellos but Amber's eyes never left my face for more than a second. I sensed anticipation. She was waiting for me to say, "Hey, Josh. I have a confession of my own to make," but it wasn't going to happen. I wasn't sure I was ready for that.

I took my seat beside her again and waited for the pressure of her leg, the feel of her hand brushing my thigh. Neither happened. There was a sudden tension in the air between us and Amber, ever so slightly, shifted her body away from mine. The move was imperceptible to the naked eye but I *knew*. She was sending me a non-verbal message. One that said if I was going to pretend she didn't exist then she was going to act like she didn't exist. For thirty minutes she kept up a polite conversation with my brother while managing to ignore me at the same time. Josh and Jenna rose to leave to spend the night at Josh's apartment. Jenna asked if I would stop in and feed Bacon.

"There are leftovers in the fridge," she said. "Just microwave them for about forty-five seconds and he'll eat it right up."

Great, I thought. Now I'm cooking for a pig.

Amber remained stonily silent. I tried to make conversation but she refused to answer my questions with anything more than one-word responses. Finally, I'd had enough.

I rose to my feet. "Whatever your problem is– I'm going home. We can go back to my apartment and discuss it if you want but I can't sit around here all night playing games with you. I have a pig to feed."

The strangeness of my own words hit me and I smirked. Amber scowled and I turned on my heel and walked out. Within ten steps she was beside me, matching my quick march stride for stride. Not a word passed between us as we crossed the street and entered my building. In the elevator she looked at me sideways, folded her arms across her chest, and turned the other way. I was reminded of an angry cartoon character and burst out laughing.

"Yeah, it's real funny," she huffed, tapping a black Doc Marten against the elevator floor.

It looked like a tremendous effort in those heavy boots and I couldn't control the chortle that continued to erupt in my throat. Nothing could wipe the smirk off my face, not even Amber's icy stare.

Outside Jenna's apartment I was still grinning. I jangled the keys in the door and my grin only widened at the sound of little hooves tap-tapping against the hardwood on the other side. The door swung back on its hinges and Bacon ambled toward us like a happy dog. He nudged my leg with his snout and I knew what he was trying to tell me.

"I have to take him to the roof so he can go to the bathroom," I said.

Amber said nothing. Shrugging, she followed me as I led Bacon up the short flight of stairs at the end of the hall, pushed open the door, and stepped outside. The roof wasn't used often for such a purpose, only when it was too late to walk Bacon.

Ten minutes passed. Amber still said nothing. Miserably, I walked to the end of the roof and stared out across the sky. Lights twinkled in the distance. They flicked off and on in the buildings across the way like a hundred tiny fairies fluttering their golden wings and dancing through the night with all the erratic energy of summer fireflies. The moon was a giant silver globe in the sky. I loved the night.

"Got another cigarette?" Amber asked from behind me. "I ran out back at the Cauldron."

"Oh, you can talk when you want something," I bitched.

"Fine, forget it."

But I was already pulling a cigarette from the pack in my hand. I tossed it to her, along with my lighter, and turned back to face the city. A gray cloud of smoke floated past my head.

"Why didn't you tell him about us?" Amber asked. Her voice was small and frail as a child's.

"I knew that's what this was about."

"Well, why didn't you tell him?"

I turned to face her. "Don't you think he already knows? He's going out with my best friend, for Christ's sake, and much as I love Jenna she has one major fault– she is in possession of the biggest mouth I've ever seen. She couldn't keep a secret if her life depended on it. Then there's the ring. Josh saw it. He may not know what it means but he certainly knows it was our grandmother's and the fact that it's on your finger is a pretty good indication that you're more than a friend to me."

"So you're upset," she stated.

I weighed her comment, searching for its truth. There was none. "No, I'm not upset. I'm not anything. But I'm also not about to run around telling everyone I see about us either. I'm just not there yet. Can you understand that?"

Slowly, she nodded. "But you'll have to tell eventually, Meagan, because I won't be your dirty little secret forever."

"First of all, don't threaten me. And secondly, you're not my dirty little secret."

"I wasn't threatening you. I just don't want to hide us."

"Okay." I could see her point and pulled her to me. "If it will make you feel better I'll invite both Josh and Danielle over for supper one night and we can tell them together. But that's it, Amber. That's as far as I go right now."

"I can deal with that."

"Good. It's better Danny knows anyway. Otherwise she just might show up one night to find you in my bed and, much as I love having you in my bed, that's not really the way I'd want her to find out."

"Do you *really* love having me in your bed, Meagan?" she teased, kissing me.

I kissed her back. "You know I do. Are we making up now?"

"Were we fighting?"

"You weren't talking to me. I think that counts."

"So we've had our first fight. Tell me."

I frowned. "Tell you what?"

"That you love me. We'll make it a rule. If one of us says, 'tell me,' the other has to respond with 'I love you', no matter what."

"Even during a fight?" I thought I liked the idea.

"Especially during a fight. So tell me."

"It's your game. You tell me."

She smiled. "I love you."

"I love you too."

"You're going to make me insane, aren't you?"

The laugh tickled my throat. "I think we're going to do it to each other."

Lesson one in Amberology: She didn't like secretiveness. Lesson two: When pissed off she was likely to retaliate. Lesson three: she had a jealous streak.

It came on Saturday night when she took me to a gay bar on the Upper West Side of town to hear her friend Tori's band play. I'd never been to a gay bar before and found the whole thing fascinating. I gawked at my surroundings, made note of the same-sex couples dancing together and making out, smiled at how comfortable they all seemed together, then clung to Amber's arm when the catcalls began.

"Caught yourself a straight one this time, huh?" someone called.

Amber allowed herself a throaty chuckle. "Don't start, Janice."

It was hard for me to picture her in such a setting but she seemed to know each of these people by name and they yelled out hellos and waved a lot.

"How could that woman possibly know whether or not I'm straight?" I whispered.

Amber leaned into me, matching my hushed tone. "Because you look terrified, Meagan. Relax."

We approached the bar and a large woman of masculine appearance sipped her beer and leered at me. "How's it goin', Amber?" she said. Her eyes flitted over my body. "You can send this one my way when you're done."

The woman was talking about me like I was a piece of meat and I scowled then stepped behind Amber, concealing myself from the woman's lusty stare.

"It's not like that Marge," Amber said easily.

"It's always like that." Marge peered at me over Amber's shoulder. "What's her name?"

"None of your business," I barked. I wasn't sure where the words had come from but they sprang out of me and Amber looked at me with an amused expression. I gave a small shrug.

"Bitchy little thing, ain't she? I like that."

My stomach gave a nervous leap and I leaned into Amber's ear. "Can we please just get away from this person?" I whispered. She smiled. Nodded.

"See ya later, Marge," she said. We headed toward an empty table near the stage and sat down. "That's Large Marge. She's harmless. Just likes to tease the heteros and the femmes. You look like both so you're a pretty good target."

"Well, you're not exactly butch, Amber. You're probably the most feminine woman in this place." I glanced around the bar and smirked. "Except for maybe *that* guy."

Amber glanced over at the man in drag a few tables away and laughed. "He sort of puts RuPaul to shame, doesn't he? I don't want to freak you out, Meagan, but you are going to draw a lot of attention."

"Why?"

"Do men come onto you all the time?"

"No more than they come onto you."

"It's no different here," she said, nodding. "Only instead it would be women coming onto you. Either way, you're very attractive and that causes attention."

I thought about her words. "So, that's how you feel when men come onto you? That uneasiness?"

"Not really. I'm used to it."

"How do you get used to constantly being hit on by both sexes?"

She shrugged. "You just do."

"Especially when you look like you, right?"

"If you're trying to say I'm attractive, thank you."

"Attractive!" The laughter burst out of me. "You're infuriatingly beautiful."

"Infuriatingly, huh?"

A light came on over the stage and five people came out, strapping on instruments and approaching the microphones.

"That's my word, yes. Your friend's the lead singer?"

Amber nodded and gave a little wave up at the stage. Tori adjusted her microphone, strapped on her guitar, and shook her fingers through her short black hair. She had pale blue eyes, a thin, almost boyish build, and full purple lips. She looked like a celebrity. The band kicked into a pulsing alternative rock number and Tori's voice came through the room in a velvety, husky wail. She was good. She had the look, the sound, and it was obvious she loved being on stage.

I reached for a cigarette and settled back in my chair, noticing that Amber had stopped speaking. Her face had changed too, I realized. There was now a determined set to her jaw, like something was about to happen and she was preparing herself for it. With growing fear, it dawned on me that Amber had brought me to this club for a specific reason. Tori leaned off the stage seductively and I found what that reason was: jealousy. Tori was suddenly singing to Amber and Amber was grinning like she'd been waiting for this moment. She'd known this was going to happen and she'd brought me to this club because she wanted *me* to know she had other options. She was still pissed about what happened with my brother and she was playing the old "You may not want me all the way but someone else will" game. Hadn't I played that game a few times myself?

I knew what she was doing. Instead of confronting me and telling me she was still angry, she was childishly encouraging this scene.

"You're twenty-five," I snapped. "Grow the hell up."

Tori continued her rock serenade and Amber gave me an innocent look. "What are you talking about?" She was smirking.

Jealousy crept in but I fought its effects. Decided I would have to get away from her for a minute if I was going to remain in control. I would not give her the satisfaction.

"I'm gonna get a drink from the bar. Want anything?"

At those words she did the most amazing, infuriating thing. Without turning to look at me, she said, "Vodka and grapefruit," and waved me away like I was an annoying bug in her ear.

My eyes saw red. It took every bit of my self-control to walk away and by the time I reached the bar there was a rage in my head so thick, I thought, *fine --she wants to play? I'll play.*

Amber was watching me from the table. I could feel her eyes on my back as I ordered our drinks and quickly sized up the bartender, an attractive woman in her early thirties with long brown hair and brown eyes. She'd do. I struck up a conversation.

Ten minutes later the drinks I ordered still sat on the bar between us and the bartender and I were bantering back and forth like old pals. We were talking, laughing, flirting, and all the while Amber was back at the table stewing in the ramifications of the game she'd started.

"I think your friend is getting upset," the bartender said, nodding in Amber's direction. "She keeps giving me dirty looks."

I glanced over at Amber, who was indeed shooting emerald daggers. I sipped my rum and coke, and resumed my conversation. Amber stalked up to me.

"I'm leaving," she growled. "You can stay if you want." A hard look at the bartender. "Yeah, why don't you stay? You seem comfortable enough now."

She moved to march past me but I crossed my arm over the bar, blocking her way.

"Amber, it's just—"

"Fuck you." She doubled back the other way and disappeared into the crowd.

"Shit." Why did I always have to react when provoked?

"Aww, let her go," the bartender said, giving me the eye.

I stalked away from the bar and pushed my way through the crowds until I reached the doors. Outside, Amber was nowhere to be found.

"Long gone," a flirtatious male voice offered from the left.

I turned to find Zeppo, dressed like a man tonight in black jeans and a black shirt, his long brown hair pulled back in a ponytail. He was leaning against a stop sign smoking a long brown cigarillo.

"You were bad," he admonished, waving a thin finger at me.

"Me?" I was incredulous. "You should have seen what she was doing in there, trying to making me jealous with her little singer friend." I nearly spat those last words.

Zeppo shook his head knowingly. "I told her not to go there. Jealousy, ha, it's for children." He chewed on the end of a red swizzle stick. "I suppose you'll want to catch up to her. Took a cab home. And I just happen to be heading in that direction."

Zeppo lived on the second floor of Amber's building. Folding forward in a royal bow, he stated grandly, "So I shall drop you at her door as I am a most wonderful advocate of love."

"Can we just go?" I snapped. I was angry at myself for letting Amber convince me to leave my car parked outside her building and Zeppo had a way of getting under my skin. He let out a put-upon sigh.

"Amber always did pick the prickly ones," he complained. "But let us go find my chariot."

Zeppo had been drinking. I drove. We arrived at Amber's apartment and she refused to let me in. Zeppo convinced her she had two choices: she could open the door voluntarily or he would unlock it with his spare key. The door swung back on its hinges, Zeppo said "*Bonsoir*, ladies," and I was suddenly left alone to face the darkness inside. The apartment was black and I struggled to find the lamp on the end table. My fingers grasped the pull chain and the room filled with a soft yellow light. Amber sat on a loveseat under the window, staring outside.

"You shouldn't have started with me," I said, dropping down beside her. I wasn't aware of how self-righteous I sounded until Amber sprang to her feet.

"Fuck you, Meagan."

"Stop saying that to me. Am I swearing at you?"

"Well, do you think I'm blind? Do you think I didn't see

what was going on between you and that bartender?"

"I *know* you saw it," I said, smirking. "That was rather the point, wasn't it? And it's no different from what was going on between you and that wannabe Melissa Etheridge up there. If you're going to play games, Amber, expect that I'll do the same."

Her eyes narrowed to slits, concealing all remnants of the green I had come to love. Her next words were so quiet I wasn't sure I had heard them at all but the determined set to her jaw proved I had.

"You're a bitch," she whispered.

I was unbothered. "Sometimes. But only when provoked."

Then she wanted to know if I was really attracted to that bartender, and why didn't I just go and be with her since I obviously enjoyed her attention, and how many other women in that bar was I attracted to? On and on she went until finally I said, "Please, Amber. I'm not even gay."

Wrong, *wrong* thing to say. If there were any words that could have made matters worse those were the ones. Now she wanted to know just what I thought I was if I wasn't gay.

"Don't we share a bed?" she demanded.

"Most nights, yes."

"Do you have sex with me?"

"Yes."

"Do you *enjoy* having sex with me?"

"Of course, that's not—"

"You're gay okay!" She yelled the words so loud I was sure her neighbors must have heard them. "You're a fucking dyke just like I am and you know what? You better get used to it because you can't live in denial forever. Eventually the real world is going to catch up to you and you're going to have to face your sexuality the same way the rest of us have to." She was venomous.

"I want to hear you say it," she went on, in that same angry tone. "There's no one here but the two of us. Why should it matter?"

I remained silent which only added to her fury.

"You can't even say it, can you?" she yelled. "Not even to me. I'm the woman you're *fucking* and you can't even say that one stupid word!" She seemed near hysteria and I couldn't understand what was driving her to such excesses.

"Look," I said, when I couldn't stand to hear anymore, "if

you want to be defined by labels, go right ahead. But I won't be. I didn't fall in love with you because you're a woman. In fact, I fell in love with you in spite of it. I fell in love with the individual living inside and it wouldn't matter what sex you were, what race or color. The skin your spirit dwells in has little to do with it. Calling me gay is to insult me. It's saying that I only love you because you have breasts and a vagina – and I hate that fucking word but every other one is worse – essentially it's saying that I am only in love with your body. Because that's all labels like *gay* and *straight* do, you know, is describe which bodies we prefer. And while your body is certainly lovely, it's not the reason I fell in love with you. To label me gay is to insinuate that it was and that underestimates my capacity to love on a higher plane. I find that insulting. Love is supposed to transcend physical barriers. It's supposed to surpass those kinds of conditions and I can't slap a label on it simply because you demand it of me."

She accepted my words for what they were-- the truth as I saw it. Later, as we lay in bed together, Amber asleep at my side, I brushed my fingers through her soft blond hair and wondered if we had really resolved a thing. She looked so beautiful lying there, and I had the unnerving sensation that it had only just begun, this battle over labels and sexuality, and I was afraid of where it could lead.

At work we were busily preparing our international launch and eleven-to-twelve hour shifts were no longer uncommon. Ted decided he wanted to post billboards all over Europe announcing that *Natural Beauty* was on its way. The office was a buzz. People scurried about collaborating on layout designs and discussing language barriers while Ted gave his approval or disapproval and I spent my days on the phone tracking down high-visibility locations. We were hitting every major city our enormous budget could afford: London --where we planned to set up our home office-- Dublin, Amsterdam, Paris, Edinburgh, Stockholm, Zurich, Belfast; the list was endless. *Natural Beauty* was going the way of *Vogue* and other such international conglomerates and we were readying the world for our arrival.

Ted, as usual, kept me abreast of every detail and we planned a trip to London together in an effort to steal away several important staff members from another major magazine that had the international market in its proverbial pocket. We wanted their editors, their layout designers, one of their photographers, and six of the eighteen translators they conferred with regularly. I had a list of names and spent hours at a time on the phone with these people, promising that we would be arriving soon and bringing with us a deal too good to pass up. They were loyal to their current employers but intrigued.

Ted and I flew to London, chose a building to make our head quarters, and spent two weeks in secret meetings hammering out deals and getting most of the staff we wanted. Dozens more people would need to be hired but we were off to a good start.

On the flight home Ted sat beside me chatting up a well-preserved fifty-six year old widow in the aisle across from us, dripping with expensive jewelry and reeking of Chanel, while I listened to a Tracy Chapman CD I'd brought along and fantasized about the homecoming I'd receive from Amber. In the two weeks I'd been gone we'd spoken to each other only twice and both conversations had been interrupted by Ted who'd taken up the unnerving habit of barging into my room whenever he felt like it and plopping himself on the sofa by the phone.

"Do you know who that is?" he asked now, nudging my arm as Ms. Face-lift brushed past us on her way to the bathroom.

Plucking the earphones from my lobes, I looked up at her as she passed and shrugged.

"Alana Hector," Ted said, excitedly. "*Cyrus* Hector's widow?"

"Oh."

I wasn't impressed. I'd met Cyrus Hector a year earlier at a convention in New York. He'd spent the evening talking my ear off and I remembered wishing I'd been placed at a table with Larry Flint instead. His conversation, I was sure, would have consisted of more interesting topics than how many celebrities had begged to be on the cover of one of his magazine. Cyrus Hector, in my opinion, had been nothing more than a perverted old letch with cigar-stained fingers and rotting yellow teeth set behind a seventy-five year old sneer.

"Didn't he die in the bed of one of his mistresses?" I asked, remembering the feel of Cyrus's sweaty hand as he pressed his room key into my palm with a knowing wink. I'd given it back without a word and left the table. The news of Cyrus's demise six months later had been in all the papers and his company had been left in the not so capable hands of his son, Cyrus Hector Junior, Amber's publisher.

"Who cares?" Ted said, with an impatient wave of the hand. "The man was a genius."

"So that gave him license to screw around? I doubt his wife would have agreed."

Ted peered at me thoughtfully through his wire-rimmed glasses. "The deals are going through, Meagan, and I'm going to need you more than ever."

"You've got me," I said, shrugging.

He smiled. "I think London should be your baby."

"What?"

"I've been thinking about this a lot lately," he said, nodding, "and there's no one I'd rather see at helm of our overseas operations. You're the only one I trust to handle it. It's time, Meagan. You're too good to be my publicity director forever. I want you in charge over there."

"I don't know, Ted," I said, thinking how only months earlier I would have killed for this opportunity. "Move to London?"

"I *need* you, Meagan. You wouldn't have to move there right away and you'd only have to stay long enough to get the magazine off the ground. A year, tops. Don't answer now. Just say you'll think about it."

"I'll think about it," I said cautiously.

At home things were no less interesting. Danny had been staying in my apartment while I was gone, taking a much-needed break from our parents, and I returned to a sight that disturbed me. I would have expected anything: a wild party, Danielle having sex in my bed, anything other than what I encountered.

In the open doorway I stood, luggage in hand, and my eyes took in the scene in one sweeping movement as loud reggae music pumped in my ears and a frown creased my forehead. On the living room floor they sat, three laughing figures hunched over a game of *Operation*, drinking pina coladas and passing around a pair of metal tweezers. *Bizarre* was the word that came to mind.

"Go for the wishbone," Danny cried, as Amber pushed back her sleeves and leaned over the game, poised for surgery. There was a loud buzz and the red nose on the game's cadaver lit up.

"Shit."

Everyone laughed and Jenna caught my eye. She looked away then her head snapped back like she'd seen a ghost. "Hey—"

"Meagan!" Danielle cried. Amber turned to meet my gaze.

Was it my imagination or did the three of them suddenly look guilty?

As well they should, I thought, *sitting here in my apartment, living it up and all without* me.

I could have stayed in London indefinitely for all it mattered.

Amber teetered toward me all giggles and smiles. She glanced at Danielle, who shrugged as if to say, *I don't care what you do,* then lovingly wrapped her arms around my neck. Danielle had known about us for weeks now and paid no mind.

"I missed you," Amber murmured, burying her face in my neck. She didn't seem to notice that I failed to return her embrace.

Jenna pushed aside a pink umbrella and sipped her pina colada through a tall blue straw. "Want one?" she asked, tilting the glass at me.

Amber snapped to attention. "I'll get you one," she promised, and wandered into the kitchen.

"How was London?" Jenna asked. *At least someone cared.*

I dropped into a chair. "Tiring, busy, and then boring. Once the deals were secured Ted dragged me to every damn tourist attraction he could find. The only bright spot came yesterday when I took off before he woke up and wandered London by myself."

"You're such a loner," Danny teased.

"It gets me by. Keep bitching and I won't give you the gifts I brought you."

"What did you buy?" she asked excitedly, jumping to her feet.

I shrugged. "A few things from Harrods and a few things from some other shops. A union jack shirt, some jewelry I found in a head shop. The black bag is yours. I got stuff for everyone. Jenna, your stuff is in the Harrods bag and the other few bags belong to Amber and me."

Jenna and Danielle raced for the bags like giddy children and Amber came into the living room carrying a tall glass of pina colada, minus an umbrella. For some reason that bothered me. It was a disappointing drink and I stared at it as she placed it in my hand. It looked nothing like the ones they'd been drinking. Theirs had umbrellas and straws and little pineapple quarters balanced on the rims. Mine looked like a tall glass of skim milk. Disgusted, I set the drink on the table beside me and manufactured a yawn.

"Sorry, guys," I said sleepily. "I'm so tired. I think I'll just go to bed. Finish your game though and I'll see you in the morning."

Danielle and Jenna nodded. "Sure, we understand." But Amber furrowed her brows and glanced at the untouched drink on the table while I grabbed my luggage, along with the bags of gifts, and carried them into the bedroom. I didn't care if she was upset. The welcome home I'd imagined was a far cry from the one I'd received. And that drink! What a sorry excuse for a beverage.

Amber emerged in the bedroom, closed the door behind her, and leaned her back against it. "We ran out of umbrellas," she said softly.

The blood rushed to my face. "What are you talking about?" I'd been caught in my childish anger but I would admit nothing.

"If it's not about the umbrellas," she said, sauntering toward me, "then what are you upset about?"

I started unbuttoning my shirt. "Nothing. I had a long flight and I'm tired."

She moved closer, slipping the shirt off my shoulders. "Are you *really* tired?" she teased, trailing a finger down the length of my throat and across my breasts. She opened the front clasp of my bra and flicked a nipple with her tongue as the bra slid off my shoulders and fell to the floor. "Or are you just too tired to do *some* things?" Her mouth covered my breast and I laughed.

"Did you ever notice you use sex as a way out of potentially stressful situations?"

"Yes." Her mouth moved to the other breast as her hand slipped under my skirt, stroking me with expert fingers.

"So what if I refuse?"

"Why would you?" She didn't stop her seduction and I laughed again because I'd never known anyone with more confidence.

"For one, because my sister's in the next room."

"No she's not." I felt the matching panties slip to the floor and was glad I'd decided against wearing jeans. "She's spending the night at Jenna's." The skirt went the way of the panties and Amber's head dipped between my legs. "What's two?"

I grabbed the bedpost. "What?"

Her turn to laugh. "You said, *for one.* What's your second reason?"

I couldn't concentrate. "I don't know," I said slowly, feeling myself being carried away by her touch. Her breath warmed my thigh. "I guess I don't have one."

"Good."

I dropped to my knees in front of her, peeling the clothes from her body and loving her. Her legs slid apart. I touched her and she moaned, kissing me, tugging playfully on my hair. My mouth met hers as I continued to touch her, caressing the way I knew she liked. Then came across something different, something *metallic.* I stopped what I was doing and Amber grinned.

"That's not—"

"A clit ring," she said, amused at my befuddlement.

For a second I was impressed. "Let me see."

"Do you like it?"

Then the jealousy set in and I felt my face change to something angry. "Who did it?" I asked, giving the little silver stud a flick. Amber groaned and my eyes widened. "That feels good?"

Her hips pressed forward. "Oh God, yeah."

I stopped touching her. "Who did it?"

Amber reached for me. "Meagan."

"I asked you who did it," I growled, sitting back on my ankles and finding myself surprised by my own reaction. "Are you going to tell me or not?"

She leaned back on her elbows. "Zeppo's friend, all right? Zeppo's *faggot* friend."

"Oh." That shut me up. I flicked the ring again and she moaned. "Does it hurt?"

"No. Twist it a little. It feels good when you twist it."

"I don't think I care to know how you discovered that," I said, doing as she asked.

"You were gone for two weeks," she groaned. "Like you didn't?"

"With Ted bursting into my room every two minutes? I

don't think so."

"Well, I did," she said easily. "And I thought of you while I was doing it too."

I stroked her again. "Maybe you thought of Tori."

Her breathing quickened. "Get real. You know you're the only one I want. Now are we going to do this or what?"

"You're impatient."

"You're teasing."

"It's a skill. Do you paint, Amber?"

She sat up to look at me. "Do I what?"

"Paint." Reaching into the bag on the floor, I gave her a wicked grin. "Harrod's wasn't the only place I stopped yesterday."

Amber reached for the bag, smiling. "You stopped at a sex shop? What do you have in here?"

"A few things that caused me more than a little embarrassment at customs."

She roared with laughter, peering into the bag. "You are *so* made for me."

"I thought we'd start with the chocolate body paint. Are you in?"

"Definitely. I really like these silk ties."

"Aren't they pretty?" I asked, smiling. "I knew you'd like those. And the Ben Wa balls, those are yours too."

"Is that all you bought me is sex toys?"

"No, that's not *your* bag, that's our bag. You can check out your real gifts later."

"And where are your Ben Wa balls?"

I laughed. "I'm far too neurotic for that. I'd be paranoid I couldn't get them out."

Amber twisted the top off the chocolate sauce, chuckling at my neurosis, and reached for the tiny paint brush it came with. "Okay, lie back and you'll see what an artist I am."

"I know you're an artist."

"In how many ways?"

"Too many."

"Do you like my clit ring, Meagan?" The paint brush touched my left nipple.

"There's nothing on that," I pointed out.

"I know. You're not the only one who can play."

"All right. And, yes, I think your ring is sexy."

"My clit ring."

"Yes."

"Say it." The brush trailed across my stomach and along the inside of my thigh. "Say, "I like your clit ring, Amber"." I said it. She grinned. "Those words don't come out of you easily, do they? Now tell me you want to eat my pussy."

My face flamed with embarrassment. "Come on, Amber."

The chocolate sauce spilled on my stomach. "Tell me, Meagan."

I smirked. "I love you."

"Not that *tell me*," she said, laughing. The paint brush slipped between my legs and I moaned.

"I know you can say it," she whispered, teasing me with the brush as her lips met mine. "Just say it. For me?"

"Why do you torment me?"

"Are you going to say it?"

"I'll *do* it."

She shook her head. "I know you can *do* it, and remarkably well I might add, what I want is to hear you say it. Tell me you get off on eating me."

"I do."

She twirled the brush in the chocolate sauce and swirled it around my stomach. *"So?"*

I thought I'd go her one better. Not only would I say it but—

"I get off on eating you!" I screamed.

Amber fell against the floor, howling with laughter. "Your sister's in the living room!"

"No!" Embarrassment quickly turned to rage. *"How could you do that?* You're such a fucking—"

"I'm joking!" She rocked back and forth, gleefully. "I told you, your sister left with Jenna. You should see your face!"

Lesson four in Amberology: She loved a good practical joke every bit as much as I did.

I burst out laughing. "You're so immature."

"*You* fell for it. I even got you to scream it."

"Are you proud of yourself now?"

"Quite."

Grabbing the bottle of chocolate sauce, I dumped it over her breasts and it slid down the length of her, covering her body and dripping to the floor.

"Oh, you're making a mess," she cried, giggling.

"Don't care."

"You don't care? The same woman who only two weeks ago yelled at Danielle for forgetting to use a coaster? The same woman who spent three hours scrubbing my oriental rug to get out two year old wine stain?"

"I got it out, didn't I?"

"Yeah, after you insisted on going out and renting a carpet shampooer."

"The club soda wasn't working. Now you're covered in chocolate, it's all over my floor, and I don't care."

"You're so progressive. You know what else it's all over?"

"What?"

"You!" She threw her body on top of mine and ground herself against me until we were both smeared with the sticky brown sauce and laughing hysterically.

"You're licking all that off too," I told her.

"Damn right, I am. I missed you, Meagan. I fucking hate when you have to leave."

Now was probably not the best time to tell her about my job offer. "I missed you too."

And we went about removing the chocolate sauce.

Over breakfast, Amber shocked me again.

"So I met Basil," she said. She poured cream into her coffee and studied my face for a reaction that wasn't forthcoming.

"You did?"

She plucked two sugar cubes from the bowl on the table and dropped them into her mug. "Um-hm. Tell me something; have you always been attracted to walking hard-ons?"

I saw an opening and took it. "Hard-ons, women with clit rings. What's the difference? I seem to attract the same kinds of people regardless of gender."

"Ha, ha."

"You asked." Lighting a smoke, I settled back into my chair. "So, are you going to tell me about it?"

"Aren't *you* interested?"

"Not really."

"Bull-shit."

I shrugged. "Don't tell me then."

"You know I'm going to."

"Okay."

"Okay, what?"

"Amber!"

"Meagan!"

We broke out laughing and eventually Amber got around to telling me how Basil had shown up at the Cauldron the previous Thursday while she was up on stage trying out some new material. She'd recognized him immediately, remembering his face from when he used to stroll into the coffeehouse looking for me.

"I used to hate that," she admitted. "He'd wander in there, cock first, so sure everyone was looking at him, and I'd watch him approach you, and of course he'd have to start making out with you, right? I can't even tell you how much that annoyed me."

"It wasn't like you thought," I said. "Usually he was just sucking up for money."

"Like your prostitute?" she sneered. "Is that how it worked?"

"I fucking hate when you say things like that. You're always assuming shit and then acting like your little fantasy scenario is correct. Basil was a good fuck but I certainly wouldn't pay him for it."

"Well, maybe you'll get your opportunity to fuck him again," she snarled.

I sighed. "I can fuck him whenever I want, Amber. But I don't. And what are you even talking about?"

She matched my angry glare. "He said he was coming in there to see if you still had his leather jacket."

"I don't. I gave it to the Salvation Army."

"It doesn't matter because he was only there to check me out anyway. Josh was in there with Jenna and Danielle and the asshole had the nerve to ask your brother if he thought you'd be into a threesome. He was leering at me and ribbing Josh and I thought your brother was gonna knock him out."

"Did he actually say that?" The idea of Basil telling my brother he wanted a threesome with Amber and me was amusing. Amber didn't like the grin.

"I'm not doing it, Meagan." Her voice was a growl.

I laughed. "Of course, you're not doing it. Do you think

I'd want to?"

"Do you still love him?"

"No, I love you. I never loved him even half as much as I love you. I didn't give Basil the ring, Amber, I gave it to you and you know what that means. Do you know what it means?"

The anger fled her face and she glanced down at the ring and smiled. "Yes," she said, softly. "I do know what it means."

Amber drove me crazy sometimes. She hated my insistence that sexuality was fraught with meaningless labels and it angered her that she could never get me to agree to calling myself gay. Often she fought me to say the word, but for me, the label was a lie, and I was as unbending in my opinion as she was in hers.

I was spiritual enough to believe I didn't need to be defined by a label. Amber was not so spiritual and believed everyone fell within a category. I said no, she said yes. The fact that I had never been with another woman before her also disturbed her. She thought it meant eventually I would want to go back to a man. I told her she was my soul mate and she said I used that as an excuse to skirt the issue. If she was really my soul mate why did I keep her hidden and flinch every time she touched me in public? It was an excellent point and all I could say in response was that I was working on it.

When the issue crept up for what seemed like the fifth time in one day, I snapped. We were watching TV in her apartment and my patience had finally worn thin.

"Do you have PMS?" I barked, crushing my cigarette in the ashtray on her coffee table.

"Oh my God!" She threw up her arms. "You sound like a fucking man."

"A straight man, no doubt."

"As a matter of fact—"

I couldn't take anymore. It made me blind with rage that I was being drawn into yet another debate about my sexuality. Well, I wasn't going to sit through it. It was as simple as that.

"I've had enough," I said, shoving my arms through the sleeves of my jacket. "You want *my* solution to this problem? Well here it is: I'll go out and fuck some other woman, okay?" I knew I couldn't because Amber was all I wanted but her face turned to stone. "I'll fuck someone else because that seems to be the only way you're going to accept me as your equal."

"Oh, you're just dying for an excuse," she snapped.

"You're the one who's telling me that's the way it works, that a person has to have had more than one lesbian encounter in order to be truly committed to you. And you're so goddamn condescending about it! So, I'll do it just to make you feel better about us. For some reason you need me to have sex with someone else to prove I love you. Fine-- I don't get your sick logic but I'll go along. Maybe I'll go see if that bartender's available. I'm sure if I told her I'm not dyke enough for my girlfriend she'd be happy to initiate me into the fold. Wouldn't that make you happy then, knowing I'm capable of sex with other women?"

With that I stormed out of her apartment and childishly allowed my answering machine to fill with her messages for two days. They ranged from the pleading, "I'm sorry, can we talk about this?" variety to the angry, "You're probably out fucking her now" sort.

I didn't call her back and my heart didn't soften until I heard the desperation in her last message and knew I'd gone too far.

"I don't know what's going on between us," she said, in that last call. "I haven't eaten or written a thing in the last two days." She sounded exhausted. "Just call me, okay Meagan? I'm sorry. I suppose I deserved this because I don't always know how to be gracious about our differences. I love you."

Her words touched my heart and I called her. Within twenty minutes we were back in each other's arms.

"Don't do that to me, Meagan," she pleaded. "You really scared me. Don't ever shut me out like that."

I loved her. But sometimes I thought we just weren't going to make it.

Chapter 7

"Danielle, I don't know if you should be drinking."

"I'm nineteen, Meagan. Just pour the freaking shots."

I glanced at Amber and Jenna who both shrugged like they didn't think it was such a big deal. We were celebrating the publication of Jenna's first column.

"Ted loved it," I praised, pouring four level shots of tequila while Amber unwrapped a bowl of lemon wedges.

"Did he really love it?" Jenna was excited.

I nodded. "The readers are going to love it too. Wait till you see the letters we get."

"Did you talk to Mom?" Danielle interrupted. I had lunched with our mother that afternoon and Danielle was anxious to hear the results. "Did you tell her to leave me alone?"

"Yes, you big baby, I told her. Doesn't mean she's gonna listen though."

"I'll bet I know something you didn't tell her," Danny singsonged, her head indicating Amber who appeared not to be listening.

"Shut up, Danny," I mumbled. She loved to stir up trouble.

Jenna came to my rescue. "Everyone ready for their first shot?" She questioned loudly. We picked up our glasses, licked the salt off our wrists, and downed the poisonous liquid with a collective, "*Ugh*", four hands reaching for the bowl of lemons.

Danielle poked the top corner of the glass door on the stereo and it bounced open. She sifted through the CDs on the bottom shelf. "Got any *Garbage* or *Wild Strawberries*?" she asked, digging through the pile.

The rest of us downed another shot. "There's a Garbage

CD in the bedroom, and a few others I took to London with me."

Jenna jumped to her feet. "I'll grab 'em. Gotta pee anyway." She left the room and Danielle started laughing her head off.

"What?" I demanded.

She yanked a CD from the back of the pile and triumphantly waved it in the air. "You didn't do a good job of hiding *this*," she taunted.

Amber squinted. "What is it?"

"Nothing."

"Nothing, my ass!" Danielle squeezed her sides and rocked back and forth on her knees, her face contorted with unabashed glee. *"B-Barry Manilow,"* she yelled, and Amber broke out laughing.

My face reddened. "That's not mine!" And because my lie was such an obvious one, they laughed even harder.

"Bull-shit," Danielle cried. "When we were kids she used to dress up like Chiquita Banana and dance around the house singing *Copa Cabana*."

Amber lost it.

"It was *Halloween*," I said, defensively. "I think you need to stop coming around here so much." Danielle and Amber continued laughing. "And as for you," I said, turning to Amber, "you can sit here laughing all you want, but the last time I checked, Conway Twitty was not headlining the lesbian cavalcade of stars, if you know what I mean."

Amber's jaw dropped open, flabbergasted that I'd discovered her collection of, decidedly, uncool music hidden behind some mainstream fiction she'd apparently thought no one would reach for on her bookshelf.

Jenna emerged from the bathroom and joined in the laughter as Danielle taunted us. "Conway Twitty! Barry Manilow! You two are a match made in heaven. Two closet geeks!"

Amber and I exchanged a look and burst into embarrassed giggles. Danielle was right; we were closet geeks. Well into our twenties and both immature enough to be hiding music we didn't think we should like.

We sat on the living room floor. Jenna sat cross-legged under the window, Amber with her back against the couch, Danielle on guard at the stereo, and me, beside Amber but with my feet hooked under her thighs and my knees up. Amber's arm rested on the top of my knees.

"Wanna play truth or dare?" Danielle asked suddenly. There was a mischievous note to her voice I didn't like.

"Don't you think we're a bit old for that?" As usual, my words proved my age.

Amber gave my shirt an affectionate tug. "C'mon, it'll be fun." Jenna shrugged her usual noncommittal shrug.

"Okay, I'll go first," Danielle said excitedly. "Meagan, truth or dare?"

I took a drag of my cigarette and exhaled a stream of smoke. "I knew you'd pick me. You probably think I'll pick *truth* too because it's easy and boring."

"Pretty much."

"Dare."

There was a combined, "Ooohh," as Danielle scratched her chin in thought. "Okay," she said, "I dare you to prank call Mom."

I laughed. "You're so predictable. And that's such a lame dare I'll go you one better. I'll prank call Mom *and* I'll tell her I'm a big old dyke."

Amber sat up straight, her curiosity definitely piqued. Danielle started egging me on and Jenna said, "Meagan, don't."

Jenna knew that once a year I got drunk and called my mother to confess some outlandish thing about myself that usually turned out not to be true. It was immature but funny.

Danielle started chanting, "Call, call, call," the way people at a frat party chant, "Chug, chug, chug". Amber smirked, and Jenna watched in stony silence as I dialed the number and switched the call to speakerphone so everyone could hear.

On the third ring my mother's familiar hello boomed through the scratchy speaker.

"Hey, Mom," I said, reaching for the emery board by the phone and scratching it across the chipped nail on my index finger. "Just wanted to tell you that for the past few months I've been having sex with a woman named Amber. I like it too. Talk to you later."

I pressed *link* and the line cut out as Danielle and Amber burst out laughing. Jenna shot me a disapproving look. One minute later the phone rang and Danielle snatched it up. She listened for a minute then said, "Mom says to go sleep it off".

Tequila clouded my brain. "Tell Mom," I said loudly, "that I probably will be going to bed soon but I doubt I'll be getting much sleep."

And I started laughing because I knew my mother didn't believe a word of it. For once she was getting a real confession but she had no idea.

Danielle hung up the phone. "I can't believe you did that," she said, shocked and impressed.

I was beginning to like the taste of the tequila, or maybe I just liked the whole salt and lemon ritual. "What?" I asked, snottily, as Amber refilled our glasses. "Don't you know by now that I never refuse a dare?"

Jenna shot me a look and turned to Danielle. "Your mother doesn't believe that," she said, purposely bursting my bubble. "She doesn't believe it anymore than she did last year when your sister called to tell her she had anal sex with her boss on the table in the board room. Or the time before that when she confessed to being a dominatrix who specialized in degradation fantasies and golden showers."

I burst out laughing. "That was so gross; even I can't believe I said it. I think that was the first one too. Remember the sound of her voice when she said, "I will not hear of you urinating on people. Go to an AA meeting for Christ's sake". I thought I'd die laughing. Then there was the way the speakerphone made that loud cracking sound when she slammed down her receiver. God, I thought she must have broken the thing in two."

Amber laughed. "So you do this to your mother all the time? What if your father answers?"

"Oh," Jenna snorted, "then she hangs up. She'd never offend her father like that. You shouldn't do it to your mother either."

I didn't like this new, self-righteous Jenna. It occurred to me that since Jenna was going out with Josh she might just start becoming more sister-in-law than friend.

"You always laugh though, don't you?" I said defiantly. "What's going on?"

"Nothing. I just don't think it's all that funny anymore."

"Oh." I threw up my hands. "And we all have to live by the rules of little Miss Jenna, don't we? Perfect Jenna. Miss holierthan-thou. I'm so sorry, next time I consider doing anything even slightly off color I'll check with you first, okay? God knows what I'd be if you weren't there to moralize everything for me."

Truth was, I sensed Jenna was right and it annoyed me. She remained silent, apparently willing to let me rant, while Danielle looked at her feet and Amber wrapped her arms around me from behind.

"It doesn't matter, honey," she said. "Just let it go." Her words were a soothing whisper in my ear, and while I wanted to take her advice, I couldn't. Reaching for the phone, I again dialed my mother's number.

"What are you doing?" Danielle screeched.

The phone started ringing. "Making things right." On the second ring Mom answered again and I said simply, "Hey."

"Oh Christ," she muttered. "What is it now? Let me guess-- you moonlight at a funeral home because you're secretly a necrophiliac. I don't have time for this, Meagan."

The room broke into quiet snickers and I waved my hand for silence.

"I know," I said into the speaker. "I'm calling to apologize for my behavior. It was disrespectful, and I'm assuming, bad for my karma."

I gave Jenna a sideways glance and my mother called out, "Thank you, Jenna," knowing by my mention of karma that Jenna had been the impetus behind my apology. Jenna laughed.

"So what you are saying," Mom continued, "is that you are, in fact, not having sex with a woman."

I looked to my cohorts. Danielle's face remained impassive. Jenna shrugged, and Amber smirked, her eyebrow slightly raised. No help there.

I proceeded with caution. "What I'm saying is that I'm sorry if I offended you with my rudeness."

"Hmm."

"What?"

"Of all my children, Meagan, you are the most outspoken and the most evasive at the same time."

"I'll take that as a compliment. Good night, Mom."

"Good night, dear."

Then I turned to my audience and bowed in recognition of their fervent applause. "How was that yoga girl?" I joked, falling on the pillow beside Amber and resting my head in her lap.

"Impressive", said Jenna.

"I know."

Amber bent her head over mine. "And evasive," she whispered.

I saw where her comment could lead and decided to ignore it. No way was I going to go down that road. That road led to arguments about secrecy and labels, and everything else I most definitely did not feel like getting into.

By ten-thirty Danielle was ready for bed and asked Jenna if she could crash on Bacon's futon.

"Aren't you staying here?" I asked.

Danielle adjusted her ponytail. "Nah, you guys look like you can go on partying. You don't mind, do you Jenna?"

Jenna shook her head. "Of course not. But I have to warn you, your brother is coming over later and Bacon might wake you with his squeals of delight when he sees him."

Jenna and Josh-- it still seemed strange.

It didn't feel like anyone was drunk anymore. A glance at the half-full bottle on the floor revealed that, indeed, no one had been in the first place. Between the four of us we'd barely touched the tequila, which meant my phone call to my mother had not been a drunken attempt to reveal the news of my love life without actually having to tell her. My subconscious mind, crafty little thing it was, had tricked me into thinking I was intoxicated so I'd make the call. Mom, of course, had been reaction-less.

In the morning, Amber showered and dressed in a baggy old pair of my jeans and a blue sweatshirt. The jeans had frayed holes in the knees and the sweatshirt was marked with a bleach stain in the front. She looked great.

"Where did you find that?" I asked, noting the way the awful clothes hung off her slender body in a manner that smacked of casual style.

Amber tied her boots. "At the back of your closet in a box marked *cleaning attire.* Only you would be so methodical as to have an entire wardrobe set aside specifically for housework."

"Well I don't actually *use* them," I defended. "I just couldn't think of any other reason why I might wear them." There was a knock at the door. "Maybe I should give them to the homeless or something."

Amber reached for her jacket. It was ten-thirty and she'd promised herself she'd be in her apartment, working on her new book by noon.

"On the other hand, maybe it's condescending to think the homeless would want to wear a bleach-stained sweatshirt simply because they're homeless."

My hand twisted the doorknob and Amber laughed. "*I'm* wearing it."

"True, I--" My words trailed off as my eyes met what stood in the open doorway. "Oh-my-God."

"Close," Basil said, stepping passed me into the apartment. "Hi, Amber."

Amber looked from me to Basil, dropped her jacket on the chair, and said hello.

"Going somewhere?" Basil asked.

"What are you doing here?" I crossed the room and reached for the cigarette smoldering in the ashtray. "And how the hell do you keep getting up here without buzzing?"

Basil grinned. "Wanna smoke a joint?"

"No. It's ten-thirty in the--"

"Sure."

My head snapped in Amber's direction. Had she actually just said that? Basil blazed up, inhaled deeply, and passed the joint to Amber who did the same before passing it back. I couldn't believe what I was witnessing. My ex-boyfriend and my current girlfriend, who I hadn't even known smoked pot, were sitting on my couch, stinking up my living room with a cigarette-sized joint.

"I don't have your leather jacket," I said suddenly, thinking that must be the reason Basil was here.

Amber took another enthusiastic toke and I grabbed the tequila bottle from the coffee table and carried it into the kitchen where I slammed it down on the countertop. Amber jumped. Basil continued to contentedly smoke his joint.

Grabbing a clean ashtray from the bottom cupboard, I re-entered the living room and banged it on the coffee table beside Basil's feet. Then I went about plumping the pillows, smacking them between my palms and viciously tossing them end over end.

Basil offered Amber the joint again and there was a glint of fear in her eyes as her gaze met mine. She waved the joint away. Basil shrugged and sucked it between his lips.

"I was thinking about us," he said, licking his fingers and pressing them to the lighted end of the joint. There was a small sizzle as it extinguished, and Basil placed the roach in his cigarette pack. "The three of us."

Amber cast a worried glance in my direction and I thought, *Not liking Basil so much now, are you?*

"There is no three of us," I said, dryly.

"But there could be."

Amber was beginning to fidget in her seat. The fact that she'd agreed to smoke his pot after I'd said no was getting under my skin and a sadistic part of me wanted to scare her into thinking I might take Basil up on his offer.

"Whadda ya say?" Basil pressed. "The three of us? In there?" He pointed at the bedroom and I gave a harsh laugh. Much as I wanted to get Amber back for her little trick, I couldn't do it.

"You're such an asshole," I said, shaking my head. "I'm in a *relationship* with Amber. It's not some free-for-all sex thing you can just join in on."

Suddenly, Amber yanked me to her and kissed me, passionately. At first I thought she *was* trying to start something up between us, but when Basil groaned and readjusted his fly the look of disgust on her face said it all. Still, I didn't much care for the stoned exhibitionist she'd suddenly become.

"Weren't you going somewhere?" Basil asked Amber. He leered at me. And the look seemed to indicate that the minute she stepped out the door he and I would go at it like animals.

Amber smiled sweetly, always the picture of composure. "I can stay awhile," she said. It was going on 11:05 and I grinned at a jealousy only I knew to be going on within her. "I'm too stoned to write anything coherent now anyway."

"Really?" Basil was surprised. "I do my best writing when I'm stoned."

"How would you know?" I asked, sarcastically. "You've never been straight in your life."

Amber snickered.

"Yeah," Basil said. "Well that stoned writing was good enough to land Dimestore Ganja a recording contract."

"Seriously?" I must have sounded too excited because Amber's head snapped in my direction and Basil grinned.

"So whadda ya think, baby? Want on for the ride?" He

didn't even care that Amber was sitting there. Her face clouded over.

"No thanks, Baz," I said, thinking of how only a year earlier I would have been happy to ride his coattails into the world of celebrities and rock stars. Now it didn't matter. "I've ridden you before, and the experience was uneventful at best. Besides you always take on more passengers than I'm comfortable sharing my seat with."

"Ouch." Amber shook her head. "That's gotta hurt."

Basil shot her a look and groped my wrist. "I hope you don't end up regretting that decision someday," he said, running a finger across the inside of my palm. I closed my hand. "You know, when you get tired of playing dyke." He strolled out of the apartment with a triumphant gait.

Jerk!

Amber sat cross-legged on the arm of the couch, grinning, and picking at a loose piece of rubber on the sole of her boot. She might have been impressed with the way I handled the situation but the feeling wasn't mutual. And for the second time it occurred to me that, in Amber, I might have chosen the female equivalent of Basil. Charming, intelligent, possessive, highly-sexed, and now, add pothead to the list. Hard-ons and clit rings--there was truth to that joke.

On the other hand, Amber was all the things Basil wasn't: Faithful, compassionate, affectionate, and breath-takingly beautiful. Even stoned she looked like some wide-eyed waif and an aura of innocence permeated the air around her. I struggled to maintain my anger but felt it dissipating like fog. No one had ever affected me to such extremes. If there was one emotion I'd always been able to hold onto, it was anger. Now I didn't know if my insides were healing, or if Amber consumed so much of my heart that being angry at her would have been like unleashing that anger on myself, pointless and self-destructive. I loved her, but sometimes I wished she'd get the hell out of me.

Amber reached for me. "You have a problem with casual drug use, don't you?"

Duh.

I felt decidedly uncool, like my secret CD. "Define 'casual'."

She shrugged. "You know, occasional."

"Well, if your *occasional* is the same as mine, then no. It's when people start walking around in a state of perpetually stoned stupidity that I get turned off. How often do you do it?"

"Barely. I'd say once every few months."

That didn't appease me. Rightfully, it should have because if Amber was being honest she averaged less than six joints a year. It was the *why* I had a problem with. Why did an intelligent, creative person feel the urge to blur her mind? Was being intelligent such a mixed blessing that along with the success it brought, came the need to occasionally escape it?

I wanted to tell Amber I didn't want her getting high at all but realized I had no right. It was her body and she could do whatever she wanted.

She came to the decision of her own volition. "I can see why it would bother you," she said, tenderly rubbing my arm and nodding at the door. "After dealing with *that* anyone would have some drug issues. So, I just won't do it."

"Amber, you can do whatever you want." Even to me the words sounded hollow.

She shrugged. "Why bother? It's stupid anyway."

I thought I never loved her more.

Chapter 8

Josh Summers' apartment was a yuppie playboy's fantasy come to life. It was an ultra-modern abode furnished in leather, glass and chrome. There were mirrors on the walls and a wine rack in the corner of the open-concept dining room that held several bottles of vintage merlot. Or perhaps it was pinot noir. Burgundy? I didn't know a thing about wine. Josh was a connoisseur of the finer things. I simply liked what tasted good on my tongue.

Dinner was a casual affair. Jenna was comfortable in denim overalls, and Amber and I both wore jeans-- hers black; mine blue. It was Josh who added a touch of formality to the evening. In his black pleated pants and button down shirt, matched up with a Ralph Lauren tie, he reminded me of an anal retentive tightwad. The thought irked me.

"You really need to get that stick out of your ass, Joshua," I said, scrutinizing his handsome face and lighting a cigarette.

He looked up from his apple pie. "What does that mean? And I told you, no smoking in my house."

"This isn't a house, it's an apartment, and I *am* smoking in it. Now quit your bitching and go change into something comfortable."

"I am comfortable." He frowned at the ash growing on the end of my cigarette. "I'm not giving you an ashtray."

"I'll use your plate."

"You always have to have your way, don't you?"

"Yes. Is it the plate or the ashtray?"

"Second drawer beside the fridge," he groaned.

"Thank you." I grabbed the ashtray and came back to the table. Offered Amber a cigarette but she looked at my brother and shook her head.

"Go ahead," Josh said. "Meagan's gonna do it all evening

anyway."

Reluctantly, she took a cigarette.

"When are you going to quit?" Jenna complained. She'd been trying to get me to give up smoking for years.

"Soon, I think. Elaine grows more haggard-looking every day and it freaks me out."

"Why not tomorrow?" Jenna pressed.

"Why not when I'm ready?"

Amber laughed. "We probably should quit, Meagan. You're so worked up over this London deal you're smoking a lot more than usual." I'd told her about the job offer but I'd also told her I was going to try to work out a way I could remain in charge without ever leaving home. With fax, phones, and email, how hard could it be?

"We'll quit together," she stated.

"Tomorrow?"

"Monday. Who wants to quit on a weekend?"

I nodded. "All right-- Monday."

"I'm gonna watch you, Meagan," Jenna warned.

"Go ahead. I can quit whenever I want."

Josh gave a harsh laugh. "Fifty bucks says if you quit on Monday you'll be smoking again by Friday."

I crushed my half-smoked cigarette in the ashtray. "Five hundred bucks and I'll give you better odds. Say, three months?"

"Don't do it, Josh," Jenna warned. "She'll win if money's involved."

"Your loyalties snap away easily," I told her.

"They do not. We just can't afford to lose five hundred dollars right now."

It was the "we" that grabbed my attention. "Why's that?"

Josh and Jenna grinned at each other and Jenna squealed. "'Cause we're getting married!"

I choked on my wine.

"That's great," Amber gushed.

"We know it's quick. We've only been together five months but we also know it's right. Josh wanted to announce it over a big family dinner but I told him no, Meagan has to be the first to know."

"I'm stunned," was all I could manage.

"I'll tell you this," Josh said. "It wasn't easy stealing Jenna away from you." He laughed at his own joke and I manufactured a tight smile.

There was truth to his words, joke or not: He was stealing Jenna away.

"What about Bacon?" I inquired, knowing Josh's uptown apartment came with a *no pets* clause in the lease.

Amber snickered. *"What about Bacon?* That's what you come up with? Congratulate them!"

I thought I wanted to silence her in a very physical way.

"Of course I'm happy for you," I cried, crossing the room to hug them. "When are you telling everyone else?"

"Sunday night at dinner," Josh said. "You'll still come, won't you?"

My mind flashed to a family dinner in which Josh announced he was marrying Meagan's flakey friend from across the hall and I grinned. "Wouldn't miss it for the world."

"And the bet?" Josh asked.

"If I win--which I will--you don't have to pay me until after the wedding. Or whenever you feel like it, really. Now that you've gotten Jenna involved I'd feel guilty about taking the money."

"Oh, but you'd gladly take just mine," Josh laughed.

"I've taken it before. You always lose but you never learn your lesson. We can call it off right now if you want."

His eyes flashed an ambitious fire. "No way. This time *you're* going down."

"No," Jenna said, quietly. "She's not."

I grinned. "That's right, Manicure-Man. Listen to your bride because I don't lose."

"You have a snide little nickname for everyone, don't you?"

"Are you telling me you *don't* have a manicure? You probably bathe with a loofah and floral scented soaps."

Jenna giggled. "Bubbles and candles too."

"Jenna!"

I smirked. "You're a big girl, Joshua."

His eyes sparked a hint of amusement. "Then I guess you're attracted to me," he shot.

The laughter burst out of me. "That's not bad."

"Liked that did you?"

"I'm impressed," I said, nodding. "When did you learn how to be a smart ass?"

"Around the same time you stopped blowing Koreans for quarters."

"What?" I doubled over with laughter. "Koreans for quarters!" My legs gave out on me and I fell to my knees, slapping the carpet and howling with unabashed merriment.

My laughter was infectious and Jenna erupted into girlish giggles, while Josh chuckled and Amber strained to help me to my feet while staggering about herself. Josh was not known for his humor, or his sarcasm, and he'd knocked us over with both.

"I slammed you, Meagan. Am I a member of your club now?"

"Oh, you're in," I screeched. "With one nonsensical comment you yanked the stick out of your ass and I couldn't be more proud."

"Good," he sneered. "Because your approval is what I live for."

"Easy Josh," I warned. "Don't press too far on your first try. You're likely to get hurt."

"Your razor tongue must be hell on Amber," he joked.

Amber burst out laughing. "I think he's winning, Meagan."

"I think so too. Get out of my game, Josh. You're a little too good at it."

"Naw." He shook his head. "I've been saving that one up for a while."

It rained on the ride home. The wipers swooshed back and forth but not fast enough to clear away the water that continuously splashed the windshield, impairing my view of the road. The light was red. Amber fiddled with the radio, switching from one station to the next in search of only God knew what, while my fingers rapped an impatient beat on the dashboard. The good mood had passed and I found myself once again thinking of how my brother had craftily stolen away my best friend.

"This is WBL--"

Switch.

"--persisting till morning."

Switch.

"Be the tenth caller and win--"

Switch.

"Can you leave it at one fucking station?" I barked.

Amber's hand retreated like she'd touched a hot stove. "The light's green."

My foot pressed the gas pedal and the car crept forward. "I'm sorry-- I just really hate the rain."

I hated surprises too, so I'd been hit with a double whammy tonight.

"That's because you've never made love in it," Amber said. "If you replace the unpleasant memories you have of rain with something good, like making love, it will cease to bother you." She shrugged like someone who had all the answers.

"That's an interesting theory," I said, signaling a turn. "Unfortunately, it doesn't work."

"You know that for sure?" It was a loaded question.

My thoughts drifted to Basil, his wet hair dripping in my face, a determined-to-come expression on his own, and I smirked. *Tell me you love my cock,* he whispered in my head. I laughed out loud. "Yes, I know that for sure."

Wouldn't you like my cock in you now?
No.

Amber was watching me, her green eyes boring a hole through my forehead. "You miss sex with a man, don't you?"

"No." I pulled in front of her building.

"Not in the slightest bit?"

"No. Are we going to get into this again? I do not miss sex with Basil."

"Who said Basil?" Her eyes narrowed on my face. "I said *a man.*"

"Whatever. I said I don't miss it and even if I did, it wouldn't matter because I *love you.*"

Satisfied with my answer, I cut the engine.

"Prove it."

"What?" I felt my annoyance grow.

"If you love me as much as you say you do, prove it."

"How?"

Amber crossed her arms and rested her boots on the dashboard. I felt a frown crease my forehead. "Tell you parents about me," she said, defiantly. "Sunday night, at dinner."

Grabbing her ankles, I placed her feet on the floor, where

they belonged. "No."

　　　　"Why?"

　　　　"Because it's not the proper time. Sunday is for Josh and Jenna and I'm not ruining their big announcement by springing from the closet and making the evening about me --or you. I can't believe you'd even be selfish enough to suggest it."

　　　　She flung open the car door. "Oh, and it's not selfish of you to keep me as your dirty little secret, huh?"

　　　　Rain splattered against the upholstery. "Stop saying that. You're not my dirty little anything." She stepped out into the rain and I followed her up the front steps and into her building. "Amber."

　　　　"What?"

　　　　I groped for words and came up with, "Why can't you accept that it's going to take some time? Do your parents know about *me*?" I knew I had her.

　　　　"Yes."

　　　　"They do?" I had nothing. Amber rarely saw her parents because they didn't get along, and her words surprised me. "Why?"

　　　　We were inside her apartment now. "Why what? Why do they know about you?" I nodded dumbly. Amber sighed. "Because I love you. Because if it were legally possible I'd marry you. I want for us the same things Josh and Jenna are capable of having. At the very least I'd like us to live together."

　　　　The evening was becoming one surprise after another. I had no idea Amber felt the way she did and I couldn't stop myself from grinning like an idiot.

　　　　"You'd marry me?"

　　　　She grinned back. "Yes."

　　　　And I never felt more loved, or more pressured, in my life. "You make me insane," I said, laughing and pulling her to me.

　　　　"Well you don't do much for my lucidity either," she retorted, sharing my laughter.

　　　　I didn't know how to respond to the living together comment. It seemed reasonable enough --we practically lived together already-- but what Amber was looking for was the sense of permanency complete cohabitation offered. And while I thought I would enjoy living with her, I'd just gotten out of a living together arrangement and wasn't sure how ready I was to jump back in. I kind of liked living on my own. I liked the freedom. I also liked waking up with Amber beside me.

I vowed to consider it in London. The new staff had been set up and I was asked to fly over to offer some quick training on what Ted expected before anything began.

On Sunday I rode to my parents' house with Josh and Jenna, and managed to appear interested throughout an hour-long discussion on whether or not Danielle's Greek studies qualified as a viable elective.

"Amber took Greek mythology," Danielle asserted. It warmed my heart to see the way Danny looked up to her.

Dad cleaned his reading glasses. "Who's Amber?"

The room fell eerily silent. "Meagan's friend."

"What's the difference?" I interjected quickly. "It's an *elective*, meaning she has *elected* to take it. Correct?"

Dad laughed and Mom scowled. She didn't like my role as Danielle's protector.

"Dinner will be ready in ten minutes," she said, escorting me into the kitchen to help her prepare.

Grabbing a mixer from the cupboard, she handed it to me, and indicated the bowl of potatoes she wanted me to whip. "You know," she said, pulling a roasting pan from the oven with plain white oven mitts. "I appreciate the fact that you watch out for Danielle, but honey, she has to learn to fend for herself."

I laughed uproariously. "For once, Mom, we are in complete agreement."

"We are?" She was pleasantly surprised.

"Definitely. I've been telling Danny the same thing for months."

"Good."

Jenna appeared in the kitchen, perfect daughter-in-law smile frozen in place. I choked back a laugh. "Can I help?" she asked.

"I think we have it under control," Mom responded, scanning the cluttered counter top. "Perhaps you could get everyone into the dining room."

"Sure." Jenna disappeared.

"I like her," Mom said, wiping her hands on her June Cleaver-esque apron, and I thought, *I'm glad.* Josh *will be glad.*

Dinner consisted of medium-rare roast beef, mashed potatoes, creamed peas, steamed broccoli, and a salad made with a variety of colorful vegetables. A small bowl of cherry tomatoes sat off to the side.

"I didn't put these in," Mom said, passing the bowl. "Because Meagan would have a fit if a tomato touched her plate. Isn't that right, dear?"

Everyone laughed. My little eccentricities were a constant source of amusement.

"What can I say? I don't like things that aren't as they appear." I plucked a small ball from the bowl. "See, here you have a tomato. It looks appetizing enough. Plump. Firm. But the second you bite into it, it splits open, filling your mouth with mushy goo. I abhor such trickery."

The laughter came again and Danielle shrugged, slapping a spoonful of potatoes onto her plate. "A tomato is the edible equivalent of a person with a secret," she said. "Maybe that's why you hate them."

"How do you mean?" Dad inquired, suddenly interested.

Danielle ignored the look I shot her. Once she was in the spotlight there was no stopping her. "Exactly what Meagan said: They're not as they appear. Their exterior presents one image but it's what they hide on the inside that counts." Dad seemed satisfied with her response, and thankfully, Danielle let it go.

Sometimes I wondered why I bothered defending my sister when she seemed to relish putting me under the microscope.

Dinner ended and we adjourned to the living room for drinks. It was time for Josh and Jenna's big announcement and I could feel a charge in the air. Briefly, my mind wandered to Amber, as Josh cleared his throat, helped Jenna to her feet, and the two of them stood before us. I couldn't wipe the grin off my face.

"What's going on?" Mom asked, all honey and sugar. She didn't like surprises any more than I did and her smile was set in concrete.

Josh rested his arm across Jenna's shoulders, gripping her bicep. "Mom, Dad-- Jenna and I are getting married."

Danielle squealed and Dad jumped to his feet, clapping Josh on the shoulder and pulling Jenna into a paternal hug. "That's wonderful," he said, giving her an extra squeeze. Her eyes darted nervously to my mother who, surprisingly, broke into a genuine smile, and said, "We couldn't be happier."

It had been that simple. Jenna's transition from Meagan's

flakey friend to Josh's fiancé had been as smooth as silk. And it threw me. Jenna was not without her charms, but they were more of an earthy sort, something my parents didn't usually respond to.

"We'll throw a bridal shower immediately," Mom said, excitedly. She didn't believe in wasting time.

"Whoa," Josh said. "We haven't even set a wedding date."

That got him an impatient wave of the hand. "You can decide that later." She checked her date book. "We'll do it here at the house. It'll be nice." Her finger scanned the page. "How about the twenty second? Sunday?"

Jenna shook her honey-blond head. "Can't. My maid of honor might not be able to make it here on time. She has to fly in."

"From where, dear?"

"London."

I snapped to attention and Jenna giggled.

"Me?"

"Of course you, silly. You're my best friend in the whole world, not to mention the groom's sister. So what do you say? Will you be my maid of honor?"

I crushed her with a hug. "Duh."

Josh laughed. "I think that's how articulate people in the publicity game say yes."

"Fucking right it is."

"Meagan!" But even Mom couldn't keep the disapproving frown on her face. It was too happy an occasion.

Chapter 9

"Have you given any more thought to moving to London?" Ted asked. We were sitting in his office and I'd just returned to work after another two week stint in England. Amber and I had discussed the situation and we'd come to an amicable conclusion.

"I'm not prepared to move there just yet, Ted," I admitted. "But I think I have a solution that will make us both happy-- temporarily. Right now we're still dealing with the billboards and setting up the offices so my presence isn't required on such a full-time basis."

Ted was nodding the way he did when he wanted me to cut the bullshit and get to the point. "Give me the solution, Meagan."

"Ten days a month. We set up the flat above the offices with some furniture and I'll live there ten days a month. The rest of my duties can be fulfilled via fax, phone and email."

"And what about when we're ready to get down to business? Will you go over and be my President of overseas production?"

"Possibly." In passing I thought Amber could move to London with me. "It's a great opportunity and I'm not shrugging it off; I just want to ease myself into the situation and see if I like it."

"You love to leave me hanging, don't you Meagan?" He chuckled.

"Does that mean you accept my temporary solution?"

"I accept it. But we can talk further when the time comes. You drive me crazy, Meagan."

I rose from my chair. "I get that a lot. What are you doing for New Years, Ted?"

"I don't know. It's still a few weeks away."

"Not that many. If you're still into art, Amber's friend is throwing a party at a gallery that displays his work. Wanna come?"

Ted shrugged. "Sure. Have you told your parents about Amber yet?"

"Christ," I groaned. "You sound like her."

"So, that's a no."

"What do you care? You don't even know my parents and you've met Amber twice."

"Secrets are never good, Meagan," he said, sagely. "You're a pit bull in business and a worm in your personal life."

My temper jolted at the sound of his words and I reached for the door. "Stick to what concerns you, Ted. I fulfill my obligations here and the rest has little to do with you."

He rose to walk me out. "I'm a friend, Meagan."

"No, in here you're my employer."

"And when we go out for drinks together? When you try setting me up on blind dates--what am I then? You can't cancel a friendship the minute you get to work. That's not how it works and you know it."

I sighed. "You're right-- I'm sorry. I don't know when I'll tell my parents. Amber is really pushing me and it's got me on edge. Then there's this whole flinching thing."

"Flinching?" We were standing at the door but neither of us made a move to open it.

"I flinch when she gets too close to me in public. I don't mean to and I know it hurts her, but something comes over me and my body just reacts. She gets this wounded look and I don't mind telling you-- it breaks my heart."

"So, what are you going to do about it?" he asked sympathetically.

I didn't know. There were times when I thought I should end things with Amber to spare her the pain I always seemed to cause but I was unwilling to give her up. I knew I was hurting her, but I loved her. I was locked into who I was, knowing that who I was caused disappointment, and yet, change wasn't coming about easily. I was trying, but time was beating me, and each day Amber became more distressed over my lack of growth. I had caged her somehow. She had come to me free, a person comfortable with her sexuality and who she was, and I had turned her around. With a look I could make her silent. With words I could keep her hidden.

And with my love I had taken away her freedom. I had taken Amber into bondage and she had done nothing but allow it. Would no one intervene on her behalf?

"I don't know, Ted," I said softly. "I'm trying to work it out."

I didn't mention that I thought I was losing the battle.

Chapter 10

"You want me to take it off, don't you?" Amber bitched.

A plump woman of forty-seven with short brown hair passed in front of the car on her way to the house and glared at me through the windshield. My knuckles whitened on the steering wheel, jaw clenched. Amber looked from the woman to me.

"Who's that?"

"My bitch of an aunt, Celia. She's hated me since I was a teenager and the feeling is mutual."

"Why?" Amber twisted the ring on her finger.

I glanced down at it. "Because she's a religious nut and I was a bit wild when I was a kid. My uncle Seamus--in Ireland-- she blames him for corrupting me. That would be her word. Seamus is the black sheep and he and I have always been extremely close. It annoys my family. I hate that my mother even had to invite that woman here. It's Jenna's bridal shower and my mother invites a woman who thinks Jenna is a freak and I'm a slut."

"This should be fun," Amber groaned. "Do you want me to take this ring off or not?"

"No, I don't *want* you to."

"But you're going to make me. Fine." She began pulling the ring off her finger as more relatives passed the car, smiling and waving. "I'll be your secret, Meagan," she said, quietly. "I'll walk in there with you and watch you pretend I don't mean a damn thing."

"It's not for me," I barked, growing tired of the endless battle. "It's for Jenna."

"Whatever."

"Amber." My eyes met hers. "I don't want you to take the ring off; it's our bond."

"Well, would you rather I walk in there and flash it under

your mother's face? You can't have it both ways, Meagan."

"Wear my chain."

"What?" She didn't understand and her eyes were hard.

I unclasped my necklace, slipped off the silver moon pendant, and looped the ring through the chain. "If you wear it under your shirt no one will know."

She took the chain and angrily clasped it around her neck. "Anything else I can do to oblige you? I can't believe you sometimes. It's so fucking important to you that I wear this ring but not important enough to let me wear it in plain view."

"I'm not trying to hurt you."

"But you're doing it anyway, *aren't* you?" She flung open the car door. "Let's just go."

Inside, the house was a clatter with family and friends, all women (except for Dad), and all gossip-mongers. I hated family functions. They served only one purpose; the eyeing up and whispering of one relative to another. Family loyalty was a joke. The only real loyalty came in the forms of those who remained silent, and they were seldom popular among an Irish clan such as ours. The men were okay but they weren't around to ease the henhouse jabbering and I found myself saying, "I don't want to hear it" a lot.

Over greetings in the foyer: "Did you hear Nelson's getting a divorce?"

"I don't want to hear it."

Over hors d-oeuvres and wine: "Elizabeth miscarried again. When is that woman gonna realize she wasn't meant to have a baby?"

"I don't want to hear it."

Over brunch: "Look at how fat Mary's gotten. She looks like a--"

Patience was never my virtue and profanity was my vice. "I said I don't want to fucking hear it!"

Forks dropped around the table for twelve. Jenna had requested a small bridal shower, something intimate. She was getting that now. Celia choked on her wine across from me. Amber's head bounced up to look at me from her place beside my mother at the end of the table. Cousin Laura, the one who'd been jabbering in my ear gasped, Jenna cleared her throat, and my mother let out a shocked, "Meagan!"

I threw my napkin on the table. "*What?* How many times do I have to tell you people I have no interest in family gossip?"

"I was just making conversation," Laura defended.

"Well, make it with someone else."

Laura threw her napkin beside mine. We had been close once, when we were worriless children, then fate had brought us a tragedy and we'd drifted. Laura was one of the regular gossipers now and I couldn't handle it.

"What is the matter with you?" she demanded. "We used to be close, Meagan. You, Janie and me--we did everything together. Then Janie goes and gets herself killed in a crash because she was never anything more than a drunk anyway--"

"Shut the hell up," I commanded. The table descended into silence. No one talked about Janie Metcalf. Everyone knew that and they were waiting for the explosion. "She was twenty-one years old." And I was supposed to be with her that night. I'd never lived down the guilt.

"She shouldn't have been driving at all and you *know* it."

The knife twisted in my heart. "Because I was supposed to, right? Because I was supposed to be there to take away her fucking keys? That's right, Laura. I was supposed to be in that car--and so were you."

"And we'd both be dead!" she cried.

"So better that it was just Janie, huh?" The accident had happened five blocks from the bar where we were supposed to meet her. Laura had distracted me and Janie had gotten upset and taken off because I was late. I'd never really forgiven Laura or myself.

"*She* got behind the wheel, Meagan."

"I'm telling you to drop this." Amber was watching me, listening, and the rest of the table took on a sort of tension. Mentioning Janie was a big mistake.

"I won't drop it. You blame me. Admit it."

"I blame the both of us," I barked. "If I hadn't stopped to listen to you whining about your boyfriend Janie would be alive right now."

"Meagan, that accident was never your fault," my mother said. Amber stared at me like her heart was breaking. In one conversation she was learning about my guilt.

"Whining about my boyfriend!" Laura scoffed. "We

should have dumped Janie in high school."

My head snapped around to glare at her. "No, Janie and I should have dumped you. She may have had her problems but she was *always* there for you."

"Do you wish I was in that car, Meagan?"

"No, but I spent two years of my life wishing *I* was. You have to bring this up *now*? Fine Laura. Let's talk about it. Let's talk about how after two hours of consoling you while Janie was waiting for us you refused to come with me to the bar. Or maybe we should talk about how I walked up that fucking street to find it loaded with cops and paramedics--"

"I don't want to hear it. It's over."

"Yeah, for you. You weren't there. You didn't see Janie's dead body lying on the hood of her car with her head twisted at an impossible angle, her eyes open and filled with blood. Did you see her legs sticking through the broken windshield, and the glass stuck in her forehead? Did *you* have to call her parents and tell them what happened? No, that was me! I was the one who had to explain to her parents that their daughter was dead because you and I never showed up at that bar."

"She's dead because she was drunk and speeding." Laura had no sense of guilt whatsoever.

"And she was both of those things because of us. Accept your goddamn part in that. We both knew her temper, Laura. We both knew she was gonna get mad and take off if we didn't get there soon. She sped off angry and drunk because of us, because she thought we stood her up. It *was* our fault."

"It was her fault! And I refuse to feel guilty about it."

"Yeah? Then *you* tell her that when you see her cold dead eyes coming at you in *your* sleep. But you won't see that, will you Laura? When you think of Janie you see her on the beach, or driving her jeep, or passing you notes in chemistry class--well, lucky you! You wanna know what I get to see? Every fucking time her name comes up? Every time I have to look at *you*? *I* see her lying dead in a pool of her own blood. I see the torn clothes and the broken glass all around her. You ask me why I stopped calling? It has nothing to do with moving downtown, or getting my job at the magazine, or the dozen other ridiculous things you'd like to blame it on. I stopped calling because every time I see you I have to see her and relive the entire nightmare of what we did. You remind me of the friend I failed to be and truthfully, I can't even stand to look at you."

"Meagan, that's enough," my mother hissed. "There are other guests at this table."

"Oh, I see. We can talk about each other behind each other's backs but don't dare say it where it can be heard, right? Go sit beside Celia, Laura. I'm sure I've given you plenty to gossip about now."

"Got to hell, Meagan. You were always such a bitch."

Amber stiffened at the end of the table. She wanted to say something in my defense but bit her tongue.

I glared at Laura. "Fuck you."

"Always the lady," Celia muttered snidely. Laura moved to sit beside her.

"You make me sick, Laura," I barked. "It's my best friend's bridal shower and look at what you've forced me to do."

"Forced you?" Celia demanded. "You have no one to blame for your nasty mouth but yourself."

"And just who's talking to you? You bible-thumping pin cushion."

Amber coughed into her napkin. My eye caught hers and I knew the cough was really a stifled laugh.

"That's enough," my mother said rising from her chair. "In the kitchen. Now!"

"I'm not twelve, Mother."

"I said, now!"

Respectfully, I rose from my chair. "Jenna, I'm sorry. I let my cousin get a rise out of me and I lost my temper."

"It's okay, Meagan," she said. "I know how you feel about Janie."

"The other bitch," Laura shot. Celia nudged her.

My teeth ground together. "Say it again, Laura," I threatened. "Say something else about Janie. What's that? Are you silent now?"

"I'll say whatever I want, Meagan. You don't control the world. Obviously. You couldn't save Janie's life, could you?"

Tears threatened to spring to my eyes. Her words were like razors. "You're really sick, Laura. I hope you fucking rot in that acid you use for blood."

On a turned heel I left the room, passing Amber who

looked up at me with shocked sympathetic eyes. I followed my mother into the kitchen.

"Why can't you ever be on my side?" I complained, when we were alone in the sunlit kitchen.

"Meagan, you are embarrassing me. How do you think it looks that I'm the only one with a daughter who has a mouth like yours? Can't you ever keep your opinions to yourself?"

"No. Not where Janie's concerned. Would you like me to leave?"

"I would like you to behave. No one blames you for that accident and it is not appropriate for the maid of honor to be insulting the bride's guest. Your friends are out there too. Aren't you embarrassing yourself? I have a published author sitting to my left and just imagine what she thinks of your behavior."

"Amber?" I burst out laughing. "That's what concerns you?" It was too funny. My mother was worried about what my lover thought of me.

"She's a very intelligent woman, Meagan. We were discussing Elizabethan poetry when suddenly we were rudely interrupted by your disgusting use of profanity at the *dinner* table. I was absolutely mortified."

"Don't worry about, Amber," I said. "I can assure you, she likes me."

"You could learn a lot from that girl."

They were condescending words but instead of my head filling with anger it was greeted with an image of Amber lying beside me in bed and the laughter burst out of me.

"I have," I managed.

Then it struck me that my mother still failed to put the pieces together. I had told her I was having sex with a woman named Amber and she had flubbed if off as easily as she'd flubbed off the dominatrix confession. Perhaps she thought I'd only used Amber's name that night because it was convenient. Whatever the reason, she failed to make the connection.

Back in the dining room, everyone had finished eating and we began clearing the plates. Some women helped and others adjourned to the living room to gab and set up the bridal games.

Dad sat on the deck out back, smoking a cigarette--he'd been out there all day--and I peered at him through the glass, thinking the cigarette looked pretty good. I hadn't touched one in three weeks. True to her promise, Amber had quit with me and the withdrawal we suffered in the beginning did little to help our volatile but passionate relationship. We'd moved passed it and now laughed at how easily we'd bitched at each other during that first week.

The bridal games began and I excused myself from the festivities. Went outside to sit with my father.

"Your friend Amber seems to be keeping your mother entertained," he said, flicking a cigarette over the fence into the neighbor's yard. "Have you known her long?"

The last thing I wanted was to talk about Amber, but my Dad put his arm around my shoulders and I said, "A few months. She's a poet." I didn't know why I felt the need to comment on her profession.

He took a sip of beer and nodded. "Pretty girl."

I didn't respond and only stared at the overgrown rose bushes lining the back of the property. Nothing could have prepared me for what would happen next.

"Happiness," Dad went on, as if we'd been deep in conversation when neither of us had actually said a thing, "is very important." He covered my hands with his and studied my face for a moment. "Does she make you happy sweetie?"

I nearly fell off the step in shock, and my first reaction was to lie. To say, "My God, Dad what are you thinking?" But one look in his big brown eyes told me lying would be futile. He *knew*.

I bowed my head and said quietly, "Yes, Dad. She makes me happy."

Nodding, he pulled me to my feet and crushed me to his chest. "Then your secret is safe with me," he said. "Come on, let's go back inside."

The house looked impossibly full. It was forbidding and full of my lie, my *secret*. "You go ahead," I said, reaching across the deck for his abandoned beer. "I think I'll get some air first."

He turned toward the sliding glass doors. He was almost through them when I said, "Hey, Dad--"

His brow furrowed in thought, and then he stepped back onto the deck and smiled. "It's the way you look at her," he said. "Your eyes light up every time she passes and its written all over your face." He disappeared into the house and I was left outside to ponder his words.

It was a crisp December day, not cold, just breezy enough to leave a slight chill in the air. We had been blessed with a warm fall and it looked like winter was going to be just as mild. My mind drifted to Janie and the hurt filled my heart. I hadn't been the friend I was supposed to be that night. I hadn't been a very good friend to Jenna today either. I almost ruined her bridal shower. The room recovered quickly after my departure but I had kept it on edge for several minutes before that. Goddamn Laura. She knew what mentioning Janie would do and I walked right into it.

The sliding doors opened and Amber stepped outside.

"You all right?" She asked, sitting beside me on the step.

"Yeah, I'm just not good with my guilt."

"I'm sorry about your friend, Meagan."

"Me too."

"When you left the table Jenna told everyone Janie was a closed topic and she'd appreciate it if no one mentioned her. That got your cousin a lot of glares."

"Christ," I groaned. "I almost ruined her shower."

Amber took my hand and I glanced worriedly at the door. She dropped it with a small sigh.

"My mother really likes you," I said. "She was actually worried about what you, 'a published author,' thought of my behavior."

Amber smiled. "I know. She asked me not to hold it against you. She said, and these are her words. That you hurt more deeply than others and that you've always felt responsible for Janie's death and couldn't handle anyone mentioning it. That's why you're like a rabid dog when it comes to protecting the people you love, isn't it?"

"I suppose. My therapist tells me I'll have to drop my heroine role eventually but I don't think she's very good because I don't see it happening. Maybe I should find a new shrink."

"To be honest, Meagan, I don't think you need therapy at all. I don't see how there's anything wrong with you; not anything that would require weekly therapy sessions, anyway."

"I think that myself sometimes," I agreed. "But if you've never been in therapy, it's kind of like a mind spa. Instead of relaxing the body you're relaxing the mind and it almost becomes addictive in itself because it's a good release. We should probably get back inside."

Amber rose from the steps and followed me into the house where my father greeted us with a shy glance. Josh had arrived just in time to let everyone congratulate the new couple before the party ended. One by one they sidled up to the smiling duo, said a few polite words, and headed out the door. Celia and Laura were among the firsts to leave and I breathed a sigh of relief.

Amber and I helped Josh and Jenna load our two cars with gifts and were ready to make our escape when my mother came rushing outside, my father in quick pursuit.

"I almost forgot," Mom breathed, winded from her short jog. "This is our number." My eyes widened as she pressed a piece of paper into Amber's palm and tossed back her pretty auburn hair. "Let me know what you think of that idea."

"What idea?" I snapped.

Mom's head cranked in my direction and I guiltily looked at my feet.

"Your mother wants me to give a lecture at the university," Amber said. My mother was an English Professor. My heart locked in my throat and Amber continued speaking. "I'm sorry, Joan, but I'm right in the middle of working on a new book and it just isn't possible right now."

Relief flooded my body and my mother gave a wounded little look. "I understand. Why don't you keep our number though, in case your schedule should clear?"

Nodding, Amber pressed the paper into her coat pocket and turned to me. "Should we go?" She gave my arm an affectionate squeeze and I yanked it away. Dad's eyebrows shot up. Mom looked at him with that "our daughter's so rude" expression, and Amber's eyes narrowed to emerald laser beams on my face.

"Yeah, let's go," I said quickly.

We drove home with nothing in the air between us but music. Amber was mad at me and I was filled with guilt. I had done it again. I had turned her into a lie and when she'd touched me in a way that any friend might have I'd behave like a paranoid bitch.

In the garage beneath my building neither of us made a move to exit the car.

"I'm sorry," I whispered.

"I know."

Her hands were folded in her lap and I took one of them.

"No, I mean I'm really sorry, and not just about what happened when we were leaving. I'm sorry for the whole fucking day. I'm sorry I made you lie about who you are and I'm sorry I haven't been able to tell my family how much I love you. But that's not entirely true either because my father knows."

"He does?"

"He said he could see it in the way I looked at you, the way my eyes followed you around a room. That's why he was out on the porch all that time; he was debating whether or not he was okay with it. Surprisingly, I think he is. My siblings know, my father knows, my uncle Seamus knows--"

"Your uncle in Ireland? He knows?"

I nodded. "I tell Seamus everything. The problem is, you seem to require more from me, and I understand that, I really do, but I don't know if I actually *have* what you require. And what if I never do, Amber? I couldn't bear to keep hurting you like that."

"Let's go inside," she said, shaking her head. "I don't want to talk about this here."

She gave my hand a squeeze and we headed upstairs. Josh was in the hallway and I tossed him my car keys. "The rest of the gifts are in my trunk."

"Should I make coffee?" Amber asked when we were alone in the apartment.

It struck me that she took everything in stride, like she expected I'd hurt her, and the thought filled me with shame. I didn't want to be the source of anyone's pain, especially Amber's.

"Coffee?" she repeated.

"Move in with me." The words sprang from my lips, shocking me.

"No."

"No?" That was an even bigger surprise.

"That's what I said. Now do you want coffee or not?"

I was speechless. I fully expected she'd be all for the idea--hadn't she been the one who'd first mentioned it? A small ball of relief formed in my stomach but it was too small to ease the sting of rejection.

"Why?" I finally managed.

Amber threw herself on the couch and expelled a great sigh. "Because you're nowhere near ready for that and only asked because your guilt is getting the better of you. You don't want me living here right now any more than you want your mother to find out about us."

"My mother doesn't come here," I said. It was the wrong thing to say and Amber fixed me with a glare that could take down an elephant.

"I see. So I could live here and still maintain my status as your secret fuck, right?"

"That's not what I meant."

"Isn't it? You're so fucking spineless. Oh, you've got a big mouth all right but you won't use it when it comes to us. You wanna know what else your mother said to me today? She said she wished you'd just settle down with someone but that it would probably never happen because you're such a commitment-phobe. She said you're more capable of loving an entire race of people than you are of loving one individual."

I was dumbfounded. Commitment-phobe? *Hello*, had she forgotten the three year term I'd done with Basil? And where did she get off talking about my love life anyway?

"Do you know how that made me feel, Meagan?" Amber pressed. "To sit there listening to your mother talking about how she wanted you to find someone who could make you happy while staring directly into the face of the person who does? It took every bit of my self-control to remain quiet when I really wanted to say, 'I love her and I make her happy'."

Her words frightened me. She was admitting she'd been tempted to out me and I didn't like it one bit.

"I doubt my mother was referring to you, Amber," I said sarcastically. "She meant a man. *Someone,* to her, does not mean someone of the same gender."

"What's the fucking difference?"

"You need me to explain that?"

"Maybe I do because if your happiness is all that counts I don't see why it should matter who provides it."

I laughed, bitterly. "My happiness is *not* what counts."

Amber didn't think clearly sometimes. She saw things from her perspective and her perspective alone. I thought she didn't understand the heterosexual thought process one bit.

"Are you going to give me children, Amber?" I said. "Are you going to make her a grandmother? Those are the things she wants. She wants what any mother wants for their daughter-- a house in the suburbs, a dog, and 2.5 children."

"And I suppose you've never heard of adoption or insemination, right?"

She was truly delusional.

"I've heard of the Immaculate Conception too but that doesn't mean I believe in it. The last thing I'd want is to bring a kid into this."

"What *this?*"

Frustrated, I pushed my fingers through my hair and stared at her. It would be nice if we could skip the arguing just once. "You don't need me to spell it out," I said. "I think you're smart enough to know what I'm saying."

Amber shot to her feet, her eyes wild with disgust and rage. "You are really something else! Are you honestly saying gay people shouldn't be allowed to raise children? God, you just make my skin crawl sometimes."

"I'm saying it's a fucking challenge!" I yelled. "Everyone has the right to raise a child but you and I have no business doing so."

"Why?" she demanded, pacing before me.

"Do you want children, Amber? Or are you just fucking with me for no reason? I'm really not in the mood."

"*You* brought it up. I'm only pointing out the possibilities. Why do we have no business raising a child?"

"Look at us, for Christ's sake."

"So, you're saying you never want kids?"

"I don't know! I'm certainly not considering it now, are you?"

"No, but that's not the point."

"It's precisely the point. We're arguing over something that has no relevance in our lives."

"It's relevant if eventually you'll use it as an excuse to break up with me."

"With the way you're acting," I growled, "I wouldn't need an excuse. I asked you to move in and you turned me down— fine. Do we have to make a federal case out of it?"

Amber dropped on the couch and crushed a throw pillow to her chest. "Your mother's right-- you are the most evasive person on the planet. You'll do anything to avoid confronting the truth."

My turn to stand and pace. "Oh, and is that the truth according to you or the truth according to my mother?"

"Semantics. See what you do?"

"No, I don't see. I don't know what the hell you're talking about. If you're trying to say I'm not straightforward enough, then by all means, *say it.*"

"You're not."

Sighing, I crossed the room and sat beside her. There had been enough fighting for one day and my head was starting to ache. "There's nothing evasive about the way I love you," I said, in my best "let's be reasonable" tone. "That's one truth that's as timeless as it is honest."

"Fuck off, Meagan," she threatened. "Now you're going to go into your 'forgive me because I love you so much' routine and I'm in no place to hear it. Do your sales number on someone else—someone who hasn't yet discovered it's all bullshit."

Now she was pissing me off. "Well, if that's what you think then maybe you should leave."

Angrily, she rose from the couch and snatched up her purse. "Maybe I will. Call me when you get a spine."

My heart leaped up and choked me. "If this is a break up, Amber, don't expect the phone to ring because I *won't* call. I don't do that."

She spun around like a tilt-a-whirl. "I wouldn't expect you to because it's your way or no way, right? Who the fuck do you think you are?"

I didn't want her to leave, not like this. I should have let her walk away but I couldn't. "The person who loves you," I said softly.

Her expression tightened. "You're not done fucking with me yet, are you?" she demanded. "Or maybe you're just not done fucking me."

My head dropped between my shoulders. Amber could really exhaust me. "Why do you have to make it about that?"

"Because that's the only time I get a hundred percent of you. We have to be locked away together for you to be the real you."

"Six months," I groaned. "We've been together six months and you've been pushing me since day one. 'Be gay, Meagan. Tell your family about us. Quit flinching.' I think I've done rather well in that short amount of time. Almost everyone knows about us and I've been working on the other problems. I don't know what you want from me. You've had to change nothing for this relationship, Amber, while I've had to change my whole identity. And I've been doing it, *for you*. I've been working my ass off and just when I think I'm getting ahead a bit you hit me with more demands. Why did you even come after me in the first place?"

She dropped her purse by the door, suddenly willing to stay. "Because I wanted you. Because I was so drawn to you nothing else mattered."

"Everything else matters."

"I just want—fuck." She pressed her fingers through her hair. "I just want you to stop being afraid. It's hard for me too, Meagan. And I have had to change, I've had to lie. I know you don't mean to hurt me, but Christ, you really do sometimes. In all honesty, what happened today is not even the whole reason I'm upset. I'm also hurt for what I know is going to happen in two weeks."

I looked up at her, confused. "What's in two weeks?"

"Christmas, Meagan." Her eyes got teary. "You're going to dump me on Christmas because your mother doesn't know about me. You'd rather be without me on the holiday than to admit I matter."

My heart ached. We hadn't discussed Christmas but if I was honest with myself that was exactly what I planned on doing.

"Amber, don't cry," I said, approaching her. "I won't go for Christmas. I'll stay with you."

Sadly, she shook her head. "You just don't get it, do you? I don't want to pull you away from your holiday; I want to be a *part* of it."

"We'll make our own holiday," I soothed.

"No, go to your parent's house, Meagan. It's time for my annual visit with mine anyway."

What could I do but agree? We both knew I was not taking her to my parents' house and introducing her as my lover on Christmas day. Then another thought occurred to me. One as inappropriately stupid as any I had concerning Amber.

"Why don't you come with me?" I suggested, seeing a solution that wasn't really one at all. "Jenna's come for many holidays. My mother won't think anything of it."

My words had the effect of knives and Amber burst into sobs of frustration.

"I don't want to be there as your *friend*," she cried. "You want me to lie again? Isn't it bad enough I'll have to do it when the wedding rolls around?"

I just couldn't win. "Amber, you would have to do that even if my mother did know. On the off chance that she actually accepted it, she still wouldn't want us putting it on display for hundreds of guests."

"And neither would you, right?" Furiously, she wiped her eyes.

"No," I hushed. "I wouldn't want it on display."

"You're that ashamed of me?"

"Are you telling me you never monitor your behavior? If you're saying you'd go to a family wedding with some other woman and be all over her, you're lying. Some things just don't work in certain company and you know it."

"*Are you ashamed of me?*" She didn't care to hear my reasoning.

I pressed my palms into my eyes. "No! For fuck's sake— no! If I was *no one* would know about you. I just don't like being a public spectacle. I don't like the spotlight. I never have. And as for Christmas, I'm not going."

I pulled away my hands and my eyes caught sight of a picture I kept on my bookshelf. It was of Seamus and me, smiling outside a pub in Dublin, and a new, more thrilling thought occurred to me. "Why don't we go to Ireland?"

"*Ireland?*"

"Yeah." The idea was quickly starting to appeal to me. "We'll spend Christmas with Seamus. He'll love you."

"No, Meagan." Amber was adamant. "You go your way and I'll go mine."

"I don't want that."

"I don't care. You're not dragging me halfway around the world because you have one relative who'll like me. Deal with the relatives you have here. We'll go our separate ways Christmas afternoon and meet back here later."

"Are you going to be okay with that?" I questioned.

"It's my suggestion, isn't it?"

"Okay, don't get bitchy. We'll do it your way. Stay with your family as long as you want but I'm only spending three hours with mine."

Exhausted, she dropped down beside me. "My parents live over an hour away so it'll take me longer. You don't know how much I dread even having to see them at all."

"Or we could go to Ireland," I said, stroking her hair, glad the crisis had passed.

"No."

I chuckled. "You can be downright stubborn. Whatever you want then. I'll come back here around eight and wait for you."

"Alone?" She curled up to me.

"Why not?"

"On Christmas?"

"Doesn't bother me," I said, shrugging. "I've spent Christmases alone in New York, Montreal, and once even in Hong Kong – though I can't recall for the life of me what I was doing there. I think it was the first time I found out Basil was cheating and I took off."

"To *Hong Kong?*"

"When I run – I *run.*"

"I guess you do."

"But it wasn't just the cheating that made me flee," I said, thinking back to the horrible day I'd been betrayed by two people I loved. "It was also who the cheating had been with."

"Who?"

I'd never told anyone this except my therapist and a small breath of fear escaped me. "Will you take it to your grave?" I asked, double checking before I uttered a word. "No matter what happens between us, will you promise never to mention it to anyone?"

Amber stared at me. "You're killing me here, Meagan. Who was it?"

"My sister."

"Danielle!" she shrieked. "Oh my God! The two of you must have had one hell of a blow-out."

I shook my head. "She doesn't know I know. It happened while I was away on business. Danny was seventeen and Basil— sick fuck that he was—was twenty-seven. Danny was the first person he ever screwed around with and I came home to find him sobbing. He confessed everything. How she'd stopped by, came onto him, and, well—he was Basil. Danny had always had a crush on him so I also knew he was telling the truth. Obviously, it didn't matter who initiated it but Basil took some comfort in the fact that he hadn't gone looking for it."

"And you *stayed* with him, Meagan? He cheated on you with your sister!"

"Did I ever claim to be the picture of sanity? I thought it was an isolated incident. Danielle couldn't look in me in the eye for almost a year. She was always waiting for it to come. She'd look at me and I knew she was sizing me up, trying to see if I knew anything and if I did, why didn't I just confront her so she could get it out and ask my forgiveness? It bothered her more, I think, that it never got mentioned."

"But you look out for her," Amber said.

"Yes, and I always will. I see no point in telling her what I know; she's suffered enough with her guilt. She was an insecure kid, and in some sick way, the experience with Basil helped make her more confident. She wasn't a virgin, that was for sure, but it was the conquest. She seduced her older sister's boyfriend into bed. It gave her ego a much needed jolt."

Amber was shaking her head in awe. "You have the strangest outlook on things. You're almost saying it's okay that Danny did what she did."

"No, it's not okay but I forgave her a long time ago. I never really forgave Basil because he could have destroyed my relationship with my sister, but I did forgive her. She was young. But changing subjects to one that's far more important to me—do you forgive me, Amber?"

She let out a slow breath of air. "That's the eternal question, Meagan."

"Then let me rephrase it. Will you put the moonstone back on your finger?"

"No."

"Oh." A sudden ache pulsed beneath my ribs and I felt a wetness growing behind my eyes. Amber gave me a sly grin.

"You will."

Relief flooded me. "You should have waited about two seconds longer," I said laughing. "Because I was about to burst into tears."

"You were?"

"Definitely. Your 'no' went straight to my heart and I almost sobbed."

"I think I would have liked to see that."

"Too late." Smiling, I unclasped the chain from around her neck, removed the ring, and slipped it on her finger. "Please, don't take it off again."

"You told me to."

"I was wrong."

"And the wedding?"

"That's still a few months away, at least. Maybe by then it won't matter."

"I want to believe that, Meagan."

A dull throb pumped behind my eye. "So do I."

The next two weeks passed quickly. *Natural Beauty* was being swamped with faxes and phone calls concerning the billboards that were causing a wave of interest across Europe. What was *Natural Beauty*? People wanted to know. When was it coming? We were flooded with curious emails and our website was being accessed twenty-four hours a day. Ted was pleased with the result.

In London the new staff was acclimating themselves to their duties and each other while the building we chose passed inspection and was being renovated. The staff worked around the decorators and carpenters, setting up new web sites—to take some of the pressure off their North American sister—discussing possibilities for the first issue; layout design, print type, graphic art and content, and moving into their offices as they were finished one by one. The London staff was working hard and I stayed in conference with them on the phone an hour a day, and emailed back and forth the rest of the day. I found I enjoyed being in charge and thought I might enjoy it even more in person. Would Amber ever consider moving to London? It was a question I just might pose when the time came.

Natural Beauty's stock continued to rise and I allowed myself a sneaky happiness for what that meant to me. I had done what Jenna would consider the unspeakable, but I had done it as much for Ted as I had for myself. He was going to make me his partner sooner than even he suspected, I'd taken care of *that*.

Professionally, I was on top of the world. Personally, I

was still waiting for the other shoe to drop.

Chapter 11

"You'll have to tell sometime," Dad said, cornering me on my way to the bathroom. It was Christmas Day and he'd been urging me to tell my mother about Amber. He didn't want me to tell her *then*, but soon. Two weeks, he had known and he was driving me crazy.

"If you love this girl," he went on, sagely, "it's not fair to keep her hidden away like something you're ashamed of. Give your mother the benefit of the doubt. She may surprise you."

I didn't know why it was so important to him that I fess up. *I* was the one who had to endure a forty-five minute lecture on how it had been long enough since Basil and I broke up and that I should start dating again.

"Someone intelligent," my mother had said, wishfully. "Not like that awful Basil." I could have laughed out loud.

"You know who's smart?" Danielle cut in. "Amber." For some reason she'd been riding me all day.

Mom missed the irony in her voice. "A lovely girl," she agreed.

I shot Danielle a look. There was a thump under the table and Danielle looked accusingly at her new boyfriend, Mark, a preppy nightmare in the making. "Did you just *kick me*?" she demanded. Mark shook his head and piled another forkful of turkey into his mouth.

"Oh, I'm sorry," Jenna said, tossing me a secret smile. "That was me." Josh grinned behind his napkin.

"Well, I'm gonna get a bruise now."

"Sorry."

Dad looked at the faces of his three children and his soon to be daughter-in-law. "I'm glad we're all here together," he said, his eyes misting over.

Mom sipped her wine. "It's lovely." Lovely seemed to be

her word of the day and I didn't know what was more perplexing: Dad getting all mushy, or the fact that for once, my parents were in agreement.

Dinner ended with the customary shot of Bailey's. It was tradition in my family to toast the coming year with a shot of Irish Cream and a resolution, or goal for the next twelve months. One by one we went around the table rattling off our desires. Mine was to try to consider all things from a place of love and acceptance but came out, "to be more like Jenna." Everyone laughed.

Danielle wanted to find a major and stick to it. Dad wanted to have a large family reunion. Josh wanted to buy a house, Jenna wanted to continue to be successful with her column, and Mom wanted to get "that damn flower garden under control." Danielle's new boyfriend Mark wanted to "get a goal." I laughed and Mom frowned, which definitely wasn't going to be good for Danielle.

"I've changed my major four times," Mark went on, digging a nice little hole for Danielle to fall into. I decided it was time she got a bit of her own medicine.

"There's nothing wrong with indecision," I said, sweetly. "Some people don't know what they want until they're forty. As long as you're happy, that's all that matters." I grinned, knowing my mother considered decisiveness the most important quality in a man.

Mark agreed he was indeed happy and Danielle sulked, noting the annoyed expression on our mother's face. She was in for a *big* lecture on her choice of men and the only person who didn't know it was Mark.

Satisfied, I began clearing the dishes from the table and brought them into the kitchen. Mom followed with the glasses, and Danielle just followed.

"How *is* Amber?" she inquired, as I readied the plates for the dishwasher. I shrugged and Danielle pressed further. "Well, you *do* see her a lot, don't you?" Mom glanced at me.

"Sure. I see her all the time. She's been pretty busy with her new book."

"What is your obsession with this Amber girl?" Mom asked Danielle.

"I just find it fascinating, the way she's become such a fixture in Meagan's life." She folded her arms across her chest and attempted to stare me down.

"You know how your sister is," Mom responded, grabbing the detergent from under the sink. "She makes a few close friends and they become her surrogate family. If only she had as much interest in her real family."

Danielle stalked from the room and I hid my amusement behind a careful expression of mock indignation. "I love my family," I asserted. "I just don't need to spend twenty-four hours a day with them."

"Or twenty-four hours a year," Mom said, but she laughed.

Dad was fiddling with the hinge on the bathroom door, pretending not to be listening. He waited for Mom to leave the room then said, "You see? If you don't tell her soon your sister probably will."

I was unaffected. "Danielle won't do anything more than drop hints Mom doesn't seem to catch on to anyway."

"Meagan, *I* don't like lying to your mother."

"I'm not telling you to." I drew a long breath. "Listen, I've already decided to tell her anyway, I'm just waiting for the right time. Maybe after she's over all of her 'holiday stress'." Mom was notorious for getting all wigged out around the holidays. Part of her "everything must be perfect" anxiety.

"You really love this girl, don't you?" my father pressed, fixing me with warm brown eyes and a slight frown.

"Does it bother you, Dad?"

He thought about the question. "I don't think bother is the right word. More like *baffle.* It baffles me because I never would have expected this from you. You've always gone for a certain type of man."

"It was a surprise to me too," I said, chuckling.

"But like I told you two weeks ago-- if you're happy, that's all that really matters. What concerns me is I don't think anyone can be truly happy living a lie."

I was saved from having to respond by a dull ring that came from my purse a few feet away. My cell phone. It was my link to the outside world. Reaching inside the bag, I pulled it out, and flipped it open.

"Hello?"

"Oh, good." Amber's soft voice greeted my ears. "I'm

glad you answered."

"What's up?" I asked with a smile, thinking I missed her already.

"I'm running late. My parents have guests, which saved me from having to spend too much time talking to them, but I won't be able to make it back to the city till after ten."

"Good thing we exchanged gifts last night," I joked.

Mom came into the kitchen to make coffee and sighed at the phone pressed to my ear. "You're not doing business on Christmas?" she complained.

I shook my head. "It's Amber. She called to wish us a Merry Christmas."

"You get by on half-truths, don't you?" Amber said in my ear.

"Oh, that's so sweet," my mother said. "Let me say hello." She held out her hand.

"I—no."

"I'm not gonna out you, Meagan," Amber said. "Just give her the phone because you sound suspicious."

I handed my mother the phone. "Sorry, I thought she had to go."

"Merry Christmas, Amber," Mom said into the receiver. "Are you enjoying your holiday?"

I paced the kitchen while Amber talked to my mother and Dad watched. On my mother's end I listened to her discussing food and gifts and what my parents were doing for New Year's until, finally, she said goodbye and handed me back the phone. Smiling, she left the room and Dad followed.

"Did you talk long enough?" I bitched into the receiver.

"Well, after I told her I've been fucking you for six months I couldn't exactly hang up."

"Funny." I grimaced.

Amber chuckled. "Why don't you stay there a while longer and I'll meet up with you around ten-thirty."

"Okay. How are you getting back to the city?" Amber didn't believe she needed a car.

"One of my parent's friends."

"I miss you."

"What?"

"You heard me." I glanced at the open door to the dining

room. "And I love you."

"You're getting brave," she teased. "I love you too."

By the time Amber arrived I had showered, poured a glass of wine, and was sitting at the kitchen table working at my laptop. Just because it was Christmas didn't mean there wasn't work to be done. There was a budget to review, emails to respond to, and web sites to scan for prospective advertising clients. I pulled up several U.K web sites and listed companies that looked interesting on the notepad beside me. These were the companies I would get to buy advertising space in the other *Natural Beauty*, the one I was going to take even farther than its North American sister.

Amber stepped through the door and groaned. "Damn it, Meagan. It's *Christmas*. Put the laptop away."

I folded shut the machine and reached for my wine. "I was just killing time till you got here."

"How much time?"

"About two and a half hours."

Amber poured herself a glass of wine and pulled me toward the living room. "Forget about work for one day. I thought we agreed you were going to stay later with your family."

I shrugged. "How did it go with yours?"

"No better or worse than it ever does." We sat on the couch and she leaned into me. "I wish you could have been there with me."

"You didn't ask."

"Are you saying you would have gone?"

"Sure."

Her head flopped back against the cushions. "Why didn't you tell me?"

"And invite myself?" The idea was preposterous. "I do have some manners you know."

She let out a little chuckle. "I can't believe you would exercise your 'manners' with me. You're so outspoken and then you're so shy. It's *me,* Meagan. If you wanted to come you should have said so-- I would have been thrilled."

"I didn't want to pressure you."

"The way I pressure you?"

"I didn't say that. I just thought if you wanted me there you would have invited me. You didn't, so I assumed you'd rather go it alone. I understood. How could I not? As Danny would say,

I'm the biggest loner there is."

"Why is that?" Amber asked. "You have a huge family and, according to Jenna, tons of friends, but mostly you stick to yourself. Don't your friends get upset when you don't bother for them?"

I shook my head. "Most of my friends lead busy lives too. We get together when we can and no one ever bitches because we're all pretty much the same way. That's probably why I'm so close to Jenna; she's not like that."

"I think you'd be close to Jenna even if she were. The two of you would *make* time for each other. You're so close it's almost incestuous."

"Same thing with you and Zeppo. By the way, Ted's bringing a date to the party, some chef named Vicki. I thought we'd all go out for dinner first."

Amber shrugged and my ear caught the sound of a distant ringing. It was faint but audible.

"Do you hear that?" I asked.

"Sounds like your cell phone."

I reached for my purse to find my phone missing. The ringing continued. "I don't know where I put it," I said, searching the living room.

The ringing grew more annoying and my search became more furious. I turned over cushions, checked under the coffee table, squeezed my hand down the sides of a chair, scanned the bookshelf, and all the while the phone continued to ring.

"Where's it coming from?" I asked, three seconds short of losing my mind. "I'm gonna kill whoever's letting it ring like that when I find the damn thing."

I reached into my coat pockets and Amber gave a curious glance at the door. She walked over and swung it open. "There's your problem," she said.

Jenna stood in the doorway with her cordless phone in one hand and my ringing cell phone in the other. "How many rings before you lost it?" She giggled.

Amber laughed. "About five."

"Why do you do such things?" I snapped, snatching the phone from her hand.

She pushed in the antenna on her cordless. "Because it's funny. You left your phone on the kitchen counter. Your mother almost spilled gravy on it."

I tossed the phone in my purse and fixed the couch cushions. "Where's Josh?"

"Home."

"And you're not there?"

"I don't need to spend every minute with him. We have a whole lifetime for that." She grinned mischievously. "Did you see Danielle's face when I kicked her? She looked like she wanted to kill Mark. I kicked her hard too."

"Why?" Amber asked.

Jenna was suddenly without words and the question required an answer.

"She was dropping hints," I admitted, sipping my wine. "She talked about you all evening until my mother finally asked her why she was so obsessed with you. Danny pretty much shut up after that."

"Your mother shouldn't talk," Jenna said, throwing herself in an overstuffed chair by the window. "*She's* obsessed with Amber."

"She is?" Amber was smiling.

"Big time," Jenna confirmed. "She's dying to get you on campus. Danny told her Meagan would never allow it."

My jaw clenched. I hadn't known about that. "I've had just about enough of Danielle's shit," I bitched.

"She's just playing with you," Jenna soothed. "And you got her back, didn't you? With all that talk about Mark's indecisiveness being a good thing. I knew you were setting her up and the minute Mark left your mother gave it to her about her choice of boys. Danny said, 'Just be grateful I date *boys*,' and that time Josh kicked her. Your mother really doesn't put the pieces together, does she? Danny did everything but outright say you're sleeping with Amber but your mother just didn't get it. Anyway, I better go. Bacon still needs to go out and I'm beat. I'll see you guys in the morning."

"I can never get used to the fact that she owns a pig," Amber admitted when Jenna was gone.

Who could? Jenna was as strange as I was peculiar.

On New Year's Eve Amber and I met Ted and Vicki at a busy Italian restaurant a few blocks from Amber's apartment. Vicki Slater was a petite woman of thirty-three with mousy brown hair and violet contact lenses. She was a quiet woman, somewhat shy, but her personality opened like a flower after a few of the cocktails Ted ordered for us. She was pretty, in a non-confrontational way, the sort of woman who could look attractive or unattractive depending on the time of day and the amount of light in the room. Sitting beside Ted, with his Wall Street executive look, she was attractive.

Amber was stunning in a shimmery gold slip dress, and I wore a form-fitting sarong with a delicate oriental pattern woven through the folds of red in little lines of blue and gold. The matching top had the same detail, held in place by super-thin spaghetti straps, and no one would ever guess that it wasn't one complete outfit.

Ted and I discussed business over drinks and Amber and Vicki let out a simultaneous groan.

Ted laughed and patted Vicki's hand. "Okay, we get it. No business tonight."

We were squeezed into a dark booth in a corner, Ted and Vicki across from us, and the talk turned to art. Amber had guided Ted into it on Zeppo's behalf and I smiled at her initiative but remained silent. I knew nothing of art. Like my wine palette, I only knew what I liked. And I found myself getting bored.

The table cloth was long, I noticed. It dropped down to an inch above the floor and I found myself considering a way to ease my boredom. I stared down at the olives at the bottom of my drink and a strange thought amused me. What would Amber do if I--?

I almost burst out laughing and realized I must know the result of such an action. Discreetly, I plucked the olives from my drink, ate one, and carefully moved the other under the table. So far, no one had noticed a thing. Amber's legs were crossed and she didn't think anything of it when I gently urged them apart to rest my hand on her thigh.

"Tell them about the pieces Zeppo has sold," I encouraged.

Amber began speaking and slowly I trailed my hand along the inside of her thigh. Still, she didn't react. I pressed further and her eyes suddenly widened with alarm as I gently brushed aside her lacy panties and eased the olive between the folds of her lips. Her words fell short and her head snapped to look at me.

"That last piece went for three thousand, wasn't it?" I asked, smiling.

"I-- yes." She glanced down at her lap and her head popped up again as the olive circled her clitoris. She made no move to stop me but her face was beginning to flush and I urged her to continue speaking.

"Where did you meet Zeppo, again?"

I added more pressure and Amber began breathing a bit heavier. "At…At the grocery store," she managed, shifting slightly so I could reach her better.

"And you became friends?" Ted asked.

She bit her lip. "Yes."

"She found out he lives in her building," I offered, helpfully.

The movement continued under the table and Amber suddenly squeezed her legs, trying to stave off a cry of pleasure as she came.

Grinning, I dropped the olive under the table and reached for my martini like nothing had happened. She snapped back to attention.

"Do you enjoy art?" I asked Vicki.

"Honestly, I don't know much about it."

I nodded. "So we can stare at the paintings in wonder together."

She chuckled. "I guess so. Perhaps someone will explain it to us."

"I'll do my best," Ted said.

The salads arrived and everyone dove in. We planned on leaving for the gallery shortly after dinner so I ate slowly, knowing we were in no rush. A burst of yellow at the side of my plate caught my eye and again came the wicked thought.

"I didn't know they put baby corn in salads," I said.

"Sometimes," Vicki said. "Do you like them?"

"I like their texture."

"Texture?" Amber swallowed. She knew what I meant to do.

"The little ridges," Ted agreed.

"They're bumpy."

Nervously, Amber cleared her throat. "Bumpy?"

"Why do you keep repeating me?" I asked.

"I…I don't know." Her eyes were pleading with me, wanting me to do this but begging me not to at the same time.

Everyone went back to their salads and when I was sure no one was watching, I dropped a tiny ear of corn onto the napkin in my lap. The corn made the same journey the olive had and soon Amber's breathing was quickening again. She continued eating, trying to ignore what I was doing, and when her fork stabbed a piece of corn, I smirked.

"See what I mean about the texture?" I asked, stimulating her with the tiny vegetable. "The bumps?"

"Yes." She couldn't look at me.

Vicki glanced up from her salad. "You've had baby corn before haven't you?"

"Not like this," Amber managed.

A small bubble of laughter escaped me. "Amber steams all her vegetables," I lied.

"They're good steamed," Vicki agreed.

Amber silently climaxed again and I dropped the corn.

The entrees arrived. House special. Baked manicotti smothered in a meaty tomato sauce and garnished with sprigs of fresh parsley. Ted ordered a bottle of red wine to go with our meal and Amber smirked down at my plate as if to say, *what now, smart ass?* There was nothing I could use so I left her alone through dinner. The desserts arrived.

"That's interesting," Vicki said, inspecting the small lump of cake before her. "We usually top it off with raspberries but the sliced strawberries they've used here are good. It allows for that whole one to be placed at the side as garnish. It's much prettier."

I grinned down at the plump red fruit and Amber caught the look.

"I don't like strawberries, Meagan," she said, quickly.

"What are you talking about? I once watched you eat a whole tray of them in Montreal."

"I knew it!" Ted exclaimed. "There was no way you went through four bottles of champagne and all that food on your own."

"What?"

"Your expense account, Meagan. I do check these things, you know?"

"So what? How many trips have I taken where I haven't billed the company for a thing?"

"That's why I didn't complain," he said easily. "I'm not complaining now."

"No business talk," Vicki admonished.

"Right." I nodded, and by the end of dessert Amber had reached her third orgasm. The strawberry had gone even further than the olive and the corn. It had caressed her, plunged gently inside of her, until she was gripping the end of the table, biting her lower lips, and internally rocking with orgasm. Ted and Vicki noticed nothing.

Discreetly, I pulled the napkin from Amber's lap and dabbed her with it. The strawberry greeted the other foods on the floor and Amber's eyes widened with horror when I placed the napkin on the table. She needn't have worried. I had a plan for the linen as well.

Clumsily, I reached for my glass of wine and knocked it over, spilling its contents across the napkin with a little cry of embarrassment.

"It's okay," Ted said. "You only got the napkin."

"Yes," I agreed, looking at Amber. "Only the napkin."

With a sigh of relief Amber settled back against the wall of the booth and grinned at the once white linen that was now stained red. I picked it up and tossed it on my empty plate. The waiter carted away the dishes and left the bill on the table. I reached for it.

"Forget it," Ted said, snatching it away. "I got the pleasure of dining with three lovely ladies so I'm picking up the tab."

"You're so corny," I said, laughing. Then I thought of the corn under the table and laughed even harder, causing Amber to smirk.

"Should we go to the party now?" Ted asked.

Amber wasn't letting me off the hook that easily. "Can we meet you there in about an hour, Ted?" She asked. "I completely forgot I was supposed to let Jenna's pig out while Meagan was in the shower."

"Her *pig*?" Vicki looked shocked.

"Long story," I said. "A farmer, an ax, and a woman who heard of a pig about to die."

"An hour?" Ted repeated.

Amber nodded. "We just have to let him run around a bit

and then we won't have to worry the rest of the evening."

Ted turned to Vicki and gave a little wink. "Want to go for a drink somewhere while we wait?" Vicki giggled.

"Drink, my ass," I teased.

"Yeah," Ted retorted. "And you're really going home to walk a pig."

Laughingly, we strode from the restaurant and headed for our separate cars.

"I can't believe you did that to me," Amber said, as we pulled away from the parking lot. "Three times. In front of your *boss*– and with food no less!"

"You could have stopped me."

"And miss having a memory like that? I doubt it. I just want to know what on earth possessed you to do it." A motel approached in the near distance.

"I was bored, and I wanted to see how you'd react. You should have seen your face when I gave you the olive."

"Turn here," Amber said, pointing at the seedy inn as we passed.

"God, no. Look at that place."

"Who cares? Turn."

"We're three blocks from your building."

"Okay, just hurry."

"Hurry?" I laughed. "You've had three orgasms."

She laughed back. "I liked your little trick with the napkin. I thought I was going to have a heart attack when you threw it on the table."

We pulled in front of her building. "I thought of dropping that under the table too but I just couldn't, in case there was, you know, something on it."

She was amused by my evasion of what could possibly be on it. "You kill me sometimes, Meagan. You can jerk me off in a crowded restaurant, right under your boss's nose, but you can't say the word come. I've never met anyone who has as many problems with the use of certain words as you do."

"What words?" I asked, following her into the building.

"You need a list? Come, pussy, lesbian, cunt – and I'm sure that can't be all of them."

I thought about her list as we climbed the stairs. "Did you happen to notice a connection between those words?" I asked, outside her door.

Amber turned her key in the lock. "If I think about the connection I'm gonna get upset. I'd rather think about what you did to me in that restaurant. That's the woman I want to be with now. I don't want *scared* Meagan, I want *locked away with me* Meagan. I want the woman who drops her inhibitions the second her clothes hit the floor. Can she come out and play now, or is neurotic Meagan gonna hold her back?"

"You make it sound like I have multiple personality disorder. The three faces of Meagan."

"Does it sometimes feel that way?"

The door closed behind us and her dress slipped to the floor. She wore no bra.

"No."

"No what?" She began tugging at my clothes.

"No, it doesn't feel that way. You don't believe in wasting time do you?"

"Not when we only have forty-five minutes."

"So, we'll be late."

" Do you want Zeppo to cry?"

"Would that be anything new?" My hands slipped into her hair. "We'll be late."

"No."

"Yes."

"I'll get dressed right now," she warned.

"No you won't."

"You're pretty sure of yourself."

"I'm pretty sure of us. We'll make love and we'll be late. It's inevitable. We might not go at all."

Pressing me against the door, she kissed me. "Maybe not," she breathed against my lips. We went into the bedroom.

"You're late," Zeppo barked when we entered the crowded gallery. He was wearing sleek black pants that hung provocatively off his slender waist and a tight black t-shirt. Zeppo was an attractive man when he wanted to be.

Amber glanced around the gallery, illuminated by the small floodlights that pointed up at the paintings on the beige walls, giving the room a warm yellowish glow. She shrugged. "Had to have sex."

"That's why you're late?" Zeppo shrieked. "The two of

you can have sex any time!"

Six people turned to look at us with amused expressions and I cringed. "Would you lower your goddamn voice?"

Zeppo glared at me. "You're not the only woman in here who's fucking another woman, Meagan. Seventy-five percent of this party is gay."

"I don't care if they fuck goats. Are you announcing whether or not *they've* just gotten laid? Where's Ted?"

"If you are referring to your boss, he hasn't arrived yet."

"Actually, I was referring to Ted Danson," I sneered.

Amber laughed and Zeppo shot me a scornful look. "Mingle," he said dismissively, waving his arm about like the lord of the manor.

Lord of the Dance is more like it, I thought, and snickered to myself.

Zeppo walked away and Amber looked at me. "Did you just say, *Michael Flately*?"

We grabbed a couple of glasses of champagne from a passing waiter. "Did I?" I hadn't realized I'd been thinking out loud.

"I'm pretty sure you did. Look, here comes Ted and Vicki."

Ted and Vicki approached and we exchanged obligatory sex jokes before introducing them to Zeppo, who immediately began leading them around his art. Zeppo and Ted exchanged comments while Vicki nodded a lot and pretended she understood. I recognized the actions because they were mine. Amber and I mingled. She introduced me to her friends and I particularly hit it off with an artist named Jinx– no last name. Then Jinx came onto me when Amber walked away and I stopped liking her.

"Aren't you Amber's friend?" I demanded.

"Yeah. So?"

I turned on my heel and stalked away from her. Amber met up with me again by a sculpture in the center of the room.

"She came onto you, didn't she?" she asked, adjusting the sculpture of a half-mangled cat that was dipped in silver. I eyeballed the piece admiringly.

"Is this one of Zeppo's?"

"Yes. Did Jinx come onto you?"

"Yes. What does he want for it?"

Amber's face twisted in anger and she moved to stalk past me toward Jinx but I grabbed her arm. "Hold on there, Xena. I'm not letting you make a scene."

"That little bitch knows how I feel about you," she growled through clenched teeth.

"Maybe she was testing me."

"And what? If you'd gone to bed with her then you're no good for me?"

"It's possible."

"You're wrong, Meagan. I saw the way she was looking at you."

Jinx's eye caught mine from across the room and she smiled then shyly turned away.

"Tell me you didn't see *that*," Amber demanded.

"I saw it. Just please, Amber, don't start anything." My adrenaline started to pump and my body filled with nervous energy. My eyes pleaded with her. "Please, Amber, don't make us a spectacle for everyone to gawk at."

Amber sighed. "For you, Meagan. I'll let it go for you."

"Thank you." My heartbeat slowed. "Now, what does Zeppo want for this sculpture?"

She looked at it, trying to concentrate. "Eight hundred."

"Done."

Amber waved Zeppo over and he cried when she told him I wanted to buy the half-mangled cat.

"You don't think it's disgusting?" he wailed. "Everyone keeps saying it's disgusting."

"It is. That's why I want it. Zeppo, stop crying." My eyes caught the spectators. "You're making people stare at us."

"And your boss is buying three pieces for the office," he blubbered. "Two sculptures and a painting. This is so wonderful!"

Amber placed a *sold* tag under the sculpture and handed Zeppo a napkin to blot his eyes with. He walked away, still weeping.

"That man really tries my patience," I complained.

"I know, Meagan. He's just sensitive."

Ted and Vicki approached. "This place is great," Vicki enthused, admiring the artsy ambience and the collections of strange people. "But I can't seem to find the ladies room."

Amber smiled sweetly. "I'll show you."

"I like Vicki," I told Ted when they were gone.

"Don't hold your breath for me, Meagan. She's not very bright."

"So?"

"So that's important. You bought this disgusting cat?" He nodded at the tag with my name scrawled across it.

I liked the cat. It sat on its side, pain clearly marked in the silver eyes of the head that was sculpted to appear as if the creature was inspecting its injury – a large chunk of flesh missing from its side and three shiny exposed ribs. The back legs appeared to be crushed and the tail was nothing more than a limp stump.

"I bought it," I said, smiling, "because this I understand."

"Mutilation? That's what you understand?"

Crudely, the cat made me think of Janie. "Yes. She weeps for her soul instead of her injury and I understand that. The exposed ribs represent how many lives she has left and that's what torments her."

"That's some interpretation, Meagan."

"It's right. I asked Zeppo and he walked away bawling because someone actually got it."

Amber and Vicki returned from the bathroom just in time to ring in the New Year. The gallery counted down then erupted into cheers and glass-clinking as the clock struck midnight.

At two, the party was still in full swing and Zeppo approached, carrying my purse. "Your purse is ringing, Meagan," he said.

"Now?" Amber squeaked. "What kind of business could you possibly have at two in the morning? I really hate that phone, Meagan."

Smiling, I pulled it out of the bag and flipped it open.

"Is this Meagan Summers?" a female voice asked over loud music blaring in the background.

"Yes. Who's this?"

With a growing rage I listened to the girl describe a situation that required my immediate attention.

"Can you come now?" she pleaded.

"I suppose I don't have a choice. Wait with her and I'll be there shortly." Angrily, I flipped closed the phone.

"Be where?" Amber asked.

"I have to go," I said, tightly. "My sister is passed out in one of the bedrooms of some frat house."

"So who called?" Amber didn't sound surprised.

"That's the best part: some little fifteen year old named Charlotte. Apparently, she shows up at this party with some older friends, the girls desert her, and crying, she stumbles into a bedroom where she comes across my stupid sister who informs her to call me so I can come and get them. Now not only do I have to bail my sister out of a mess, but I also have to take care of some little girl who doesn't have the sense to realize she doesn't belong at a frat party. Mark and Danny are fighting– that's what I got out of this girl. He stormed off and left her there."

Amber was reaching for her purse. "Which campus?"

"Finly? Farley?"

"Finly," Amber said. "I'll go with you. I used to party there myself."

Across town the frat party was out of control. Amber and I entered the residence to the blaring sounds of a stereo cranked at full volume and the greetings of several amorous young men.

"Where did the two of *you* come from?" a blond boy asked, tossing his arms across our shoulders.

Simultaneously, we removed ourselves from the boy's embrace and he staggered away in search of beer.

"Does anyone know Danielle Summers?" I called out.

"*Everyone* knows Danielle," one boy snickered. Several others laughed and exchanged high-fives.

"Jesus Christ," I muttered. "My sister's the frat house whore."

Amber pointed in front of us. "Those stairs go to the bedrooms."

I glared at her. "You'd know that too, wouldn't you?"

"Yes, I would, and if you think I'm gonna apologize for getting laid in college you can just think again."

I nodded. "I'm sorry. I'm not mad at you."

"Danny's upstairs," a girl yelled over the music. "Passed out in the third bedroom."

"Thank you."

Amber and I climbed the stairs to the second level, passing several couples making out on the steps, and slapping away the hand of one particularly randy boy who tried to grope us as we passed. The door to the third bedroom stood ajar and I pushed it the rest of the way.

A small girl jumped from the side of the bed and ran toward us. "Are you Meagan?" She looked terrified and relieved.

"*You're* fifteen?" I demanded, observing the tiny body and the young, innocent face. "How did you get into this party when you don't look any older than twelve?"

"It happens, Meagan," Amber whispered. The lump on the bed groaned.

"Is that my sister?" Danielle slurred. "I told you she'd come. Meagan always comes."

Danielle took for granted that I would always be there for her and her words angered me.

"You are in serious shit," I scolded, stalking past the child and approaching the bed. My eyes took her in and anger crept further into my head. She lay on the bed, sprawled out in a DKNY t-shirt and nothing else. "Where the hell are your clothes?"

"Don't yell at me."

"Yell at you? I get called away from a party to come down here and collect your drunken ass and you're telling me not to yell? You're lucky I don't drag you out of here by your bouncy little ponytail. Where are your clothes?"

"I-- I don't know." Her head shook wildly, eyes darting around the room. "I lost my pants."

Amber burst out laughing and I whirled around to face her. Charlotte giggled behind her hands.

"You find this funny?" I demanded.

"No," Amber said. "It's just...well, yeah. I'm sorry but I really do."

My eyes scanned the room and spotted Danielle's jacket on a chair. I tossed it on the bed, walked to the door, and slammed it shut.

"I don't believe this," I muttered, searching the room for the missing garment. "How the fuck do you lose your pants? Never mind, I know how!"

Amber helped me search and young Charlotte fidgeted by the door.

"They're under the bed," I growled, yanking out a pair of faded blue jeans and tossing them at her. "Where's Mark?"

"He...He left," she sobbed. "We got in a fight."

"About what?"

"I don't remember."

"Get dressed," I said coldly.

Nervously, she pulled on her jeans. "I'm sorry, Meagan," she whined.

"No, but you will be. You're going home."

"*Home?* No, I want to stay with you."

"We're beyond what you want, Danielle. You freaking disgust me." I thought of the boys downstairs and the thought did little for my anger. "How many boys have you slept with tonight?"

Her jaw dropped. "What are you implying?"

"I don't need to imply anything; there are enough implications flying around downstairs. Why does *everyone* know Danielle, huh? Why did some little yuppie prick say *that* with a snicker?"

"I don't know," she sobbed. "I don't know what you're talking about. I was only with Mark, then he left and I passed out. Then that girl came in." She pointed at Charlotte.

I was not appeased, and furiously, I paced the room. "And what do you suppose might have happened to you in the time between Mark's departure and her arrival?"

"Stop it!" she wailed. "You're scaring me."

"You should be scared. I'm making you a doctor's appointment. When was your last pap?"

"You're not *serious*?"

"Meagan, calm down," Amber soothed.

My stare was ice. "My sister is the frat house fuck and you're telling me to calm down? Only God knows how many STD's she might have."

"You're overreacting."

"I'm not a slut!" Danielle yelled, bouncing against the headboard. "And I'm not diseased."

"Yeah, well you're getting bloodwork anyway—if I have to drag you down there myself."

"The same way you dragged me down to the birth control center to get the pill when I was fifteen?" she shot.

"Were you not sexually active, Danielle? If it wasn't the birth control center it would have been the abortion clinic. Someone had to take you by the fucking hand and someone always ends up being me. Are you using condoms?"

"Yes! I'm not stupid!"

"I'm not so sure about that."

She whipped a pillow at me. "Just go. I'm sorry I even told her to call you."

"Fine." I turned toward the door. "I'll have Mom come and pick you up."

Danielle shot from the bed like a bolt of lightning. "*Okay,* I'll do whatever you want! Please Meagan, don't tell Mom. She'll throw it in my face for the rest of my life."

She started crying and my heart softened. My sister was a definite weakness of mine. Sighing, I pulled her into a hug and stroked the back of her hair as she cried. "Okay, I won't tell Mom. Don't cry. It's not a big deal." I glanced at Charlotte over Danny's shoulder. "Where do you live?"

"Oakridge suburbs."

"I don't think I know it."

Amber cleared her throat and instinctively I knew the news was going to be bad. "It's about thirty miles from here."

I nodded. Tried not to let Charlotte see I was frustrated. "Okay, let's go."

Amber helped me guide Danielle down the stairs where we were greeted with cheers and shouts of, "Yeah, Danielle!"

"Shut up," she groaned as we reached the bottom step. "You're gonna get me in trouble."

"Looks like you've done that all by yourself," a skinny, boyish girl with a shaved head pointed out. "Are those the two who are gay?"

My head snapped at Danielle.

"You're gay!" she cried at the girl.

"Well, duh! You said your sister's gay too and I am assuming *that* is your sister." The girl gave an ugly grin and her head bobbed up and down. "I'd fuck her." The room broke into hysterics.

"Don't ever end up here like this again, Danielle," I growled. "Because I won't come for you."

"I'd fuck the other one too. She's hot."

Amber ignored the girl as we led Danielle toward the door.

"Aw, don't go," a muscular boy called out. "Throw Danny back in the bedroom and the two of you can party with us."

"Thanks, but no."

"Come on," persuaded the skinny girl. "The two of you can party with *me*." She winked and it was more than I could take.

"And wouldn't that be a treat?" I sneered. "Why don't you grow some hair and some breasts and then maybe we'll talk. Better yet, grow a dick because you're tipping the gender scale as it is."

Again the room broke into laughter and the girl scowled at me.

"All right, Danny!" someone yelled. "Your sister rocks!"

Amber chuckled, shaking her head. "You can't control that mouth of yours for long, can you?"

Charlotte trailed behind us and, maternally, I took her hand.

"Oh, I see the problem," the skinny girl commented, nodding, "you like them even younger than me."

"Oh shit," Danny groaned.

I dumped her off on Amber and whirled around to face the skin-headed stick. "You're pushing your luck, G.I. Jane."

"G.I. Jane!" someone screamed, and the party roared with laughter.

"Meagan, that's my *friend*."

"Do you think I give a shit, Danielle? Get your drunken ass out to the car. Come on, Charlotte."

The bald stick had nothing to say after that, and finally, we were outside shivering in the cold January air and dragging Danielle to the car, little Charlotte scurrying along at our side.

"G.I. Jane," Amber muttered, laughing quietly to herself as we helped Danielle into the backseat. Charlotte climbed in beside her and I got in the passenger's side. Told Amber to drive because she knew where we were going.

Amber got behind the wheel, started the car, and I turned to face Charlotte. "And as for you, do your parents know you were attending a frat party with people almost twice your age?"

"N-no," she stammered. "They're not home."

"Lucky you."

"G.I. Jane." Amber was still chuckling over that one and I looked at her. She glanced at my curious expression and burst into boisterous giggles. "I can't help it! It was so funny. Did you *see* her face? She had no idea how to respond. I'll bet everyone was thinking it but no one had the nerve to say it. *You* said it and the boy beside you nearly wet his pants."

"Glad I amuse you."

"*Grow some hair and some breasts*," she mocked, laughing and wiping her eyes as she drove.

"*Better yet grow a dick*," Charlotte chimed in from the backseat, "*cause you're tipping the gender scale as it is*."

Amber lost control. "Wait," she screeched. "I have to pull over before I get us all killed." She pulled to a stop at the curb on a quiet street.

"I'm gonna puke," Danny wailed. Charlotte inched away from her.

"Not in this car, you won't."

Danielle hunched over and started to gag.

"Jesus, open your door, Danny," I cried. She made no move to do so. "Open the fucking door!"

I leaped over the seat, still half-leaning in the front, flung open the back door and started shoving her outside. "Get out of the car! Oh my God! Get out of the fucking car!" I gave her one last shove and she fell to the street outside. Amber and Charlotte continued to laugh.

"It's not funny," Danny cried, puking on the side of the road.

"No, Danielle, this is the only funny thing that's happened since we found you. You want to get all loaded, you can suffer the consequences."

She was vomiting while trying to hold her hair and I continued to berate her.

"Please, Meagan, just shut the hell up," she wailed. "I'd almost rather deal with Mom."

"That can be arranged," I snapped, scanning the backseat. "Did you puke in this car?"

"No, I didn't puke in your precious car!"

"Well, are you done puking now?"

"No! Leave me alone!"

I turned in my seat to find Amber still grinning. "Then I have to turn up the radio because if I listen to you gagging out there for one more second *I'm* gonna be sick."

"So, turn it up!" she yelled. "And just shut your fucking mouth for five minutes!"

"I am going to kill her." I muttered and cranked the dial on the radio. Danny remained outside and a feeling of remorse crawled over me. Had I never been drunk? How many times had my high school friends held back my hair while I puked on the side of a road?

Muttering to myself again, I whipped open the car door and went to help Danielle. I held back her hair until the vomiting stopped then helped her back in the car. We drove the thirty miles to Charlotte's house in relative silence. She thanked us profusely and we headed back to the city. Twice more we had to stop to let Danny vomit and it was four-thirty by the time we reached the building and dragged her onto the elevator, half-asleep. We were noisy. We clanked around in the elevator and grumbled in the hallway, trying to get Danielle to walk, at least some of the way on her own. I fumbled with my keys, Amber held Danny upright against the wall, and Jenna's door swung open.

"What are you doing?" she mumbled, rubbing her sleepy eyes.

"I thought you were staying at Josh's. Where is he?"

"Sleeping."

"Good, keep him there because if he sees Danny like this he'll freak."

"Well, I imagine you've already taken care of that so I'm going back to bed." The door closed behind her and we helped Danielle into the living room and onto the couch. Amber threw a blanket over her and I placed a bucket beside her head, praying she'd see it if she woke up to vomit again. Amber and I went to bed.

Hours later the high mid-morning sun streaked in through the window, burning my closed eyelids, and I rose from the bed to make coffee and lecture Danielle on her behavior and her big mouth. Amber followed in a pair of jeans and a t-shirt from the small collection of clothes she now kept in my closet.

"How do you feel?" I asked Danielle, noting that the bucket by the couch was as clean as it had been when I'd placed it there.

"Headache."

I went in the bathroom to grab the aspirin from the medicine cabinet. "Take those," I said, handing Danielle two aspirin and a glass of water. She washed down the pills and I handed her a cup of strong black coffee.

Jenna strolled through the door, minus Josh, and plopped herself on the couch. "So, spill it," she said, interested in hearing the tale of the previous night's event.

Amber delved into the story, telling it in precise detail, and Jenna remained silent. Finally, she couldn't resist a small lecture of her own.

"You amaze me, Danielle," she said. "Your sister is always there for you and instead of being grateful for that you call her to pick you up at a party where you've told everyone about her sex life."

"I didn't' tell *everyone*. I told Jane."

Amber burst out laughing. "Her name is really Jane?"

Danny nodded her aching head. "That's why everyone lost it when Meagan called her that – because they call her G.I. Jane behind her back."

"And what do they call you, Danielle?" I asked.

"Nothing. Whoever told you *whatever* only meant I'm popular. Everyone knows I'm with Mark. And we're fine. I called him this morning and we worked it out."

"You shouldn't do that, Danny," I said, shaking my head. "He walked out and left you drunk and alone at a party. If you're so certain you still want him then let *him* call you. When you call you're only showing him you're willing to put up with his shit. And if I *ever* hear of you discussing my private life with anyone again you and I are going to have some serious problems. I will not stand around being ridiculed by your little bald-headed friends."

"Okay," she groaned. "Would you let it go already? Christ, you harp on shit worse than Mom does."

"I'm not harping. How would you have liked it if I'd loudly announced to everyone downstairs that you couldn't leave the bedroom because you couldn't find your pants?"

"You would have humiliated me."

"Well, what do you think you did to me? My personal life is exactly that, Danielle-- personal. At the very least you could have warned me that you'd opened your big mouth."

Danielle shivered with annoyance. "What is the big deal? All she said was that she'd fuck you-- that's a compliment."

"You're delusional. Do you think I care that some little bald girl would fuck me? If you think that does something for my ego, you're mistaken."

"I thought it was funny," Amber said, grinning.

"I know."

"Come on, Meagan, just picture little Sinead O'Connor saying she'd fuck us. It *is* funny."

"Sinead O'Connor has hair now," I pointed out.

"Whatever."

"And she's pretty. That Jane couldn't be pretty if she stapled a picture of Gwyneth Paltrow to her forehead."

"Nicole Kidman," Jenna said, sipping her coffee.

"Is that your type of woman, Jenna?" Amber teased.

Jenna shrugged. "If I was ever going to be with a woman-- yeah. She's gorgeous."

"What about you?" Amber asked Danielle.

"No offense, but I wouldn't."

"You're lying," I said. "It's a hypothetical question so there *is* a hypothetical answer. There has to be."

Danielle pondered. "Drew Barrymore, I guess. Now Amber."

"How do we always end up in these silly little games?" I asked, shaking my fingers through my hair. "Get four women together and suddenly they're thirteen again. Besides Amber's gay so the list could be endless. She has to pick a man."

"Are you calling me a slut?" she asked curiously.

"It has nothing to do with that. It's about attraction. You'd fuck half the woman in Hollywood the same way the rest of us would fuck half the men."

"No, that doesn't sound slutty," she joked.

"You know what I'm saying. So, who's your guy?"

She warmed her hands on her cup. "Alec Baldwin or Tom Cruise."

"I'll give you that, though I find Alec a bit hairy. No Brad Pitt?"

"Too pretty."

"David Letterman," Jenna breathed, wistfully.

My head cranked in her direction. "Jenna, that's gross!"

"You never went, Meagan," she pointed out.

"Sure I did. I agreed with Amber."

"You never said a *woman*."

"Oh." Nodding, I sipped my coffee. "Easy. Andrea Corr."

"Who the hell is Andrea Corr?" Danielle demanded "You made that up."

"For what possible purpose? Andrea Corr is the lead singer for The Corrs."

"Who?"

I went to the bookshelf and pulled down a video tape, opened the mahogany doors on the entertainment center and popped the tape in the VCR. "They're an Irish band. Seamus turned me onto them."

The TV screen sparked to life and music poured out of the speakers. "He taped this concert last time he was here and forgot to take the tape. See the girl with the tin whistle?" They gathered around the screen. "That's her."

"I think I'd like to change my answer," Jenna said, giggling at the TV.

"Me too," Danny chimed in.

Amber only shook her head. "The woman is stunning."

"The whole family's good-looking," I said. "The band's made up of three sister's and one brother. She's just the most breath-taking."

"Incredible eyes," Jenna said. "They look as black as her hair."

"Yeah," Amber agreed. "Then there's the pale skin, the face and the body – you know how to pick 'em don't you Meagan?"

I laughed. "You're conceded."

"Who did you say this was?" Danny was enjoying the music.

"It's right there on the stage – The Corrs. They're going to be big too, mark my words. What I should do is try to contact their publicist and see if they'll give the magazine an interview. They're pretty well-known in the U.K – but I mean for this *Natural Beauty*, in North America where they're still relatively unknown."

"She's probably not gay, Meagan," Amber suddenly said.

"What? What are you talking about?"

"I'm just pointing out the obvious."

"Why should I care whether or not she's gay? I'm talking about business. Are you getting jealous over a hypothetical response to a hypothetical question?"

"It wouldn't be hypothetical if you met her. Then it would

present itself as a real problem."

I burst out laughing. "You're not *serious*? As you just finished saying, the woman is most likely not gay. Even if she was, what makes you think she'd have any interest in me? Furthermore, I'm not--" My words fell short. That was the wrong road to trek down.

"Gay, Meagan?" Amber knew where I was going anyway and her emerald eyes took on a hard edge. "You're not gay?"

"No," I snapped. "And I'm not gonna fight about it either."

She sighed. "No, I don't feel like fighting."

"Meagan, pause that," Jenna said, pointing at the screen.

I pressed the button and the picture stilled on a wide angle shot of Andrea Corr at the microphone, hands wrapped around the pole, body suggestively leaning into it.

"Who does that remind you of?"

I studied the picture. "Oh my God, you're right."

"Who?" Amber asked.

"You."

"What?"

I nodded. "That's exactly what you do on stage-- you look like you're having sex with the mike."

"Now play it," Jenna said, "and I'll show you what else I noticed."

I pressed the play button and the image bounced back to life.

"Do you see it?" Jenna cried.

"Am I blind?"

"See what?" Amber asked suspiciously.

"Her eyes," I said. "The way they flirt with the crowd. Look at the audience; she has them completely spellbound. They don't even *see* the other band members. That's what you do, Amber. You seduce your audience the same way she's seducing hers."

"Come on," Amber laughed. "The two of you are pushing it."

"Are you so inherently sexy that you don't even realize what you do?"

"It's true," Danielle admitted slowly. "I've only seen you on stage a couple of times but even I couldn't help noticing it."

"Because she charges the room," Jenna said, ever-aware of atmospheric energies. "She fills it with her presence."

"You guys are making me uncomfortable," Amber complained. But she was smiling and I knew she secretly enjoyed the compliments. Amber was inherently seductive; there was no denying it. She could pull a person in and spin her around, all the while appearing as if she had no idea she was doing so. That was the true mark of her seductivity: the feigned naiveté behind it.

Stretching, I reached for my coffee and felt the empty ache in my stomach. "Why don't we go out for lunch or something?"

"Out?" Danny whined. "I'm such a mess."

I glanced at her crumpled clothes and her disheveled brown ponytail. "You're right, you are."

"So?" she pressed. "Can we order in?"

A bored sigh escaped me and I dropped on the couch beside Amber. "I really must stop giving you your way, Danielle."

"Greek salads and vegetarian pizza it is," she said, reaching for the phone. "Who's in?"

"Whatever." I waved my hand at her in a backwards manner.

"You love me, Meagan," she teased.

My sister was too cute for my own good.

Chapter 12

It wasn't easy loving Amber. She was kind and considerate but she was also stubborn and opinionated. We fought -- a lot. Then the fighting would come to an abrupt end and we'd be in each other's arms apologizing and proclaiming our undying love. Things would be good for awhile. I'd ignore her comments about my sexuality and she'd ignore my flinching. We'd go back to laughing-- the other staple of our relationship, for we were as passionate in our laughter as we were in our battles.

Not once did I stop believing Amber was my soul mate. There was a chemistry between us beyond what I recognized as regular earth plane love. We were drawn to each other the way my gran and Rosalie had been decades before. Amber was my Rosalie. She was the one with the guts and the fire. I was the one with the ice. Amber could explode in a burst of beautiful fireworks while I could shut down behind a glacier and block out the noise of my heart, for a time. It was a trait that distressed her.

But Amber had a fear of her own: abandonment. She was afraid of being left behind and afraid I'd be the one to do it. She was likely to throw a fit if I annoyed her but the instant I suggested perhaps things weren't working between us she would shift moods and tearfully list every reason why they were. She said 'tell me' a lot during those times and I always gave the appropriate response, even when I thought it might be better for her if I didn't. What good was loving someone if you were always hurting them? Amber was strong but she was fragile. Her brilliant mind could be a weapon but her heart was her disease. After awhile I discovered I wasn't the one with the cure and the end would strike us down like lightening.

For her, I would tell myself when the lies and the cruelty poured out of me: *This is my act of altruism for her*.

It had started innocently enough. Jenna and I were sitting at our usual table at the Cauldron and Amber was up at the mike doing her thing.

Pridefully, I watched her and smiled at the way she bewitched the crowd while at the same time speaking her words directly to me. Often she did that and the audience rarely failed to notice her affection for me. I told her the attention made me uncomfortable, but my complaints didn't matter, she insisted on making others aware of what she felt for me. Certainly everyone at the Cauldron knew it anyway but that never eased my discomfort. I didn't want them to know it. I didn't want their eyes following hers to land on me. I wanted to be left alone and Amber never understood why. She thought my quest for privacy was about her, and it was in part, but the greater reason was that I had simply always been a private person. She insisted on exposing me and the insistence annoyed me.

Tonight was to be her last set for awhile. Her manuscript was almost done and the next few weeks would be spent adding the finishing touches and turning it in for publication.

Amber had finagled herself a great deal with Hector. Because he had stalled publication of her previous book for almost two years --his father's death being a contributing factor-- Amber had marched into his office weeks earlier and demanded her next book be printed within two months of handing it in or she would shop it elsewhere. Cyrus Hector Jr. had never been a smart man and Amber was a force of furious beauty-- he caved to her demands. When she returned home to relay the story, I'd laughed, called her "the Hammer," and went out the next day and bought her a little golden mallet to wear on her chain. Like Gran's moonstone, once the mallet went on it became fused to her body. She was very gracious about gifts and found it endearing I always attached a symbolism to them. Rarely did I give her something that meant nothing. Everything mattered, and as she now smiled at me from up on the stage I knew it always would, regardless of where we ended up.

Jenna sipped her cappuccino beside me. "I can't believe this is the last one," she said. "It's gonna be strange coming in here and not finding her up at the mike."

Amber finished her last poem and I watched her gather her notes from the table beside her.

"Mitch almost begged her to stay but she told him she'd be back," I said. "You know Amber, she wouldn't dare write another book without audience approval on each poem first. She's so confident and then she's not."

Amber approached our table and happily tossed her notebook on top of it. "So, I guess that's it."

"I guess." She'd been great tonight. "Determined to go out with a bang. huh?" I said.

"Always."

She leaned in to kiss me and in that exact moment the awful thing happened, the one destructible action that would change our lives forever. Her lips moved in to meet mine and something horrible within me snapped away in terror. Eyes were upon us; dozens of pairs of them, and a terrible feeling of loathing for the woman I loved crept across my skin and seeped into my pores. She was centering me out. She knew I hated that but she was doing it anyway. People were watching. People were always watching when Amber was in the room. And before I could stop myself, my body involuntarily jerked backwards and my face distorted with the horror of one who had never been kissed by a woman before and I heard the awful shriek spring from my lips as if it had come from someone else and not from me at all.

"What the fuck are you doing?!"

Jenna choked on her cappuccino and Amber stared at me as if I had cut her through with a dull blade. Instantly I was on my feet. "Oh my God, I'm so sorry. I don't know where that came--"

My words were halted by a startling flash of flesh before my eyes. The hand swung out, whipped from the left and smashed against my cheek. It took a few seconds to realize she'd slapped me.

"Fuck you, Meagan!" she yelled, and stormed out of the Cauldron in a whirl of black clothes and platinum hair.

I stood at the table, stunned. The eyes were upon me like spectators at a boxing match but my feet refused to move.

"Did you see that?" a female voice whispered.

Jenna was on her feet. "Meagan, why did you do that?" she hissed.

"I-- I don't know."

"Come on." She pulled on my arm and dumbly, my feet followed her out the door and onto the dark street where Amber sat on the steps of our building hunched over with her face pressed into her knees. Crying, I realized vaguely. Crying because of me. Again.

Jenna dragged me across the street, patted Amber's shoulder and went inside, leaving me there to deal with the mess I'd created.

Numbly, I sat on the step beside her. "Are you okay?" I asked, leaning into her a little. The snow fell around us but she didn't seem to notice.

"No, I'm not okay." She wiped her eyes with the underside of her palm. "How okay would you be if I flinched every time you touched me? If I shrieked out something like *that*?"

"It was an accident," I whispered.

She rose from the steps and paced before me. "It's always an accident, Meagan. If our hands touch in public you jump ten feet-- if only you could see the look that crosses your face. You look at me like you've never seen anything more disgusting."

She didn't disgust me. She was the most beautiful woman I'd ever seen. I loved her. But with a growing dread I knew what I must do.

"I can't do this, Meagan. I can't live this way."

On weak legs I stood to meet her gaze. "I know."

"*You know?*" Anger flashed on her face and her temper confronted me again. In one swift move she pinned me to the building and stared into my eyes. There was a desperation about the move that forced me to look away. "That's all you can say? Not *I'll change* just *I know*?"

She kept me pinned at the shoulders but I didn't struggle against her. Didn't have the heart to. The fight had fled my body and a defeated sigh escaped me.

"Yes," I whispered. "That's all I can say."

"It's unacceptable."

"Yes."

"I'm *telling* you I can't live this way."

Once again, I could muster no more than a quiet "yes".

Sadly, my eyes met hers and she let out a horrified gasp. Her face fell forward and pressed into my neck. Her forehead rolled from side to side.

"Don't do it, Meagan," she pleaded. "Please. I know what you're doing."

Yes, she knew. There wasn't anyone who knew me quite like Amber and with one look in my eyes, she knew I was about to break her heart. My own heart cracked and grew cold with self-loathing. The end crept over my body and I shuddered at the chill of our dissolution. Amber was crying into my neck. I fought off tears of my own and gently eased her away.

"I'm sorry," I said, meekly. "It just isn't working."

"Meagan, don't do this."

The sob was at the back of my throat and I turned away from her. "I'll have your things sent to your apartment tomorrow."

I moved toward the stairs but Amber latched onto my arm. "We'll work it out," she pleaded. "Maybe if I stop pressuring--"

"No!" The word came out of me like a threat. "Just go home, Amber. I won't ever be what you want."

And for a second I watched the shock register on her face. Her mouth fell open and her eyes widened in surprise that I had actually done it. She shivered slightly. Tears blurred her emerald stare and I watched these things happen to her as if someone else had caused them.

Then I was in the building and darting for the elevator and it wasn't until I was behind the door of my apartment that my wall of ice came tumbling down. The glacier slid down my body and dripped with me down to the floor. With a splash and a thud, I hit the hardwood in a wave of defeated sobs.

It was over. That much I knew and understood. I simply could not go on hurting her with no more intention than only being myself. I didn't deserve her. Perhaps I didn't deserve anyone.

The sobs wracked my body and I curled up on the floor like a broken child. The phone started ringing. I ignored it. It rang once, twice, five times before the answering machine picked up and Jenna's voice filled the room.

"Meagan, pick up," she said. "At least unlock your door so I can come over. Didn't you hear me knocking?"

I'd heard nothing. Only the sounds of the cries in my head.

"Will you pick up the freaking phone?" she demanded. "Okay, listen. Amber's here. I went downstairs and got her so if you wanna come over and talk, she's here. Are you listening to me, Meagan? I'm coming over."

I heard her walking across her apartment. Her footsteps came through the answering machine and I knew she was getting closer. I heard her door open and then the click of her hanging up the phone on the other side of the metal barrier that separated us. The answering machine went dead and the knocking began.

"Open it, Meagan. Don't make me use my key to get in there. You know I hate doing that."

She wasn't going to leave me alone. Reluctantly, I snapped open the lock and slid back down the wall beside the door.

"Just leave me alone, Jenna," I whined.

She came in and crouched down beside me. "Meagan, you don't have to do this. Let Amber decide when she's had enough. You're not protecting her, you're taking away her choice."

I stared at her blankly. "What do you mean?"

"I know why you're breaking up with her. You're trying to spare her but you don't have to." She tucked my hair behind my ear. "This isn't like Janie. It wasn't your job to save her and it's not your job to save Amber. Please, just come talk to her."

"I can't," I whispered. "Jenna, I'm hurting her. You saw what happened tonight. How many times am I going to hurt her like that? I can't do it. I can't be the source of her pain."

"Do you think she's gonna let you go so easily? She loves you."

"I'll find a way. Just go be with her, Jenna. She needs you now more than I do." I wiped my eyes and rose to my feet. I could not be weak right now. Control was a must.

Jenna saw the change register on my face and sighed because she knew the walls were going up around me. I felt them rise from the floor with me, shielding me within their cold, crystalline enclosure. And then I was locked inside. The cryogenic chamber sealed shut, impenetrable. I became one with the coldness of indifference.

"Take care of Amber." The words slipped out of me like rivulets of melting frost. "I have work to do anyway."

Jenna studied my face for a change in the block of ice. "Are you sure? You won't come over?"

"I'm sure. Please Jenna, just go be her friend now. I'll deal with me."

Defeated, Jenna left the apartment and I quickly went back to crying, silently this time, and in the bedroom where I was sure I wouldn't be heard. The tears fell till morning and I rose from the bed, still wearing my clothes from the night before, and went to get ready for work. My insides continued to ache but I battled the effects it could have on my mind and prepared myself for the day ahead.

With a purse slung over my shoulder and a briefcase in my hand, I dared to make my escape. My feet whispered across the living room floor, fingers reached slowly for the door handle like the next victim in a slasher film. Amber knew what time I left for work and I wanted to sneak passed Jenna's door without incident. Quietly, I turned the knob and stepped into the hall. Amber was already there.

"Did you get any sleep?" she asked, reaching to touch my hair.

I backed away. "Sure."

"Really?" She cocked her head to the side and engaged me with a grin. "'Cause you look like shit."

It was a joke that normally would have made me laugh but not today. "I gotta get to work," I said, turning away from her. She snatched my wrist.

"Meagan, wait."

"What?"

Her fingers made a soft trail across my hand. "Come by after work, okay?"

"Why?"

It was difficult to ignore the way my body wanted to respond to her touch. She took a step forward, I stepped back. Her hand reached to touch my face, I turned my head. If I let her touch me any more than she already was I was a goner, and she knew that. I could feel my heart softening and in a moment of weakness, I said, "I'll stop by around five." Then I became angry with myself because we both knew if I said I'd do something I'd do it. Now I would only be prolonging the agony for both of us.

Amber gave a triumphant grin. As far as she was concerned the hard part was over. She'd gotten me to agree to come by and now all she had to do was wait for me to keep my word.

I found myself grinning back, but only for a second and only because I admired the way she had callously used my own sense of integrity against me. I had a healthy appreciation for those who would do anything to get what they wanted.

"I have to go," I said again, forcing a strong note into my tone. If I looked at her much longer, feeling this admiration, I was going to cave. Another minute and I'd be embracing her and telling her how sorry I was and I couldn't risk that. I had to let her go for her own good.

At work I spent the day in my office trying to figure out how I was going to handle the situation when I arrived at Amber's apartment. How would I again tell her I honestly couldn't see her anymore? If I told her I was doing it for her own good she would take away my altruistic act by telling me she could deal with the problems and that I didn't have to protect her. But I did have to protect her-- from me. From the hurt I was causing.

Finally, I came to a decision. If I had to, I would lie to her, just this once. If she forced the issue and I found myself backed into a corner I would turn my head so I wouldn't have to look at those truth-grabbing eyes, and I would lie my way out. There had always been a cruelty within me, a sort of masochism I tried to keep in check, but if Amber called it out I would use it. Sometimes hate was the only way out of love.

At 5:15, I arrived at her apartment and she greeted me at the door wearing faded blue jeans and a green sweater that made her eyes impossibly beautiful. I tried not to look. Smiling, she acted as if nothing had happened the night before. She threw her arms around me and kissed me as only she could. My arms wrapped easily around the small of her back and my mouth returned the kiss. She smiled again against my lips.

"I knew you didn't mean it," she murmured, and the words snapped me back to reality.

Quickly, I drew away from her and struggled to free myself from the energy that had always drawn us together like a magnetic pull.

"I'm sorry," I whispered. "Coming here was a bad idea."

I turned to leave but she blocked my path. "Meagan, don't do this," she pleaded for the second time in two days. "I love you and I know you love me."

We had loved too greatly, that was the problem, and I saw no other course of action than the nasty one my mind produced. It had to be cruel. If it wasn't cruel, she would never give up on me and I couldn't bear that. Either way I would hurt her. At least this way it would happen once and no more.

I turned on her fiercely and yanked my arm from her grasp. "But it isn't enough, is it Amber? Don't you see? I don't know how to be what you need. Half the time I don't even *understand* what you need."

"So that's it? You just walk away?"

"Yes. I just walk away."

"I don't believe this," she raged. "I can't believe you can do this when you know how hard it was for me to get involved with someone like you."

"*Someone like me?*" I demanded. Her words angered me. "Don't play the victim, Amber, it's not becoming. And I didn't exactly twist your fucking arm. If I remember correctly it was *you* who came after me. I was perfectly fine in my little heterosexual existence but every time I turned around there you were, forcing your way into my life. I don't regret it, but let's be honest: We both knew the challenges we'd face going in. We just didn't know they'd be this insurmountable." I thrived on challenge but this was beyond my abilities.

"They're not," she barked. "You're just too fucking selfish to try."

I threw up my arms. "Whatever."

"How can you be so cold-hearted?"

The comment hurt. I had heard it a few times in my life and to hear it from her turned me to ice. I was giving her up for *her* sake.

"You want cold-hearted?" I growled. "How's this? You were never anything more than a rebound."

"You're lying."

"No, that's the truth. Basil cheated on me and I dumped him. You showed up all willing to take his place and I thought, why the hell not? This should be fun for awhile. You were never going to be permanent, Amber, no matter what you did. I used you to fill the void."

She crossed her arms in front of her. "I don't believe you. You're not that kind of person. You love me."

"*Loved* you, maybe," I said, cruelly, "but very briefly at that. You were never anything more than someone to kill time with. That you grew on me I won't deny, but like I've told you a hundred times before, Amber, I am not gay. That should have been your first clue. How could I ever stay with you if I'm not even gay? You were an experiment, now it's done. And I suggest you move on because I'm doing so even as we speak."

Tears sprang to her eyes. I held back my own.

"Stop this," she cried. "It's going too far. If you have to end it, for Christ's sake, don't do it this way. End it on the truth because I don't believe your lies. You weren't faking what we've been to each other."

"I was."

"Yeah?" A new fire danced behind her eyes and she flashed her hand under my face, flaunting the moonstone. "What about this, huh? What about your fucking precious ring?"

It was a stinging revelation and the lies exploded. "Do you really think I'd give you something that means anything to me?" I demanded. "It's a piece of junk." *Forgive me, Gran.* "It never meant anything. It's just some stupid ring I got one year at Mardi Gras and I wore it as a good luck charm."

"Then you won't care if I do this." She yanked the ring off her finger and stalked toward the garbage bin in the kitchen and I watched with horror as the metal lid popped open and the ring dropped inside. I didn't react. She looked at me and I cringed as she grabbed a jar of blueberry jam from the fridge and poured its contents into the garbage receptacle.

My body sprang into action. "What the fuck --?" I stopped.

"Doesn't mean anything though, does it?" she sneered. "You're ready to yank it out of the garbage but it doesn't mean a goddamn thing!"

I threw up an emotional wall. "Do what you want. It's *junk.* My grandmother never had a secret lover and that wasn't her ring."

"You made me hide it at the shower."

I shrugged. "Part of the game."

"You're really sick."

"Yes."

"Do you even know how transparent you are?" she yelled. "I see through you, Meagan. I know what you are and it isn't this."

"You don't know anything," I barked. Had to end this soon. Had to get out before the lies choked me and the tears burst free. "I *never* loved you, okay?" I avoided her eyes. "I liked you.

You were fun. But not once did I ever think I actually loved you."

My words were razors and she was back to crying. "Why do you have to do it this way?"

"Because it's the truth."

"Then look me in the eyes and say it."

I couldn't. How could I look in those eyes and lie? Her eyes were her soul. They were emerald truth-finders. Her eyes exposed me for what I really was. The walls were ready to tumble and Amber was goading me on.

"Do it, Meagan. Look me right in the eyes and tell me you don't love me."

I pulled up my anger and my cruelty. I tapped into the rage for Janie, the hurt of Basil, the love of Amber, and most importantly, the calculating mind for business. My heart fused them together like a cold ball of metal and slowly my stare met hers.

"I don't love you, Amber," I said quietly. "I never did."

And I watched my words destroy her. The jaw tightened in pain. The lips curled in rage. The body trembled. And the eyes-- oh God-- the eyes filled with hate!

"Get out," she hissed.

Suddenly my feet refused to move and Amber's rage exploded.

"*Get out!*"

She picked up an ashtray and hurled it at me. I ducked and it crashed against the wall behind my head and shattered to the floor in a million sparkling pieces.

"Are you fucking crazy?" I screamed. The ashtray was thick and made of crystal. "You could have killed me!"

"Don't flatter yourself. You're not worth murder."

My heart squeezed me. "Goodbye, Amber. It's been fun."

And I stepped out into a freedom I knew I didn't really want.

Gran's ring was gone. I thought of it on the way home and cried. With one lie, I'd wiped out forty years of my grandmother's love. I could scarcely see the road for my tears.

A horn blared beside me and a car swerved around me. I was halfway on the wrong side of the road, eyes blurred with tears. Part of me wished the car had hit me. The driver yelled something, shot me the finger, and sped off.

It was a short distance between Amber's home and mine, mere blocks. I roared the distance home and locked myself behind the big metal door. Within seconds Jenna was pounding on it. I curled up on the couch, ignoring her. She used her spare key to get in.

"Meagan?" Her pale blue eyes scanned the room, landed on me, and her head fell in a sympathetic tilt. She came to the couch. "Meagan, what did you do? She's sobbing over there."

I burst into sobs of my own. "I-- I told her I never loved her and that-- that I *used* her-- and, many-- many horrible things!"

Jenna pulled me into her arms and I cried against her shoulder.

"It's not right, Meagan" she said. "You lied to her."

"I had to," I sobbed. "I thought if she hated me she'd hurt less and she *does hate me.* Oh God, she really does! You should have seen her face, Jenna. She looked like I'd killed her."

"Shhh." Jenna rocked me in her arms. "It's okay, Meagan. She doesn't hate you. She's hurt. I called there. I'm sorry but I had a really bad feeling and I called. There was something wrong with your head."

I wiped my eyes and looked at her. Jenna sometimes had what she called "*flashes*"; little bursts of psychic knowledge.

"My head?" I asked.

Jenna looked frightened. "In my mind, I saw it bleeding. You were standing by the door and I yelled at you to duck."

I choked on another sob. Had Jenna been responsible for saving my life from eight blocks away?

"She threw an ashtray at me," I managed.

"Crystal?"

I nodded. "It whizzed by my head."

"Oh." A little cry of pain escaped her and she pulled me tighter into her arms. Jenna didn't have the flashes often but they could be frightening. Instinctively, she began picking at the air around my head.

"Oh Jenna, don't," I groaned. "Just leave my aura alone."

"Okay." She stopped her cleansing. "So, what happens now?"

"I don't know."

"You can make it right, Meagan. You can call her and tell her it was all a lie."

The pain ripped through me again. "*I can't do that.* Would you give up on someone if you knew they still loved you?"

"You know she still loves *you*," Jenna pointed out.

"It's different. I also know I have to end it or I'll go on hurting her for only God knows how long. And you have to keep this a secret, Jenna. You can't go telling her I love her or you'll only prolong her misery. Do you understand that? There's no going back from this and I need you to help protect her."

Jenna didn't like the idea but she agreed. My logic may have been backwards but she understood it. Understood *me.*

"However you want to handle it, Meagan," she said. And I knew she meant it.

Another sleepless night followed and the next day I packed up Amber's things and sent them over with Jenna. I then scheduled an emergency appointment with my therapist, Helen Nisku.

Helen hadn't been much help from day one but I'd continued to see her. She remained silent a lot. In her stereotypical wing-back leather chair she'd sit with her thick legs crossed before her and her analytical eyes peering out at me from behind tan-framed glasses that were far too big for her round face. She had heavy jowls and, often when I looked at her, I was reminded of a bulldog. However, her smile was kind and her tone soft, and those were the things that continually drew me back.

"I'd like to try something different today, Meagan," she said as I sat across from her, dry-eyed and as cold as the leather chair beneath me. Helen had listened to me relay the previous day's events as dispassionately as if I were describing what I'd eaten for lunch. "I'd like for you to cry."

I blinked. "Excuse me?" She'd *like* me to cry? As if I could cry on demand.

Helen nodded. "I want you to allow it, Meagan. You sit in this chair session after session and you explain things that would make other patients howl in agony but you never shed a tear. The safest place to cry is within these walls. Let it out."

I didn't like the idea. My tears were a private matter. "I cried at home," I said. "I think I'm dry now."

"Does Amber hate you?"

The tears welled quickly and I fought them. "Don't do that," I pleaded.

Helen left her chair and kneeled before me. I stiffened. We didn't have that sort of relationship. She stayed in her chair and I stayed in mine.

"You saw a dead body in the forest when you were ten," she said, softly. Her eyes peered into mine and she took my hands. I knew what she was doing, she was going to yank the tears out of me whether I wanted her to or not.

"You loved your gran," she continued, kindly, "and she died that same year. You didn't cry." Slowly she was drawing out the horrors. "You took the pain in because you believed someone had to be the strong one and for some reason you decided that someone had to be you. You were ten years old but you took charge of the scene. It was Meagan handing out tissue at the wake and pouring the coffee. It was Meagan holding her Uncle Seamus' hand and stroking her mother's hair."

"I did what my Gran would have wanted," I said, quietly.

"Yes, and you learned to deal with her death in your own way. Let's move a little further, okay Meagan?"

"Okay," I said weakly.

Helen handed me a tissue and I knew we were going to go more than a little further. She was preparing me for greater pains.

"You've always had a strained relationship with your mother," she continued. "When you were an adolescent you learned to make your friends your family --"

"And Seamus."

She smiled. "Yes, always Seamus. People give you a hard time about your relationship with him but he has always been the one constant in your life."

"Because he's an alcoholic."

"But you accept that. So, we have your friends and Seamus. And then there was Janie. You loved Janie like a sister and you protected her as fiercely as you still protect your sister and your friend, Jenna. And now, Amber."

The tears were slowly sliding down my cheeks and I looked away.

"But Janie died and you saw the horror of that. You saw her dead on the hood of her car and you live with the guilt of failing to be at her side that night. You refuse to hear that it wasn't your fault and it gives you nightmares but still you do not cry."

"You're making me cry," I said hoarsely.

"Yes, because it's time. Let it go, Meagan. Cry for the man in the forest with the rain dripping over his dead lips, and for your Gran, and for Janie. Cry for the way your sister betrayed you when she slept with Basil. Cry for how Basil continued to betray you after that. And for your soul mate, Meagan. For months you've sat in this chair telling me Amber is your soul mate, so cry for the loss of her."

The sobs poured out of me and I thought they would never stop. For thirty-five minutes I cried while Helen patted my knee, nodded a lot, and repeatedly handed me tissues and glasses of water. When I left her office I felt worse than when I'd gone in.

Jenna was waiting for me when I got home. There was a cardboard box by the door and I knew what was in it-- the things I had left behind at Amber's apartment. I sifted through it slowly. Mostly clothes. No ring. Then I remembered she'd thrown out the ring and the ache came back to my soul.

I'm sorry Gran. I didn't do it right. I lied and my lie destroyed what you and Rosalie created.

Would my gran ever forgive me? More importantly, would I ever forgive myself?

There was a small unfamiliar box at the bottom and, curious, I plucked it out and snapped open the lid. The gold hammer. My heart hurt and my head ached.

"This isn't mine," I said.

Jenna's eyes darted away. "She won't keep it. She said --"

Fresh tears welled in my eyes. "That I'm the real hammer," I whispered.

"I'm sorry, Meagan. I didn't correct her impression of you but are you sure this is how you want to leave it?"

"I'm sure."

Miserably, I went in the bedroom and closed myself inside. I'd never felt so horrible in my life.

Chapter 13

"Get up."

My father was tugging on my arms and I felt myself being lifted from the couch. I had been there for days. I had taken the week off work and settled into my misery while Josh and Jenna did everything they could to bring me around. Danielle had practically moved in and between the three of them I never got a moment's peace. Now someone had contacted my father and he was in my face.

I stared up at him through eyes that refused to close all the way but refused to stay open. "Dad? What are you doing here?"

He pulled me to a seated position. "Go get dressed. We're going out for supper."

"No, I don't feel well."

"Please, honey." He sat beside me on the couch and a part of me wished he was Seamus. Seamus could get me through this but he had to work and I didn't have the energy to fly to Ireland.

"This place is a mess," my father said. "Jenna says you don't eat and you don't sleep and Danny says you've been wearing those flannel pants for a week."

"They're warm."

"And the mess? The magazines and pop cans littered about?"

"Danny's," I groaned. "Her mess-- she can clean it."

"Meagan, I'm worried. You were practically born with a dust-buster in your hand and look at this place. This isn't like you. You got over Basil and you'll get over Amber."

I rubbed my itchy eyes. I didn't know how to tell my father Amber was nothing like Basil. Basil hadn't been my soul mate. I hadn't *destroyed* Basil.

"I'm fine, Dad," I pleaded. "Please, just go away. I go back to work tomorrow and everything will go back to normal then, okay?"

I must have been the only one who didn't know how utterly wrong I was.

Days drifted slowly into weeks and my depression grew more severe. I tried to stay focused on work but even that had become a challenge. The London decision was getting closer every day and Ted was beginning to want an answer. I continued to put him off. Aware of my fragile situation and the battle going on within me, Ted let it go for awhile. My presence in London still wasn't a must but the day was coming and soon I would have to decide.

Word from Jenna was that Amber had locked herself away in her apartment and refused to see anyone but Zeppo. She was working, Jenna said, but I couldn't imagine on what because I knew her manuscript had been almost ready weeks ago.

Zeppo showed up at my office. Ted had commissioned another painting and Zeppo decided to hand-deliver it. I was in the board room with Ted when I saw him pass and he looked in at me, spotted Ted, and knocked on the glass door. Ted rose to open it and I scurried away to my office like a rat.

My evasion didn't affect Zeppo. He handled his business with Ted and five minutes later burst through my door.

My head snapped up from my work. "Zeppo! What the hell --?"

"Do you have any idea what you've done to her?" he yelled, slamming the door.

"Get out. I have work to do."

"No, little Miss Thing, you and I are going to have this out." He stalked over to my desk. "Jesus, look at you."

"What?" I demanded. I still hadn't been sleeping much. I was working non-stop and food was a necessity I was only able to choke down in small lumps.

"You look like the walking dead."

"Fuck you. Get out of my office."

"You still love her," he sneered.

"So?"

I didn't deny it. Amber was a ghost who wouldn't leave me alone. Her image filled every space of my apartment. I couldn't sleep in the bed we'd shared. Her memory filled every particle of air and I sometimes felt like I couldn't breathe. I was suffocating in the energies she'd left behind.

Jenna was studying Reiki and I let her practice on me but every time I felt something negative leaving my body I stopped her. "I can't get it out if you won't let it go," she'd say, gently pulling on something invisible. She thought she was pulling the bad stuff out of me but I felt like she was pulling the Amber out of me and I wasn't yet ready to give her up entirely.

"Are you leaving?" I demanded of Zeppo, who continued to stare at my face like it amazed him.

My eyes were itching again, a sure sign that they were red and inflamed, and I reached into the top drawer of my desk and pulled out a bottle of Visine; tilted back my head and squeezed three drops into each eye. The itching subsided.

"How many bottles of *that* do you go through each week, Meagan?" Zeppo commented snidely.

I shrugged. "At least one."

"You don't even care, do you?" he barked. "You ripped out her heart and you don't even care. You cold, fucking cunt."

"Didn't I ask you to leave? Don't make me call security, Zeppo."

"Yeah, I'm leaving." He turned toward the door. "And honey, all the makeup in the world isn't gonna hide those swollen eyes and sunken in cheeks. You look like shit."

"And I suppose you'll put that in your report too," I snapped.

"Sure will." He yanked open the door.

"I'm sorry she's hurt, Zeppo."

"Fuck you."

The door slammed behind him and I pulled a compact mirror from my purse. Yes, I was getting thin. Not horribly so but the signs of stress were there. The hair still fell in pretty brown-auburn streaks and the makeup was smoky perfection, but the eyes -- behind the irises lived the dull look of misery. If the eyes were the windows to the soul, I was without one.

Sighing, I closed the compact and went back to work.

Chapter 14

"Wanna go to BeBe's?" Jenna asked.

It was Friday night and I'd just stepped off a plane from London only to race to a restaurant to have dinner with Ted and Peter Gregory. Jenna had accosted me as soon as I'd gotten home.

"I just stepped through the door," I complained, feeling jet-lagged and distressed. London had been another ten day trip and my plans for the evening included nothing more than curling up on the couch with a book.

"They're having live music tonight," Jenna persuaded. "You haven't been out in weeks. We'll call Danny and make it a girl's night out."

I checked the messages on my machine. Three hang-ups. "Where's Josh?"

"Weekend ski trip with the boys. We're going out."

Jenna didn't wait for a response. She picked up the phone, called Danielle, and told her we'd be picking her up within the hour. Then she turned to me and told me to get dressed, as if she really thought I'd wear a business suit to a club.

An evening out didn't sound so bad after all, and, nodding my agreement, I went into the bedroom and changed into a creamy wool sweater Seamus had sent me from Ireland and a pair of blue Versace jeans that hung more loosely on my frame than when I had purchased them a few weeks earlier. The reflection in the mirror told me they looked better this way. For makeup I decided on subtlety; nude lipstick, a touch of bronze across the cheekbones, brown eyeliner and mascara.

Forty-five minutes later we were strolling through the frosted doors of BeBe's. The club was dark and noisy, and as packed as it ever was. Smoke rose to the ventilators in the ceiling in great purple-gray clouds and the dance floor was jammed with swaying bodies decked out in their best club gear. I didn't plan on dancing. I felt tired.

"Wanna grab a drink?" Jenna asked loudly.

"Let's grab a table first," Danielle suggested.

Our eyes scanned the room as we walked and Danielle suddenly stopped short, causing me to walk into her back.

"Oh my God!" she gasped.

"What?" I pushed her aside to see what she was looking at and my mouth drop open in sheer disbelief. Amber! And as if that wasn't bad enough, she was sitting with *Basil!*

A wave of nausea swept over me and Jenna said, "Look there's a table," and forced me into a chair.

Danielle looked from Amber to me. "Jesus, you're as white as a ghost."

My eyes refused to budge from Amber. My heart ached. The smoke in the room filled my head and I couldn't speak. She was staring back at me and the rest of the club could have been empty for all it mattered. Vaguely, I was aware of Basil's eyes upon me but he was unimportant. All that mattered was the eye-lock Amber and I were frozen into. Danielle and Jenna remained silent at the table. Amber and I remained dead locked, when suddenly; an exotic looking Asian woman approached Amber and sat in her lap. My heart stopped.

Amber gave me an evil grin, turned the woman's head and kissed her. Passionately. Basil laughed, and I felt the nausea reach the back of my mouth. I was going to be sick.

"I gotta get out of here," I said, lifting myself on wobbly legs.

Amber spotted movement out of the corner of her eye and broke her lip-lock with the voluptuous woman, fixing me with her cold green stare. Now all three of them were staring at me, their eyes daring me to make a move.

"Okay," Jenna agreed, her eyes flitting back and forth between Amber and me. "Let's go."

Jenna took my hand and we turned to leave when Danielle stunned the both of us. "Fuck this," she roared, and stormed off in Amber's direction.

Jenna tried to stop her but Danielle was quickly across the room and leaning over their table. Her arms flailed wildly, the way they did when she was angry, and I began feeling very faint. The last thing I wanted was a scene.

"Oh God Jenna, go get her."

I steadied myself on the back of the chair. Jenna approached Danielle and tried pulling her away. The Asian woman whispered something in Amber's ear and Amber suddenly shoved her off her lap, her face a mask of rage. For a second her eye caught mine and she gave me a curious look. The kind she used to give when having an insight on what was going on inside of me.

Danielle was yelling at Basil now and Jenna was desperately trying to remove her from the scene. Even from a distance I could see the determined set to Danielle's jaw. No one was getting her away from there until she was good and ready. Amber said something to the Asian woman, who glared in my direction, then stalked away.

Finally, I could take no more. Staring directly at Amber, I slowly but deliberately, began walking toward their table. Amber was watching me but listening to Danielle, and as I drew closer I could hear Danielle saying, "She doesn't eat. She doesn't sleep. This is the first time she's been out in weeks and look how you behave," while Jenna was doing everything she could to silence her.

Amber's eyes never left my face as I approached Danielle and began rubbing her arm. "It's okay, honey," I said in the most soothing tone I could muster. "Let's go home." I couldn't believe how tired I'd suddenly become.

Jenna wrapped her arm around my waist and I thought she might be holding me upright. Amber continued to stare like a spectator at the scene of an accident but remained silent.

"Come on, Danny," I pleaded. "Let's go home."

"Meagan, you're slurring," Jenna whispered.

"Huh?" My concentration was gone and I realized Jenna was indeed holding me on my feet. She tugged on Danielle's jacket with her free hand.

"Let's go Danielle," she said in a tight voice.

Danielle suddenly burst into tears. "No!" She shook off Jenna's hand. "What's the matter with you people? Don't any of you *see* it?"

"See what, honey?" I reached out to wipe a tear from her cheek but she yanked herself away and I stumbled forward. "What the hell is wrong with you?" I yelled. The stumble embarrassed me.

"Not here, Danny," Jenna said, her eyes clearly indicating that whatever Danielle had to say should not be said in front of Basil and Amber. "Not like this."

"What are you talking about?" I demanded. But the words caught in my throat and went unheard below the music around us.

Angrily, Danielle grabbed my wrist and twisted it. "What do you see when you look in the mirror?" she barked.

"Danny don't," Jenna pleaded, her eyes wide with fear.

"What do you see?" Danielle was in a rage and she yanked on my arm, shaking me. I hadn't the strength or inclination to fight her off.

Amber shot to her feet but Danielle pointed an accusing finger at her and said, "Sit the fuck down," to which she promptly did.

Amber protecting me from my sister? It was crazy enough to make me want to laugh.

Violently, Danielle rummaged through her purse with one hand while the other remained clamped to my wrist. She thrust a small mirror in my face.

"Look at yourself," she demanded.

"Danielle!"

"It's dark, Danny," I offered, reasonably. "But I think I know what I look like."

"*Do you?*" she pressed. "Do you see the sunken in cheeks when you look at yourself? The eyes that always look battered and half-shut? Did you happen to notice the way you start swaying on your fucking feet, or how you start slurring your words like Seamus on a bender after nine?"

"Don't talk about Seamus, Danielle."

"How much do you weigh, Meagan? A hundred pounds?"

"Now you're exaggerating." I pulled myself together and stood on my own. The movement was an effort but it was time to take control. Danny was tearfully shaking her head and I pulled her into a hug, rubbed her back. "I'm fine, Danny. Please --" My eyes scanned the bar and the few people who were watching. "Please, Danielle, you're making a scene."

Wrong words to say to someone in a rage. Disgusted, she yanked herself away from me and the arms went back to flailing wildly.

"Everything's a scene to you, isn't it? Well, I don't care, Meagan. I don't give a shit who's looking!"

"You're pissing me off," I growled. The others at the table remained cloaked in their silent awe and Jenna sank into a chair, sensing we were at an impasse.

"No," Danny squeaked. "*You're* pissing *me* off. Do you have any idea what it's like being around you anymore?"

"So stop coming around," I threatened. "Why are you at my apartment twenty-four hours a day, anyway?"

"Because someone has to be around to force the fucking food down your throat. Without me you'd be dead in a week."

"I fucking eat! Now shut the hell up. I'm taking you home-- to *your* home and from now on you can leave me the hell alone."

Danny was not about to calm down. *"Would you fucking look at yourself?* You're a zombie, Meagan."

"Danielle, that's enough!" Jenna's voice was a harsh yell and she shot to her feet. Jenna never yelled at anyone and her tone, mixed with the anger in her eyes, stunned Danielle into silence.

A sigh of relief expelled from my body in a great stream. It was over. I thought we could just go home and turned on my heel only to slam into a tall dark-haired woman who'd suddenly appeared behind me. My forehead crashed into her shoulder and I looked up. The woman grinned and puffed a cigarette.

"Hi Meagan," she said.

She didn't look familiar and I was in no mood for pleasantries. "Who are you?"

"You don't remember me?"

"No."

"Sure you do, I'm Jinx."

Jinx. The woman who had come onto me. Amber's friend. I glanced at Amber and her expression was tight but still she said nothing. I wondered if she would ever utter a word.

"You guys broke up, huh?" Jinx's head indicated Amber.

Amber scowled. "Yeah Jinx, she's all yours now."

"Thank you," Jinx sneered.

My head whipped around at Amber and she shrugged. Rage ripped through me like a hungry snake and I turned back to Jinx and spewed my venom.

"Get the hell away from me," I snapped. "You fucking

dykes are like sharks smelling fresh blood and I have no interest in *you.*"

Her face turned to concrete. "Eat me."

"Not without a latex body condom and a blindfold."

Jinx stormed away from the table and I heard Basil snicker. Amber smirked down at her drink.

"*Now* can we go?" I demanded of Danielle. "Or do we need to wait around for something else to happen?"

Danielle shrugged and the phone in my purse started to ring.

"For Christ's sake," I groaned. It was one thing after another and I could feel myself becoming unglued. Frustrated, I snatched the phone from my bag and flipped it open with an annoyed, "What?" It was Ted.

"You gotta come back to the restaurant," he pleaded. "Peter's had a few drinks and he's asking for you."

"Well tell him you couldn't get a hold of me."

Exhausted, I dropped into the chair across from Amber and she gave a little jump, startled by the action. I didn't care. Annoyance was quickly turning to anger and I was ready to snap. Absentmindedly, I snatched up Amber's vodka and grapefruit, took a sip, and dropped it back in front of her. She stared at the glass in disbelief.

"I can't do that," Ted was saying. "He really wants to see you."

"I don't give a shit what he wants." The whole table was listening to my end of the conversation and my patience was thinning. "Listen Ted, you have no idea what kind of shit I'm dealing with tonight."

"Business first, remember? Aren't you the one who's always saying that? Just come back."

Business first. Yeah, that was me but I was goddamn tired.

"Do you want me to burn out? Christ, I just left his freaking side an hour ago. Didn't I jump off a fourteen-hour flight just to race to that restaurant and hold his fucking hand through a teary conversation about his ridiculous dead grandfather? That's not in my job description, Ted." The music played around us but it seemed quieter now. "I'm not coming back."

Ted didn't like my attitude and pulled one of his own. "Do

I have to remind you I am your employer?"

The words were a growl and I shot to my feet, rage coursing through me like a new disease.

"Are you pulling rank on me you son of a bitch?"

"For Christ's sake, Meagan," Danny hissed beside me. "That's your boss!"

I silenced her with a look while Ted bitched in my ear about how important Peter was to the magazine's success and that he had taken a liking to me.

"He wants you back here."

Ted was pushing me. "And if he wants a blow job should I get down on my fucking knees too?"

"Meagan, shut up!" Danny was getting scared.

"Are you in a bar?" Ted demanded.

"It's none of your fucking business where I am!" I paced in front of the table. "Tell Peter I said he can shove his millions of dollars up his ass. He doesn't own me, Ted, and neither do you."

"Do you like your job, Meagan?"

Ted's tone was as threatening as I'd ever heard it and it was the last thing I needed tonight. Reasoning snapped away like a rubber band.

"You fucking little prick!"

Jenna was pulling on my arm. "Meagan, don't." Basil's mouth was open, as was Amber's, and Danielle was shaking her head in horrified fascination.

"You wanna threaten me, Ted?" I kicked over a chair. "You think you fucking can? Well, try this -- I quit!"

"Oh my Goddess! Meagan, no!" Jenna desperately yanked on my sleeve and I tore my arm away.

"You what?" Ted shrieked.

"Are you hard of hearing too you slave-driving son of a bitch? *I quit!* Find someone else to be your little whore because I'm done." I slammed the phone on the table. *"Fucker!"*

"Meagan, *why did you do that?* Have you lost your fucking mind?"

The rage grew to an unbearable height and I knew I was losing control. I whirled around on Danielle.

"You really like scenes, don't you Danny? Well here, have a fucking thrill!"

In one wild moment I yanked the beer from Basil's hand

and crashed it down on the phone. The bottom flap splintered away and shot across the table at Amber. Jenna pleaded with me to stop. People began turning to check out the commotion. I didn't care. I had slipped over the edge and continued to pound the beer bottle against the phone, smashing it to pieces.

For Basil sitting with Amber. *Smash.* For Danny's outburst. *Smash.* For Jinx. *Smash.* For Amber kissing that woman. *Smash, smash.* For Ted and his demands.

"Get a fucking grip on yourself," Basil shrieked, his face contorted in horrified anger.

"Fuck you!"

The neck broke away from the bottle and the base of the glass sliced across my palm.

"Shit!" The broken bottle slipped to the table and blood gushed from my hand.

"Meagan!" Amber was instantly on her feet.

The shattered phone started ringing again and I stared at it like a homicidal maniac who had failed to kill her victim. Jenna caught the manic look and snatched up the phone before I completely lost my mind.

"It's still ringing!" I shrieked. Blood poured down my fingers and Jenna was shoving the broken bits of phone into her jacket pocket. "Oh my God. It's still *ringing!*"

Vaguely, I was aware of Amber grabbing my wrist, Basil walking away from the table, Jenna taking my hand and Danielle demanding, "What kind of freaking therapist do you have?"

"Be quiet!" Jenna yelled.

The fit had passed and people went back to their drinking and dancing.

"We have to get this clean," Amber was saying. "There's beer in it, maybe glass. Jenna, it looks deep."

Jenna inspected the damage in the dim light. "You'll need stitches."

"I quit my job. Can you believe it? I quit my job."

"Don't worry about that now. We have to get you to a hospital."

I didn't care about the cut. My adrenaline was pumping so high I couldn't even feel it. "Jenna, did you hear me? I quit my job."

Then I remembered the stocks and suddenly burst out

laughing. It didn't matter if I quit. I could quit thirty times a day and it would never matter.

"What could you possibly find funny about this?" Danielle demanded. "You're over the edge. You've completely lost your mind."

"Yes." I couldn't stop laughing.

"Let's go in the bathroom," Amber suggested.

They were pulling me through the crowd while the blood continued to pour down my hand. I continued to laugh.

"Hey Jenna, ya think your uncle Steve has room for one more in his padded room?"

Danny waved three girls out of the facilities and locked the door.

"You're not supposed to lock that." I said.

"Shut up, Meagan."

"Unlock it. What if someone has to get in here?"

"They can use the other bathroom. Do you really want people coming in here and seeing what a fucking maniac you are?"

"Shut up, Danny," Amber barked. "Haven't you done enough?"

"Me?" Danny was getting angry again. "This is your fault, Amber. My sister's life is a fucked up mess and I hold you responsible for that. Why couldn't you just stay the hell away from her?" She took a menacing step forward. "I'd really like to punch you out, you little bitch."

"Stop it!" I gave Danielle a small shove. "Apologize right now."

"You're protecting her? Do you have any idea what went on here tonight? You quit your job, Meagan. You sliced open your goddamn hand and you're losing your fucking mind and it's *her* fault."

"No, it's mine."

Jenna started running the cold water and Amber pressed my hand under the tap.

"*I* did those things, Danielle," I said, wincing at the burst of pain as the cold struck my hand. "And don't worry about my job; I'll have it back by the time we get home."

"You quit."

"It's impossible for me to quit. I can't tell you why but it just is, all right?" Amber's hand pressed mine further under the tap and I struggled against her. "That hurts, Amber. Just let go."

"We have to get it clean." I thought she looked like she wanted to cry. "Please Meagan, don't fight me. There might be glass in there."

Amber was trying to take care of me and it was suddenly breaking my heart. I didn't deal with heartbreak well.

"I said let go." I yanked my hand away and the inner rage crept up again. "You're so concerned now but you tried to kill me a few weeks ago."

"I didn't try to kill you."

"Yeah? Well that ashtray could have cracked my head open pretty damn good. Then you have the nerve to drop me off on Jinx tonight like I'm nothing more than some sex toy you can just pass around. Go back to your little Asian girlfriend, Amber."

"She's not my --"

"I don't care. Go away."

"I'm trying to help you."

"I don't need your help. My sister will apologize for her behavior and then we'll be leaving."

"I will not," Danielle snapped. "Look at the way *you're* talking to her."

"That's me. *You* will apologize."

"She doesn't have to," Amber said quietly.

I threw up my hands. "Fine. Whatever." The gash didn't appear so bad once the blood was washed away and I shrugged at it. "I won't need stitches."

"Meagan --"

"No Jenna. I appreciate your concern but it will be fine. We'll just break off a piece of your aloe plant. Let's go."

"I'm coming with you," Amber said, quickly.

My eyes widened in alarm. "No, you're not." What exactly did she think was going on here?

"I need to talk to you, Meagan. I've done something. Something I really need to talk to you about."

"What?" A new fear grew within me.

"I can't talk about it here," she said, looking around the florescent-lit bathroom. I was too tired for games.

"Then you can't talk about it at all."

I marched away from her and grabbed a paper towel from the dispenser on the wall. I swung open the bathroom door and walked out with Danny trailing along at my side.

"I'm sorry, Amber," Jenna said, and quickly followed us out.

Swiftly, we moved through the club and out the back doors to the parking lot where people milled about smoking cigarettes and joints. Jenna got behind the wheel of the car and suggested we bring Danny home. For once Danielle did not protest.

With a paper towel pressed to my injury, I watched the city pass by and thought of Amber. She'd looked great tonight, all platinum hair and emerald eyes. I thought of the way they'd focused on me and the way she cried out my name when I cut my hand, and I cried silently. Jenna and Danielle pretended not to notice.

Amber had said she'd done something. I didn't want to know what, but the curiosity was like an insecurity carving its way around my stomach and the nausea settled in once more. Fear dried the tears as we entered my parent's quiet neighborhood and pulled into the driveway.

Glumly, Danielle got out of the car. She seemed guilt-ridden over what had happened; like she thought she had been the one to make me lose my mind.

"It wasn't your fault, Danny," I said. "I'm responsible for my own actions."

"I love you, Meagan," she whispered, leaning through the window to hug me.

I patted her back with my good hand. "I love you too. Just go inside and I'll talk to you tomorrow."

At home the answering machine was already blinking with messages. I played them while Jenna ran across the hall to break off a piece of her aloe vera plant. The first message was from Ted. He said he was sorry for pushing me and did not accept my resignation.

"*You're right,*" he said. "*Your time is your own but I expect an apology too. Monday morning.*"

I smiled to myself and walked into the bathroom to pour peroxide over my wound. The liquid stung and I winced. The answering machine beeped for the second time and Amber's voice filled the room, noise in the background. She was still at the club and said she'd try again later.

The machine beeped again. Amber again. She was back at home now and repeated her earlier assertion that she'd try again. I hoped she wouldn't while at the same time wishing she would.

I sighed and went back in the living room to let Jenna tend to my hand.

"Ted forgives you?" she asked, bandaging my palm and nodding at the machine by the phone.

"Yeah, and now Amber's been calling."

"I know. I just talked to her."

"You did?"

"She called my place."

"Oh." I admired Jenna's bandage and the phone beside me rang. Once, twice.

"Aren't you going to answer it?" Jenna asked. I shook my head and let the machine take the call. Amber's voice filled the room.

"*I know you're home now, Meagan. Pick it up. Please, it's important that I talk to you.*" There was a slow pause. Breathing on the line. "*I'm-- I'm not with Ming if that's what you're thinking. That woman. She's not --*"

I couldn't control the impulse and I snatched up the receiver. "Didn't I tell you I don't care?" I demanded. I cared desperately. Seeing Amber kiss that woman had really been the thing to push me over the edge. "Why are you calling me? We haven't talked in weeks."

"Just listen to me," she pleaded. "I was mad at you and I did something."

"I know what you did. The whole bar knows what you did."

She sighed. "That's not what I'm talking about. It's something worse. Meagan, I--"

"I don't want to hear it," I interrupted. Her voice was like torture. "I don't give a shit what you've done. If it has anything to do with us, let me be the first to remind you-- I don't love you!"

It was a stupid, childish thing to say and Jenna kicked me.

"Yeah, I've heard that story," Amber said. "And you never did right?"

"That's right." It was easier to lie on the phone, the ache of deception less severe. "You never meant a thing."

"You're such a fucking bitch!" Amber yelled. Jenna

flinched in the chair across from me. Even she could hear Amber's scream from five feet away. "I can't believe I almost felt bad. Well, I won't now. In fact, I can't wait. It's gonna hit you like a ton of bricks and I can't fucking wait!"

"What is?" Fear terrorized my heart. "What the hell have you done?"

"No, you don't want to hear it. I was calling to warn you but fuck you!"

Now I was becoming petrified and I dealt with fear about as well as I dealt with heartbreak. "What the hell did you do to me you dyke bitch?"

"Real mature, Meagan," she scoffed. "Dyke? That's the best you can come up with?"

"Amber, if you've done something to embarrass me I swear to God you'll be sorry."

"No," she barked. "You're the one who's gonna be sorry. You never lose, right Meagan? Well, you've never come up against *me* before."

"I'll sue you."

She laughed. "For what? You don't even know what I've done. But you will --soon enough." The phone slammed in my ear.

"She's bluffing," I said. But a terrible feeling told me she wasn't. Amber had done something that was going to make the world come crashing down around me. My heart knew it even as my lips expressed their hopeful doubt.

The rest of the night drifted by slowly. Jenna left because I needed some time alone, and I took up my usual fetal position on the couch. The bedroom was off limits. It was where I went to change clothes and nothing more. It was filled with Amber's energy and haunted by her ghost. In the beginning I had tried sleeping in there, but then the walls would close in around me, and the bed would grow uncomfortably large and bare, and I would float through the night sleepless and teary.

I pulled the blanket to my neck. The ceiling was high and paneled with oak beams that met at a point in the middle like the ceiling of an attic. Amber's face had passed through waves of emotion tonight. It registered the shock of first seeing me, the evil of wanting to hurt me by kissing Ming, the horror of Danny's words, the anger of Jinx's arrival, the worry over my cut hand.

Meagan. She had cried out my name with the love of one

who would never abandon me fully and she raced to my side like one who would always belong there. She tried to take care of me and her care had been a torture I could not endure. It brought out my cruelty. Her compassion tore through my guilt and my heart hurt more than my hand.

When she said she was coming home with me I wanted her to, and the want turned me into a monster. I could not afford to have Amber around me. If I found myself alone with her the walls would crack and I would beg her forgiveness. Then we'd be back to square one. I'd hurt her again. I'd flinch, or I'd fight her over my sexuality, or I'd refuse to come out of a closet I didn't believe I was in. There would be no peace for either of us until I learned how to be what she needed. And I thought I might never truly learn how to be *that.*

My mind drifted to a thousand different things then coiled itself around one disturbing thought--what had she done to me? There was no sleep. Perhaps there wasn't even hope of ever sleeping again.

At 11:45a.m., the buzzer by the door sounded and I rose from the couch like one who had been there mere minutes instead of hours. My finger stabbed the button for the intercom.

"Yes?"

"Open up," came the firm male voice. "I'm here in my capacity as a friend."

"Basil?" I rubbed my eyes. "Do we have such a capacity between us?"

"Yes-- now open up. I don't need the whole world seeing this."

"Seeing what?" I didn't unlock the lobby doors.

"What I have for you. Just unlock the freaking door."

Curiosity got the better of me and I pressed the button marked *door.*

There was a short buzz and the click-click of the lobby doors swinging open and closed. I opened the apartment door and went back to the couch. Waited.

"You're a real pain in the ass," Basil said, strolling into the living room. He was carrying a picnic basket and a plaid blanket, and his long black hair waved in the air behind his head as he moved toward me. I burst out laughing.

"You brought me a picnic?"

"If you're gonna make fun of me I'm gonna get mad. Yes, I brought you a picnic." He whipped open the blanket and spread it across the floor. Then he reached for my hand and pulled me down to join him on the blanket.

"Why did you do this, Basil?" He'd never done a kind thing for me in his life.

Shrugging, he ignored my question and began pulling food out of the basket. "I've got sandwiches, fruit, beer, Twinkies-"

"Twinkies?"

Basil cocked his head at me and smiled. "Don't you remember? I was the first person who ever gave you a Twinkie."

"You're right." I chuckled. "And I don't think I've had one since." The food spread out before us kept me smiling. "Basil, this was really sweet."

"How's your hand?" God forbid anyone should think Basil sweet.

"Fine."

"And your job?"

"Still a corporate slave. Apparently my shackles don't remove so easily."

"You wouldn't want them to." He handed me a tuna sandwich and frowned when I placed it on the floor beside me. "Eat it."

"Can I have an apple instead right now?"

Nodding, he handed me an apple. "I want to apologize for last night."

"You didn't do anything."

"Fuck, Meagan." He whipped back his hair and tore into his sandwich. "I don't know how we all ended up where we did last night. I saw Amber when I went into BeBe's around nine so I just went up to her."

I bit into the apple. "To hit on her, right?"

Basil laughed. "After three years together I guess you know me pretty good, huh? But it didn't happen like that. Next thing I know we're talking about you, and we're both getting a little pissed off, so we sat together -- a sort of 'been dumped by Meagan and we hate her' club."

"That thrills me."

"You can't hate what you haven't first loved."

"You grow wise," I teased.

Basil shrugged. "It's common knowledge. Hate isn't the opposite of love, indifference is."

"Have you become a sage? Maybe you should change the name of your band to Dimestore Philosopher."

"Keep forcing me to think and I might. Anyway, we're sitting there talking about you, when all of a sudden this chink shows up."

Basil, the ambassador of political correctness. I frowned at his choice of description but said nothing.

"And Amber says she knows her from the dyke bars, you know, that she once fucked her a few years ago."

A stab of jealousy twisted in my gut and the apple turned to sulfuric acid in my stomach. I got up to throw it away and Basil's voice followed me into the kitchen, seemingly unaware of what his words were doing.

"So they're talking about muff-diving, right? And I've got the biggest hard-on of my life when who should I spot out of the corner of my eye walking in but your sister, followed by Jenna, then you. I nudged Amber in the ribs, and when she spotted you, she quickly asks Ming-- the chink -- to go get her a drink. That's when you saw us. No, let me correct that. That's when you saw her, you barely noticed me at all."

I laughed. "That's not true." Basil cracked open a beer and took a long haul.

"But you know," he said, wiping his mouth with the back of his hand, "I felt bad for her when she saw you. She looked like she was gonna cry. Then Ming shows up with her drink and I watch Amber's face distort into something evil."

"Yeah," I said. "I know that look."

"Yeah." He took another sip of beer. "And when she kissed Ming my hard-on deflated to nothing because, up close, you could see how cold and calculated the action was. She wasn't into it. She was doing it to *hurt you*, and I know I've done some shitty things to you in the past but what she did really bothered me."

"You laughed," I pointed out coldly.

Basil rested his beer on his knee. "A nervous reaction. I didn't know what to do. All I knew was you were hurting and don't even try denying it because I've hurt you enough to know what it looks like. But the thing is, this time it seemed more real. You never looked at me the way I saw you look at her. And when your sister came over to the table I tried playing it cool but felt like shitting my pants. She yelled at us, especially Amber. Telling us to grow the fuck up and that we didn't know shit about what you were going through."

"I wish she hadn't done that."

"I know-- you lost it. But we'll get to that later."

"Why did Amber shove Ming?" I was more interested than I should have been.

"She said something about you."

"What?"

"I don't know but it pissed Amber off good. Then she sort of got her shit together and just asked Ming to go get her another drink. What the fuck were you on last night, anyway?"

"Nothing." What a stupid question.

"I couldn't believe it. I thought, *Christ, she's on coke or something*-- look how skinny she is-- but I knew you didn't do drugs so it really threw me."

"Did I look that bad?"

"That's the scary part-- you looked great. You had that model-on-heroin look going."

"Model on heroin!" I laughed.

"Your eyes were all smoky and seductive, sort of half-closed. Danielle was still yelling at us when Jenna came over, and then you started to come over and Amber muttered something to herself. Something like, 'and of course she has to look so fucking hot too'."

"She did not." I smiled.

Basil shrugged. "Don't believe me, then. But you were a lot skinnier up close and the surprise was definitely on her face. And then that Jinx woman, fuck, I thought Amber was gonna snap. But she didn't, you were the one who snapped. I'm sorry, Meagan, but I had to walk away. You scared the freaking shit out of me when you smashed up that phone. I've never seen you lose your cool like that in my life. I went back to the table when you guys took off for the bathroom, and then when *you* left, Amber came back to grab her cigarettes."

"Wait. She's smoking again?"

"Did she quit?"

"We both did."

"Well, then I guess she's smoking again. I think she only

had one, though. Does it really matter?"

I thought of her health. "Yes."

"*I* smoke," Basil pointed out, after a little concern of his own.

"You should quit too," I said, giving him the response he wanted. "Does your story end here?"

"No." He shook his head. "I told her to sit with me because she looked kind of freaked, and she did, but she wasn't really there. She just said, 'Shit. I really have to get a hold of her.' I asked her why and she tells me she's done something so vengeful she wished she hadn't. 'Did you see her tonight?' She says, 'Oh fuck, I've made a horrible mistake.' And she was about to tell me what but then that chink comes back to the table and she starts thrusting her big tits in Amber's face. She's coming on to her, big time, but Amber just gives her the brush-off. So Ming gets all pissed and she's squinting her eyes and I start laughing my ass off because a chink squinting may as well be asleep on her feet if you know what I mean. How can you squint when your eyes are naturally half-shut anyway?"

"Basil!"

"Oh, don't go all Mother Theresa on me, like you don't get off on me calling her a chink. You'd just never say it yourself but you're thinking it inside and you know it. Maybe not about all of them, you'd call them Asians, or some political shit. But in your heart, Meagan, I know you believe this one is just some rice-munching, karate-chopping dyke who wants to fuck your old lady."

I laughed in spite of myself.

"A-ha," Basil cried, triumphantly.

"A-ha, nothing. Racial slurs are not what comes to mind when I think of Ming --the word 'slutty' does-- and Amber is not my *lady*, old or otherwise."

"Semantics."

I threw up my arms. "I need to get a dictionary. Why does everyone keep saying that word to me?"

"Don't know." Basil twisted the top off another beer and handed it to me. He grabbed one for himself. "Anyway, as I was saying, Ming starts throwing a fit and Amber's just sitting there looking at her nails, like she's bored with the whole thing. Finally Ming says, 'What the fuck? You only used me to get back at that anorexic girl?'"

"What anorexic girl?" I asked. Sometimes I just didn't get it.

Basil looked at me like I was insane. "You really don't look in the mirror anymore, do you?"

"Me?" I was incredulous.

"Duh."

My eyes narrowed. "So you're the one who taught me that ridiculous expression."

He laughed. "You say it?"

"I've said it at work."

"Why do you think I brought all this food over? And look, all you've eaten is an apple."

"I'm okay, Baz," I said, smiling. "But thanks for the effort."

Basil stayed the afternoon and we spent the day on my living room floor. We played cards, watched TV together, and marveled at what better friends we made than lovers.

Later, as he was leaving he kissed my cheek and said, "I'm curious, Meagan. Why would you dump her if you still love her?"

Why indeed? There was no ready answer and I shrugged. "Thanks for a nice day, Baz. I'm glad you stopped by."

We were at the door and he grinned. "How glad?"

"What?"

"Glad enough to have sex with me one last time?"

I groaned. "I was waiting for it."

"Just checking," he said, chuckling. "So, we're friends now. Okay. I can deal with that. Just know my services are always available."

"They're always available to everyone, Basil," I said, chuckling back.

He kissed my cheek again. "That's true. You know where I am if you need me."

"I'll keep that in mind."

He turned to leave and I watched him walk toward the elevator and smiled. The man knew how to wear a pair of jeans.

"Hey, Baz?"

He was getting in the elevator. "Yeah?"

I shook my head admiringly. "You always did have a

great ass."

And I heard him chuckle again as the elevator doors glided closed.

Chapter 15

The wedding date was set. Josh and Jenna decided on a spring ceremony and booked the back garden of a lovely church in the suburbs. It was to be an earthy affair, for Jenna, but presided over by a Catholic priest, for Josh; Jenna began the three week crash course in her conversion to Catholicism.

"Why are you doing this?" I asked when she first sprang the news on me as we stood in a small seamstress's shop getting fitted for our dresses.

Jenna's dress was silvery-white and very flowy and when she tried it on I was reminded of a moon goddess. On the big day she would wear a wreath of fresh flowers on her pretty blond head and I couldn't help thinking how lovely she would look.

The dress she'd chosen for me was light brown and made of a satiny material. It was a sleeveless design with a bit of a plunging neckline that dipped down between my breasts but was modest enough not to reveal anything. It was earthy but sexy somehow, precisely what Jenna wanted.

"Why am I doing what?" She studied her dress in the mirror and turned to the seamstress. "Iris, can this be cut in at the waist a bit more? I'd like it to sort of flow from there."

Iris pinched the material around Jenna's small waist and pulled two pins from between her teeth. "Yeah, we can do that." She pinned the dress in the appropriate places.

"You're changing your religion," I said, tugging at my own dress and frowning a little at the fit. "This is too big. You'll have to take it in."

Iris moved over to me. "Gain some weight, Meagan. It would be nice if we could use at least some material."

"I'm not that thin," I barked. "Besides," my tone softened, "I'm taking kickboxing now and my appetite is improving." I'd started the course as a release for my nervous energy.

"Then we won't take it in just yet. Let's wait and see what happens with your weight first."

"Okay." I took off the dress, pulled a shirt over my head, and turned to Jenna. "Why do you want to be Catholic?"

Jenna shrugged. "It's just a label, Meagan. If anyone knows about *that* it's you, and I'm doing it for Josh. Your brother wants to be married in a Catholic ceremony. After that I can practice whatever religion I want. Why is it so important to you anyway? You're Catholic."

"By birth-- not choice."

"So?"

"So, I just worry you'll change who you are. You're *Jenna*."

"What does that mean?" She frowned at her reflection in the mirror and I pulled on my skirt.

"Jenna equals aromatherapy, yoga, and Reiki. Jenna equals crystals and tarot cards, meditation, spirituality and Goddess love. You're special, okay? You've always been unique and I hate to see you abandon your individuality. It's too high a price."

She smiled sweetly. "I won't abandon myself, Meagan. I appreciate your concern but you have to remember, your brother is sacrificing something for me too. My sacrifice only has to last a few weeks but your brother will always be married to a woman who isn't really Catholic."

"He doesn't care about that, Jenna. It's not like he goes to church or even prays. It's my mother's influence. She wants the Catholic wedding and Josh is still too much of a chickenshit to disagree, even if he wanted to."

"So I'm doing it for your mother too. What have *you* done for love, Meagan? Why do you stand before me now, a woman struggling to get her life back on track? Because you made your own sacrifice and these are the results."

"Okay." I raised my palms in the air. "I get it. Are we almost done here? I'm on another flight in about an hour and a half."

Jenna groaned. "You're going back to London?"

"Montreal. Tye's bitching about something new. He's a great guy on a personal level, but professionally, he's a nightmare."

"How long are you gonna be gone?"

"I'll be back tonight."

Jenna eyeballed me curiously. "You're flying there and back all in one day?"

"I hate Montreal."

"Do not."

"Okay, I hate the *memories* of Montreal."

"That tastes true. What time will you be home?"

My mind calculated the flight schedule, the time of the meeting, the hours in between. "Probably around midnight."

Jenna nodded. "I'll be home tonight if you find yourself too wound up to sleep."

"What am I going to do without you?" I said, hugging her. "Once you guys are married the building is gonna be so empty."

"I know." Jenna's eyes misted. "It's gonna be strange."

"Did you find a house yet?"

"No, we're still considering that Victorian. It's so pretty and we absolutely love it but Josh is concerned about the roof. It's pretty bad and it will be expensive to put a new one on. I'd like to take the money from my parents but I just can't bring myself to do it."

"Jenna, your parents have more money than God."

She groaned. "And it's always been a problem."

I saw only one solution. Grabbing my jacket and my purse, I turned to her and said, "Buy the house."

"What?"

"Buy the house and I'll pay for the new roof. Consider it part of your wedding gift."

"No, Meagan, it's too expensive."

"Will you let me be a friend for once? You want that house. Josh wants the house, and I can *afford* to do this, all right?"

"But --"

"No buts, I've already decided. Tell Josh to go down and make his offer today. The change of ownership takes thirty days, right? So in exactly thirty-one days a new roof is going on that house no matter who owns it. Make sure it's you."

Iris pulled the pins from her mouth and chuckled. "This woman doesn't screw around."

Jenna burst into tears and yanked me into her arms. "I love you so much but I can't let you--"

"Stop right there, Jenna, because in my head it's already

done. I'm telling you the place is getting a new roof in thirty-one days and I mean it. The house can be yours or someone else's but the roof is going up regardless."

There was nothing she could do but agree. We both knew once I set my mind to something nothing would get me to change it.

"I wish you could move in there with us," she whined.

"A threesome with my brother and my best friend?" I joked. "We'd end up on Jerry Springer for sure."

She giggled. "Your sister is nuts about that show, but you know what I mean. We've been bursting through each other's doors for almost seven years. How are we gonna manage without that?"

Instinctively, my mind drifted to thoughts of London. Was there really anything holding me back anymore?

"We'll manage," I said, quickly. "Everything changes."

"Yes," she agreed. "And often too quickly."

So the wedding plans were underway. Amber's revenge still hadn't presented itself and I drifted through my days focusing on work and setting my mind to other things. The kickboxing course I signed up for at Preston College seemed rudimentary and I switched to a gym a few blocks from my building. Found I really enjoyed working out and began doing it four times a week. It was a good release, better than therapy with Helen, who I continued to see on a weekly basis.

Slowly, I was coming out of my depression. The Purple Cauldron beckoned from across the street but I ignored its call. I hadn't been in there since the night Amber slapped me and I had no plans of ever going back again. I didn't think she would be there but my heart couldn't handle the memories the place invoked.

Kickboxing was a good escape. The activity brought back my appetite and the work-out strengthened my tired body. It was also good for my inner turmoil. When the pain got to be too much I'd head for the gym and beat the hell out of a punching bag.

It was the sparing that presented a problem for me. I couldn't bring myself to hit my opponent with anything harder than a tap and often ended up sprawled out on the mat because of it. There was just something about striking another person that wasn't in me and my instructor often berated me for my passivity.

"Fight back," he'd say. "You're making it harder on the other students. They don't want to hit someone they know won't hit back."

In time I learned how to strike out without bringing up the rage I was so afraid of and my sparing abilities improved. Eventually, I even won a match.

The gym was broken into three smaller gyms-- one for women, one for men, and one co-ed. I stuck to the women's gym and after weeks of losing, I took down my opponent with a single kick and happily bounced around the room to the praise of my fellow classmates. Our workout came to an end and I helped my blond opponent to her feet, feeling somewhat guilty.

"I'm sorry, Amber," I said absentmindedly, lifting her to her feet.

She just looked at me. "It's no problem, but my name is Tina."

Of course her name was Tina. "What did I call you?"

"Amber."

"Oh." The name struck me with a jolt. Was that why I refused to hit my opponent? Did my subconscious believe I was hitting Amber? "I'm sorry, Tina. I know your name. I must have been thinking of something else."

Tina giggled. "Well, considering you finally won one, I'd say the person you were thinking of is the person you were hitting."

"No." I shook my head. "I'm not mad at her."

Tina did a little plunge and stretched her legs. "Then I'd hate to see if you were. Whatever gets you by, though. If I were you, I'd use it."

"What do you mean?"

"I have a sister," Tina said. "She pisses me off and when I want to win a match I think of her. I wanted to win today but apparently your Amber is stronger than my Susan." She shrugged. "You got me down."

I didn't like the conversation's direction. "Next Wednesday then?" I asked, sipping a bottle of Evian.

Tina reached for her gym bag. "Sure, if you leave Amber at home."

"I said I was sorry."

"You're not supposed to be, Meagan. It's what we're here for, remember? If it bothers you to hit maybe you should switch over to the yoga class. Actually, there's a good one down at that healing center on Riverview."

I smiled. "My soon-to-be sister-in-law is the instructor. I can't even tell you how often she tries getting me to *breathe* with her, or stretch into some strange pose."

Tina nodded. "So if we get paired up again next week it's gonna be your turn to hit the mat." She was grinning and I laughed.

"If you're making that a challenge you should know I don't plan on losing."

"Good." She turned to the door. "Now we're getting somewhere."

Tina left and I finished my water and headed for the locker room. The gym had a short hallway that all the smaller gyms flowed into and I rounded the corner with expert speed. I had signed up for the morning class because I liked to exercise before work, and I was running late. Not by Ted's clock but mine. I didn't have to be at work by eight-thirty but I liked to be. An hour less of my day was an hour less and I tried to fill every minute I could possibly fill. Calling Tina by Amber's name had thrown me and I was in a rush to leave the gym.

The locker room door was ajar, but in the process of making its slow, whispery close and I wondered if I could reach it before the handle met the frame. It was one of many silly games I played with myself now, a way to occupy my mind. If I could round the corner and jam my foot in its way I'd win.

My body darted into action and I sprinted for the corner at the exact second someone else was rounding it from the other side. My shoulder crashed into a thick, fleshy wall and my feet swept out from under me.

"I'm so sorry," a kind, male voice said as hands reached to help me to my feet.

"It was my fault." I looked up at the handsome face and a small gasp escaped me. *"It's you."* The man from the retro party months ago. The one with the soft brown eyes and the floppy sand-colored hair.

He smiled. "Meagan Summers, right? I'm Ken Faigan."

I shook his extended hand and thought of what a disaster I must look in my white sweatpants with the drawstrings hanging down in the front, and my cotton t-shirt, and my hair tied into two small braids that dangled from behind my ears.

"I never got the chance to thank you for the new statue. I

love it."

"It was the least I could have done," he said, shyly. "Considering I broke the one from Ireland."

"Ireland." I laughed. "I can't believe you remember that."

"Remember it? It haunts me. Would you like to get a cup of coffee, Meagan?"

I looked at my clothes. "Can I get cleaned up a little first?"

"Why? You look great."

I laughed. "Five minutes okay? Just let me run to the locker room and get dressed."

"Are you gonna stand me up again?"

"Stand you up?"

"You never showed up for our date by the fountain, remember? But I'll forgive you if you have coffee with me now."

"Five minutes," I pleaded.

"Okay, five minutes." He looked at his watch. "But if you're not back here by exactly 7:06, *I'm* standing *you* up and then you'll never know what a great guy I am." He gave another grin and I laughed.

When I returned from the locker room at 7:15 to find him waiting in the front lobby I folded my hands across my chest and smirked at him.

"I knew you'd wait."

He shrugged. "I was just curious to know what you'd change into. Ready to go? There's a coffeehouse up the street, right across from your building."

"The Purple Cauldron," I said.

"I've heard it's a nice place."

"It is, but I don't want to go there. Could we go somewhere else?"

He shrugged. Didn't press the issue. "Sure. I'm on call today so I should have some time."

"On call?"

"At the hospital. I'm a pediatrician, but I pull duty there too."

"Oh." I thought that was sweet. He spent his life caring for children.

We decided on a little cafe uptown, three blocks from the *Natural Beauty* offices and three blocks from the hospital where he was on call.

"Do you mind if I ask you something, Meagan?" he said, staring down into the coffee he'd ordered with two creams and two sugars. Mine was black, one sugar. I took a sip and nodded.

"I've seen you here and there," he continued, "and I always wanted to approach you but usually you were with someone."

"A blond woman?"

He chuckled shyly. "That's where I was going with this, yes. Is she your-- are you and she --?"

"Not anymore." The question was a hell I had no patience to wait for.

"But she was?"

"Yes. And as for your next question, the answer to that is yes, too."

He frowned. "Yes?"

"Yes, I do like men."

"Oh." Another shy chuckle. He was so cute. "Wanna take a crack at what my third question might be?"

"If it's gonna be what I think, then no."

"No you won't go out with me?"

"You had to ask, didn't you?"

"I'm an inquisitive guy."

I shook my head and thought of how adorable he and Danielle would look together. "I'm sorry, Ken. You seem really sweet and under other circumstances I would definitely go out with you, but I just got out of a relationship and I can't get involved in anything more than friendship right now."

He held his cup in both hands. Gave a sly grin. "But you'd have a weekly coffee date with a friend, right?"

I smiled back. "Yes."

"So, meet me here every Wednesday after your workout. It'll be fun."

The laughter bubbled out of me. "It'll be fun, huh?"

"I'm a fun guy, you'll see."

"You don't waste time, do you?" Hadn't I once said the same thing to Amber?

Ken shrugged. "Life is short and I'm almost thirty-two. I'm not saying that's old but I want to grasp every opportunity in life I can."

His attitude was refreshing and encouraging. "I'll tell you what-- why don't we start with next Wednesday and see how it goes from there?"

"Okay Meagan," he said with a disarming grin, "but I give you fair warning-- too much time in my presence and you'll want to marry me."

"What?" Again the laughter bubbled.

"I like your laugh."

"Forget my laugh. What makes you think I'd want to marry you?"

"I don't know. I think you'll like me."

"I already like you but I'm not picturing picket fences and children named Junior."

"Well, that's good," he said, smirking, "because I don't want to marry you either."

"You're strange."

"But cute, right?"

"Ego-maniacal is what comes to mind."

"But am I cute?" The grin never left his face.

"Yes." I smirked back. "You're very cute."

"You could fall for me."

I liked his game. "Could not."

"Oh, but you could. You just finished saying I'm cute, you agreed to be my friend, and you like that I'm a pediatrician."

"What makes you say that? I'm not the sort of woman who gets all weak in the knees just because a man happens to be a doctor."

"No." He signaled the waitress for a refill. "It's not the doctor part-- it's what *kind* of doctor. You wouldn't be impressed if I was a brain surgeon but it's the kids part that gets you. Admit it."

The waitress refilled our cups and I smiled. "Yes, it's the kids part. I haven't known many sensitive men."

"Have you known many men?"

"That's a loaded question if I ever heard one. Have you known many women?"

"Have *you?*" he countered, smirking.

"You have a challenging personality."

"Why do I get the feeling that impresses you?"

"Because it does."

"See, you're falling for me already. With every minute

that passes you become more infatuated. And you're wondering if I'm good in bed."

Who was this man?

"Don't get too flattered," I said, easily. "I wonder that about everyone."

"You do?"

"Don't you? You're wondering it right now. You only say I am because you're the one who's really thinking it. You're picturing me naked and you're wondering what it would be like if we got together."

"You said you'd only be my friend," he pointed out.

The waitress passed again. She was a heavy set girl and she was eyeballing Ken, waiting for him to request something else.

"I will only be your friend," I said, "but that won't stop you from picturing me in bed."

"Now who's got the ego?" he joked.

"I have a very healthy one, in fact. And as for marriage, well, you'd propose right now if you thought I'd accept."

"I've known you thirty minutes."

"But you don't waste time, remember? You think I'm attractive, you like my personality, my laugh, and you're a romantic."

"I am?"

I nodded. "You believe in love at first sight, don't you?"

"A doctor shouldn't say this, but yes. Do you?"

Briefly, I thought of Amber. "Yes."

"But you don't think that's us."

"Neither do you. What I do sense is the chemistry for what could be a very easy and comfortable friendship."

He smiled around his cup. "I can see that. We seem to be on the same wave length."

"Right, but there isn't a sexual charge."

"Oh, there is. You're just in no place to allow it."

"Possibly."

He shrugged. "So, we'll be friends."

"We'll be friends."

"And we'll meet for coffee."

"Yes."

The grin again. "And later, a few months from now, we'll get married."

"Okay," I laughed. "We'll get married. You can buy me a house in the suburbs and I'll quit my job and stay at home tending to the house and the cooking and the sixteen children in the yard."

He shook his head. "Three children and I wouldn't expect you to quit your job. I think you're probably too good at it."

"I am. But there's something else."

"What?"

"I don't cook."

"I do."

"Really?"

"Mm-hmm. I'm very good at it too. Would you like to come over for dinner sometime?"

"I thought we were starting with coffee?"

"I see, you'll marry me and raise my children but dinner is out."

"What can I say? Genetically, you look pretty good."

Ken burst out laughing. "Are you neurotic, Meagan?"

"Yes."

"You don't care to lie to me?"

"Why should I? If you're going to be my friend the truth is nothing to fear."

"So, what's your truth?"

"You want a summation?"

"Sure."

"Will I get yours then?"

He stirred another teaspoon of sugar into his coffee. "If you want it."

"My truth." I thought for a moment. "I'm a twenty-seven year old world-traveled neat freak with tons of ambition and the love of a good dare. I don't back down from a challenge easily, except in one case that proved beyond my capabilities. I don't like being the center of attention, I do appreciate privacy, and my sister Danielle calls me a loner but I spend my life looking out for her. My best friend and soon to be sister-in-law is a woman named Jenna who is the personification of the New Age movement. She's also a little bit psychic. I have been with one woman and she was the challenge I lost. I hurt her in the worst way I possibly could but I still love her and that's why I can only be your friend. Is that a fair enough summation?"

"More than adequate," he said, nodding. "Will you go

back to this woman?"

"No." A small pain stabbed my heart. "She hates me now and for the past few weeks I've been waiting for her revenge."

"What do you mean?"

I sighed. "She threatened that she'd done something to me. I don't know what but I sort of walk around waiting for it to happen."

"You're living in fear?" Ken was concerned. "Is she dangerous?"

"No," I chuckled. "Nothing like that. I think maybe she made it up just to scare me but the problem with that theory is that Amber doesn't lie. Anyway, now you."

"You want my summation?"

"Yes."

Ken took a sip of coffee. "Thirty-one year old pediatrician who comes from old money. Twin brother who died at birth. Engaged once in med-school but it didn't work out. I coach a softball team for disabled kids. I live uptown and have never been with a man." He grinned. "I came to your party with Jeff Henderson and wasn't dressed in retro clothes because he didn't tell me it was a theme party. You weren't retro either. When I accidentally broke your fairy statue I was secretly glad for the excuse to talk to you. I was hurt when you stood me up for who I now realize was Amber, but I knew you didn't do it on purpose so I forgave you. I saw you in BeBe's one night a few months later but you were with her and another woman-- Jenna, I presume, because she was very earthy-looking. I was too shy to approach you. Today, when you bumped into me I knew I was going to ask you out for coffee whether you were seeing that woman or not. Now we're in the cafe and that pretty much brings us up to date."

"Good summation." I looked at my watch. "Unfortunately, I'm late for work."

Ken rose to walk me out. "Next Wednesday then?"

"Next Wednesday."

Next Wednesday turned into the next which drifted into Thursday and Friday and Ken got me to agree to dinner at Jade Gardens, a Chinese restaurant three doors down from my building. His charm was an accessible kind and I found I was not as impervious to his smile as I'd previously thought. Still, I insisted it was not a date.

"Right," Ken said, agreeably. "Just a couple of friends getting together for dinner."

Dinner consisted of almost everything on the menu. It was the combo platter and Ken wanted to try it all. His zest made me smile.

"So, the other shoe hasn't dropped yet?" he asked, around a mouthful of chow mien.

I plucked a sweet and sour chicken ball with my chopsticks. "What do you mean?"

"The woman scorned."

"Oh." I shook my head. "Not yet."

"Maybe she did make it up," he said, shrugging. "Did you know you can see the Bank Street Bridge from your living room window?"

"No, you can't."

"Mm-hmm. I admired it that night."

"You're wrong." I reached for my water and had the feeling I was being set up. Oddly, I didn't mind. I enjoyed Ken's company.

"Ten bucks," he challenged, his eyes dancing with the dare.

"You're on."

We finished dinner, Ken paid the bill, and we walked the short distance to my building. Ken grinned all the way like he had won some small victory and we rode the elevator to the tenth floor.

"You don't believe me, do you?" he asked, as the elevator door glided open and we stepped into the hall.

I jangled around in my purse for the keys. Jenna's door opened a few feet away and light streamed into the hall. No one came out and I thought she must be readying Bacon for his evening walk.

"I think this is a really cheap ploy to get in my apartment," I said.

"Nope, you can see it. But assuming it is a ploy, you'd let me into your apartment just to win ten bucks?"

We neared the door. "Well, it's not like you're going to rape me."

"How do you know?"

"Are you going to rape me?"

"No."

"So, there you go." I glanced at Jenna's open door. "What is she doing?"

"Who?"

"Jenna. She's got her door open but she's not coming out." Turning the key in my door, I called out over my shoulder, "Hey, Jenna?"

"Maybe she heard us and wants to keep her door open in case I attack you," Ken joked.

"Maybe, but you gotta give me my ten bucks first." The apartment door swung open.

"Oh my God!" Ken suddenly shrieked. "Meagan, don't move!"

"Why?" Fear crept into my heart and I stood like a block of stone, facing my living room.

"There's-- I don't believe this but there's a giant pig behind you and he's wearing what appears to be a hemp parka."

"A pig?" I burst out laughing and turned to pat Bacon's head.

"Don't touch it!" Ken yelled. "It could bite you."

"He won't bite me." I crouched down and stroked Bacon's head and he gave a happy grunt. "This is Bacon," I said, letting the animal nuzzle my hair. "Aren't you, baby? You're just a big fat pig, huh?"

Ken stared in horror. "Meagan, that's disgusting."

"What?"

"You're cuddling on the floor with a *pig*."

"His name is Bacon," I said, "and he's probably cleaner than you are. Pat his head."

"No way."

"Then you can't come in my apartment."

"You're serious?"

"I'm serious."

"You're honestly saying I have to touch this pig in order to have sex with you."

"Sex with me?" Again I burst out laughing. "Where on earth did you get that idea? I'm not having sex with you."

"Why not? How else are you going to raise my children?" He was grinning again.

"Are you gonna be one of those friends who never stops trying?"

"Only until you give in. Then I'll be a better kind of friend."

"You're conceited. Touch the pig."

"No."

I shrugged. "Then go home."

"Why do I have to touch him?"

"Because I wanna see you do it."

"I'm sorry, Meagan, but I just can't."

"Okay." I patted Bacon's head again. "Jenna, come get your pig!"

"It lives across the hall?" Ken shrieked.

"Yes, *he* lives across the hall and you need to get over this because no one bad-mouths the pig."

Ken laughed. "You said you were neurotic, Meagan, you didn't say you were insane."

"What's insane about loving an animal? Why does a pet have to be a dog or a cat? It's different, yes, but it's not insane. What's insane is that you're so completely anal you can't bring yourself to touch a pig."

"Okay, I'll touch him."

"Not with that attitude, you won't."

Again Ken laughed. "What attitude? You're the one getting all uptight about a pig."

"I told you his name is Bacon."

"Is this how you really behave?"

"All the time." I smirked. "And you know you like it."

He smirked back. "I do."

"So, okay. *Jenna!*"

Ken stuck a finger in his ear and wiggled it. "You have a big mouth."

I sighed. "Hang on. I'm just gonna put him in there. I don't know where Jenna is."

Ken looked at the floor. "I do."

"Huh?"

He picked up a note that had been stuck in my door. "*Gone to Josh's*," he read. "*Bacon taken care of.*"

I glanced at Jenna's open door. "So, who's in there?"

"Maybe the pig opened the door," Ken teased.

"You're funny. Just go in my apartment. It's probably my sister Danielle thinking this is real cute."

"Okay."

Ken went inside and I walked Bacon into Jenna's living room. "Danny?" No response. "You left the freaking pig in the hall."

"Danielle's not here," a familiar voice growled from near the bedroom. My heart caught in my throat. Amber! "And you're just a ten-dollar whore, aren't you?"

Anger festered. Bacon's leash was on the floor like she'd suddenly dropped it there in an effort to get away and I picked it up and tossed it on the couch as she came toward me.

"If you're taking care of him," I barked, "then fucking take care of him. He doesn't belong in the hall by himself and his leash doesn't belong on the floor. When's Jenna due back?"

"In the morning." She threw herself on the couch. "I came to walk him and then I was leaving."

"No little Asian girlfriend tonight?" I sneered.

"Maybe later. Back to dick with a vengeance, huh?"

"Yeah, and it's waiting for me. Why don't you go have something pierced?" I turned toward the door, stomach churning with want and self-loathing.

"Soon enough, Meagan."

It was the threat again and I spun around to face her. "You keep saying that but I don't see anything happening."

An evil grin. "At this point you're one of the few people who doesn't know."

"Know what?"

"What's happened to you."

"You don't scare me, Amber."

"I think I do."

"Goodbye."

"That's the easiest word in the world for you, isn't it?"

"Well, you don't make it difficult. Now, if you'll excuse me, I have a guest."

"Did he pet the pig, Meagan? Did he do his sleep-with-you duty?"

"You're quite sick, Amber."

"*You're* telling someone they have to pet a pig and give you ten dollars for sex and *I'm* the one who's sick?"

"That's not what was said and you know it. But you're back to creating your own little fantasy scenario, aren't you? For the record, I don't have to explain my actions to you. Whether or not I decide to sleep with him is really none of your business."

Her eyes narrowed. "And whether or not I slept with Ming that night is none of yours."

"You're right--" I smirked. "But seeing as how I already know you didn't, it wasn't a very impressive try."

"Maybe I'll call her tonight."

The jealousy twisted in my gut. "Maybe you will; it's none of my concern. And for the last time, *goodbye.*"

I stalked out of the apartment with my heart in my mouth and slammed the door.

"I'm sorry, Ken," I said, once inside my apartment, the door closed behind me. "I didn't expect to be gone so long."

"Problem with your sister?" he asked, sympathetically.

"Not exactly. She wasn't the one in there."

"Jenna?"

"No."

His eyes posed a question. "But someone who upset you."

"Yes."

"Amber?"

I nodded. "I wish Jenna had put *that* in her note. She heard everything we said out there."

"I'm sorry."

"Don't be. You didn't do anything wrong and neither did I. Amber and I are through. I don't want to hurt her but I don't have to answer to her either." I managed a weak smile. "So, where's your Bank Street Bridge?"

He smiled back. "I owe you ten bucks."

"Yeah, that's what I figured."

Ken caught the drawn out sigh in my voice and fixed me with soft, understanding eyes. "You'd like to be alone now, wouldn't you?"

"Is that terribly rude?" I thought my voice sounded frail.

"No." He walked toward me. "It's not rude but I'll only leave if you promise you'll be okay?"

"I'll be okay."

"Can I call you tomorrow to make sure?"

Another weak smile. He was just so sweet. "Yes, you can call me tomorrow. Maybe we'll get together and do something."

"Okay." He reached for the door. "But it has to start with

coffee or we're breaking the deal. Goodnight, Meagan."

Nervously, my eyes scanned the hall for Amber. "Good night."

I thought Ken must have sensed my trepidation because instead of waiting for the elevator, he walked down the hall to the stairs at the end and disappeared with a little wave. Relieved, I went back inside to wallow in my hurt.

Amber came back from walking Bacon. I heard her footsteps in the hall and the tap-tapping of Bacon's hooves and went to my peephole to peer out. Amber unlocked Jenna's door, then glanced at mine as if sensing my presence. She tried to urge Bacon into the apartment but for some reason he refused to budge and Amber began looking distressed. Nervously, she glanced at my door again and began pushing on Bacon's backside.

"Go," she pleaded. "Please, just get in there."

Her eyes kept darting to my door like she was afraid Ken and I would hear her and soon she was tugging on Bacon's leash.

"Please Bacon," she begged. "Just get in the freaking apartment. Hurry."

Bacon cranked his head to the left and the leash pulled, yanking Amber forward. He gave an angry grunt and she looked like she would burst into tears. I couldn't bear to watch a second longer.

I swung open my door, stepped into the hall, and addressed the pig. "Go inside."

Bacon looked at me but didn't move and Amber nervously stared down at her boots. I took the leash from her hand and kneeled to meet Bacon's eyes. He always listened so his reaction tonight was a peculiar one.

"What did I say to you?" I asked. He looked away and I forced his eyes to meet mine again. Ken would really shit if he saw this, a magazine executive down on all fours trying to reason with a pig. My tone softened.

"It's okay, Bacon. Go inside and I'll check on you later." Still he didn't move and my tone hardened again. "You have three seconds. One, two--"

Bacon tore away from me and ran into the apartment. I stood up to face Amber. "Jenna has some cookies in her cupboard. She doesn't know but I give him one when he seems down, and I don't need your little 'Meagan's so fucking strange' look. Just go give him a cookie and he'll be fine."

"Okay," she said, meekly. "Thank you."

My heart gave a little thump of sadness at her quiet tone and quite suddenly I felt I deserved whatever revenge she had planned for me. The emerald eyes tore through me and the pain was as sharp as the day I first told her it was over.

"It's okay if you've hurt me, Amber," I found myself quietly saying. "Whatever you've done, it's just --it's okay."

I brushed passed her and went inside my apartment, leaving her shocked and pale. I feared what she had done, and perhaps the anger would come later, but for now I felt strangely deserving. Minutes later there was a short rap on my door and I opened it slowly.

"I can't take it back, Meagan," Amber said. Her eyes looked teary. "By tomorrow you'll know and by Monday everyone else will. It's already in motion."

"I thought everyone already does know," I said, snidely, feeling the coldness creep over me again. I couldn't handle the game much longer.

"People know," she nodded.

"Well, then I hope it was worth it."

I slammed the door in her face and watched her walk away through the peephole. I could have chased her down and demanded to know what she'd done. Certainly at this point she'd tell me because her guilt was a battle that kept erupting inside her but a part of me still didn't want to know.

Tomorrow, I thought glumly, heading for the bedroom. *Tomorrow her vengeance will be exacted.*

Chapter 16

It was a wonder I slept quite soundly that night. The bedroom was quiet and I was trying out sleeping in there again. The noise from the city below fell into an urban hush. After midnight the cars whispered past, muffled voices murmured in the wind, music pulsed from distant vehicles, and then quite suddenly, it all stopped. The city fell asleep and I wrapped myself in my blanketed cocoon and floated away into a dream about rings and promises and apologies till morning broke free and the newborn light cleansed me with its glow of fresh possibilities.

My eyes opened to D-day and I wasn't in such a bad mood. It was the morning of my doom and the world was eerily quiet.

Rising from the bed, I reached for the clock on the nightstand, groaned at how early it was, and went to take a shower. Then I waited. All day I waited for the world to tumble down around me but *still* nothing happened. Ken called and we agreed to get together for lunch on Sunday. Basil called and we agreed to drinks on Tuesday. He had good news, he said, and couldn't wait to tell me.

At three o'clock I decided to take advantage of a quiet Saturday and went down to the office to get some work down. Ted showed up and we went out for dinner together. He went back to the office afterward and I went home.

At nine-forty-seven the world came down with a crash.

"I have to show you something," Jenna said, coming through my door and brandishing a book with a giant silver butterfly on the blue cover.

For a second I burst with pride. "Is it Amber's new book? Let me see."

"You're not gonna like it, Meagan," she warned, handing

it over. "It was sitting on my kitchen table this morning and it took me all day to build up the nerve to give it to you. Meagan, it's bad."

The butterfly winked at me and a wave of nausea flitted through my stomach. Instantly, I knew. "*When Butterflies Wear their Armor*? Oh God. It's about me, isn't it? My tattoo-- and this book. *It's her revenge!*"

Jenna eased herself beside me on the couch. "She doesn't use your name but anyone who knows you is going to know it's about you."

Fearfully, I flipped through the pages and felt my horror and rage grow. Every damn poem was about *me*-- and the very worst of me! Amber had destroyed me in prose. She'd revealed me, insulted me, poured out her hate and called me names. The worst part was instinctively I knew the book was going to be a hit. It was so passionately hateful, so *passionate,* that anyone who read it would not be able to stop themselves from hating the antagonist she referred to with names like *butterfly* and *cunt*. She knew I couldn't stand attention and she knew I couldn't stand being disliked. The bitch couldn't have stuck it to me any better.

"It hits bookstores this week," Jenna said.

"That fast? How is that even possible? It should take months at least, not *weeks."* Cyrus Jr. must have been in one hell of a hurry.

Something in me broke. I felt it snap away like someone had reached into my chest and punched through the glass that was my heart. But there was no time for tears.

"Hand me my purse."

"Meagan, you're not going over-- "

"Hand me my purse!"

Jenna did as I commanded. "I'll go with you."

I dropped the book in my purse. "No, I can manage on my own."

"Meagan-- "

Jenna couldn't reach me and I was already out the door and heading for the stairs. Amber was going to have to deal with me face to face on this one.

My mind burned with pain and rage. How could she do this to me? It didn't matter that she hadn't used my name, Jenna was right, anyone who read the book would know it was about me. In one week's time the whole world was going to hate me. People who had never seen my face were going to read this book and loathe the person who had caused the poet so much pain. *I* loathed that person. But right now I also loathed the poet.

The car screeched to a halt in front of Amber's building and I darted up the stairs to the third level and banged on her door.

"Open it, you fucking bitch!"

No answer.

I banged louder, kicked her door, and yelled out curses until her neighbor's door swung open.

"What's going on out here?" the woman demanded.

"Where's your little bitch neighbor?"

"She left." The woman was not offended by my words. "Try her weirdo friend downstairs."

Zeppo, yes! "Thank you."

I stalked away and sprinted down the stairs until I reached the second level and Zeppo's door and began banging on that. Again no one answered.

"Fine!" I yelled. "But you can't hide forever, you sick, twisted bitch!"

I reached into my bag and yanked out my new cell phone. I dialed Jenna's number and paced in front of Zeppo's door while I waited for her to answer.

"Hello?"

"Where is she, Jenna?"

"I don't know, Meagan. Just come home."

"You called her and warned her, didn't you?"

"No, she hasn't been home all day. Meagan, please just come back here. You're not in a good place and you're going to do something stupid."

"I'm not coming back until I find and kill that little bitch!"

The phone flipped closed and I marched back to my car. Next I tried the Cauldron. Mitch said he hadn't seen Amber since the night of her last set and a few customers eyed me curiously.

"Is it the book?" he asked, sympathetically.

"You've read it?"

"Sure. I got a reviewer's copy. Critics all over town have it. You didn't know that?"

"No," I said tightly, and stormed out.

Amber wasn't at BeBe's either. There was only one place she could be hiding. The one place she thought I'd never venture into alone. She was wrong. Within minutes I was on the Upper West Side strolling through the doors of Vox, the dreaded gay bar, and the catcalls and pointing began almost instantly.

"Well looky who's here," Large Marge said with a sneer as I approached the bar. "Straight girl's back."

I crushed her with a look. "Fuck you."

"Oohh," she shook her hands in front of her like she was pretending to be afraid. "Feisty. Whadda ya think Trish?" she said, turning to the bartender who was pouring draft beer from the tap. "Is straight girl on the prowl tonight?"

"No." I ordered a Jack Daniel's on the rocks and downed it in one gulp. "Straight girl is looking for Amber. Not that it's any of your business."

"I remember you," Trish chimed in, wiping the bar with a checkered towel. "You're the one whose girlfriend walked out because you were talking to me."

"Amber," Marge corrected. She shook her head, tearing the label from her bottle of beer, and crumpled it in her fat hand. "Poor girl never did learn to stop trying to convert the semen slurpers." She chuckled at her own wit.

"Ease back, Marge," Trish said, filling my glass for the third time. I was getting buzzed very quickly.

Marge took a sip of beer and poked me in the ribs with a chubby finger. I flinched. "What's the matter?" she taunted, "Amber's strap-on not big enough for ya?"

"Why don't you shut the fuck up?" My words were a death sentence and the next thing I knew I was sprawled on the floor with Marge above me like an angry giant.

"That's for what you did to Amber," she snarled.

Trish jumped over the bar and began helping me up. "Jesus, Marge." Her arms hooked under mine and she lifted me to my feet.

Wham! The second shot came out of nowhere, just like the first, and I felt every knuckle of Marge's fat fist penetrate my eyeball. The punch sent me reeling backward into Trish, who yelled, "What the fuck was that for?"

Marge shrugged. "For calling me a fat pig."

"She never called you that!"

"Nah, but she was thinking it."

My temper got the better of me and I came up against the

beast, like a squirrel picking a fight with an elephant. "Fucking right I was, Shamu!"

"Oh no," said Trish.

"Shamu?"

My eye was already beginning to swell shut but through the other I managed to make out the image of Marge's fat meat hooks reaching out to wrap around my throat. Trish jumped between us, my uninvited but appreciated protector, and the scuffle began as Marge groped around her, trying to get at me. Bar stools toppled to the floor and three burly bouncers appeared and began pulling Marge toward the door.

"Let go of me," she screamed.

"Yeah," I yelled back, full of a fire I'd never known before, *"Free Willy!"*

Several people laughed and Marge struggled even harder against the men who held her. She almost got free and my heart pounded. The woman would pulverize me.

"You're fucking dead," she yelled, as the bouncers dragged her through the doors. "I'll be out here waiting for you."

I wiped the blood from my face with the back of my hand. "Are you sure you can live outside of water that long?" More laughter.

The bouncers dragged Marge outside and I turned in time to see Trish slap an ice pack on my swollen eye. "I wouldn't fuck with Marge like that," she said, oblivious to my wincing at the sudden burst of cold.

"Screw Marge, hermaphroditic whale that she is."

Trish laughed and placed another drink on the bar in front of me. "This one's on the house, seeing as how you took a few shots from Large Marge and managed to stay conscious long enough to mouth off some more. That's a real first around here."

"Yep, I'm a pioneer, alright," I said, reaching for Amber's book which had fallen out of my purse during the scuffle. I tossed it on the bar. "I've even been immortalized in print."

Trish scanned the pages of the book while I slammed back yet another JD on the rocks. *"You're* the punishing pussy?" she exclaimed.

My mouth dropped open. *"What?"*

"My friend is a book reviewer over at *Downtown People*. He got a copy of this a few days ago and swears it's going to be huge."

"Great."

"Amber Reed," Trish said, staring at the cover and putting the pieces together. "That's the blond. And you must be the elusive butterfly she writes about."

"That's me," I responded, lifting the back of my shirt to expose my tattoo as the evidence. "Bitch of the century." Suddenly the tattoo felt like a brand. That's what Amber had done: branded me. From now on I would carry on my body the result of what I'd done to her. A tattoo that had meant nothing the day before was now a painted on regret and I would never be clean again.

"No wonder you're so pissed," Trish said, grabbing the pack and throwing more ice in it. "She really gives it to you in that thing."

"You think?" I threw the book in my purse and a twenty on the bar. I hopped off the bar stool.

"Hey, wait a minute," Trish said as I turned to leave. "You can't go yet. Marge is probably still out there, you know. She can live on dry land longer than you'd think."

For the first time in eighteen hours I laughed.

"I get off in about five minutes," Trish continued.

Oh shit, was she coming on to me? My thoughts drifted to Amber and a nasty voice in my head said Trish would be the perfect way to get back at her. Amber was jealous of Trish and if I left with her, she would surely find out about it. If I *slept* with her, well that would take a hell of a lot more alcohol, but Amber would be eating crow for a long time to come.

I felt an evil sneer cross my face. More alcohol. Much, much more.

"Should I take that as a yes?" Trish asked eagerly.

I looked at the long brown hair, the womanly form, the patient smile, and found myself nodding my agreement.

"I'm right upstairs," she said, referring to her apartment. She hoisted herself up on the bar to climb over it.

"Wait." I yanked a fifty from my purse. "Grab that bottle of Jack Daniel's too."

"The *whole* bottle?"

"Why not? We'll party."

And I'd definitely need it to do what I already decided I was going to do. Trish grabbed the bottle off the shelf and I followed her out the back door and up a flight of stairs outside, eyes peeled for Large Marge as we went. She led me into a small apartment with dingy beige walls and I hoped all of Amber's friends had seen me leave with her. If they hadn't, there was no point in going any further. Trish went to change in the bedroom and I cracked open the new bottle of Jack Daniel's and took a greedy sip.

"Do you have any glasses?" I called. The place didn't look like it had a single fork.

"Above the sink," came the reply.

Trish returned from the bedroom wearing shorts and a t-shirt and laughed at my easy consumption of the tan liquid.

"Geez, for such a little person you can really put that stuff away."

Her words surprised me. "I'm five-seven. That's not little."

"I didn't mean your height." Her hand reached out to touch my eye and I flinched. "We should put some more ice on that or by morning it's gonna be completely swelled shut."

"I'm okay." The effects of the alcohol were kicking in and I couldn't help laughing at my situation.

"What's so funny?" Trish asked, smiling.

"I'm --" The laughter choked me. "I'm a kick boxer."

Trish looked at my eye and the blood on my shirt and broke into hearty chuckles. "But you're not very good at it, are you?"

"Guess not."

We howled with laughter and brought the Jack Daniel's into the living room where we went about consuming it like spring water. It didn't take long for Trish to make her move. Almost instantly her mouth was on mine and I swallowed back the revulsion that crept up in my throat. We didn't ask for last names. It was easier that way, and I followed her into the bedroom, drunk enough now to allow it all to happen.

In the morning, Trish slept soundly and I crept from the bed where she lay naked and satisfied. I stumbled into the bathroom to throw up. The vomit poured out of me and the rational voice in my head screamed, "What have you done?" And with every flash of flesh that danced behind my eyes I gagged out my misery and disgust. I had used Trish. I wasn't kidding myself into believing she hadn't used me right back, but it was a deed that brought up the self-loathing nonetheless. And the action-- the *sex*-- oh God, the memory made me puke even more.

Trish slept through the retching, through my departure, and when I returned home Jenna was waiting in my apartment, alternately wringing her hands, and eating a cream filled doughnut. She glanced up at me when the door swung open and gasped.

"Oh my Goddess!! What happened to you?"

My eye was swelled shut and there was blood crusted on the front of my shirt. "I got beat up by a three hundred pound butch."

"You what?"

Meekly, I explained the story and watched Jenna's expressions go from pity, to shock, to amusement, to sympathy.

"All this and you never found Amber?" Her tongue darted into the pastry, lapping up the cream, and a horrible image came to mind. Trish. Me.

The gag exploded in my throat and I darted for the bathroom to vomit again. The episode lasted twenty minutes and I returned to the living room to ask Jenna to please stop eating doughnuts.

"Your friend Ken called," she said.

"Oh, I was supposed to meet him for lunch."

"You're off the hook. One of his patients broke an arm and he can't make it. He said he'll call you this evening."

"Have you heard from Amber?"

"Not a peep. She must have gone underground the second she left that book on my table."

"Everyone's reading it, Jenna," I groaned. "Every critic in this city has a copy and I know of at least one already who's giving it a great review."

"So what are you going to do?"

"There's nothing I can do. She didn't use my name so I have no legal grounds for a lawsuit and I wouldn't do that anyway."

Jenna's face showed her surprise. "You're not gonna fight back?"

"No." Tears stung the backs of my eyes. "I love her."

"Last night you were hunting her down to kill her."

"That was anger. Today it's just pain. She really hates me, Jenna. And in about one week the whole world is going to hate me too. That's what hurts. I don't really care that she's written the book it's *what* she's written. She could have printed 'Meagan Summers is a big old dyke' on every billboard from here to China, but it wouldn't hurt half as much."

"I know," Jenna hushed. "I read it three times before I gave it to you. But Amber *does* love you. That's why she did this and also why she tried to warn you."

"She turned me into a joke. Look at me, for Christ's sake. I have to go to work tomorrow with a black eye. I have to face Ted and Elaine, and everyone else I come in contact with for the next week or two with a black eye and the knowledge that at any moment someone could whip out that book and shriek, 'You're the one!'. How the hell am I going to live with this? She humiliated me."

Jenna sat beside me and patted my hand. "Why don't you call her?"

"For what?"

"To tell her you still love her and you want her back."

"Are you insane? There's no going back from this. Even if I wanted to --which I don't-- Amber has made it quite clear she hates me. Jenna, she branded me!"

I burst into tears. "For the rest of my life I have to wear the result of hurting her."

"Meagan, if you mean your tattoo you can have it removed. Laser --"

"No." I shook my head and wiped my eyes. "It's my price and I'll pay it. I have so much to pay for. My gran's ring, breaking Amber' heart, breaking my own-- you're the one who's always going on about karma, Jenna. Imagine my debts. I don't think I'll ever stop paying."

"I think you're on the wrong track with that. What about the good you're done in your life? Do you think karma would overlook that? It's not about punishing you, Meagan; it's about teaching you."

"Oh, I'm learning. Believe me, I'm fucking learning."

"And Amber?"

"Her love is as destructive as mine, but worse, because hers turns to hate."

"She doesn't hate you."

"She hates me, Jenna." I tossed the book on the coffee

table. "She's made it quite clear with that."

And I wouldn't seek retaliation. There was simply no point in it. Instead I would do what I did best: let the pain eat me from the inside out and try to pick up the pieces of my shattered self-worth.

Amber had split me open with her words. She'd reached into the darkest part of my spirit and pulled out the ugliness for the whole world to gawk at. There would never be a path back to cleanliness after this. From now on I would be soiled with the filth of my lie and I thought I could smell it odoring the air around me already. I tried to wash it away. I showered, I cleaned the apartment from top to bottom, but the stench kept seeping in like gas and I knew I would smother in its toxicity.

Ken called later that evening and insisted on stopping by when he heard the frailty in my voice. I told him it wasn't necessary, but he refused to take *no* for an answer and arrived an hour later with pizza and a movie.

Make up did little to hide the bruising under my eye and Ken was shocked to see it.

"Who did this to you?" he demanded, protective as a boyfriend.

"Would you believe me if I told you I walked into a wall?"

"No."

Again I explained the story, only this time omitting the episode with Trish. I watched Ken's face move through the same expressions Jenna's had, hours earlier. I handed him the book and he scanned the pages in shocked silence.

"So, she got her revenge after all," he whispered.

"I'll bet you're sorry you wanted to be my friend now. Honestly Ken, this is not the sort of thing that usually happens to me. For twenty-seven years I've managed to live a quiet life, but these last few months, God, I don't know what's happened. I've never been in a fist fight in my life and now, at my age, I find myself sitting here with a black eye given to me by someone who herself, was at least thirty-five. It's insane. How can people behave this way?"

"I don't know."

"Oh, I wish you hadn't insisted on coming." The humiliation was intolerable. "I can only imagine how this must look to you."

Ken squeezed my hand. "It doesn't look any way. You didn't do these things, Meagan. All you did was end a relationship with someone you loved because you feared hurting her. The things that have happened in response to that are because of the immaturity of others. I would never look down on you because someone else can't control her fists."

He pulled me into his arms and I allowed it because it felt safe. I let him kiss me because it took away the brutality of my appearance.

It was a soft kiss, more friendly than passionate, and my lips were comforted by the tender sincerity of his.

"Ken?"

"Yes?" He brushed back my hair and stared into my eyes.

"I don't usually make out with my friends either."

"Well, you're just full of firsts this weekend, aren't you?" he asked, chuckling. "It's okay, Meagan. I won't kiss you again."

"Why did you?"

"Honestly?"

"Please."

"Your vulnerability touched me. You look so sad and so pretty and I guess I have a bit of a kiss-it-better mentality."

"Odd perspective for a doctor," I said smiling. "Is that how you cure your patients?"

"No, but there isn't an antibiotic or plaster cast in the world that's going to mend this one for you."

"It's not your duty to mend me."

"No, it's my desire."

"Why?"

The smile was as kind as the rest of the man. "Because I'm always there for my friends."

"We have something in common then."

He wrapped his arm around the back of the couch and urged me to lean into his chest. "And I'm sure we'll find much more."

"In common?"

"Mm-hmm. Do you want to watch the movie?"

I squinted at the box on the VCR. "What is it?"

"*Jerry McGuire*."

"That's gonna make me cry."

"Show me the money, makes you cry?"

"You complete me, makes me cry."

His chuckle was endearing. "Good thing I didn't rent *Ghost*."

My laugh matched his. "It's a very good thing. I'd need a bucket to catch the tears, but don't ever tell anyone that."

"Are you saying you'd cry in front of me but no one else?"

"I'm not sure. Maybe."

He grinned. "Call me a jerk but I really like that."

At work on Monday I gave everyone the lie I had tried, unsuccessfully, to give Ken. Questions about my eye were responded to with, "I walked into a wall", and I felt as transparent as Amber had once accused me of being. My torment didn't end there. After work I returned home to find three ecstatic messages from my mother, requesting I call her back immediately. She sounded too happy to have heard about the book, so I reached for the phone, and started chopping vegetables for a stir-fry.

On the second ring she answered and I forced a cheery note into my voice. "What's up?" I asked, monitoring the green onions that were beginning to sizzle on the stove.

My eye caught the small box with the gold hammer inside I had tossed on top of the fridge several weeks before. I felt the wrinkles form in my forehead as my hand closed around it and pulled it down. The gold hammer sparkled in the light and I fought the urge to cry.

"I had a wonderful discovery today," my mother said chipperly.

"Yeah?"

"Yes, this morning I got a copy of your friend Amber's new book. It arrived at the school and I read it to my class."

"You what?" Terror ripped through. Smoke rose from the wok on the stove. The knife I'd been holding in my left hand slipped from my fingers and narrowly missed stabbing me in the foot. The gold hammer mocked me from its velvet prison.

"Yes," my mother continued, "she certainly is an angry girl, isn't she? I never would have guessed it from her demeanor at the shower but in this book --her words-- my goodness, her rage is certainly palpable. Have you read it?"

Read it? I could have burst into maniacal laughter.

"Yes," I said, stiffly. "I've read it."

The onions burned on the stove, filling the apartment with an odorous smoke. Jenna burst through the door like a honey-blond firefighter.

"What are you --?"

I waved dismissively at her and she darted for the stove, turning off the gas, and throwing the smoking wok in the sink. She turned to face me and I shrugged, an action that spoke volumes about my lack of interest in the near-fire.

"Then you know," my mother said in my ear.

"I know."

"So?" Her gossipy nature was creeping into the conversation and I knew where we were going.

"So what?"

"So, why didn't you tell me she's a lesbian?"

"Why is her sexuality any of your business?"

Jenna was watching me with eyes that said she knew who I was talking to and she knew what was going to happen.

"It's just surprising," my mother said. "She's such a pretty girl."

"That's a stereotype, Mother." It seemed whenever she upset me I found myself calling her "Mother." It had been happening since childhood and the fact that I had once believed in the same stereotype only annoyed me further. The "Mother's" were going to pour out of me, and if I became too annoyed, I was going to tell her exactly who the book was about.

"So why didn't you mention it? It's not a big deal."

"Isn't it?'

"Meagan, this is the nineties. People are gay."

Her tone was condescending and something snapped in me. "Well, I'm glad you feel that way because I did indeed tell you she's gay."

"No, you didn't."

"Yes, I did. Danny was staying over and I told you on the phone."

"No," my mother corrected, impatiently. "What you said was that you were having sex with a woman and then you took it back."

My fist closed around the gold hammer and the truth burst out of me with the anger and the pain. I just didn't care anymore.

"I never took it back," I snarled. "I was very careful about that."

Jenna's eyes widened and my mother gasped, "What in God's name are you saying?"

It was over. The secrets, the lies, the hiding.

"Exactly how stupid are you, Mother?" I demanded, my tone sarcastic and filled with hate.

"Meagan!" Jenna kicked me and I turned away from her.

"I told you I was having sex with a woman named Amber," I continued, viciously. "You now know Amber is gay. Danny's been dropping hints for months but you just never clue in. Check out the cover of your book. Does it look familiar? Doesn't one of your daughter's have a tattoo of a butterfly at the base of her spine?"

"This book is about you?" my mother shrieked.

"That's right. I'm the cold-hearted cunt on page three, the punishing pussy on page twenty-five, the porcelain princess on page thirty, and the snickering snatch on page eighty-one."

"Meagan!" She was horrified.

"Well, you wanted the truth," I yelled. "Now you have it! And in case you couldn't tell from the tone of the book it's over now so there's nothing to concern yourself with."

"I read it to my English class!"

"So, who the fuck told you to do that? Thank you though for only adding to my humiliation."

I slammed the phone down and whipped the gold hammer across the room. *"Fuck!"*

Jenna shook her head disapprovingly. "When you're being honest," she said, "you're downright brutal."

Fiercely, I turned on her. "Really? Then why stop with my mother? Who the hell are you that every time I turn around there you are, judging, moralizing, like you're so fucking perfect! Why don't you just get the hell out? Go home and squat in a lotus position or something and leave the matter of my immortal soul to me."

Jenna's face flashed anger. "Hey, Meagan."

"What?"

"Fuck you. I'm sick of you taking your shit out on me, so fuck you."

She turned to leave and my mouth fell open. Jenna didn't swear, ever. It was the strangest thing I'd ever heard and the laughter burst out of me. Jenna reached the threshold of the kitchen and turned back to face me. Our eyes locked and within seconds we were both in hysterics.

"Say it again," I squealed, knowing she couldn't resist a good joke.

Jenna repeated her threat, only this time she added a tough New York accent and I dropped to the floor howling with laughter. Jenna doubled over.

"We're okay," I said.

"Yeah." She helped me to my feet. "We're okay."

Forty-five minutes later we were sitting in front of the TV, eating a fresh batch of stir-fry when the buzzer by the door sounded. It was my mother. She was downstairs in the lobby demanding to be let up at once.

"Want me to go?" Jenna asked, as I buzzed my mother in.

"About as much as I want to contract an incurable venereal disease."

"Is that a yes or a no?" she deadpanned, and I couldn't help grinning.

"I'm gonna miss you."

Jenna's eyes got teary. "Me too. But look at it this way: In a few weeks we're gonna be family."

"Yep. And you're about to get a taste of what that's gonna be like right now. I *should* make you leave. You might not want to marry my brother after this."

Jenna laughed. My mother burst through the door and angrily marched toward me.

"Meagan Summers," she huffed, "how dare you talk to me like that? And *then* you have the nerve to slam the phone in my ear! I've had just about enough of your childish behavior. This is not the way I raised you."

She had a point. But I had an evil inner child and little Meagan's sarcasm broke free.

"You didn't raise me to have sex with women either," I said snidely. "Some things are self-taught."

Her hazel eyes darted back and forth between Jenna and me. Christ, when she was angry she really did look like me.

"Who knows about this?" she demanded.

"Everyone."

"Oh God." Her hand pressed against her heart and she

very dramatically, but very cautiously, fell into a chair by the door.

"Give it up, Mom," I reprimanded in a bored tone. Jenna hid a smirk behind her hands. Even she was aware of my mother's little charade.

"Are you gay?" The words were a shriek.

"No. It didn't matter when you thought it was just Amber, but no, I am not gay."

"Bisexual?"

"Not really." I was calmer now. "But that's probably a closer description."

"So, then what are you?"

"Your daughter. And a woman who just happened to fall in love with another woman. Would you like a glass of water?"

"I-- yes. I think I better."

Jenna rushed into the kitchen and returned with a tall glass of ice water. She placed it in my mother's shaky hand.

"You were in love with Amber?"

"I am in love with Amber."

"Oh, Jesus. Meagan, I don't know what to say to you. I don't know how you can fall in love with a woman and then love her *still* after she's done this to you. What's *wrong* with you?"

"I don't know," I said, quietly.

"There's nothing wrong with her, Joan," Jenna soothed.

"Jenna, she's in love with a *woman*."

Jenna shrugged. "It happens. It doesn't change who she is."

"Why did you keep this from me?"

I sat on the floor in front of her like a disobedient child. "At first because I was afraid of what your reaction would be. Then by the time I realized I did have it in me to tell you, it was already over."

"Why?"

"Because I'm not gay."

"You're not making any sense, Meagan. You're telling me you're in love with a woman but you're not gay. What about this man you've been seeing?"

"Ken's just a friend. He'd like it to be more but I'm in no position to get involved with anyone right now. Amber and I are definitely over, you don't have to concern yourself with that, but I do know in my heart that I will always love her. When I say we broke up because I'm not gay I mean I didn't know how to be what she needed. I hurt her, repeatedly, but it would take forever to try to explain to you how. In the end, I broke her heart and that's why she wrote the book. I won't lie and say it's not killing me inside but I won't do anything to try to stop it either."

"Why the hell not?"

My voice lowered to a whisper. "Because it's my due."

"Meagan, do you know what my students were saying about the subject of that book? Amber has written her pain so well, they tore you to shreds."

"Yes." Sadly, I bowed my head.

"And you're just going to *accept that?*"

"Yes."

"No, you're not," my mother blasted, filled with a passion for vengeance that was normally mine. "My daughter does not go down without a fight."

"This time she does."

"For Christ's sake-- why?"

"Because I deserve it!" The scream boomed out of me and the tears sprang from my eyes. "Everyone will hate me and *I deserve it!"*

Jenna crouched on the floor beside me. "You don't deserve to be hated, Meagan. I think it's honorable that you refuse to try to hurt Amber in return but I do think you should talk to her about this. What if she comes to the wedding?"

"The wedding?" my mother shrieked. "Oh no! That girl is being taken off the guest list."

"No, she's not," I corrected. "She's Jenna's friend and she's been invited. She may elect not to come anyway but the invitations have been sent and it's her choice now. If she does decide to come, each of us is going to behave as maturely as we possibly can, including you." I pointed at my mother. "This is your son's wedding --and Jenna's-- and no one has any right to tell them who they can or cannot invite."

My mother tugged on her auburn locks like I was driving her insane. Rising from her chair, she paced the living room. "And what are you going to do when you see her there? After this book is in every bookstore across the country and you're staring at the face of the person who did this to you?"

My arms wrapped around my raised knees and I battled

the tears that wanted to come again. "I won't look at her. If she approaches me I'll walk away. I will not ruin my brother's wedding and I will not deny Amber the opportunity to see one of her friends get married."

"You better start seeing your therapist more than once a week," my mother barked.

"I doubt I'll be seeing her at all anymore."

"Why?"

I thought of London and shrugged. "She doesn't help me." *And if things get bad enough I'm running away.* Secretly, I thought I had already made the decision. London was a great opportunity and I couldn't figure out what was keeping me from going.

"I think you'll do fine, Meagan," Jenna encouraged.

Her support always helped.

Chapter 17

Basil Waite's apartment was a grungy, dark hole littered with pizza boxes, dirty clothes, and empty beer bottles. Ancient tables in the living room housed peculiar collections of things like lava lamps and water bongs, and the walls were decorated with flags depicting rock groups and a giant poster of Jimi Hendrix-- Noel's idol. We'd agreed to meet here as I was too embarrassed to be seen in public with my black eye, and I now found myself regretting the decision.

"How the hell can you live this way?" I bitched, accepting the beer Basil offered.

"What can I say? We need a woman around here. What's in the bag?" His hand indicated the plastic bag I was holding and I grinned. It was a gift I'd picked up to thank him for the picnic.

"It's for you," I said.

"No shit?" Basil peered into the bag and smiled. "You bought me a leather jacket?"

"To replace the one I gave to the Salvation Army. It's also my way of saying thank you."

"For what?"

"The picnic. *Duh!*"

Basil laughed. "I'll wear it on the tour."

"What tour?"

"That's my good news." He handed me a CD with a giant marijuana leaf on the cover and the words, *Dimestore Ganja*, emblazoned across the top. "The label wants us to go out on the road to promote the CD while the first single gets released."

"It's gonna be on the radio?" I squealed excitedly.

"Yep. In a couple of weeks. We leave for the tour next Thursday."

"How long?" I found myself a little saddened to hear of him leaving. After three years of fighting and fucking, Basil and I had finally developed a friendship and it would be strange now to let it go.

"Three months. If the song hits it could be longer." He nodded at the disc in my hand. "That CD is yours."

"Thank you." Something frightening occurred to me and I frowned suddenly. "There aren't any, 'Meagan's a bitch' songs on here are there? I think I've had my fill of slander for awhile."

"Naw," Basil chuckled. "I'd never do that. Sorry about Amber, that was a really low blow."

"Yeah."

"Fuck, Meagan." His eyes studied my face. "I wish you could come with me."

"What?"

Smiling, he cocked his head. "You don't know, do you? I was an asshole and I really screwed things up between us but -- shit, Meagan-- I never really got over you. You took care of me for three years when I was nothing but a bum playing one-night-a-week gigs in local bars. I wasn't good at showing it, and maybe I can only say this now because I'm leaving, but I really did love you. You're the one that got away."

"Basil, you're stoned," I said, trying to lighten the mood even though his words touched my heart.

"Not stoned, baby, just honest."

"I know, Baz. There's a part of me that will always love you too." I grinned. "You gave me my first Twinkie."

"Yeah," he agreed, laughing. "We always cling to our firsts."

An image of Amber popped into my head. "Some firsts are better off forgotten," I whispered.

"Especially when they write books about you, huh? I know where your head is, Meagan. If you're still in love with her, quit fucking around and go after her, because believe me, someday you'll find it's too late."

"Good luck with the tour, Baz."

"Is that your way of changing the subject?"

"Yes."

"And it's your goodbye?"

"I suppose it's more like *see ya later.*"

"Okay." He walked me to the door, then stopped and gave me a hug. "See ya later, Meagan. I'll give you a call when we get back from the tour."

A better thought occurred to me. "Why don't you give me a call while you're on the tour? Call me from some place far and I'll fly out to catch a show."

"Really?" His face lit up. "You'd really do that?"

I shrugged. "Why not? I certainly don't have a fear of flying."

"Okay then. I guess this really is just *see ya later*. Take care, baby." He hugged me again.

"You too."

I left his apartment and walked toward the stairs at the end of the hall.

"Hey, Meagan?" Basil called after me.

"Yeah?" I turned in time to see the grin stretch across his face.

"You always did have a great ass."

Laughing, I descended the stairs and said a final farewell in my head. I wasn't sure I'd ever see Basil Waite again.

Chapter 18

The boardroom was filled with the usual staff. Twelve faces of *Natural Beauty* higher-ups convening for another Friday morning meeting. Ted sat at the head of the long glass conference table with Rick to his left and me to his right.

Elaine sat across from us, scowling as usual, and her two assistant editors did the same. Elaine wanted London. Ted was holding out for me. The assistant editors were angry because if Elaine went to London one of them would be appointed editor-in-chief, and I was screwing that up for everyone.

"How long are you going to let her put you off?" Elaine demanded of Ted, changing the conversation from our next issue to my indecision over moving to London. "I told you *I'll* go. She doesn't even know what she's doing. She's in publicity. She doesn't know how to run a magazine."

The table remained silent, waiting for my anger to erupt, but that wasn't going to happen. Calmly, I reached for the black carafe in the center of the table and poured myself a glass of water.

"I know more about this magazine than you do, Elaine," I said. "I don't brush off my duties onto my assistants. Seems to me your only real function around here is to write your little "Letter from the Editor" each month. What exactly is it that you do? Your assistant editors raid the slush pile and come up with new article ideas on their own, your secretary screens your calls, and Ted always has the final decision on what will or will not be printed. The way I see it, your duties around here consist of having lunch and chain-smoking in your office. I should be so lucky as to get paid for *that*."

Rick snickered and Ted nudged him. The last thing he wanted was for Elaine's temper to top the charts. The woman could really explode when riled.

"You're just a little corporate kiss-ass, Meagan," Elaine barked.

I shrugged. "Possibly. But I'm a kiss-ass with the opportunity to go to London and take up the second highest position at this magazine."

"Yeah, and you'll sink it. You're too damn young and you don't have the experience. I've been doing this for twenty-five years. My experience dates back to New York and starting out as a goddamn gofer at *Mademoiselle* when I was eighteen. I've worked for *Cosmo*, *Glamour*, and *People-fucking-Magazine*!"

"Well, that just sounds to me like you can't dedicate yourself to one publication. How can you expect to successfully run London when you obviously have no company loyalty? That's the difference between you and me, Elaine. You want the position of power while I just want this magazine to reach its highest potential. And you're kidding yourself if you think I can't do it. I can do it better than anyone in this room, except maybe Ted, and that's why he wants me over there."

"You've been in publicity for seven years!" she yelled. "What are your qualifications? Did you even go to college, Meagan?"

"No, I didn't. But I don't see your qualifications and experience helping you any. London is open to me because I've spent those seven years at Ted's side learning the magazine business in and out. There isn't a thing about *Natural Beauty* that I don't know. I know the finances, the stocks, employee salaries. I know the ins and outs of every department within this building. My hand is in distribution, sales, marketing. I know the little gray-haired man named Vince down in printing, and even the janitors and the co-eds in the mailroom. Believe me Elaine, I know every detail of what goes on around here, right down to the make and model number of the print press we use to who supplies the goddamn paper we print the magazine on. *Those* are my qualifications."

"Are you going or not?" she demanded, unaffected by my little speech.

"It's a good question, Meagan," Ted said. "We're getting down to the crunch here and someone is going to have to fill that position."

"I know." I nodded sympathetically. "I was in London last

week and they're just about ready to get started. The flat needs furniture--"

"We'll deal with that."

"It needs phone hook-ups, appliance --"

"You're evading the question," Elaine snapped. "Either get your ass to London or back off so someone else can go."

"This doesn't concern you, Elaine," Ted barked. "Even if Meagan doesn't go, I can assure you the position will not be yours. Worst case scenario, *I'll* go, and Meagan will run things here."

"What? I'm the editor-in-chief."

"And as Meagan pointed out, you don't know half of what she knows."

"Maybe I will stick around," I sneered at Elaine. "Just to be *your* boss."

"I'll quit! I will not take orders from some twenty-seven year old kid who shows up at work with black eyes because she's out getting into bar brawls with lesbians."

My mouth fell open. Elaine shot me a triumphant look.

"You think you're the only one who knows things, Meagan? *Walked into a wall!*" She nudged her assistant editor. "Tell her, Sue. Tell her how you saw her on the Upper West Side getting punched out by a woman named Large Marge."

Sue's eyes darted to the table.

"You were there?" I screeched. I didn't care that the rest of the table had fallen into a stunned silence. What else was new? That seemed to happen to me a lot these days.

Sue's eyes darted to Elaine and anger crossed her face. "I can't believe you just outed me and I'm not even gay!"

"You were in a gay bar," Elaine pointed out snidely. She didn't care who she hurt.

"I was there with friends. Gay people go into straight bars all the time; it doesn't make them straight."

"Can we get back to business?" Ted demanded. "Who cares how Meagan got her black eye? She does her job and she does it well -- that's what concerns me. And Elaine, your manipulative, self-serving ways do not impress me. I'm getting very tired of your back-stabbing around this office."

"What did I do? I didn't know the truth had become taboo."

Ted rose from his chair. "This meeting is over. Meagan, I

expect your decision by the end of next week. Everyone back to work."

The boardroom cleared and Rick ambled up beside me. "That woman is such a bitch. Can you imagine if she knew about Derek and me?"

Derek was our reviews editor and Rick's boyfriend of four years.

"I don't know why you guys keep it a secret anyway," I said, grabbing my notes from the table. I should talk. Ted was the only one around the office who knew about Amber. "Everyone knows Derek's gay -- he's pretty flamboyant -- and as for you, well, everyone loves you. And we're not exactly concerned about sexuality around here."

Rick hoisted his briefcase. "It's not the gay thing; it's the interoffice romance thing."

I laughed. "Do you really think anyone around here actually believes the two of you are just roommates? That's right up there with, 'I walked into a wall.' I love Derek, but come on, Rick, the man is two fingers snaps away from being Ru Paul."

Rick chuckled. "You have a thing about Ru Paul, don't you?"

"What do you mean?"

"You compare everyone to Ru Paul."

"I do?" The smirk never left my face. "I suppose it's because the guy awes me. He just makes such a pretty woman. Anyway, what did Derek say about the wedding?"

"I'm allowed to be your date."

"Great."

"Why didn't you ask this guy you're seeing?"

We left the board room. "I feel like I've been saying this a lot lately but Ken is just a friend. The problem with taking him is that he wants it to be more than friendship and that would just make me uncomfortable." *And I wouldn't want Amber to see it.* "I'd rather be with someone who isn't going to try groping me on the dance floor. Ken isn't like that but you know what I mean."

Rick nodded. "Two weeks from Saturday, right?"

"That'd be the day."

He slung an arm across my shoulders. "Let's get lunch."

Amber hadn't surfaced in two weeks and I hadn't tried contacting her. *When Butterflies Wear Their Armor* turned up in bookstores everywhere and critics all over town were giving it excellent reviews. I couldn't pick up a newspaper or weekly variety without seeing my soul being recommended as a good read in black and white print. It clawed around my insides and chewed at my guts like a hungry parasite. The book was going to be a hit and the curious looks and the whispers were already beginning.

In the Chinese restaurant on the corner there were hisses of, "That's her", as I walked in to pick up my order. The man who played guitar down the street on the other corner took to disgustedly shaking his head at me when I passed instead of smiling and making small talk like he used to. Now he glowered at me. The woman in the deli two blocks over good-naturedly teased me about being a cunt. In BeBe's people pointed, and in the laundry room of my own building I came across a man eagerly reading a copy of the book and sadly shaking his head. It seemed the whole world had suddenly taken an interest in poetry and everywhere I turned, I was faced with the book.

People who didn't know me discussed the book at tables beside me in cafes and restaurants. They picked apart the antagonist, showed pity for the angry poet, and did not see the wetness in the eyes of the person sitting four feet away.

And this was only the beginning, I thought despairingly. It was going to get so much worse.

Ken glued himself to my side. With each day that passed he became more involved in my life and I grew to count on his support. He took me out, stayed in with me, teased me about how if we ever ended up married my name would be Meagan Faigan. He made me laugh and the laughter began turning into something more: attraction.

Ken was boyishly handsome. His grin was impish and his eyes were soulful and sincere. His arms weren't thick, but they were safe and warm, and I found myself spending more time with them wrapped around me. His hugs were comforting, his kisses kind. The friendship was quickly turning into something else and I wasn't quite sure what we were doing.

"You know what we're doing," Ken teased, when I posed my concern. "You're falling for me."

"Am not."

"Oh, but you are. The same way I'm falling for you."

He called me his little black-eyed pea and we ended up in

bed making slow, leisurely love.

"Do you do *that* with your friends?" he joked, when the lovemaking came to an end. He lay beside me grinning.

I was shocked at how easily I'd been seduced by his kindness and could manage no more than a simple, "Not exactly."

It had been over a year since I'd last been with a man. Ken was about as good as any previous experience I remembered, but quiet. He was a whisper instead of a roar. I thought I liked the silence. Amber had been a talker and a murmurer, and Basil had been a groaner and a sometimes-shouter, but Ken-- Ken was a romance novel instead of a porno. He was tender, slow, playful, and we ended up doing it again.

"Twice with your friends?" he asked.

"I think we better stop this."

"Why?"

"Because I'm not ready for anything serious."

"I understand that. I won't pressure you."

"I don't want to hurt you, Ken."

"You won't."

"How can you be so sure?"

"Because I can accept your terms. You don't want to rush into anything and I'm okay with that."

"Are you sure?"

Shrugging, he gave me his grin. "You'll come around. Eventually you'll realize you're not immune to my charms."

"And then I'll marry you, right?"

"Why is that such a joke between us?"

"You started it."

"I think I'd like to end it," he said.

"Why, are you afraid someday I'll think you're being serious?"

Ken shook his head. "No, I'm afraid someday you'll think I'm not."

"But no pressure, right?"

"I'm not proposing."

"No, you're just setting up a future proposal."

"I'm not setting it up. I just don't want to discredit the possibility either."

"You don't love me, Ken."

"How do you know?"

"Are you saying you love me? Never mind, I'm not ready for that answer."

He chuckled. "It could be 'no', Meagan."

"Maybe we should change the subject."

"Do you love me?" He asked.

"Let's change the subject."

"Okay, subject changed."

The book continued to taunt me everywhere I went and the pain was a battle that continued inside me without cessation. I reached my decision about London. I told Ted. I told Ken. After the wedding I would tell everyone else. There was only one way out and no longer would I hasten to use it.

On the Friday night one week before the big day I threw Jenna a bachelorette party at a sleazy male strip club and the guests included several friends, Iris the seamstress, Danielle, and a bar full of women we didn't know. Everyone was drinking and having a wild time. Danielle was on stage dancing with a cowboy and wearing his hat. Iris was licking whip cream off another stripper's thigh. Women were dancing on the tables and applauding Danielle and Iris. The DJ called out that we'd picked a sleazy enough club to get away with our behavior. Jenna looked serious.

"I have to talk to you later," she said, as I shoved money down a stripper's g-string.

"You pick the strangest times. Look at where we are."

"I just don't want to forget."

Three gorgeous grooms came out on stage to the strains of Salt-n-Pepa's "*Whatta Man*", and began dancing toward our table, undressing all the way while the women hooted and howled and Jenna giggled nervously.

"Time for your surprise," I said, jumping to my feet.

"Oh no! What have you done?"

The DJ's voice boomed over the music. "We have a bride in the audience tonight, ladies. Do you think we can get her up on stage?"

"Oh my Goddess!" Jenna buried her face in her hands. The rest of us screamed.

"Let's get her up here," the DJ called.

The dancing grooms placed a chair in the center of the stage and I handed Jenna a garter belt with a fifty dollar bill taped to its side.

"Put this on," I ordered.

Her face flushed. "No way!"

"Come on," I persuaded. "One last night of fun."

Reluctantly, Jenna pushed the garter belt up her thigh. The grooms pranced around entertaining the rest of the audience while Jenna's friends began shoving five-dollar bills in strategic places on her body for the men to "find." We stuck them between her breasts and between her thighs, in her mouth, between her toes. We turned Jenna into a money tree and the men were starving for paper.

"Let the search begin," the DJ called out when I gave him a small wave to let him know Jenna was ready.

The rest of us went back to our table to watch with amused expressions as the grooms went about digging for the bills with their mouths. They dove their heads into the most intimate parts of Jenna's body. The blush never left her face. The women in the audience went wild.

When all the bills were removed, Jenna was given the choice of which hunk got to try for the garter. Shyly, she pointed to the one with the biggest g-string and the women roared with laughter as he pushed up her skirt and tongued his way up her leg in search of his fifty dollars. Slowly, he pulled the garter down with his teeth and slipped it over her foot. Like a wind animal, he posed on all fours and shook his head from side to side; a sexy beast shredding apart his dinner. Jenna covered her face with her hands and was finally allowed to leave the stage. She returned to a table full of congratulatory shots.

At two in the morning the party ended and Jenna and I returned home to have our own celebration with a bottle of champagne. We were sitting on the couch and I raised my glass to her.

"To my new sister," I said. "And to a long and happy marriage."

Jenna tapped her glass to mine and tiredly dropped her head on my shoulder. "She's coming to the wedding," she said, quietly. "That's what I wanted to tell you."

I didn't respond and Jenna lifted her head to meet my gaze.

"She's coming, Meagan," she repeated. "And not alone."

That grabbed my attention. "Just tell me it's not that Ming

person," I groaned.

"I don't think so. Honestly, I don't know who she's bringing only that she checked the "and guest" part of the reply card when she RSVP'd. I thought I should warn you ahead of time."

"Okay." I rested my head on the back of the couch.

"Are you bringing Ken?"

"Rick. I think Ken has too much of an emotional attachment to me to be able to deal with the whole Amber thing. I figured she'd be there; that's why I invited Rick. I wanted to be with someone whose lack of emotions would ease the tension. I didn't figure on Amber bringing a date, but who am I to bring one and expect that she shouldn't?"

"That's a pretty mature attitude," Jenna said.

"Yeah, now let's see if I can pull it off."

Jenna rested her head on my shoulder again and gave my hand a small squeeze. "Did I ever tell you I had a crush on you when you first moved into the building?"

I choked on my champagne. "What are you talking about? You're not gay."

"Are you?" she countered.

"Good point."

"But that's not what I'm talking about anyway," she said, refilling her glass of champagne. "I had a crush on you but it wasn't a sexual thing. I was attracted to your personality, your spirit."

I gave a harsh laugh. "That only leads to trouble."

"It didn't. We became best friends."

"True."

"And you know why?"

"Enlighten me."

"Because we connected on a level that surpasses sex and lust and all things earthly."

Again I laughed, only more sincerely. "So you're the one who keeps filling my head with all that crap. Okay, are we playing confession now?"

"Sure. Whadda ya got?"

The last of the cool liquid slid down my throat and in a flat voice I said, "I'm jealous."

"Of *me?*"

"Of Josh. Of the fact that he's taking away my best friend and now your loyalty will be to him and we might not ever be as close again."

Jenna shook her head like she'd never heard anything crazier. "The only thing my marriage to your brother is going to change is now you'll have an ally in the family. Besides, like I just finished telling you-- we're soul mates. Non-sexual soul mates."

"You know you're a little bit nutty, right?"

"No more so than you."

"So she's gonna be there." I whispered.

"She's gonna be there," Jenna confirmed.

It was going to be the hardest day of my life.

Chapter 19

"What a dreadful flight," Alexandra Bradshaw complained, clutching her Gucci luggage on my parents' front porch. It was the night before the wedding and Jenna's parents had just flown in from Boston.

"Don't complain, Alexandra," her husband, Charles, admonished. "At least the peanuts were edible."

"Indeed." Alexandra nodded.

I stood at the door with my mouth agape. No matter how many times I met Jenna's parents, their snobbery never failed to amaze me. I wasn't sure where Jenna had come from. She certainly didn't fit in with these two.

"Come in, please," I said, ushering them into my parents' formal living room. "Let me take your coats."

Alexandra threw her brown mink over my arm and Jenna frowned at the sight of the fur. I frowned too, but for a different reason. It was May. Who the hell needed a mink in May?

"Where is Josh, dear?" Alexandra questioned, straightening the gold clip affixed to the back of her honey blond head. She wore her hair in a tight chignon. She had Jenna's pale blue eyes but looked very little like Jenna. "We haven't seen him since your last trip home."

Jenna's parents lived in a mansion. I had been there twice and the place was cold and sterile but extremely elegant. Jenna, I knew, had hated growing up there. Her father had invented some sort of computer software when she was three and they'd been filthy rich ever since. Mostly, she'd been raised by maids and nannies.

"We decided to go traditional," Jenna responded, still frowning at the coat. "Josh is staying at his apartment tonight. The men will get ready over there in the morning and the women here."

Alexandra smiled a genuine flash of capped pearly whites. "My daughter the traditionalist," she gushed.

Charles laughed. "Who would have thought it possible?"

My parents entered the living room, carrying two trays of hors d'oeuvres.

"Hello," Dad said, extending his hand. "I'm Patrick and this is my wife, Joan."

The parents exchanged hellos and quickly launched into a round of small talk which resulted in the discovery that Jenna's father was still a chauvinistic pig and her mother still served on the board of directors for several "affluent charities" -- whatever that meant.

"We brought beluga," Charles offered, swilling a glass of my uncle Peter's homemade wine. Sometimes I forgot there were people out there even more pretentious than my mother. "It would go well with this wine, don't you think?"

Danielle bounced into the room. "Caviar?"

"Of course, dear," Alexandra giggled, an amused expression on her wrinkle-free face. Her plastic surgeon was an artist.

"That's really gross," Danny said.

Jenna and I burst out laughing. My mother cast a worried glance at my father, and Alexandra frowned.

"I'm with the girl," Charles agreed. "But caviar is a must."

His words confused me. He had just stated he did not like caviar but he would eat it because he believed he should.

"This is Danielle," my mother said, placing her hands on Danny's shoulders. "Our *youngest*."

"Is that supposed to make up for my lack of refinement?" Danielle questioned, releasing herself from our mother's grip. "I'll get a dish for your fish eggs." She flounced out of the room and I smirked. Danny was becoming a bigger mouth-piece every day.

"So, my little girl is getting married," Charles boomed, crushing Jenna to his chest.

"Yes," Alexandra agreed. "We worried she'd be alone forever, or end up shacked-up with some long-haired weirdo." My mind flashed to Basil. "She's always been such a bohemian."

Bohemian? I choked back a laugh and my mother assured Jenna's parents that everyone loved their daughter and found her positive outlook on life refreshing. They in turn proclaimed their approval of Josh.

"Such a level-headed boy," Alexandra said, dreamily.

Except that he's a man, I thought. I was biting my tongue and it was absolutely killing me.

Charles clapped Jenna on the shoulder. "Finally, a son to take over my company when I die." He laughed uproariously and my parents exchanged a look.

"Dad," Jenna interjected. "I told you, Josh and I do not plan on moving to Boston. We're happy here."

My mother breathed a sigh of relief and Charles gave Jenna a patronizing squeeze. "Sure you are, Princess. I wasn't planning on kissing the dirt any time soon. I just want to know that when I'm dead and gone my little girl will be taken care of. You're going to be a very rich lady someday and you'll need a smart man to run the company for you."

"Not that she couldn't run the damn company herself," I muttered. Jenna smirked.

It was late in the evening and Charles and Alexandra were tired after their "dreadful" flight. They elected to stay with us and my mother showed them to the guest room upstairs. By midnight, everyone else followed their lead. Jenna took my old room, Danny stayed in hers, our parents in theirs, and I took Josh's, with its shelves of trophies and medals. I was the last one to go to bed. I brushed my teeth and was about to double-check that everything was in order for the morning when I heard a small groan coming from down the hall. It came from the direction of my old room and I went to check it out.

Jenna sat at the foot of the bed, her head in her hands. "Hey," she groaned.

I crouched on the floor in front of her and folded my arms across the top of her lap. "Are you okay?"

She pressed her forehead to mine. "I'm terrified, and it's making me sick to my stomach."

I smiled and brushed the hair from her eyes. For a second my mind flashed to doing the same thing to Amber on the plane to Montreal. I drove away the thought.

"Do you love my brother?" I asked, knowing full-well the answer.

"Yes."

"Do you want to marry him?"

"Yes."

I scuffed her hair like you would a silly child and sat on the bed beside her. "Then there's nothing to worry about."

"Easy for you to say."

"It certainly is." I rose to leave.

"Meagan?" Jenna grabbed my hand. "Would you mind, you know--?"

"Staying?"

"Yeah." She nodded.

"No problem, but you better not be a blanket hog."

Jenna laughed and we got into bed. Within fifteen minutes she had talked out all her nervousness and we fell asleep. At seven we were startled awake by the sound of screaming.

"Oh my God!" a female voice shrieked.

My eyes snapped open. Jenna's arm lay across my face, her knee pressed painfully into my back. She remained asleep.

"*Oh my God!*"

I nudged Jenna and her head snapped up. "I think there's something wrong with your mother."

Together we jumped from the bed and ran toward the guest room, where the shrieking continued.

"What the hell is it?" Charles demanded, as we burst through the door, followed by everyone else in the house.

I'd never walked in on such a sight in my life. Alexandra lay in the bed, blankets yanked up to her horrified face, with her confused husband beside her and a fat, squirming pink body between them.

"Pig!" Alexandra screamed. She jumped from the bed in her lacy white negligee.

Charles jumped out the other side, his gray hair poking up like horns on the top of his head, and my eyes fell to his waist and the little white boxer shorts he wore with the red hearts and pouting mouths all over them. There was a trap door flap in the back with two little white buttons holding the flap in place and I burst into raucous laughter.

"Meagan!" my mother reprimanded. But my laughter was infectious and soon everyone in the room was in hysterics, all except for my mother and the Bradshaws.

"Come here, Bacon," my father called, wiping the tears from his eyes. He'd developed a special affection for the pig.

Bacon jumped down from the bed and we laughed even harder as my mother tried to explain that the pig was to be the ring bearer at the wedding and she'd allowed Jenna to keep him in the basement for the night. She couldn't understand how he'd escaped. My guess was the smirking Danielle.

"Let me get this straight," Alexandra said, cinching her white silk robe and glaring at Jenna. "Not only do you have pig for a pet but you plan on having the filthy animal in your wedding party?"

"Yep."

"Oh, the Noltey's will have a field day with this one," Alexandra complained, referring to some snobbish couple who had flown in from Boston with them.

Charles only shook his head. "I'm glad you're getting married, dear. Josh must be a saint."

The morning flew by. Josh called at ten to tell Jenna he missed her and couldn't wait to make her his wife and she giggled into the phone, endearingly. At twelve we began dressing and Jenna insisted no one be allowed in the room with her but me. She told her mother she considered dressing for the wedding to be a strictly bride/maid of honor thing and her mother sulked away. We giggled like children as we dressed. I affixed the floral crown to the top of Jenna's head with a few well-concealed bobby pins. She looked radiant in her satiny silver dress-- every bit the Goddess I knew she'd be.

"You look so beautiful!" I gushed.

"Are you girls almost ready?" Alexandra called from the other side of the door.

"In a minute," I called back happily.

Jenna stepped back from the mirror and took my hands. "I want to thank you for last night. It was really sweet of you to stay with me."

"Don't be silly, Jenna. That's what we *do*."

Jenna laughed and I pushed a loose daisy back into the crown on her head. Tucked a honey blond wisp of hair behind her ear.

"Did you know," she said nonchalantly, "that you talk in your sleep?"

I felt my face redden. "No. I'm sorry. Did I keep you up?"

"Naw, you just woke me a few times. That's not the part

that disturbs me. The part that disturbs me was to hear you pleading."

"Pleading?" Her words freaked me out.

Jenna nodded. "You were pleading with Amber, Meagan. At first I thought you were talking to me but you weren't. I think you should take today as an opportunity to talk to her because I'm pretty sure last night wasn't the first night you spent tossing and turning and telling her how sorry you are."

"Are you sure?" I asked, suspiciously. Maybe Jenna was setting me up.

"Positive."

"Are you girls coming out?" Alexandra called again.

I reached to open the door and Jenna said, "Will you talk to her?"

"Hey, quit with the serious stuff. It's your wedding day so let's get at it and not worry about the rest right now."

Jenna smiled and I swung open the door so she could greet her admirers. One hour later we were pulling up in front of the church. The service wasn't to begin for another forty-five minutes and I was surprised to find Rick in the parking lot trying to squeeze his BMW between one of the bridal limousines and a catering truck, who's driver had obviously confused the church address with the hall address.

Quickly, I raced over to them, directed the caterer back to the hall and helped Rick find a more suitable place to park.

"You're early," I said. We climbed the steps, passing through the chapel and out the back doors to the garden where the service was to take place. The sun was out in full force. It was a beautiful day for a wedding.

"I wanted to make sure I got a good parking spot." Rick scratched the top of his head and looked around like something confused him. "Don't think I'm a weirdo, but when I was out front I could have sworn I saw a pig wearing a tuxedo getting out of a stretch limo."

I laughed so hard I thought I'd split the sides of my dress. Bacon never failed to shock.

"I really did see it," Rick insisted.

I grabbed his arm for support. "I know," I managed between gasps for air. "There's bound to be a few things at this wedding that people have never seen before."

Rick steadied me. "Like what?"

I gathered myself and took a breath. "For starters, the pig you saw was not a figment of your imagination. He belongs to the bride and is also the ring bearer." Rick's mouth dropped open and I grinned. "You'll also notice if you look down that I am barefoot. All of the bridesmaids will be. This is to symbolically ground the wedding vows, giving them roots. It also expresses Jenna's connection to and appreciation of the earth and its bounty."

Rick shook his head. "Wow. Anything else?"

He was very handsome in his black suit, with his blond hair curling around his ears, and I smiled at him. "No, I think that covers it."

People began filling the foldout chairs and I led Rick to his seat. He said something else and as I leaned in to hear him more clearly I spotted Amber sitting three rows away. My heart caught in my throat. She was wearing a short black dress and, a silver pendant rested high on her chest. She looked as amazing as ever. More so, if that was possible.

Nervously, I cast an unwilling glance at the seat beside her and I could have burst into joyous and relieved laughter at what I saw: Zeppo. It was only Zeppo. Decked out in an elegant gray suit and looking as normal as any man in the garden. Probably why I didn't notice him in the first place.

I must have been grinning. I must have looked utterly gleeful because Amber's curious glance turned to a glare and Rick said, "So you're okay with that then?"

I shook my head. "I'm sorry what?"

"I was saying Derek will be pissed if I'm not home by nine but if you want me to stay longer I will."

"That's okay; you can leave right after dinner if you want."

"Are you kidding?" Rick asked. He pressed his lips to my hand and I thought of what a sexy and chivalrous thing his kiss would have been if he wasn't gay. "I'd be a fool to leave before dancing with the most beautiful woman at this wedding."

I smiled and thought, *no, the most beautiful woman is sitting three rows away giving me dirty looks.* "Ah," I said knowingly, "but you haven't seen the bride yet."

Amber was still staring at me. Only now her eyes were narrowed, her lips pressed into a thin line, and she was rubbing her forehead with her middle finger. I couldn't believe my eyes. Was she actually *giving me the finger?* Flipping me off because Rick had so sweetly kissed my hand? I couldn't believe she'd be that immature but my suspicions were confirmed when Zeppo noticed what she was doing and forced her hand down into her lap. I watched his lips form the word *behave,* but I had no time to deal with them. The garden was filling with people and I had to get back to Jenna who was probably having a nervous breakdown, considering the length of time I'd been gone.

Scooting past Amber and Zeppo without so much as a nod in their direction, I raced through the chapel doors and found my way to the preparation room where I was scolded by my uptight mother for being gone so long.

Jenna grinned. "Did you talk to her?" she whispered, as the hairdresser made some final adjustments to her head wreath.

I shook my head and reached for my purse. "I almost forgot," I said, removing a small package and placing it in Jenna's hand. Inside was a silver toe ring. "It's been magically charged," I told her, "with the intention that each step you take today is a step toward total enlightenment in love." I grinned, knowing Jenna's love for all things magical. "It's a happiness guarantee."

Jenna's eyes misted. "It's the best present anyone's ever given me," she said, as I clicked the ring around the second toe of her left foot.

"Don't cry," I admonished. "You'll ruin your makeup."

Jenna wrapped her arms around my neck and Charles popped his head through the door. "It's time, Princess," he said. Jenna stepped into the hallway, followed by her bridesmaids.

We lined up in the back of the chapel the way the minister had suggested at the previous evening's rehearsal, and began our walk outside.

Rebecca, Jenna's six-year-old cousin and flower girl, went first, walking Bacon down the aisle with a floral-decorated leash, the two wedding bands swinging from his collar. People *ah'd* and laughed. Rebecca reached the front of the garden and handed Bacon over to Paul Bradshaw, Jenna's cousin and Josh's best man. She moved to the far left like an old wedding pro.

One by one the bridesmaids followed until the only people left in the chapel were Jenna, her parents, and me. Quickly, I kissed Jenna's cheek, wished her luck and began my painstaking trek down the aisle, noticing that Amber was watching Rick who was watching me, and I caught her eye for a second, in which she gave a rare smile. I smiled back as I passed her row, grateful my ordeal was almost over. Then I reached the altar, kissed my brother's cheek, and moved to stand beside Rebecca.

Jenna began her slow march up the aisle on the arms of her parents and people actually gasped at her beauty. Rick glanced at me and I nodded in Jenna's direction with an *I told you so* smile on my face. Jenna reached the altar and Josh squeezed her hand. They beamed at each other and I thought them the most beautiful couple I'd ever seen.

The ceremony began. The priest started his blah-blahing in that boring monotonous tone Catholic priests have and I found my concentration slipping. I had a habit of daydreaming at weddings and, quickly, I began drifting off on the rows of flowers and the birds chirping overhead. I picked a hangnail, counted the number of pews, admired a lone squirrel in a tree a few feet away, and before I knew what was happening Josh was removing the rings from Bacon's collar.

Thank God, I thought, and glanced out at the rows of faces only to find Amber staring at me with a grin on her face. I frowned, wondering what about me she found so damn amusing, and inconspicuously gave my appearance a quick once-over. I checked my hands, my dress, my feet, and upon discovering nothing out of place, shot her a look.

Amber continued smirking and just when I'd had about enough of her head games, I realized why she found me so amusing-- she *knew.* She'd been watching me and she knew I'd spent the whole ceremony daydreaming and hadn't heard a thing that had gone on.

I allowed myself a grin, then turned away, wondering how much of my daydreaming might have been captured on video tape. Had it caught me twirling my hair around my finger and holding it up to the sun in search of split ends? Or had it merely caught me tapping my toes to the song that played on in my head?

Focus, I told myself. But by then it was too late. The ceremony was over and Josh and Jenna were in the middle of their marital kiss. They pulled apart and I was the first one to cheer, as if I'd been paying attention the whole time. Amber shook her head good-naturedly and the crowd followed my lead into a roaring round of applause. Josh and Jenna made their way back down the aisle as husband and wife.

The banquet hall was filled with balloons and illuminated by the candles that sat on every table. Three hundred guests picked at their dinners and listened to the speeches being given by each person at the head table. We were twelve deep and I sat at my brother's side with little Rebecca on the other side of me. I helped her with her dinner as the microphone passed from hand to hand, heading toward me. I did not plan on giving a speech. I planned on weaseling my way out of it.

Amber and Zeppo sat at a table ten feet away and I tried not to look at her. Twice her eye caught mine and I saw Zeppo's mouth form the words, *ignore her.* He was such a pain in the ass.

Rick was seated at a table directly across from theirs and he gave me a friendly little wave. I waved back and Amber scowled. The microphone approached me and I saw Amber arch an eyebrow when I shook my head at it. I passed it along and the speeches continued down the row until, at last, they were done and the microphone was returned to its stand in front of Josh.

I'd gotten away with it. I'd bypassed giving a speech and the only person who noticed was Amber. With a satisfied grin, I settled back in my chair and reached for my wine. A low rumble began at the back of the room and my back stiffened.

"Meagan. Meagan."

Dreaded O'Reilly cousins! Shit, they'd noticed. The chant was being led by twenty-eight year-old Joseph, the biggest troublemaker of them all.

"You know what's happening," Josh said grinning. "Did you think they were going to let you get away with it?"

I moved to jump away from the table but Josh pressed his hand to my wrist.

"Hey, let go!" The chant was growing louder and people began turning in their seats to check out the commotion. I struggled against my brother. "Let go of me!" I hissed.

"No way. You're doing it."

"Josh, please!"

But Josh was too amused to let me leave the table and I saw Amber giving me yet another of her curious looks.

"*Meagan. Meagan.*"

Eyes flitted from the back of the hall to me. People stared

with grinning faces. Amber stared. Zeppo stared. Rick stared. And I slunked down a little further in my chair.

"*Meagan! Meagan! Meagan*!"

Half the hall had joined in on the chant and the voices erupted until all that could be heard was the sound of my name being repeated over and over again.

"*Meagan! Meagan! Meagan!*"

"They're calling you," little Rebecca screamed beside me, her voice barely audible over the noise.

"Oh God!" My face flamed.

Josh laughed, handed me the microphone, and slowly I stood up and rounded the table.

"Okay!" I raised my hand for silence. "I'm doing it, all right? You O'Reilly's really suck!"

People laughed and at least fifteen O'Reilly's yelled, "*Go Meagan!*"

Leaning against the front of the table, I began, "I'm not very good at this-- "

"You're a publicity director," someone yelled from the back of the hall. "Don't you give speeches for a living?"

The hall filled with laughter and my face continued to flame. "Joseph O'Reilly, I swear to God as soon as I put down this mike I'm coming back there after you."

"All right, Meagan! Yeah!"

Again they started banging the tables and chanting my name. I threw up my arms and the bridal table behind me roared with laughter. The noise died down.

"Are you done now?" I asked.

"Done," Joseph called back.

"Good." Again I began my speech but I stumbled over my words and Joseph, grasping his opportunity, screamed out, "*Hooked on Phonics* worked for me!"

The room burst into hysterical laughter. Rick grinned at me from across the way, Amber smirked down at her plate, Zeppo looked amused at my embarrassment, and the bridal party behind me continued to laugh.

"Well, now I'm not doing it," I complained. "I really hate you O'Reilly's." But everyone knew I didn't mean it. It was all a part of the crazy game my cousins and I played with each other.

"Do you hate *all* O'Reilly's, Meggie Pie?" a gruff, friendly voice yelled out.

Meggie Pie? There was only one person in the world who called me Meggie Pie and my mouth fell open. I looked at Jenna and she nodded, grinning from ear to ear. It couldn't be. He was supposed to be--

A muscular man of forty-two rose from his seat in the back. Black hair and eyes, well cut tux, and a happy paternal grin on his handsome, masculine face.

"*Seamus!*" My scream boomed through the hall.

"Did you miss yer old uncle?" he called back.

"Oh my God! Seamus O-fucking-Reilly!" My head shook wildly with disbelief and I thought I would burst into tears of joy.

"Meagan!" my mother screeched from behind me.

But her reprimanding fell on deaf ears as I dropped the mike on the table, darted across the room, and threw myself in my uncle's arms.

"Thought I wasn't coming, huh, Meggie?" he teased. "Look at you. You look great! I heard you were skinny but you look good to me."

"Seamus, I can't believe you're here! God, I missed you. When did you get in?"

"About an hour ago. I'm sort of Jenna's surprise for you. She convinced me to take the time off work. I wanted to come anyway, but you know, it's a long flight."

"Jenna did this?" I pulled him toward the head table where he was greeted with stiff hellos and even stiffer hugs. Seamus was the black sheep but he was *my* black sheep.

"Are you shocked, Meagan?" Jenna giggled.

"Jenna, I can't believe you got him here!" I clung to my uncle's arm and buried my face in his chest. I felt Amber's eyes on my back. Even she knew how important Seamus was to me. I let go of Seamus long enough to yank Jenna into an almost teary hug. "I just love you so much! Seamus you have to sit at the head table with us."

"Naw Meggie, dat's for the bridal party."

"Dat?" I questioned.

He chuckled. "The brogue is getting thicker, huh?"

"You gotta sit with us, dinner's over. Come on." I pulled up another chair, scooting Rebecca beside Josh, and forced Seamus to sit next to me.

"Rick." I waved Rick over to the table. "You have to meet my uncle Seamus before you take off. I'm sorry I haven't been much company. I didn't expect to be stuck at this table so long."

"No problem." Rick shook Seamus's hand and they chatted awhile.

Josh and Jenna went up to have their first dance as husband and wife, and the party began. Other couples joined them on the dance floor. Rick asked me to dance at the third song and briefly, I left my uncle's side to let him escort me around the dance floor.

"See that woman over there?" he whispered, pulling me closer and pointing at the bar.

There was only one woman at the bar and my heart gave a little twist. "Amber?"

"Oh, you know her?"

"Yes," I said, tightly.

"Then you'll be happy to know Derek is giving the book her agent sent over a five flower recommendation."

My heart hardened within me. Amber didn't have an agent. She'd done that on purpose.

"Good for her."

"You don't sound pleased."

Glancing at the clock on the wall, I smiled. "It's after nine, Rick. You're gonna be in shit."

He laughed. "All right, I better get going."

"Should I walk you out?"

"No, go back to your uncle. You know you're dying to anyway."

My smile was genuine and I kissed his cheek. "Thanks for coming."

"No problem. You just have to agree to be my date next time someone in *my* family gets married."

"Agreed."

Rick left and I went back to Seamus who proceeded to get me drunk on wine and champagne. Amber flitted back and forth to the bar and occasionally her eyes caught mine. Seamus noticed.

"So dat's her then," he said, nodding in Amber's direction.

"Am I making it that obvious?"

"You both are. You should have seen the way she was watching you when you were dancing with dat boy."

"Is it obvious to everyone?"

"Naw, I just know me Meggie. She's a blond stunner, ain't she?"

"Yes."

"And yer mother knows now?"

I laughed. "You couldn't tell by the way she's been keeping her eye on us?"

"Have another drink, Meggie. We'll blot it out together."

And we continued to get drunk. Seamus asked me to dance and I followed him onto the floor and let his arms wrap around me in that protective, fatherly way of his. My head rested on his shoulder and for one song, I was safe.

"It's like when you were a kid, Meggie," he said in my ear. "You'd scrape yer knee and the first person you'd run to was yer Uncle Seamus."

"Yeah." My eyes misted. "But this is a little worse than a scraped knee."

By one a.m. the party was almost over and few guests remained. Seamus and I sat at the head table, drunk, and Amber and Zeppo sat at their table a few feet away. My parents left. Many guests left, and Josh and Jenna were preparing their escape.

"We're gonna take off," Jenna said, hugging me. "Our flight to Hawaii leaves in a few hours so we gotta get home and get changed. Danny's gonna stay at my place while we're gone." The plan was to move into the new house after the honeymoon.

Seamus rubbed his eyes and I knew he was getting tired. We'd already decided he'd stay with me for a few days.

"Why don't you go home with Danny?" I suggested. "I'm gonna stay and settle things up with the bartender."

"Are you sure, Meggie?"

My eye caught Amber's again. "I'm sure."

"Have you talked to her?" Jenna asked.

"No."

"Well, if it's any consolation, she told me she thought you looked beautiful today."

"It isn't."

"Are you gonna be okay to drive?" She peered at my eyes.

"I'm fine. I'm sobering up and by the time I settle things here…" I waved my hand like it was no big deal.

"Okay." Jenna giggled and hugged me again. "See ya in

two weeks."

She turned to leave and Seamus followed her away, glancing at me over his shoulder. I waved him off and finished my glass of wine.

I wasn't fine. I had lied to Jenna because I didn't want her to spend her wedding night worrying about me. I was broken and angry. Each time I saw Amber, the humiliation crept up in my chest and I battled to control my anger and the tears that wanted their release. When she passed me again on her way to the bar I knew I could remain silent no longer. The pain was going to burst out of me and I was going to tell her exactly what I thought.

Angrily, I marched up behind her and ordered a Jack Daniel's on the rocks. Amber was the only other person at the bar and she arched an eyebrow when I downed the drink and ordered another. On the third I could control my mouth no longer. The tears were ready to spring to my eyes and I turned to her and hissed, "You're a fucking bitch with a hell of a lot of nerve to show up here."

It was the best my weary mind could come up with and I stalked away from her and marched toward the bathroom, frustrated and wounded. Within seconds she was in there with me, locking the door behind her.

"What do you think you're doing?" I demanded.

"Keeping busy with the men these days, huh?"

I fussed with my hair in the mirror and avoided her gaze. "Whatever."

"What's the matter? Did you find Trish as much of a dead fuck as everyone else does?"

The plan had worked and I smirked. "Heard about that, did you?"

"I didn't have to, I *saw* it."

My hands stopped mid-fluff. "What?"

"I *saw* you leave with her, Meagan. I saw you creep up the backstairs to her apartment." Her head shook in disbelief. "I can't believe you had the nerve to fuck with Large Marge like that."

"*You* said she was harmless."

"She *is* harmless, until you start calling her Shamu."

"I called her that after she punched me out." Then a thought occurred to me. Amber's words sunk into my fuzzy head and I felt the ache in my heart. "Tell me something, Amber," I said. "Did you enjoy watching Marge beat the hell out of me, or did you at least have to turn your head?"

"I wasn't there for that part," Amber said softly. Her fingers moved to touch the spot that only weeks ago still bore the result of Marge's meaty left hook.

Slowly, and painstakingly, I removed her hand from my face. The charge passed between us and I drew away.

"I ran into Marge outside," she continued. "She told me what happened and when I went in to see if you were okay I saw you leaving with that *bartender*." She spat the word at me.

"Well, why the hell didn't you stop me?"

"Why should I? I'm not your fucking keeper, Meagan. Little Miss I'm-no-dyke. But you didn't miss your chance to dive between *her* legs, did you?"

"Do you want me to puke?"

"Puke! Obviously you wanted her from the second you saw her or you wouldn't have been able to do what you did."

"Actually, it's quite amazing what a bottle of Jack Daniel's and a little rage can make you do. And what about you? Did you want Ming so desperately you had to kiss her in front of my face?"

"That was a mistake."

"Mmm. As much of a mistake as sending a copy of your book to my office and to my mother? At least when I did the stupid thing with Trish I didn't know you were around; otherwise, it wouldn't have happened because I would have been too busy doing to you what that Shamuesque bitch Marge did to me. I could have killed you that night."

Amber's head dropped between her shoulders. The guilt was written across her face.

"That's okay though," I continued sarcastically. "Because you actually did me a favor. Now it's all out in the open and I'm free of the whole fucking mess."

"What do you mean?"

"I mean I told my mother everything. You didn't leave me much choice, did you?"

"I tried to warn you," she whispered.

The ache pressed against my heart. "How could you write those things about me? Do you have any idea what you've put me through? That fucking book is everywhere. I knew you hated me, but Christ, did you have to try to destroy me?"

She sat on the vanity and stared down at her hands. "I don't hate you."

"You just --" I started to cry and Amber flinched. She'd never seen me cry before.

"Meagan --"

Quickly, I wiped my eyes and pulled myself together. "Don't worry about it; I get by. Cold-hearted cunts always do."

Her eyes brimmed with tears and suddenly I was being washed up in the green again. *Please, not now!* I didn't want to comfort her but something shoved me forward and I knew what I was going to do. I couldn't stop it. Too much alcohol had torn down my walls and her eyes were reaching out to my soul and the longing it felt for her. The desperation and desire swelled within me and in one shocking movement I pressed forward and kissed her.

Her arms slid easily around my neck and her body pressed to mine. Her tongue explored my mouth like the first time and I reached up and slid the strap of her dress down, exposing a small, lovely breast. She murmured my name against my lips. I loved the sound of it. Her hand slid up my dress and I wondered if she still had her piercing.

"I can't stop wanting you." The words came out of me like a whispered cry.

"I know." Her fingers slipped into my hair. "Oh God, Meagan. I know."

We kissed and pulled at each other's clothes. When I discovered the piercing was gone she saw the question in my eyes.

"I couldn't keep it," she whispered, her forehead pressed against mine. "There was too much of you attached to it."

"Don't stop, Amber."

"No."

She slid the hem of my dress up and dropped to her knees but I followed her down and we were both on the floor, kissing, losing ourselves to the moment. Then suddenly there was a pounding at the door – or maybe in my heart. Then a laugh and a chant snapping me back to reality.

"*Meagan*! *Meagan*!"

Clumsily, I staggered to my feet, horrified by what I had almost done, by what I'd been *doing*. Amber and I stared at each other.

"*Meagan! Meagan*!"

It was Joseph and he was drunk. I was drunk and what I'd been doing was insane.

"For fuck's sake," I yelled, slapping the door. "Go away! I'm fucking puking in here!"

Silence on the other side. Then Joseph saying, "Sorry Meagan," and his footsteps walking away.

"*Fuck*." I slid down the back of the door and pulled my knees to my chest. My forehead rolled on the back of my hands and the tears burned behind my eyes. How did this happen? I'd been doing so well. Then I was alone with her for five minutes and suddenly I was vulnerable and weak. My body trembled with the waterless tears inside and I knew, at once, that the decision I'd given Ted was the best one I'd made in months. Only running would make me free.

Amber kneeled in front of me and rested her chin on top of my head. "It's okay, honey," she whispered. "I love you. I'm sorry for everything I did. Please Meagan, don't cry." She wrapped her arms around me. "Meagan, I love you. I--I didn't mean it."

The ache ripped through my heart and very gently, I pushed her away. "I'm sorry, Amber. I shouldn't have done this."

"Oh God!" She sat back against the door, defeated. "Not again."

"No." Carefully, I helped her to her feet and brushed the blond wisps from her eyes for what I knew would be the last time. "Not again, because we're both gonna walk out of here as if this never happened."

Her head shook despairingly. "How do you do it, Meagan? How do you just turn it off like that?"

"I have to," I whispered.

"Why? Especially now that everyone knows."

I didn't know how to tell her it wouldn't matter if the whole world knew. I was still the same person who didn't know how to be what she needed.

"Because."

"That's not an answer. You start kissing me and telling me you can't stop wanting me, and then you want to just walk away as if it never happened? You owe me a better explanation than *because*. Just tell me why. Goddamn it, Meagan—*why?*"

"Because I'm moving to London," I said suddenly. "And I don't know when or if I'll ever be back."

PART II

Chapter 20

Across the ocean I settled into a quiet life. *When Butterflies Wear Their Armor* was sweeping North America like a plague and I was glad to be as far away from it as possible. Its success was astronomical. A book Amber had written in less than three weeks, and without her precious audience approval, had become a giant that refused to go away without hitting every bestseller's list first. It tore me up.

London was my refuge.

Jenna had pleaded with me not to go but her pleading had fallen on deaf ears. There was only one way to get over Amber I believed-- I had to be as far away from her as was humanly possible. I also had a job to do. And with those two thoughts in mind I'd boarded the plane with a small wave to Ken and my teary family who'd gone to the airport to see me off.

I'd settled easily into the dingy gray flat above the *Natural Beauty* offices. The building was in a central location, near the underground station and several bus stops, and I decided against purchasing a car. The magazine provided a company car but I refused to drive it until the company logo was removed and it looked like any other car in London. I planned on taking *Natural Beauty* to the top-- advertising on the side of my car was not imperative to that.

The flat was disappointing but it suited my frame of mind. It had nice furniture and was stocked with the best appliances and other necessities, but it was gray. Gray walls, gray ceiling, gray trim around the windows and doors. It was reminiscent of a prison but it was where I belonged.

The kitchen was small, with no space for a table and chairs. Instead, four padded stools had been placed in front of a counter that separated the kitchen from the large living room. It wasn't as large as the living room I had back at home but it was a comfortable size, with a sofa, a loveseat, two heavy chairs, two end tables, a coffee table, a floor model TV, and a Pioneer stereo complete with a five disc change CD player and large speakers that had been hung in the top two corners of the room. The bedroom had large windows overlooking the city below, a king size bed, two dressers, and a walk-in closet large enough to store four season's worth of clothes.

I didn't plan on staying that long. I planned on working non-stop until *Natural Beauty* was a European rage, getting over Amber, and then returning to my lovely downtown apartment and my quiet little life. A year seemed an unnecessarily long amount of time. My estimation was closer to six months. Progress was already underway, and, with a dedicated staff, I knew my goal was not an unreasonable one.

The offices downstairs pleased me. The printing of the magazine was relegated to a small building next door, and the offices below the flat were clean, spacious, and abuzz with activity. *My* office was the most pleasing. I had chosen a corner office near the end of a long hall and the sign on the door said, *Meagan Summers, President.* It was thrilling to look at.

The inside had been furnished before my arrival, but I liked it. Ted had chosen a large mahogany desk with a swivel leather chair, and mahogany bookcases lined the walls. A computer sat on the corner of the desk, a black phone with a headset and several opaque buttons that would soon be flashing red with awaiting calls sat on the other corner. There were two smaller leather chairs in front of the desk and large windows behind it. File cabinets were black and unobtrusive. The room was large and carpeted and a great place to get down to business, which was exactly what I planned on doing.

Four weeks drifted by quickly and *Natural Beauty* was well on its way. I worked without cessation, only returning to the flat upstairs when my eyes refused to see straight and my mind was aching for sleep. Occasionally, I went out with coworkers and experienced the city. Amber drifted slowly from my thoughts as work accounted for each moment and Ken etched deeper into my life. He called three times a week and started arriving in London for weekends, and occasionally, a week at a time. I wondered how his patients got along without him but he assured me it had been taken care of; another doctor would go away and then Ken would take *his* place, carrying two patient loads at a time. It never seemed to bother him and Ken and I grew closer every day.

In time I realized I loved him. It wasn't the sort of love I had felt for Amber but I accepted it because I knew in my heart I would never truly know that kind of love again. Ken accepted it because I threw my all into our relationship and he knew, without a doubt, that I would never go back to Amber.

"I told you you'd fall in love with me," he often joked. "Admit it, honey. I'm downright irresistible."

And he was. Ken Faigan was handsome and kind, and the sweetest man I had ever known. I loved being with him. I loved his visits and often found myself disappointed when he had to leave.

"Oh, but I'll be back," he regularly warned. And he always kept his word.

Months drifted quickly. Danielle was having a great time living in my apartment and Josh and Jenna loved their new house. Jenna called weekly and she never failed to mention Amber and what she was up to. They were becoming closer in my absence and the idea both pleased and horrified me. I liked that they were friends but I dreaded what that meant to my return home.

Bacon died. Jenna tearfully relayed the news one day on the phone and when we hung up I burst into tears. I loved that pig. He was one of the few things I looked forward to seeing again when I returned. But with the bad news came the good-- Jenna was pregnant. Four months along and she'd only just realized it.

"How is that possible, Jenna?" I'd questioned. But Jenna had always had problems with her menstrual cycle. It wasn't uncommon for her to skip periods. When it started happening a little too frequently she went to the doctor who happily informed her that she was four months pregnant, at least, and she had better start with the vitamins and such.

Josh and Jenna were thrilled. They hadn't planned it but it was a welcome surprise and Jenna was overjoyed that she'd somehow managed to skip morning sickness and hadn't really gained all that much weight. Her doctor told her to gain some and she joyfully went about stuffing her face.

"You have to come home now, Meagan," she'd giggled on the phone. "You're going to be an aunt."

An aunt who still had work to do.

"Eventually, Jenna," I'd responded. "I'm not done here

yet."

"You're missing my pregnancy."

"So are you, apparently."

With more laughter we said goodbye and promised to talk again soon.

The news of Jenna's pregnancy brought out something in Ken. He started talking about babies and marriage and he didn't seem to be joking anymore. I tried to flub it off but often I found his words lingering in my head long after he'd gone and I wondered if it wasn't such a bad idea. I was twenty-seven years old, I loved Ken, and wasn't it time I settled down? A house in the suburbs and a quiet little marriage didn't look so bad. It would be peaceful, *normal,* and I began wondering if Ken would indeed pop the question.

My wondering came to an end three weeks before I was to return home. *Natural Beauty*, under my careful but obsessive guidance, had become the European smash Ted had hoped for, and my passage back across the ocean was planned. Ken arrived in London to celebrate my success and we sat in a crowded restaurant smiling at each other. Ken reached for my hand.

"Marry me, Meagan," he said.

I laughed. "I'm not falling for it, Ken. I'm supposed to say yes right? And then you'll laugh and tell me you were joking."

"I'm not joking."

His smile was genuine as he pulled a box from his pocket and got down on one knee. Grinning faces turned to look at us and I flushed.

"Oh God, Ken. Get up."

"Nope."

He popped open the box and there was a ring inside with a diamond so large an elderly woman at the next table took one look at it and in a lovely British accent said, "Goodness dear, if you don't marry him, I will." Ken and I laughed.

"Well, what do you say, honey?" Ken pressed. "Will you marry me?"

"Say yes," urged the British lady. "*Yes.*"

Ken squeezed my hands. "Well?"

"Yes."

"She said yes!" he shouted, and the people in the restaurant cheered.

Later, back at the flat, I was surprised to find my whole family waiting there with smiles and champagne.

"Oh my God! What are you guys doing here?"

"We all flew in together," Ken squealed, as I went around the room exchanging kisses and hugs. Aside from Ken, I hadn't seen any of my family or friends in six months. "I was hoping you'd say yes-- "

"And he flew us all in to celebrate," Danny squealed, crushing me to her. "First class."

Josh shook his head disbelievingly. "I can't believe my little sister's getting married."

I was having a hard time with that one myself. All the way home from the restaurant I wondered if my acceptance of Ken's proposal hadn't been a bit premature. Was I really doing the right thing?

"I'm twenty-seven," I said to Josh. "Hardly your *little* sister anymore."

"So, let's see the rock," he said.

"Josh!" Jenna admonished, but she was grinning. It was so good to see her again. I hadn't missed anyone more.

"I'm so glad you're getting married dear," my mother said. She fixed me with a penetrating gaze and I knew what was coming. "The past is dead now. You can forget the things you've done-- " Amber. We all knew she was talking about Amber. "And move forward with your handsome husband-to-be."

Ken *was* handsome, I'd give her that much. With his big adoring eyes and sandy brown hair I couldn't help but imagine the beautiful children we'd make.

Children? Was I honestly thinking of children? The thought had never occurred to me before.

Ken squeezed me in an embrace. "So what kind of a wedding will it be, sweetheart?" He always gave me my way, his biggest mistake. "A garden wedding like Josh and Jenna's? Though I wasn't there for that."

Thank God.

"A church? Or maybe you'd prefer if we just run off to Vegas and get it done by an overweight Elvis impersonator."

I laughed into his arm.

"Certainly not," my mother said. She never did know a joke when she heard one. My father remained silent. It seemed everyone was smiling now but me.

Chapter 21

"What's this?" I asked Cynthia, picking up the brown wrapped package that sat on my desk. Cynthia had been my assistant since my arrival in London, and if all went well with immigration, I planned on bringing her home with me. She'd make a great addition to the main office staff. Twenty-four years old and quite bubbly for a Brit.

Cynthia checked her clipboard and removed a yellow sign in sheet. "The package came this morning. Overnight delivery from--" she checked the name on the clipboard. "Amber Reed."

My heart caught in my throat. I hadn't seen or heard from Amber since the wedding.

I kept a copy of *Butterflies* on my bookshelf in the flat upstairs as a reminder of the pain I was capable of causing. I vowed to never hurt anyone like that again.

"Aren't you going to open it?" Cynthia asked.

Slowly, I removed the plain brown wrap. Another book. Oh God, I thought, had she done it again? Filled another book with her loathing of me?

"*Gemstones & Fire,*" Cynthia read over my shoulder. "What does it mean?"

I shook my head. "I don't know yet." I turned to the first page and a feeling of dread settled in my stomach.

"Hey, it's dedicated to you." My eyes followed Cynthia's pointed finger. "*For Meagan,*" she read, *"Fire purifies, forgiveness heals. Thanks for the journey.*" Cynthia nodded. "Nice. I wish someone would dedicate a book to me."

I sat at my desk. "Hurt someone badly enough and they might."

"Pardon?"

"Nothing. Can you check your rolodex for Ms. Reed's address, please?" I knew the street but I couldn't remember the building number.

"No problem." Cynthia fluffed her hair and strode from the room.

Forgiveness heals. Did that mean Amber had forgiven me for the pain I'd caused her? Scanning the book, I assumed she must have. The poems were about embarking on a new path and only one of them related to me. A beautiful saga in which the butterfly from the last book emerges from her hiding place and carries the gemstone up to the sun where they are scorched by the flaming star, then fall to the earth, seemingly dead. The butterfly lands on one end of the earth and the gemstone on the other. As the tale progresses, the butterfly comes back to life but her wings have changed color and she flutters around her new world in search of happiness. The gemstone, left in a dirt the reader would think is her grave, shines so brightly she is spotted by a pretty young maiden who picks her up, dusts her off, and makes a pendant of her that she wears near her heart. The gemstone has found a home. The butterfly's fate is undecided. The saga was a metaphor for our lives; that much was not lost on me.

The intercom beside me buzzed and Cynthia's bubbly voice filled the room. "I've got that address for you, Meagan, and your sister-in-law is holding on line two."

"Thank you." I grabbed the black plastic receiver and pressed the flashing red button marked 2. "Hey, Jenna. Why are you calling? I'll be home in a couple of weeks."

"I had to know," came the response.

"Know what?"

"Don't play dumb. What you thought of the book? You did get it, didn't you?"

"I'm looking at it right now."

"And?"

"You're nosy."

"Nope. I was nosy before I married your brother, now I'm just family." She giggled. "So what do you think? Pretty good, huh? I think it's going to blow *Butterflies* right out of the water. This one's much better. Less antagonistic, wouldn't you agree?" Another giggle. "And that dedication-- you must have been stunned. I wish I could have seen your face."

"Yes, it certainly is something," I agreed. "My assistant is handing me Amber's address as we speak. Hang on." I pulled the phone away from my ear. "Thanks, Cynthia."

"Would you like me to send out the usual thank you letter?"

"No, I'll take care of this one myself."

Cynthia left the room.

"You're writing her a letter?" Jenna asked, when I came back on the line. "What are you going to say? I didn't tell her about the engagement."

I reached for the *Natural Beauty* stationary in my top drawer. Pastel paper with the magazine logo at the top, a pretty pink flower with the letters NB woven through its vines.

"It's okay, Jenna," I said. "I'll explain it in the letter. It won't be easy but Amber has opened a line of communication between us by sending me this book and I plan on using it."

"Good," Jenna said. "Amber comes to the house a lot so if you guys could get to a point where you can at least handle being in the same place that would be great. It would be even better if you could become friends."

I stared at the blank computer screen before me, debating whether or not to use it. No, handwritten was better.

"Friends," I repeated. "I think I'd like that."

"So would she."

"Jenna?"

"Mm-hmm?"

I swallowed. "I'm getting married in three weeks."

She giggled. "I know that, silly. I'm you maid of honor, remember?"

I drew a large figure eight in the center of the paper, thinking. "The thing is, I'm really scared. Ever since you guys flew back I've been out here on my own and I'm thinking, what if I only said yes to Ken because I'm a million miles from home and I feel safe here? I love Ken. He knows the situation with Amber and he accepts it, but honestly, how fair is that to him? I'm also afraid that the minute I come home this peaceful little bubble I've been living in is gonna burst and it's going to be chaos. It feels like a premonition or something. What do you think?"

Jenna sighed. "I think you'll marry Ken no matter what I say. Don't get me wrong, Ken's a great guy-- "

"But you don't think I should marry him."

"I didn't say that either."

"You didn't have to, Jenna. There are four people in this world who know me well: you, Ken, Amber, and Seamus. You and Seamus are just the only ones I've never fucked."

"Meagan!"

"No, listen. The fact that I've never slept with you is what makes your opinion so important. You have no stake in it, so to speak. Seamus doesn't know anything yet. I know you think I shouldn't marry Ken. Amber would certainly think it. Ken thinks this could be a whole new life for us and I want to believe him. Do you see what I'm saying? That's two votes for yes and two for no, and that scares the hell out of me."

"Well this is how I see it," Jenna said. "Amber is seeing someone now who I think makes her happy. I know she doesn't love her the way she loved you, but then you are in the same predicament aren't you? Your family wants you to get married; it's pretty much all your mother talks about. You and Ken love each other, and as for me, well you know I'll back you up whatever you decide."

"So basically you have no advice."

She laughed. "Not a lick. Sorry, but this one's for you to decide all on your own. Though we both know what you'll do, don't we?"

"Yes, I suppose we do. See you in two weeks, Jenna."

Jenna and I hung up and I started to write. I wrote three pages, scratching my truth along the blank paper until I had written every bit of what I felt and exhausted myself with words. I wrote I would always love her, I was sorry for the pain I'd caused, I'd forgiven her for the book, and I was glad she found someone who made her happy. I told her about the engagement and how Ken knew everything about our history together and about what a good person he was. "*You'd like him, Amber*," I wrote, "*and hopefully I'll be able to like the person you're now with.*"

I wrote that I was on my way home and we would probably run into each other soon enough, so I hoped we could become friends. I didn't want to run anymore, and I ended the letter with nothing more intimate than *Sincerely, Meagan*. I had written enough, maybe more than I should have, or maybe it didn't really matter because nothing could change the past.

We were moving on.

Chapter 22

Airports were always a scene, the worst part of flying. People were constantly pushing and shoving and racing through the terminals, knocking each other over with their luggage as they ran to catch a flight for which they refused to be even five minutes early. Then there were the teary goodbyes, the small groups of people huddled together blocking the walkways as they cried their proclamations to write every week and call once a month.

Arrivals were no better than departures. Again you had to press your way through the small bands of people crowding the terminal. Only these people would be smiling and asserting how much they had missed the person who had finally "come home." I hated welcome committees. Especially those comprised of a group of family members the person probably fled the country to escape in the first place.

My eyes scanned the area for Ken, who had insisted on meeting me at the gate when I told him on the phone I would take a taxi and see him almost as quickly.

"Not good enough." he'd said. "I'll be there."

I'd relented and now felt strangely out of place in the crowded terminal, searching for *my* welcome committee, a solitary man.

A row of chauffeurs stood by the window holding up signs with names on them. *Johnson, Roberts, Delgado*. Then I spotted him. There at the end of the row stood my silly husband-to-be, wearing a black sports jacket, a chauffeur's cap tilted on the side of his head like a beret, and holding up a cardboard sign that said *Summers*, with a backward "s" and an upside-down "e". I burst out laughing and threw myself in his arms.

"You're crazy."

"To match my bride," he said, squeezing me to his chest

and kissing my neck. "I can't believe you're actually here. Are you glad to be home, honey?"

"Yes," I lied. The truth was I was scared to death. I had been a different person in England and dreaded the idea of possibly going back to who I once was.

Burying my face in his jacket, I lost myself to the safety of his embrace. "I'm so glad you're the only one here, Ken," I said, breathing in the inviting odor of his cologne. *Obsession for Men.* It was sexy and safe. "I don't think I could have dealt with the whole family crowding around me the minute I got off the plane. I know they mean well". I shook my head. Sometimes I felt suffocated by their love.

Ken pressed me closer. "Your mother wanted to bring the whole gang, but I asked her if she wouldn't mind letting us have this moment."

"That was a good way of putting it," I said, smiling. My mother was a sucker for romance.

Ken hoisted my bags onto his shoulder. "Geez, you travel light."

I laughed. "Are you kidding me? Those are just the necessities. The rest is being packed and shipped over next week. Prepare yourself for an onslaught of boxes."

We'd decided on the phone that I would continue to sublet my apartment to Danielle, since she loved it so much, and upon my arrival I'd move into Ken's spacious uptown apartment while we searched for a house.

Ken guided me through the airport. "There's a welcome home dinner at your parents' tonight".

I groaned.

"You have to attend, sweetheart. It will just be family. No big deal. But tomorrow," he grinned, "tomorrow I have a special surprise for you. I can't wait to show you; you'll be so excited."

I squeezed his hand. "I'm excited enough just being with you again. I loved London but every time you left I missed you terribly."

"Really, Meagan?"

"You sound surprised. Why wouldn't I miss the man I love?"

"I missed you too, though the fact that you agreed to marry me helped."

My stomach gave a nervous flutter. "Married. I guess that means I'll have to grow up, huh?"

"Don't you dare," he said. "I love you just the way you are --crazy."

"Ha ha."

Dinner at my parents' house consisted of the usual crew. Danielle and her boyfriend Mark, Josh, Jenna, Ken and me.

"This family keeps getting bigger," Mom gushed, pulling Ken into a hug after releasing me from an extended bone-crusher.

Jenna was sitting on the carpeted stairs in the foyer by the front door. "Excuse me if I don't get up." Her face looked strained.

I rushed over to her and Josh patted her hand. "The last trimester has been a bit of a bitch," he said, and Jenna frowned at his choice of word. Same old Jenna.

"Are you okay?" I asked, pressing my palm to her forehead. I didn't know what I was checking for, only that people always did that when someone was sick. Fever, I thought. Checking for a fever.

Laughing, she pulled me into a hug. "I'm fine. I'm *huge*, but fine."

Josh hadn't lost that adoring look in his eye. "You're beautiful, honey," he said. He winked up at me. "The doctor said she could go into labor any day now."

"But you're only eight months along."

Ken placed a comforting hand on my shoulder. "It's okay, sweetie. Believe me this happens all the time."

"It's true," Jenna said, nodding. "The doctor said everything looks good. We just might get our little gift a bit early."

"So you're okay?" I questioned.

Jenna giggled. "Why worry? I've got you here now to do that for me."

The others joined in her laughter. The fact that I was a chronic worrier was a real source of amusement to the people who knew me.

"How's that dinner coming, Joan?" Dad asked, rubbing his hands together.

"I think that's our cue to go in the dining room," Mom said.

Dinner was followed by drinks in the living room, where I was hit with a barrage of questions I was growing far too tired to answer. After an hour, Ken rescued me by saying, "I hate to break up the party early but I have a surprise for Meagan in the morning, one I'm fairly certain she'll want to get up for."

      I smiled up at him. Ken always knew when I'd had enough. That was the wonder of my fiancé; no matter what, he was determined to be my hero. How could I not love a man like that?

Chapter 23

Sirens screamed in my head. Ken rushed into the bedroom and slammed his palm against the top of the ancient alarm clock he refused to replace with a clock/radio. So much nicer to wake up to music, I thought.

"Sorry, sweetie," he said.

I smelled the pleasing aroma of freshly brewed coffee and struggled to open my eyes. "What time is it?"

"Ten. I thought I'd let you sleep in a bit. Would you like something to eat before we go?"

"Go where?"

"The surprise, remember?"

"Oh, right." Rolling over, I reached across the bed and urged him down beside me. The sheets fell away, exposing my naked breasts.

"I love that you've taken to sleeping naked," Ken said, nuzzling my throat.

"Thank my suffocating London flat for that."

"I will." He stopped what he was doing and moved to pull me off the bed.

"Hey."

"Come on, get up," he said, tugging on my arms.

"No. You get in."

"But I want to show you."

"Show me something else first."

Grinning, he quickly stripped off his clothes, revealing a tone but not overly-muscular body. "You don't have to tell me twice," he said, and rolled me on top of him, fitting my body to his.

He was an amiable bedmate. He wasn't wild and dirty like Basil had been, or even vocal and seductive like Amber, but he was always affectionate, always focused on the moment and losing himself to it. He had a way of making sex fun, like the goal was to be playful and enjoy the experience rather than just to reach orgasm. When he came he laughed and that always amused me. It made me think of a teenage boy who couldn't believe he had just gotten laid.

Ken was grinning now, a sure sign that we were reaching the end of our copulatory experience, and I ticked off the seconds in my head. One, two, three, laughter. I fell against his chest and his arms wrapped lovingly around the small of my back.

"Okay," I announced, jumping to my feet and feeling filled with a new energy. Sex always gave me a jolt. "Let's go check out that surprise."

"Hey," Ken laughed. "You'd just leave me here like this? Post-coital nothing?"

"I thought men didn't care about that," I teased.

"This one does. Get back here." He pulled me back on the bed and crushed me to his chest. "That's better."

"Ken?"

"Mm-hmm?"

"I want my surprise."

"Right now?"

"Right now."

"All right, go get dressed and I'll grab the blindfold."

"Blindfold, huh? Kinky."

He laughed. "I love your one-track mind."

One hour later he pulled his shiny BMW to a stop in front of a place I couldn't see and walked around the car to open my door. Guided me onto the sidewalk.

"Ready?" he asked, when I strained against the blindfold, trying to see through it.

"Ready."

He removed the material from my eyes and before me stood the most beautiful white California style house with a sold sticker adhered to the "For Sale" sign in the large front yard.

"It's incredible," I gushed, marveling at the terra-cotta front path that led up to the door and the sloped roof with the rounded peaks that could only mean cathedral ceilings and skylights inside. I couldn't help but wonder what this suburban palace would cost us. Once inside, I decided I didn't care-- I had to live in this house.

"Ken," I said. As we walked through the empty rooms I

imagined them filled with white furniture and beautifully colored tapestries on the walls. "It's what I always imagined my house would one day be."

"I know," Ken said, grinning. "Complete with four bedrooms, two bathrooms, a library, a kitchen the size of a small gymnasium for all the cooking you don't do," he joked. "A sauna-"

"A sauna?"

"Yep. Plus--" He led me to the kitchen window facing the backyard. "Look."

"Oh my God! Is that--?"

"The beginnings of the most beautiful Japanese garden you've ever seen. The landscapers will have it done by the start of summer. I can't help but have images of Jenna coming over to meditate in it."

I laughed. "She probably will. But look at the gazebo and the little wooden walkway. I can just picture all the flowers and plants surrounding it like a little jungle. Plus there is that whole cleared out area to the right that would be perfect for a playhouse and swing set." My mind was wandering to children again and I stopped speaking. Why did that thought keep coming up? As far as I knew I hadn't a maternal bone in my body.

"And a dog house, Meagan," Ken said. "You know the kids will want a Fido."

"A Fido!" He could always make me laugh with the strange things he said.

"So, what do you think? Could you make this home?"

"Could I? I say we move in tomorrow, furniture or not."

"After the wedding," he said, kissing my forehead. "We can't start our new home without first starting our new life."

He could be quite superstitious for a doctor.

Chapter 24

"Jenna!"

Two days in town and I burst through her front door like I owned the place.

"Where are you?" I called, barely able to conceal the excitement in my voice. Ken had dropped me off at home to retrieve "my" car, his black jeep, before leaving for the office.

"In case you want to show Jenna," he'd said, handing me the keys to the new house with a knowing wink.

Josh was at work but Jenna had given up her job at the holistic healing center. She still wrote her column for *Natural Beauty*, as writing the column allowed her to work from home, and I now raced through the rooms of the lovely Victorian she and my brother shared in search of the one person who would join in my fervor without question. Jenna loved a happy occasion more than anyone. By the same token, she hated confrontation more than anyone too.

I checked the living room, the dining room, the downstairs bathroom. No sign of life.

"Jenna!"

I barged into the kitchen, sure I'd find her there, making the cinnamon-and-apple tea I could smell steeping on the stove. Empty. Where could she be, I wondered, noting the three large cups on the counter with varying amounts of amber liquid inside. There had been an unfamiliar sports car in the driveway and I thought perhaps she had company, maybe out in the greenhouse in the backyard. I peered out the screen door. No one.

"What the hell?" I muttered.

There was a shuffling sound behind me and a familiar voice said, "Hello, Meagan." My heart stopped. It was the same lilting tone I heard call my name a million times in my head. My breath drew up short as I turned to face the one person who could make me awkward and unsure of my grasp on life with nothing more than a raised eyebrow.

"Amber. I didn't know you were here."

My eyes took her in with one glance. She looked as incredible as always. The look only she could pull off. Faded jeans with a rip in one knee. Black Doc Martens. Long, thin body topped with the blond hair that had grown a few inches since I'd seen her last but still fell seductively into her left eyelashes. And the eyes. Those knowing emerald eyes that haunted me still in my dreams. She stood by the stove. Neither of us moved.

"Jenna said you were back."

I nodded. "Yesterday."

Leaning forward on the counter, she looked out the window above the sink. "I got your letter."

I fiddled with the zipper on my jacket. "Thank you for the book."

After what I'd written, the cordial way we addressed each other now seemed insane. I brushed a strand of hair behind my ear and Amber frowned at my hand.

"Nice ring," she said.

I gave a little jump and glanced down at my engagement ring. The large diamond sparkled in the sunlight that streamed through the window, a glaring insult to the one who stood before me and the things I'd written her.

Managing a quick *thank you*, I shoved my hands in my jacket pockets. Glanced around the kitchen as if deeply admiring its down-home atmosphere. We avoided looking at each other.

"This is silly, Meagan," Amber said, after precious seconds of uncomfortable silence that felt like hours. She crossed the room, closing the distance between us and I moved away from the door, meeting her halfway.

"You're right," I said, hugging her. "We know each other far too well to stand here acting like strangers." I kissed her cheek, ignoring the spark that was obviously still between us, and squeezed her a little tighter. "It's really good to see you. I'm hoping we can be friends."

She squeezed back and returned my kiss with a chaste one of her own. "Me too."

I'd missed her so much it was an effort to break our

embrace and I hated that after all this time she could still have that effect on me. If there was going to be a friendship between us it wasn't going to be an easy one.

Moving away from her, I grabbed a cup from the wooden tree at the back of the counter.

"Where's Jenna?" I asked, pouring myself a cup of the delicious tea I had been deprived of for so many months. I tilted the kettle at Amber and she shook her head but didn't answer my question. "Is she out or something?"

Amber looked away. "She's up in the nursery with Gwynne."

"Gwynne?"

"My…umm…Gwynne."

"Oh." I felt a stab of jealousy twist in my heart. I wasn't supposed to feel that; I was engaged. Calmly, I reached for a cinnamon stick from the cup on the counter and dropped it in my tea. Stirred.

"Meagan, I --"

I shook my head. "Don't explain, Amber. There's no need for it. We've both moved on and if Gwynne is here, well, then I guess she's here. I'm sure she's very nice."

"Nice," Amber repeated. She threw back her head and let out a throaty chuckle that caught me off guard. "I don't know if that's exactly the adjective for Gwynne but--"

I shrugged. "She makes you happy."

Amber leaned back against the counter and smiled at me. "You know, I'm not sure you've ever let me finish a sentence in the whole time I've known you."

"I'm sorry, Amber." I said, my eyes casting a nervous glance at the empty doorway leading in from the dining room. "It's just, if we're going to have *the talk* I'd rather not do it like this."

Jenna came into the kitchen followed by a tall raven-haired woman. The woman had cold blue eyes, the color of a deep ocean, and a pretty porcelain face that cracked into a sneer when she saw me. Gwynne. She stared me down. Knew full well who I was.

"What talk?" she said, fixing her eyes on me like I was an object to loathe.

I walked up to her and extended my hand. "You must be Gwynne."

She forced herself to take it and crushed my fingers. "Yes."

I didn't flinch but I knew this wasn't going to be easy. The woman hated me on sight and I couldn't imagine the dedication in Amber's book helped any.

Gwynne hopped onto the counter and pulled Amber to stand between her legs. Her eyes never left my face as she leaned down to possessively wrap her arms around Amber's waist. Amber looked at her feet and I looked at Jenna, the discomfort in the room palpable. Jenna tried to cut through it.

"This is Meagan," she said, leaning her head on my shoulder.

"I gathered as much."

"She just got back from London."

"I know." Gwynne's head bobbed up and down impatiently.

Our eyes locked, a mutual dislike slicing through the air between us, and she kissed the top of Amber's head, daring me with her icy stare to do something about it. I didn't blink.

"Why did you come back?" she asked rudely.

Amber maneuvered herself away from Gwynne and went to the stove to pour a cup of tea. It was a move calculated for my benefit and I felt my confidence come flooding back. Amber was giving it back to me and she was doing it on purpose. I thought we would always look out for each other like this.

Smiling, I sat on the counter opposite Gwynne and matched her arrogant pose. Jenna moved beside me and leaned against my leg protectively. Amber and Jenna were both protecting me, in their ways, but I wasn't afraid of Gwynne. She was a lightweight compared to the people I dealt with professionally.

"London was a temporary thing," I said easily. I sipped my tea and refused to let Gwynne rattle me. "I was sent to make sure the magazine I worked for became an international success. It did, so now I'm back. I'm also getting married in a few weeks --" I thought that would shut her up, "-- and I'm considering an offer to co-found a publishing company with my current employer."

"You and Ted are starting your own publishing company?" Amber was impressed.

"Possibly. I'm thinking it over. Most likely I'll do it."

"What about the magazine?" Jenna asked, removing a box

of cookies from the cupboard above the sink.

"We'll still publish it. We're also looking at another we'd like to buy called, *The Watcher*. It's a tabloid that pulls in some good money."

Jenna grinned at me. "You're filthy rich, aren't you Meagan? You live like anyone else, but you were making serious money back when you were playing the stock market. And you hid it, didn't you?"

I stole one of her cookies and laughed. "Well, I haven't amassed your family's fortune. And I didn't hide it; I just didn't have any reason to go around spending it all."

"So you are rich?"

"I'm --healthily independent."

Amber laughed and Gwynne scowled.

"Anyway, we're looking at a few magazines, but we'll do other things as well."

"Books?" Amber asked. Gwynne shot her a look.

"That's the plan," I said, breaking my cookie in half. "Ted's convinced the two of us together can make even a giant like Hector obsolete. I'm not so sure about *that,* but I'm always up for a challenge." I thought of the day we broke up. "In business, I mean."

"You'll do it," Amber said, encouragingly. Gwynne pulled her back into place between her legs but Amber was unaffected. "Is that why you sounded so excited when you first came in?"

I thought of the gorgeous new house I had come to tell Jenna about and shook my head. Amber caught my reluctance and didn't press me.

"Why then?" Jenna asked, opening the lid on a jar of peanut butter and dunking an Oreo inside. "What were you excited about?" She plucked the odd mixture between her lips.

"It's nothing."

Amber stared into her tea. She knew I was trying to protect her from something.

"Meagan," Jenna urged. "Tell me."

I looked at Amber then up at Gwynne, who was sneering at me like she knew this was something she was going to love hearing.

"I have a house," I said, quietly, trying to ease the blow I knew Amber would have to take.

"You're in town one day and you bought a house?" Gwynne made sure her tone was loud and incredulous.

I looked away because I didn't want to see Amber's face when I said, "Not me."

"*Ken bought you a house?*" Jenna squealed.

Amber's eyes never left the tan liquid in the cup before her. "What kind of a house?" she asked.

I swallowed the guilt that filled my mouth. "A California-style split-level."

Jenna choked on her cookie. "With cathedral ceilings and a Japanese garden in the back?" I gave a slight nod. "Oh my Goddess! He bought you your dream house."

Amber looked up at me but I remained silent.

"Ever since I've known her she's wanted a house like that," Jenna went on. She clapped her hands excitedly. "Take us there."

"Jenna, I don't think--"

"Yeah," Gwynne chimed in, "I'd love to see it."

Before I could question why, Amber read my thoughts and said, "Gwynne's an interior decorator. That's what they were doing in the nursery."

"Oh."

"Why don't you and Jenna go?" she suggested. "Gwynne and I can wait here."

"Oh come on," Gwynne pressed. "I wanna see. Maybe I can be of help somehow."

I wasn't buying this sudden urge to be friendly. Gwynne's expression told me she wanted to keep everyone on edge. Amber and I exchanged a look and I shrugged. Gwynne was her problem.

"Are we going?" Jenna asked, jamming another peanut butter dipped cookie between her lips. She made pigging out look cute.

My eyes glanced around the kitchen, trying to buy time, then landed squarely on a white pamphlet beside the microwave with a big ink cross on the top. The pamphlet piqued my curiosity. I picked it up.

"Jenna, what's this?"

She looked nervous, suddenly, and swallowed her cookie like it was a large lump of cement.

"That's...umm...that's a service schedule from the

cathedral you're getting married in."

"*Cathedral?*" My mind forgot all about Amber while my brain digested this startling revelation. "What are you talking about? I'm getting married in that little chapel in the woods off highway eight."

"No," she said nervously.

"What do you mean *no*?"

She sighed. "I mean your mother cancelled the chapel. She changed the ceremony so that it will be held in St. Patrick's cathedral and presided over by Father O'Ryan; the priest who baptized you."

"*Baptized me*?" I nearly fell over. "Twenty-seven years ago? She dug up some tired old priest I haven't seen in twenty-seven years? Is she crazy? We can't get married in a church. Ken isn't Catholic."

"What is he?"

"WASP or something. I don't know."

"*You don't know?*"

"I'm not exactly religious, Jenna; that's why we selected a non-denominational minister. And don't change the subject. Why wasn't I told about this? Last night at dinner, everyone was there, and *no one* thought to tell us our fucking wedding has been changed?"

Jenna cleared her throat. "There's sort of more."

My eyes narrowed. "What more?"

"Flowers."

"What about them?"

"Your mother cancelled the daffodils and orchids and switched to roses because she thought they were more appropriate."

"More--?" I was stunned. I couldn't believe what I was hearing. Gwynne and Amber both remained silent, watching the anger cloud my face.

"And just when were you planning on telling me? When I strolled into a goddamn cathedral surrounded by roses? I hate roses. They're so fucking generic. Jenna, how could you allow this to happen?"

"*Allow it?* You know your mother; no one tells her what to do. Maybe you could, but you weren't around."

"And I suppose there aren't any phones in London either.

Jesus Christ. There are twelve of us. Immediate family, that's it. Twelve goddamn people in a church big enough to hold hundreds. A cathedral! Didn't I say I wanted things simple? This isn't simple Jenna. This is ridiculous."

"I know," she said, quietly.

I paced the kitchen. "Now I have to fix this. The wedding is in two weeks and I have to change it *today*."

I was tempted to call the whole thing off but told myself to calm down. I could handle this. I handled bigger problems than this every day. I scratched the back of my neck, thinking.

"All right," I said calmly. "I presume the minister has been canceled as well." Jenna gave a sympathetic nod and I reached for my purse. Pulled out my little blue book, searched the pages, and reached for the phone. "Fortunately, I happen to know a judge."

"Shouldn't you discuss this with Ken first?"

"No, I'll fix it first. How do you think he'd feel if he knew what my mother has done? He knows we can't get married in a Catholic ceremony. We don't even want to. He'd see it exactly as it looks: That my mother just cancelled our freaking wedding. The sick thing is, she wants it more than anyone."

I punched in the first three numbers.

"Meagan, are you honestly saying you have a judge in your pocket?"

"In my pocket, Jenna?" That got her a queer look. "Who am I, John Gotti? I have a *friend* who's a judge. He used to be one of the magazine's lawyers. Years ago."

The three women watched in awe as I finished dialing the number, spoke briefly to Judge Roberts, and explained the situation. After a quick check in his date book he came back on the line and agreed to perform the service. I thanked him and hung up.

"Problem one taken care of."

"You got the judge to agree?" Gwynne asked.

I nodded. "Okay, Jenna, I need your phone numbers. The chapel, the florist, and anything else my mother might have screwed up in her haste to kick me down the aisle."

Jenna reached into a drawer by the fridge and produced a small file with an elastic wrapped around it. I tore it open and sifted through the pages until I found the number for the chapel in the woods. Called and rebooked. Problem two taken care of in less than five minutes.

The third problem was the biggest. The florist was preparing the roses that very minute and did not have orchids in stock.

"Cancel the roses," I told him. "You have daffodils?"

"We've already begun the process of cutting and arranging so you'll have to pay for both."

I glared at Jenna. Nice maid of honor. "Yes, I will pay for both."

"What shall we do with the roses?"

"I don't care. Drop them off at a nursing home or something. Just don't have them sent to that chapel. Where can I get orchids?"

"You can't."

"I can and I will." I paced the kitchen, pressing the cordless phone to my ear and passing Gwynne and Amber as I moved back and forth. "My future husband requested only one thing for this wedding, purple orchids, and *you're* going to figure out how I'm going to get those. Call another florist. Fly them in from Brazil for all I care --just get them."

"You want me to *fly* them in?"

"Is it possible?"

"Well, yes, I suppose it is."

"Then do it. And in the future, you'll take your orders from me and me alone. If anyone calls you to change anything without my authorization and you do it, you can bet your ass you won't be getting a cent."

"We're very sorry Miss Summers."

"It's okay. Just get me the orchids." I hung up. As far as I was concerned the flowers were the most important part of the whole event, especially the ones Ken had requested. He had only one wish for his wedding day and he was going to get it.

I sat the phone on the table. "I've taken care of everything now, right Jenna?"

"Yes."

"No more surprises?"

"None that I know of."

"That doesn't comfort me."

"Are you really having orchids flown in from Brazil?"

I picked up the phone again. "Or wherever they come

from."

"You're intense, Meagan," Amber said. She looked like she'd be proud of me if I was using my intensity for anything other than this. "You're efficiency is incredible."

Suddenly I couldn't look at her. Too much guilt over having just planned my entire wedding in front of her face. "Thank you."

"Who are you calling now?" Jenna asked.

"Guess." I dialed the familiar number and waited for my mother to answer. Three rings later she did and I didn't bother with pleasantries.

"Who the hell do you think you are changing everything behind my back?" I didn't wait for her to respond. "I don't care what kind of fantasy wedding you had planned for me; it's not gonna happen. I've changed it all back, except now we're having a judge instead of a minister, and it's gonna cost us a goddamn fortune in flowers because you had to screw around with things that are none of your business. You're lucky I don't make you pay for them. And if you try one more stunt I'll back right out of this wedding. Do you hear me? I won't get married at *all!* I am not Josh and I am not Danielle, so don't fuck with me because I won't put up with it. I hope I'm making myself very clear because the next little stunt is the one that sends me back to London. Goodbye."

I hung up before she had uttered one word after *hello.* Pushed my fingers through my hair and smiled. "I think that's everything."

Jenna laughed. "Your mother must be having a heart attack over there after the way you just talked to her."

"I'm tired of being nice. I've been telling her to mind her own business since the day I moved in with Basil and she never does. This time she went too far. She had that coming and then some."

"Do you think that will stop her from butting her nose in your business in the future?"

I chuckled. "No." The stress had passed and I was back to me. "Speaking of Basil, I didn't tell you what happened last week."

"You saw Basil last week?" Jenna was surprised.

"Indeed I did. Ken met him too."

"No way! That must have been awkward."

"You have no idea. Ken was over for another two-day

stint. He was flying home Friday and this was--" I paused.
"Thursday. Yeah, because it was the day before he went back.
Anyway, we're up in the flat when Cynthia rings and she sounds all
excited. 'You're not gonna believe who's down here asking for
you,' she says. 'Noel Ford and Basil Waite.' Big deal, right?"

Gwynne choked on a cough. "Of *Dimestore Ganja?*" She
looked at Amber for verification and Amber gave a slight nod.

"Ex-boyfriend," I admitted. "So, anyway, Cynthia is
asking if she can send them up and Basil's in the background
saying, 'Tell her I wanna see her,' like I'm some freakin' groupie
just waiting around for his call."

Jenna sat at the table across from me. "I hear they're huge
in England."

I nodded. "Three number ones. I think only one song hit
the charts here."

"So, they came upstairs?"

I sipped my tea. "Yeah. Within minutes Basil's banging
on the door like there are bombs exploding on the other side of it,
saying, 'Come on, baby, open up,' and Ken's just looking at me
like, 'What's this?' right? Well, Basil and Noel stroll in, Ken takes
one look at them, and he's like a star-struck kid, which embarrasses
the hell out of me. He's shaking their hands and saying what an
honor it is to meet them, and Basil, being Basil, finds this highly
amusing.

"'You know Meagan?' Ken asks, awe-struck. I don't
know why but we'd never really discussed Basil."

"I can just imagine what Basil had to say in response to
that," Amber said.

"You know him too?" Gwynne demanded.

Amber shrugged. "We've met a few times."

My mind flashed back to that night in BeBe's and
inwardly I cringed. "Where was I?"

"Ken asking Basil if he knew you," Jenna reminded.

"Right. Well, you know what a mouth Basil can have. He
starts laughing his head off and says, 'Know her? Does bouncing
her on my dick for three years count?'"

"Oh my Goddess!" Jenna cried.

I nodded emphatically. "Noel bursts out laughing and
Ken's jaw drops to the floor. I don't know what to say so I come
out with, 'Basil, that's inappropriate,' which only makes him laugh

harder.

"'Inappropriate, Meagan?' he howls. 'Who are you, the Queen of England?'

He and Noel are having a great time with this and Ken is just standing there like a statue."

"What did you do?" Amber asked.

"I ask Basil why he's there but he doesn't answer me. He just tilts his head and looks at me like something about me confuses him. He's studying my face and my hair and my body, and I'm saying, 'Basil, why are you here?'

"'Is that your boyfriend?' he asks, pointing at Ken."

I turned to direct my conversation back to Jenna because this was where it was going to get a little sticky.

"What did Ken say?" Jenna asked.

"He gets kind of stiff-looking and says, 'I'm her fiancé.' Basil looks at me and I nod. He looks around the apartment.

'And you live *here?*'

Well, you've seen the flat; it's nothing to write home about."

"It's a hole, Meagan," Jenna said. "I can't believe you even stayed there."

"I was running a business. I wasn't exactly concerned with my living conditions."

Amber burst out laughing and I looked at her. "Sorry, but you're the last person I ever thought I'd hear say that."

I shrugged. "People change. Anyway, I told Basil it was just a temporary thing, but that didn't please him. He starts shaking his head and comes out with the ultimately bizarre, 'Your eyes, Meagan. What happened to your eyes?'

'What do you mean?' I ask. And Ken is getting really bitchy-looking. Basil moves closer and tilts up my chin. 'What the fuck, Meagan?' He says. 'What happened to your fucking eyes?'"

"They look okay to me," Jenna said.

"That's what I thought." I sipped my tea. "But Basil's saying my eyes are dead and the comment pisses Ken off. He says, 'Her eyes are just fine. That's my *medical* opinion.'

"Basil looks like Ken stabbed him through the heart. 'A doctor, Meagan?' he says.

Noel tells him to let it go. But Basil isn't ready to let it drop. 'No,' he barks. 'I want to know what happened to you.'"

"I don't understand," Jenna said.

"Neither did I. So I start talking to him in the most reasonable manner I can muster and for some reason it's making him more upset. He's telling me not to talk *that* way and I'm telling him I don't know what he means."

"I know what he means," Jenna offered, nodding.

"What?"

"That you talk differently now. Around Ken, anyway."

I shrugged. "Ken gets offended by profanity so I try to keep it to a minimum when I'm around him."

Amber's jaw tightened. I saw it from across the room and I knew what she was thinking. She was thinking I would change for Ken but not for her.

"Anyway," I continued, ignoring the fierce look. "Basil finally gets around to the purpose of his visit. He came by to offer the magazine an interview with the band, because he says he owes me, and to give me tickets and backstage passes to a concert at the Royal Albert that night."

Jenna was awed. "Did you go?"

"Mm-hmm." I reached for my purse. "But wait-- it gets better."

"How much better?"

"It wasn't just a Dimestore Ganja concert," I said, digging around inside my bag. I had made sure I'd gotten something for Jenna, and even for Amber, because the incident was too surreal not to share with them. "It was a benefit for AIDS or diabetes -- some disease. Basil gave four passes so I brought along Ken, a photographer, and a writer to get the story. The concert was being televised and it'll all be printed in next month's issue --which Cynthia is going to send copies of."

"What will be?" Amber asked.

"About the concert and the party afterward, which Basil got us into as his guests."

"You partied with rock stars?" Gwynne asked, jealously.

"Which ones?" Jenna interrupted.

I grinned. "I didn't think you'd believe me so I had to bring proof. Basil's band, obviously, Bryan Adams, Madonna… "

"You partied with *Madonna?*" Jenna shrieked.

"No, she didn't come to the party. But there were people there who didn't even perform at the concert. A couple of Spice

Girls, that Robbie *Whoever* guy --mostly British singers. And this is the topper: are you ready for it?"

"Meagan who?" Jenna was on the edge of her seat.

"Think Irish."

"Just tell me."

"The Corrs."

"Are you kidding me?" she squealed. "You're kidding me right?"

"What's so big about the Corrs?" Gwynne asked. "I've barely heard of them."

I couldn't help grinning. "But they're becoming known here, aren't they?"

"You did not meet the Corrs," Jenna said. "You're making that up."

"Who are you? Danielle?"

Amber was stunned. She stared at my face. "You really did, didn't you? You actually met them?"

"Yep. And I brought you guys gifts, too." I pulled two autographed CDs from my purse and handed them to Jenna and Amber.

Jenna stared at the CD insert. "This is too wild," she giggled. "Does this mean I'll meet Nicole Kidman?"

I laughed.

"What does that mean?" Gwynne asked. She eyeballed Amber's CD and she didn't look pleased.

Amber shrugged. "It was just some silly game. Thank you, Meagan." Her eyes had an unspoken question and I smirked.

"No problem."

"What did Ken think?"

"Ken wasn't there."

"He wasn't?" Jenna was surprised again.

I shook my head. "Early flight. He went back to the flat."

"And you stayed?"

"Damn right I stayed."

"Did you meet *all* of them?" Amber asked. I knew what she was getting at and couldn't resist the gag.

"Yes," I said, smiling. "I met Andrea. She's really good in bed too."

Amber's jaw dropped open and Jenna and I broke out laughing.

"I'm joking, Amber. Of course I'm joking! She was nice. They all were. My uncle Seamus would have shit."

"Did you tell her about the list thing?" Jenna asked.

"Are you insane? I'm sure I'm gonna say, 'Hey Andrea, you know what? A while back I told my friends I'd have sex with you.' Get real, Jenna."

Gwynne was not liking the conversation's direction. "That was the game? Who the three of you would have sex with?"

"That was the game," I said easily.

"Does Ken know?"

I laughed. "Jesus, Jenna. You should marry Ken. You're very concerned with what he does or does not know, aren't you? I told him when I got home. He thought it was funny."

"He would," Jenna said, giggling. She glanced down again at her CD. "So, what do they do --carry these around with them or something?"

I smirked. "You've become quite the smartass in my absence."

"Someone had to keep your torch lit."

"You're *so* funny. No, they don't carry them around. I picked up the CDs because I knew they'd be there and I looked like a freaking groupie too, but it was worth it just to see your face. *Basil* carries his CD around with him. He actually got jealous that I wasn't asking for *his* autograph so he whips out a CD and signs it for me. And you know the funniest part? I forgot it at the party."

"I don't get it," Jenna said.

"He brought it to my office the next day. Then he got mad when I started laughing and asked him if he was that desperate for a fan he'd hunt one down. I apologized and then he told me I could not marry Ken. That he *forbid* it."

"Get out." Jenna laughed. "Let me guess: Basil asked you to marry him."

I chuckled. "Do you think I walk around getting proposed to everyday?"

"Basil's still in love with you," she pointed out.

I waved my hand dismissively. "Naw, he's seeing some model or something who was waiting for him in LA. He left two days later but not before telling me I couldn't marry the 'Yuppie.' That he wasn't my type. We started fighting, of course, 'cause it's Basil and me, right? And before I knew it, we were having a screaming match in my office."

Jenna placed a plate of cookies on the table and Amber and Gwynne finally took a seat. They'd been standing around the stove for twenty minutes.

"What were you fighting about?" Jenna questioned, biting into a cookie.

"Ken, mostly. Basil was saying that I was some sort of new Meagan and I was marrying Ken to cling to conventionalism and he didn't like me much anymore. He called Ken a preppy nightmare and said eventually being with him would kill my spirit. I told him maybe I've just grown up enough to be able to spot a decent man instead of a walking hard-on. He stormed out and I'm pretty sure that's the last I'll be seeing of him."

Jenna placed another pot of water on the stove. "Why do you say that? Basil always pops up sooner or later."

"He won't. I was harder on him than I should have been. He was being a prick, but in Basil's way, it was his little act of heroism. He thought he was protecting me and he was trying to take care of me the way he did a few months back." I thought of the picnic on the living room floor and smiled. "Basil did something very sweet and out-of-character."

"In London?" Amber asked.

It wasn't easy looking at her while thinking of that day and I bowed my head. "No, I guess it was more than a few months back. I was having a hard time with something and he brought me a picnic to cheer me up."

"You only ate an apple," she said quietly.

My head snapped up in time to see Gwynne shoot her a look. "Excuse me?" How could she know that?

Her eyes darted away. "Sorry."

"Don't be sorry; just tell me what you mean."

"He called me," she admitted, staring at the table.

"When?"

"The day after."

The surprise was clearly on my face. "Did he tell you what we talked about?" I asked nervously.

"Not really. He just...well, you'd cut your hand and he wanted to tell me you were okay. He also mentioned something about you not liking that I was smoking again."

"Are you still?"

"No."

"And the apple?"

"He was worried."

I didn't care that Gwynne was watching me with hateful eyes. I had to have the details. "Because I lost it, right?"

"You were pretty scary," Jenna admitted.

I ignored her. "So, what did Basil say?"

"Just that he couldn't get you to eat and it freaked him out. You were so thin."

"I wasn't that thin."

"You were, Meagan," Jenna stressed.

"Whatever. And what did you tell Basil?"

"Honestly?"

I shrugged. "It's not like it matters now."

She nodded. "I told him you were a fucking bitch and I didn't care if you were anorexic."

That pissed me off. "For Christ's sake, I wasn't anorexic!"

"You asked," Gwynne defended.

"Yes." It was a quiet admittance of guilt and Amber threw up her arms.

"Here we fucking go," she bitched.

My eyebrows shot up. "What did I do?"

"The 'yes' shit."

"What about it?"

"I don't know. You just have this habit of saying 'yes' and it so goddamn infuriating. Someone says something to you and you respond with 'yes'. It's like a quiet acceptance of guilt or something. That night when we were out in the street after I slapped you in the Cauldron, all you kept saying was yes. I'm telling you I can't deal with what you've done and you're saying, 'Yes.'"

"Can we not get into that?"

I wanted to make this go away but Amber was angry. With one word I had somehow managed to drag up the pain for her and she struggled to maintain her composure. I could see the battle happening on her face and I knew eventually we were going to have it out. I just didn't want it to be then.

"It doesn't matter," she lied. "We should probably just talk about something else."

"How about your house?" Gwynne suggested. I got the

feeling she'd been waiting a long time to direct the conversation back to that. Jenna didn't catch the threat in her tone.

"Yeah," she agreed. "We got into all this other stuff and forgot about the house. Can we go see it now?"

I didn't know how to respond so I tried to stall. "Show me the nursery first."

Jenna and I climbed the stairs to the baby's room, leaving Gwynne and Amber in the kitchen to work out whether or not they were coming. Within minutes they were arguing.

"I don't want to go," I heard Amber say.

"You have to," Gwynne asserted. "You need to see with your own eyes that she too has moved on. She's getting married. He bought her her dream house, Amber. Once you see it, you'll be free of her. Don't you get that?"

"I've been free of her for almost a year, Gwynne." The words drew a coldness around my heart. The statement was the absolute truth but it still hurt to hear it. "I don't need to see her new house to know that we've both moved on. I just watched her plan her entire wedding twenty minutes ago. What greater proof is there?"

Jenna and I stood on the landing at the top of the stairs, knowing we shouldn't be listening but doing so nonetheless. We didn't have much of a choice, unless we spent the next half hour in the nursery.

"You see," I whispered, leaning against the sturdy mahogany banister. "What did I tell you? I'm home one full day and already chaos."

"You didn't start this, Meagan," Jenna said reasonably.

"Maybe not, but I'm still the reason behind it. What is it about me that brings out the worst in people? I didn't have that problem in England, you know? Everything here is so stressful. It's always one problem after another."

"Stop it."

"What?"

"I know you Meagan, you're thinking of running back to London right now."

"I'm not going back. I was just threatening my mother with that."

"Good. Because it's time you stopped running."

The angry voices below crept into my head and I sighed.

"I'm trying, Jenna. Honestly, I am."

"Listen to me," Gwynne hissed.

Jenna and I entered the kitchen unnoticed as Gwynne's hand clamped on Amber's forearm. The anger flash in Amber's eyes. They stood by the sink, quietly arguing.

"Let go of me Gwynne." Her teeth were clenched together. She moved to shake off Gwynne's snake hold but the grip tightened and I saw the pliable flesh on Amber's arm press up on either side of Gwynne's hand. She winced and it was more than I could take.

I crossed the room quickly. "What the hell do you think you're doing?"

Amber's eyes widened in disbelief, Gwynne whirled around to glare at me, and Jenna latched onto my wrist, stopping me in my tracks. I tried to yank my arm away but she was surprisingly strong for a pregnant woman.

"Jenna!"

"It's none of your business wedding girl," Gwynne barked. She was reminding me of who I was; a future wife. Telling me I had nothing to do with what did or did not happen to Amber. She was wrong. Amber would always be one of my concerns.

Jenna kept a firm grip on my wrist and I looked past Gwynne's fierce expression at Amber, who looked shocked that I would say anything at all.

"Are you okay?" I asked.

"She's fine," Gwynne said.

I shot her a look. "I didn't ask you. I asked *her.*"

"I'm fine, Meagan," Amber said like a dutiful little girl. This time it was she who couldn't meet my eyes.

Jenna let go of my wrist but shook her head at me, indicating I should let this drop. I couldn't. It simply wasn't my nature to let people get away with things. I also wondered if Amber was being abused by this woman. She pressed her hand over the spot Gwynne had grabbed and my mind flashed to an image of a victim hiding an injury. I frowned.

Jenna saw my expression and went to grab me again but I jumped away from her and went to Amber, remembering the scene in the gallery when Zeppo had grabbed me and the fierce way Amber had yelled at him. There was no way I could, in good conscience, let this go.

Our eyes locked and I took her hand. "May I see?" I asked softly.

Reluctantly, she pushed back her sleeve and Gwynne pounced.

"Get your fucking hands off her!" She shoved me.

My mouth fell open. The woman was clearly insane. I had never struck another person in anger in my life, but I felt a pressure in my head like the pulling of a rubber band seconds before it snapped. I shoved her back.

"Don't you ever fucking touch me."

Gwynne was unaffected by the warning. She staggered backward from the blow then came at me again while Amber's eyes darted back and forth like she was watching a particularly frightening tennis match and she didn't know which player to root for.

"Stop it!" Jenna jumped between us, pregnant stomach freezing everyone in place. She turned to face Gwynne while I inspected Amber's arm.

"Jesus, you're bleeding." I looked into her face and thought I would cry. Is this what I had left her to? To go out and find someone even worse than me?

"She's what?" Gwynne shrieked.

I ran a clean dish cloth under cold water and pressed it to the injury. "She's fucking bleeding. What did you do? Dig your nails right into her goddamn arm?"

"Meagan." Jenna pulled me away from Amber who was still having a hard time meeting my gaze. Gwynne took my place holding the cloth.

"I'm sorry, Amber", she said, tenderly rubbing her arm. "I didn't realize what I was doing."

Amber looked away and remained silent. Gwynne's words infuriated me more.

"You didn't *realize*?" I yelled. "Are you fucking crazy?"

"Shut up."

"Meagan, please," Jenna whispered. "Let them work this out for themselves."

I slapped my forehead. "Jenna, you saw her assault her."

Gwynne glared at me. "I didn't *assault* her."

"Really? What would you call it when you make someone bleed?"

"I said I didn't mean it."

"Oh, well that makes it all right then, doesn't it?"

"Will you shut the fuck up?"

Amber pressed her fingers to her temples. "Just stop it. Both of you. What is this solving?"

I stared at her. Jenna handed me my cup of tea and I placed it on the counter and walked back toward Amber.

"This woman is violent," I said quietly. "She hurt you."

Her eyes flashed a sudden anger. "And you never have?"

I blinked. "W-What?"

"It's a little late in the game to start protecting me now, Meagan."

I took a hurt step back. Couldn't believe how she had just turned on me. Thought a day that had started out so good now couldn't get any worse.

"Amber," Jenna said.

"What Jenna?" She threw the cloth in the sink and glared at me. "You've never hurt me, Meagan?"

Oh, I had. But she'd returned the favor tenfold. Now I had arranged my entire wedding right in front of her and we were back to square one.

"Why are you doing this?" I whispered. I knew why. The house, the phone calls to the chapel, the judge and the florist. All of these things said and done right in front of her face.

"Doing what? Speaking the truth?"

I looked at Gwynne who was gloating at me. At Jenna and her sympathetic face. Back at Amber who was staring at me like she hated me all over again. I couldn't take it. It was all too much for one day.

"Fuck this," I roared. "I certainly didn't come home for this shit." I walked away from Amber and yanked my purse off the table. Turned to Jenna. "I'm sorry, Jenna. Obviously none of us is mature enough to deal with this situation. I'll call you later, okay?"

I kissed her cheek and she nodded, knew this was best. I stalked toward the back door, passing Gwynne and Amber, who said, "That's right, Meagan; take up your usual habit of running away."

Gwynne snickered and I whirled around to face them. "What am I supposed to do? Stand here and let you insult me? You shouldn't forgive people in book dedications if you really don't mean it. That's *your* lie."

My hand twisted the door handle but the door refused to budge. I pushed on it. Rattled it back and forth. Looked up because it seemed to be stuck somewhere at the top and saw that it didn't want to pull away from the frame.

"What's wrong with this goddamn door?" I felt like I would burst into tears.

"It sticks," Jenna said, walking toward me. She gave the door a hard shove and it swung open. I started to step through it.

"Wait." Amber suddenly hopped off the counter.

Jenna smirked and Gwynne gave Amber a hard look. A warning look, which Amber ignored.

"Meagan, wait." She ran up to me and gently grabbed my wrist. I looked down at her hand and felt its heat like a shock to my bloodstream. "Just come back. I'm sorry, okay?"

"Amber!" Gwynne stalked toward the three of us and yanked on Amber's arm.

I felt my eyes grow wide. Protective anger filled my head once more and I fought the impulse to strike her.

"Are you *grabbing* her again?" My voice was a menacing hiss. "Are you fucking *grabbing her*?"

"You don't know how to mind your own business, do you?" Gwynne snapped. "She's not yours anymore to protect."

I shrugged. "Maybe not, but you won't ever touch her like that in front of me. Take the warning because it's your last."

"Yeah, I'm real scared, Twiggy."

I wasn't that thin anymore, just thinner than Gwynne, who was the personification of an hourglass. This decade's answer to Marilyn Monroe.

"You're like a fat Natalie Imbruglia, aren't you?" I sneered, thinking that if the Australian singer gained several pounds she'd look like Gwynne's twin. "I don't have to fight you to take you down, Gwynne. You don't know me or what I'm capable of, so I suggest you watch what you do with those hands because I *will* come after you. Bet on it."

"Okay," Amber said. "Let's not start this again." But when she looked at me I caught a glint of happiness in her eyes. My angry threat pleased her on some level.

Gwynne glared at me and I decided I wasn't finished making my point. I would show this woman exactly who I was.

"Do you have a phone book, Jenna?" I asked.

She brushed past me into the kitchen. "Sure," she said, pulling open a drawer.

"Good, I want to show you something."

Amber and Gwynne followed me back into the kitchen where I took the phone book from Jenna, placed it on the table, and flipped it open to the R's.

"See that?"

Jenna's eyes followed my pointed finger. "*Red Shoe Real Estate*. What does it mean?"

"It's me."

"Huh?"

"Remember the day I offered you the job at the magazine? You got on some kick about my ambition and said you knew I was doing something sneaky to Ted."

"I remember that," Amber interrupted. "You told her you weren't doing anything to Ted that he wouldn't thank you for later."

I grinned and nodded. "Red Shoe Real Estate is a dummy corporation I set up to buy the remaining sixteen percent of stock I needed to get controlling interest of the magazine."

Jenna gasped. "Meagan, that's criminal! How could you?"

"Well, I'm not in prison, am I? Red Shoe is no longer in business-- like it ever was-- but you know how I got the name? The woman beside me in the registrar's office was wearing ugly red shoes. I knew you'd think I was doing something ugly, so it just seemed fitting."

Jenna was disgusted. "Does Ted know?" she demanded. "Oh my Goddess! You totally screwed him over! He was your *mentor* and you stole his company!"

Gwynne's eyes were hard on my face. Amber just looked amused. She knew I'd never steal anything.

"Relax, Jenna," I said. "I did not steal his company. I just sort of --gave myself a promotion."

"You had no right."

"Oh shut up. You act like it was *your* company."

"I asked you if Ted knows."

"Why? Are you gonna run and tell him?" The thought amused me. "Yes, Ted knows. He found out when I was in London. It was the first three weeks and I was working the staff pretty hard. Eleven to thirteen hour shifts a day because I was weeding out the losers, seeing who could handle the pressure. I lost fourteen employees in the first two weeks and the ones who stayed got bonuses and raises and I eased the pressure. Then I went about hiring staff to replace the ones I'd lost and that's when Ted flew to London to confront me."

"I remember," Jenna said. She didn't sound so angry anymore. "I was turning in my column one day and Rick told me I better prepare for your return because Ted was probably gonna fire you."

"Fire me!" I laughed. "Rick always was such an exaggerator."

"So what happened?" Amber asked. Gwynne glowered at her.

I sipped my tea. "Well, it's kind of a long story so I'll try shortening it. Ted bursts into my office demanding to know what the hell I think I'm doing. He says he's getting complaints all over the place, that people are freaking out and saying I'm running London like a concentration camp. I told him I was weeding out the losers and he starts yelling about how he hand-picked that staff. 'And you did a shitty job of it too,' I told him. 'We agreed London was mine so back off.'

"He tells me, 'Not anymore,' and that really pisses me off. I start calling him a chickenshit and bitching about how I got us the investors and I was fucking running things.

"You're done, Meagan,' he says. 'I'm pulling you out. You're on some power trip and you're out of control. You're hiring people, firing people, handing out raises without my authorization—'

"He was pissing me off even more. Even without controlling interest we both knew I could do all of those things without checking every little detail with him. It was part of being in charge.

"'I don't need your authorization on a goddamn thing,' I told him.

"'Have you forgotten who owns this magazine?' He yells. I knew who owned it-- me."

Amber chuckled and Gwynne shot her another look.

"So he's pacing my office and he tells me I'm leaving London and going back on publicity where I obviously belong. 'No, Ted,' I said. '*You're* leaving London. You're tired. You don't have the balls for it anymore so why don't you just get your chickenshit ass back on the plane before *I* fire *you*.'"

"Jesus, Meagan," Amber said. "The things you do sometimes." But she was grinning.

"You're fucking insane," Gwynne barked.

I smirked. "That's what Ted said, too."

"He called you insane?" Jenna asked.

"Oh yeah. Told me I needed to get my fucked up head back in therapy before I snapped. He was screaming at me and that's when I very calmly whipped out my business registration. 'Look familiar, Ted?' I asked.

"Ted always keeps himself up-to-date on the stocks and his face turned five shades of red. For a minute I actually got scared because he looked like he was going to have a heart attack. 'I'm *Natural Beauty*'s whore, remember?' I told him."

Jenna frowned at my choice of word. "What does that mean?"

I laughed. "When we first got the investors, Ted was going on about how I'd won us the money because, as he put it, no man could resist my charms when I was on a roll. I told him he was making me sound like his little corporate whore and he said, no, I wasn't *his* whore, I was the magazine's whore."

"Maybe you're just a regular whore," Gwynne muttered.

Amber turned her head and I shot Gwynne a look. "You're pushing me, Mama Cass." I got some sort of twisted pleasure out of calling Gwynne fat.

"So then what happened?" Jenna interjected, stopping a scene between us that was about to erupt again.

I turned back to Jenna. "Ted lost it. He called me a backstabbing little bitch and was screaming about how I was going to prison. Something about dummy corporations and what would happen to a girl like me in prison. What the fuck did I care, right? He wasn't gonna do a goddamn thing."

"How could you possibly know that?" Jenna said.

I shrugged. "Because he needed me. Because if I wanted to I could run the magazine into the ground before he ever got his controlling interest back. I could pick up the phone right then and sell the 16% to an outside buyer and-- with a little constructive paper work-- still remain in control. The magazine was mine now and there wasn't a damn thing he could do about it."

"*This* is what you do to your friends?" Gwynne demanded.

"Yeah, so just imagine what I do to my enemies."

"You're sick."

"Are you gonna let me finish this?"

"Finish it," Jenna said.

"Well, Ted busted up my office a bit."

"No way!" Jenna's eyes widened in surprise. Ted was one of the most peaceful men on the planet and I couldn't help laughing at the memory.

"Yeah, he broke my computer, tore books off the shelves and whipped them at me."

"Weren't you scared?" Amber asked.

"Not really. Security came in and started grabbing him and that made me feel bad; I mean they were going to throw him out of his own office. So I told them to let him go, Ted calmed down, and I told him what I really wanted was a 50-50 partnership. He asked me why I would bother since I now had controlling interest and I told him the truth: That I never wanted it. That I'd give him the one percent and we'd be 50-50 all the way. Suddenly Ted looks around the destroyed office and bursts out laughing. 'That's all you wanted?" he says. "Why didn't you just tell me?'

"I didn't tell him because I knew his plan was to make me wait at least another five years and I just didn't have that kind of patience. Ted agreed to the partnership as long as I promised not to pull any more tricks. And once Europe did as well as it did you can bet your ass he was thanking me. I can't even show you Red Shoes' registration because he was so pleased he stuck it in the toe of a baby shoe, had the shoe bronzed, and gave it to me as a gift."

Jenna laughed. "So that's why you had that shoe on your desk the day I came down to your office with you."

"It's my good luck charm."

Gwynne was not impressed. "Was there a point to this long and boring tale?"

"You didn't find it?" I asked. "The point is I *always* do what it takes."

I glanced at Jenna and saw a thought forming behind her eyes and dread displaying itself on her face. A distant memory was coming back to her, one in which I'd said similar words in response to a distressing situation that had suddenly disappeared. 'People do what it takes,' I'd said that day, and Jenna hadn't known what it meant. Now she was looking at me and she *knew*.

"Meagan," she said, slowly. "Mrs. Johnson--"

I nodded. "It was me."

Her face fell. "I can't believe you sometimes," she whispered.

"Who's Mrs. Johnson?" Amber asked.

"An old woman who made Jenna cry every day for close to three months. She lived on the ninth floor and was always complaining about the noise, blamed Jenna for everything. Jenna always tried to be nice but every time Mrs. Johnson saw her she called her names, said she was evil --because Jenna was making a few extra bucks reading tarot cards at the time-- and once even spat at her. Finally, I had enough."

"What do you mean *you* had enough?" Gwynne demanded.

"I mean no one screws with the people I care about. Mrs. Johnson got exactly what she deserved."

"She got evicted, Meagan," Jenna said, softly.

"Yeah, and you know how many rent checks I had to intercept to pull that off?"

"You stole from an old woman?" Gwynne demanded. "How fucking sick are you?"

"I didn't steal from her. I'm not a thief."

"Your stories seem to indicate otherwise."

Jenna was shaking her head again. "It was Jimmy's old mailbox key, wasn't it? When he moved out the landlord started using his box as the rent deposit and you still had the key."

I laughed. "I'm surprised you're just figuring it out now. Every month I'd open the box and rip up her check until eventually she was evicted."

Jenna slumped down in her chair. "She was an eighty-three year old asthmatic with heart disease, Meagan."

"What's your point?"

"Meagan, she was put in a nursing home!"

"I did it for you," I defended.

"Well, don't do things for me. I don't like your way."

"You liked it just fine when that girl who refused to serve you because you were wearing a pentacle suddenly got fired from her job at Jade Gardens."

"That was you too?"

"It's always me, Jenna."

"Please," she groaned. "If you don't stop looking out for me I'm gonna come back as a termite in my next life."

Amber laughed and a bored sigh escaped me. No one ever appreciated a thing. "I got Mrs. Johnson out of the nursing home," I muttered.

Jenna looked up at me. "What?"

"I felt bad when her family put her in there and I got her out. I found her a nice apartment in a quiet senior citizen's building and hired her a housekeeper until she got back on her feet."

"You did?" A new level of respect crept into her voice.

"Yes. She milked it though, I'll tell you that." I chuckled. "Mrs. Johnson was one cunning old woman-- I liked that. She was better after a few weeks but she made me pay for that housekeeper for another five months. We both knew what she was doing but neither of us mentioned it, and I didn't mind playing her game. Her family didn't have money and when she died I paid for her ashes to be sent back to Romania with her son."

"She wasn't Romanian."

"Then her ashes went to the wrong country."

Amber laughed. She still found my antics amusing and I smiled at her.

"She was Romanian, Jenna. It was her husband who wasn't."

Jenna smiled. "So, you took care of her?"

"You're just gonna drag it out for me, aren't you? Yes, I took care of her. Remember how I'd disappear every Saturday morning? I was bringing her groceries. She'd give me a list and I'd go. Then I'd come back, sit with her awhile, make her lunch, and leave."

"Why didn't you tell me? You said you were playing racquetball."

I couldn't hide my amusement. "And have you thinking I was a good person? That's your department, Jenna. I'm only human. For the record, I don't even know how to play racquetball."

"Well, it sounds to me like you know how to be devious," Gwynne sneered. "You just don't have what it takes to follow it through. And don't you ever shut up?"

My head snapped up. "Rarely. And there have been a few exceptions along the way-- you could be one."

"Are you threatening me?"

"As long as I never see you put your hands on Amber like that again, no. Do it once and I won't be responsible for what happens to you."

Gwynne turned to Amber. "Are you just gonna stand here and let this psychotic bitch threaten me?"

I glanced at Jenna, whose face suddenly distorted in pain. "Jenna, are you--"

She fell forward into my arms, clutching her stomach. I held her upright. "Meagan, it hurts."

Gwynne and Amber shared a worried glance and Amber helped me ease Jenna onto the floor, where I cradled her head in my lap.

"Is it labor?"

She nodded up at me. "I'm having a contraction." Just then her water broke.

"Shit." I pulled her closer, thinking fast, assessing the situation.

"What do we do?" Gwynne screeched, jumping up and down like a maniac.

I looked at her. "That car out there is a Corvette, isn't it?"

"Yes."

"Okay, we'll have to take the jeep. Amber you drive Gwynne's car because we can't all fit in the jeep, and Gwynne, can you drive a stick?" I knew Amber couldn't, otherwise I would have asked her to drive. I hated the idea of asking Gwynne for anything.

Gwynne nodded, all animosity between us temporarily forgotten.

"My keys are in my purse. Go start the jeep and we can lay her down in the back."

Gwynne grabbed my purse and raced for the door.

"What about me?" Amber said. "Is there anything else I should do?"

I had been designated to take charge of the situation, or maybe I'd just jumped into action. Either way I was the only one who could emotionally detach myself long enough to get things under control. The panic filled my insides but I disconnected and told Jenna to practice her Lamaze breathing. I tilted her head forward so she could take in more air and stroked her hair.

"Do you have a bag packed?"

"Bedroom closet," she grunted.

"I'll grab the bag," Amber said.

She moved to run past us but I grabbed her leg. "Wait. Toss me that phone first. I'll call Josh at the office and tell him to meet us at the hospital."

Jenna took a heavy breath of air and smiled around the ache. "Thank the Goddess you didn't leave, Meagan. I know I can always count on you to be on top of things."

I kissed her forehead and felt like coming apart at the seams. Knew I couldn't. Someone had to remain in control and I was the only one with enough experience to do it.

She let out a little laugh. "Heck of a day, huh, Meagan?"

Amber grinned at me.

"Go," I urged. "Grab that bag so we can get out of here."

Chapter 25

The waiting room was eerily silent. Time passed slowly and I paced the small enclosure while Gwynne and Amber sat on a long corduroy couch under the picture window that faced the street outside. They flipped through old magazines. There was a coffee table in front of them, imitation wood with a dozen periodicals strewn across the top, and Gwynne had her feet on the edge of it. I paced in front of them. Crossed the room. Peeked into the corridor. It was empty except for a lone janitor in green coveralls who was washing the floor with a mop that looked like it had seen better days. He sloshed the mop in a pail of soapy water, wrung it out on the side, and slapped it against the concrete floor.

Was it concrete? It looked like concrete. It looked like the floor in any general hospital. I shrugged to myself and the man lifted his graying head and smiled at me. I smiled back. Reentered the waiting room. Amber glanced up at me and I pointed at the vending machine in the corner. She shook her head. Gwynne glanced up but said nothing. Barely a word had passed between us since Jenna had been wheeled down to the delivery room with Josh racing along at her side.

I approached the vending machine and stared at the snacks behind the glass. Dropped three quarters in the slot and pressed the button marked "F." A small bag of chips slid off the top shelf and fell in the tray at the bottom. I reached through the metal door, looked at the bag I pulled out and, realizing I didn't really want the chips, tossed them on the coffee table near Gwynne's feet. I made another selection. Dropped my quarters in again and pulled out a pack of cinnamon Trident.

I shoved the gum in my pocket and crossed to the pay phone on the other side of the room to try calling my parents for the fifth time. I'd left my cell phone sitting on Jenna's kitchen table and sighed when I now realized I was out of change. It seemed the only time I ever forgot my phone was just when I might need it most. There was a small scraping sound behind me and I turned to see Amber sliding a quarter across the table at me. I picked it up.

"Thank you. Take those chips if you want them."

She frowned at me. "Why did you buy them?"

I shrugged. Gwynne eyeballed the bag and I nodded at her. She picked it up and opened it while I went back to the pay phone. Still no answer.

Gwynne ate the chips, looked at her watch, and out of the corner of my eye I saw Amber nudge her. I went back to my pacing. Back and forth, back and forth, until Amber finally said, "Sit down, Meagan. You're making me a nervous wreck."

"Sorry." I sat but my legs continued to bounce.

Gwynne looked at her watch again. "I have to go," she said. "I have to meet with a client." She stood and I glanced up at her.

"Thank you for your help." It killed me to choke out those words. Amber knew it and I saw the amusement flash on her face.

Gwynne approached me. "Listen, before I go I just want to apologize for what happened earlier."

I nodded. "We both behaved poorly. I'm not saying I'm okay with what you did," I asserted, "but you're right; it was none of my business to get involved."

Amber stared through the open door to the corridor. "You don't think the three of us forced her into labor, do you?" she asked me.

"No, the doctor said it could happen any day. We probably didn't help matters, but I don't think we brought it on either."

Amber walked Gwynne to the door and I turned my head as they embraced. It was a chaste embrace, to all outward appearances, only I knew better: It was Amber forgiving the one who had hurt her. I'd been on the receiving end of that embrace enough times to know. Gwynne asked Amber when she'd be home and Amber said after the baby was born, that she wanted to stick around for Jenna. Gwynne didn't like leaving us alone together but she didn't have a choice.

"She's not driving you home," I heard her whisper.

Amber nodded. "Okay, I'll call you to pick me up." She handed Gwynne the car keys.

"So I'll see you in awhile?" Gwynne pressed.

Another nod from Amber. I didn't want to be seeing or hearing any of this but they stood in the doorway and I was trapped in the room behind them. I tried not to pay attention. Gwynne left and Amber stepped back into the room.

"Do you want some coffee?" she asked, sliding her hands into the back pockets of her faded jeans. They were beaten around the front pockets, ripped at one knee, and she looked casually sexy. I glanced away.

"God, no."

She grinned. "That's right; no caffeine when you're stressed."

It didn't look like the others would be arriving any time soon and I wondered how we would deal with each other alone. If I didn't know any better I would have sworn Jenna had gone into labor on purpose. She did that sort of thing. Forced people together by any means necessary. Amber sat on the long vinyl couch beside me and turned so her body was facing mine. She was close. Close enough to make me uncomfortable.

"Look at you," she said, giving my arm a squeeze with both hands. "You haven't changed a bit. I was hoping you'd be fat or something but you look as great as ever."

I laughed. "You too. And thanks for wishing obesity on me."

"You know what I mean."

"I know." I twisted my body toward hers and couldn't help wondering what it would be like to kiss her. I knew that strange energy would still be there because I could feel it wafting through the air between us already.

"It's strange, isn't it?" I said. "The two of us sitting here like civilized people after all this time. A part of me can't help feeling like nothing has changed."

"Yeah," she agreed. "I swear I had a million different ways I was going to approach this situation when it finally arrived and now that it's here and I find myself coming up empty."

"Me too. I didn't think it was going to be easy but I didn't count on it being this hard either. We really made a mess of it today, didn't we?"

She smiled. Fiddled with her bootlace. It was a nervous gesture I remembered all too well.

"Do you really think we can be friends, Meagan?"

"Honestly?"

"After your letter I'd expect nothing less."

"I don't know," I said. "I'm hoping we can be. Considering Jenna's position in both our lives we almost have to be."

"True."

"I'm glad you guys got closer while I was gone."

Amber laughed. "She's always talking about you. 'Meagan's running that whole company by herself over there. She has a staff of over a hundred and she knows every single employees name, which department they work in, and what their personal duties are' and on and on. She's so proud of you. Every time she talked to you she'd call me and tell me what you were up to. How *Natural Beauty* was becoming a European rage because of you. How you barely slept and never took a day off because you were so focused on making *Natural Beauty the* magazine all of Europe had to have on their coffee tables." She shook her head appreciatively. "And you did it too. In only seven months you turned the European magazine industry on its ear."

I laughed. "Well, I don't know about *that.* It became a success. I got us a few big interviews and the magazine just sort of took off from there."

"Jenna said that after the fifth month it was even out-selling the North American *Natural Beauty* -- that you were running the European one better than Ted was running the one here."

"It was out-selling it," I said, modestly.

"Are you blushing?"

"You know I don't deal with praise well. I was just doing my job."

The clock on the wall ticked away the minutes and my ears were met with the soft hum of music I only now noticed. I glanced at the clock.

"Can I ask you something Amber?" I said. She nodded. "What happened with Gwynne in the kitchen today," I continued, "that doesn't normally happen, right? I mean, she doesn't hit you or anything, does she?"

Amber arched an eyebrow. "Does it really matter,

Meagan?"

"Do you think it wouldn't?"

She sighed. "And evasive Meagan re-emerges. Answering a question with a question." She didn't seem to realize she'd done the same thing. "No, Gwynne doesn't hit me. I don't know what went on in that kitchen today but I can assure you it will never happen again."

"Good. Maybe I'm the last person who has any right to say this, but I just don't want to see you get hurt."

I went back to my pacing. Amber's eyes followed me back and forth.

"Meagan?"

"Sorry." I sat down beside her again.

"No, it's not the pacing." Frustrated, she pushed her fingers through her hair and I watched the platinum strands fall through her fingers like little slashes of sunlight. "Shit," she said. "Okay, I'm just gonna come out with this. There's something I need to know before I can close the book on us entirely. You don't have to answer, but I was wondering when you met Ken. He's obviously not from England so I'm assuming you met him before you left. *How long* before you left is what I need to know." She looked away. "Were you seeing him when we were together?"

She glanced back at me and I met her gaze evenly. "What do you think?" I asked.

"Goddamn it, Meagan. If you don't want to answer, just say so. Don't play word games. I always hated when you did that."

I hadn't known I *did* do that.

"No," I said. "The answer is no. I didn't cheat on you with Ken or anyone else. I've never cheated on anyone in my life. I met Ken at a party Jenna and I threw awhile back. You were there. You met him too. He was the guy who broke one of my statues."

"I remember that!" Amber cried. "It was about a month before I kissed you for the first time. Ken must have been the guy you were talking to when I interrupted."

I grinned. "On purpose."

Amber laughed. "You knew that? You knew that I did it on purpose?"

"I was straight, Amber, not stupid. By then I had pretty much figured out you had a thing for me but I was still in denial about it. I told myself that you were too good-looking to be a lesbian and that I had somehow concocted the whole thing in my head because lesbians simply did not look like you."

Laughing, she leaned forward until her forehead brushed my arm. "You always were a bit naive."

"Hey!"

"No, but that was one of the things I loved about you. You walked around like the world was full of wonderful surprises -- like you were only just discovering what everyone else had always known. You were supposed to be this big jaded businesswoman but instead you were walking around thinking all lesbians look like KD Lang."

My turn to arch an eyebrow. "I've met your friends, Amber. A lot of them do."

She thought about it and laughed. "I guess so."

"Anyway," I said, pulling a pack of gum from my pocket and offering her a piece before taking one for myself, "After the party Ken and I didn't see each other again until a few months after you and I broke up. At first we were just friends and I even considered setting him up with Danielle, but she was too young and she was also with Mark."

Amber nodded. "Same here."

"Really?" I joked. "You wanted to set Gwynne up with my sister?"

She gave me a playful shove. "You really don't change, do you? Same corny sense of humor."

I snapped a bubble in my mouth. "Yeah, and you still find it funny."

Just then Ken appeared in the waiting room. "No one's here yet?" he asked striding toward us and leaning down to kiss me hello. Amber reached for a magazine.

I snapped another bubble. "Not yet." It seemed I stopped being nervous the minute Ken arrived -- or maybe it was when Gwynne left. "Ken," I said. "This is Amber."

"The infamous Amber," he replied. He shook her hand. "Nice to meet you." He was much more civilized than Gwynne had been. Ken was a confident guy.

Amber looked Ken over and nudged me. "You never go for anything less than gorgeous, do you?" she joked. Ken laughed.

"You should talk," I countered, blowing my third bubble, which Ken popped in my face. I pulled the goo from my lips.

"Where did Gwynne grow up? On a catwalk in Paris?"

Amber chuckled and Ken sat beside me, taking my hand. "Do we know anything yet?"

"Nope."

"Well, I guess I'll have to do something about that."

I snapped my gum again and Ken held his hand under my chin. "Give me that."

I looked at him strangely. "I don't think so."

He sighed. "Then just promise not to make us insane with it. Jenna still has Dr. Lauren?"

"Mmm-hmm". This time I snapped the gum on purpose. Ken chuckled.

"You're such a child," he said.

"I'm naive too." I glanced at Amber and she smirked.

"Whatever that means," Ken said standing up. "I'll go talk to Dr. Lauren." He glanced at Amber's exposed forearm. "Right after I take care of that scratch."

Amber's face turned red. "It's nothing."

"Good, then you won't mind if I clean and bandage it. Looks like someone grabbed you a bit forcefully."

Amber and I exchanged a look but said nothing.

"Okay then," Ken said. "I'll be back in five minutes with information and gauze." He gave a disarming grin and disappeared into the corridor.

Amber shook her head. "Wow, he's exactly like you."

I frowned. "How so?"

"As Jenna would say, he's on top of it. Same way you always are -- every angle covered."

I turned to face her and my eye caught a glint of silver dangling from around her neck. I moved to touch it. Amber jumped back, startled.

"There's a switch," I said, making light of the very thing that had destroyed us. "You flinching at my touch."

A line appeared in her forehead. "Meagan."

"Relax, Amber. I just wanted to see what's on your chain."

She hesitated. Her hand hovered at her throat, and then, nodding as if she were agreeing to some great task, she pulled the necklace out of her shirt and my eyes snapped open with surprise.

"Gran's ring!" I gasped. It wasn't gone! My grandmother's

legacy had not been in vain. I thought I would burst into tears of joy and crush her with kisses. "But --you threw it out. I watched you!"

"I thought you got it at Mardi Gras, Meagan," she said, grinning. "A piece of junk as I recall. Not your grandmother's at all."

My eyes shot to the floor. More guilt. "I'm sorry about that," I said, quietly.

"It's okay. You're not a very good liar."

"And I won't be doing it anymore."

"What do you mean?" She twisted the ring on her chain.

"I'll never lie to you again, Amber," I promised. "As long as you promise to be careful what you ask me. When did you start wearing the ring again?"

"After Jenna's wedding. I pulled it out of the garbage after you left that day. I couldn't leave it there. I knew you were lying and I thought someday, if I ever forgave you, I'd give it back."

"Does Gwynne know what it means?"

"No."

"Do you?" I asked quietly. "Do you remember?"

Her eyes met mine. "Yes, I remember. I promised you I would never betray it Meagan, and I haven't." She moved to unclasp the chain from around her neck. "I suppose you'll want it back now."

"No." It belonged to Amber. She still wore it which meant she had never fully abandoned our bond.

"But it was your grandmother's."

"And I gave it to you."

"But we're not together anymore."

Her words squeezed my heart like a python. "History repeats itself," I muttered.

She tilted her head. "Excuse me?"

"My gran and Rosalie weren't together but my gran continued to wear the ring. I'm not saying you have to, only that you can if you choose to. They became friends and, we're trying, I think, to be friends. The ring is yours. I held up my end of the deal and now it belongs to you. Maybe someday you'll give it to Gwynne--" My heart twisted at the thought and I cast a nervous glance at the corridor, hoping Ken wasn't lurking around right outside this room. "--That's entirely your decision. Just make sure it's right, Amber," I added more softly. "Before you give that ring to anyone, make sure you feel it in your soul. It sounds silly but you have to *know* you're giving it to the right person, okay?"

She knew what I was saying and her eyes softened to a warm, pale green.

I smiled. "And whatever you do, don't let my mother see it. That's one headache I really don't need."

Amber laughed. "I think you're as unusual as you say your gran was."

"Probably, but I'm a bit young for her level of senility."

"You're awful." She gave me a playful shove and I frowned.

"I thought we established that long ago."

Amber was saved from having to respond by Ken who appeared in the doorway holding a bottle of solution and a package of gauze. There was a knowing grin etched across his face.

"Well," he said. "It looks like the three of us are going to be the first to meet Samuel Joshua Summers."

Chapter 26

Ken and I were married in the little chapel in the woods two weeks later. The ceremony was small and intimate, like I'd wanted. Ken wore a black Armani suit and I wore a white Calvin Klein dress that wasn't quite a wedding gown. We had our white daffodils and purple orchids. Guests included Ken's parents, who had flown in from Vancouver; my parents, my siblings, and baby Sammy who weighed in at 6 pounds, 3 ounces.

I'd chosen not to take my husband's name, for obvious reasons, and Ken didn't mind. Judge Roberts married us; we signed the papers, and then headed off to an expensive French restaurant to celebrate. Ken loved French cuisine. He smiled all through dinner and exchanged happy comments with my mother who was thrilled I'd "finally" done it. Josh grinned a lot, glad he wasn't the only Summers who was married anymore, and we teased Danny about how now our mother was going to start bugging her.

"Forget it," she said. "I'm only twenty. I've got at least another ten years before I'll even consider it."

Secretly, I thought she was the smartest Summers yet.

Gwynne Patterson had been hired to decorate our house while Ken and I were to take leave on a two week honeymoon that would start in the south of France and end in Ireland. I wasn't pleased with the idea but Gwynne, I learned, was one of the best decorators in the city. A few of Ken's friends had used her and had been thrilled with the results. Ken wanted to be thrilled, and I was shocked when he returned home from work one day only to tell me he'd heard of an excellent decorator he wanted to use for the new house.

"Her name's Gwynne," he'd said.

"No." The word came out of my mouth quickly and Ken laughed.

"But you haven't even heard the rest."

"Her last name's Patterson, right? Do you know who that is? It's Amber's new girlfriend, a woman who would rather see me dead than anything else."

"I'm sure you're exaggerating. Can we at least just meet with her? She's really good, honey."

I'd said no several times but Ken kept pressuring, and, reluctantly, I'd agreed to go down to her office with him.

Gwynne had been amused by our request but she was also all for the idea. She'd shown us her remarkable portfolio, we'd gone to the new house together, and by the time it was over, there was little I could do but agree to her assistance. The woman was good. Ken and Gwynne got along wonderfully, and it bugged me. Wasn't it enough that Jenna was going to find ways to thrust us all together? We were going to have to see each other whether we wanted to or not. Ken's insistence we hire Gwynne to do the house was only going to make that harder.

After dinner at the restaurant, Ken and I went home to change then headed downtown to Gwynne's office for a meeting. It was the only chance we had before leaving for our honeymoon and I wasn't pleased. I was even less pleased when we arrived at her office only to find a note on the door asking if we could please meet her at home, as she wasn't feeling well but wanted to go over the plans.

"Is she serious?" I demanded, tearing the note off the door. Ken didn't see the ploy.

"We have to go. This is the only time we can meet with her before we leave."

"Forget it, then. We'll hire someone else."

"We've already signed the contracts and made a deposit," Ken pointed out.

Gwynne was playing a game and I was getting angry. "I see --so you want to spend our wedding night sitting around an apartment where your wife has been fucked in every room."

"Do you have to talk like that?"

"It's Amber's apartment!" And I hadn't been there since the night we broke up.

"So what? Handle it like an adult, Meagan."

"You're pissing me off."

"Are we going to fight on our wedding night? Let's just go

and get this over with. We won't stay long." He started toward the car. "Are you coming?"

"Yes," I hissed. "I'm coming."

Ken opened the door for me and glumly I got in the car. This was not the wedding night I had planned. Actually, I hadn't planned anything, but this was the last thing I *wanted.* What if Amber was there? She knew we'd hired Gwynne but certainly she didn't think she'd have to have us in her home. Gwynne Patterson was proving she was going to be a thorn in my side.

Ken followed my directions and within minutes we were pulling up outside Amber's building. My heart gave a sickened twist as we climbed the stairs to her apartment, the same stairs I had almost stumbled down in my haste to escape the last time.

Smiling, Gwynne opened the door and ushered us into an apartment that hadn't changed a bit those many months. There were a few new things. A lamp I didn't recognized, some pictures of people I didn't know-- Gwynne's additions I figured. Ken and I followed her into the living room and sat on a loveseat Amber and I had made love on several times. Had she and Gwynne done it here too? The idea sickened me and I swallowed back my disgust.

"I'm glad you could meet me at home," Gwynne said, pouring coffee from a pot on the table and offering us cake. Ken took a piece but I waved it away.

"You don't look sick, Gwynne," I said.

She smiled sweetly. "It's a menstrual thing."

Ken sipped his coffee. "Where's Amber?"

"Poetry reading. Some author's club or something."

I settled back in my seat, somewhat relieved. "Okay, let's do this."

"Impatient?" Gwynne giggled.

"Wouldn't you be on your wedding night?"

"Good point."

We began discussing the kitchen and the downstairs bathroom when there was a rattling at the door. Keys! Oh God! My stomach gave a nervous flop as Amber stepped inside. She didn't notice us right away. The keys got tossed on a table by the door and she turned in time to see Gwynne rise from the couch, a satisfied sneer on her face. I kicked Ken in the shin.

"What?" he demanded.

What did he think?

Amber's eyes darted to the loveseat as Gwynne kissed her cheek.

"I wasn't feeling well," Gwynne said quickly. "So I asked if they could meet me here. You don't mind do you?"

Amber's eyes were hard on Gwynne's face. "No, I don't mind," she said tightly.

"How was the poetry reading?" Ken asked. Nothing affected my husband.

"The what?" Amber looked confused.

"Oh, that's *tomorrow* night." Gwynne smacked her forehead. "Sorry."

My lips tightened. Sorry, indeed. Gwynne had done it on purpose. She'd wanted Amber to see me on my wedding night and it was the sickest thing I'd ever witnessed.

"Are we done here?" I demanded.

Ken looked at me strangely. "We've only started."

"Then I'll leave you guys alone," Amber offered, turning toward the bedroom.

Ken rose from the loveseat. "Don't be silly; you can join us. It's no big secret and this is your home."

"We're sorry for the imposition, Amber," I said quietly.

Gwynne waved her hand in the air. "It's no imposition. Amber knows I sometimes do business from home. Sit with us, sweetie."

Amber shot Gwynne a look but followed her to the couch across from Ken and me.

"Oh, I didn't ask how the wedding went," Gwynne suddenly realized, grinning. "That's so rude."

I scowled at my coffee and Ken said. "Quiet. My wife likes things quiet. But it was very nice."

"Congratulations," Amber managed.

Ken smiled. "Thank you."

"Hey, we should celebrate." Gwynne jumped to her feet. "We have a bottle of wine, don't we Amber?"

"That's not necessary," I said.

"Sure it is. It's your *wedding* night and I've pulled you away from it to handle business. The least I can do is offer a congratulatory drink."

"That's very kind," Ken said, nodding. "We'd appreciate it very much."

I shot him a look. Gwynne rose to grab the wine and Ken politely asked if he could use the bathroom. Amber pointed it out and suddenly we were alone.

"I'm really sorry about this, Amber," I whispered.

"It's okay."

"We were supposed to meet at her office."

"I know."

"Are you mad at me?"

"No."

"I am. I shouldn't have let Ken convince me to come. We'll finish this quickly, okay?"

"Don't worry about it, Meagan. You know you're always welcome here."

I managed a weak laugh. "No, I didn't know that."

Amber smirked. "Okay, maybe you haven't *always* been welcome but we're trying to be friends now, right?"

"It's not looking good, is it?"

"I suppose it'll just take some time. When do you leave for your honeymoon?"

"Thursday." The word caught in my throat.

Gwynne appeared with a bottle of wine and four glasses as Ken returned from the bathroom.

"To the new couple," Gwynne said cheerily, pouring the wine and raising her glass.

"Thank you." I sipped my wine. "Can we do this now? I've got three buildings to look at in the morning and meetings all afternoon."

"Buildings?" Amber asked.

My smile was genuine. "Markham-Summers Publications will need a place to set up office."

"You're doing it?" She squealed. Ken let out a little chuckle and wrapped his arm around the couch behind me.

"Yes. My wife has delayed her own honeymoon because she'd rather spend time crawling around abandoned buildings with her partner. You probably should have married Ted."

"He didn't ask."

"Funny. What is it with you and that guy, anyway?"

"Is the new groom jealous?" Gwynne joked.

Ken laughed. "Sometimes I think I should be. That man is everywhere but in our bed. He's at the office, he's on the phone--"

"Not the cell phone," Amber groaned. "She's still doing that?"

"Are you kidding me? That phone is glued to her ear. She gets calls from London at four in the morning and do you think she'd ignore it? No way. She gets up and starts emailing these people back and forth. Last week I had to call Cynthia and tell her to stop calling so late."

"*You* did that?"

Ken grinned. "Yep."

I was not impressed. It now made sense why Cynthia had been so upset for no reason. "You made her cry, Ken."

"All I said was stop calling so late."

"Cynthia is sensitive and she works very hard."

"So?"

"So, stay out of my fucking business."

"Meagan!" Ken was shocked. Amber and Gwynne exchanged a look. I sighed.

"I'm sorry. You just can't get involved in my work, Ken. I didn't mean to yell at you but I handle things a certain way. I never bitch about your emergencies so don't bitch about mine."

"You're right." Ken nodded. "I shouldn't have gotten involved."

"And?"

"And what?"

"And you're going to call Cynthia tomorrow and apologize."

"Okay."

"I think I hear the snapping of a whip," Gwynne teased.

Amber burst out laughing and shook her head at Ken's curious look. "I'm sorry, Ken. It's just too funny."

"What is?"

"Your balls, I guess. To mess around with Meagan's business? They must be made of steel."

I couldn't help joining in the laughter. Strange that the four of us should be laughing together, but it felt nice.

"You know what's even funnier?" Ken chortled. "Spending your wedding night with your wife's ex-lover."

The laughter came to an abrupt halt and everyone got nervous. Gwynne cleared her throat, Amber shifted in her seat, Ken looked surprised by his own words, and I was desperate to lighten the mood again.

"That's a good one, Ken," I said. "It's a wonder you don't have your own sitcom."

Amber laughed again and Ken smiled.

"Maybe we should get back to discussing the house," Gwynne suggested.

"Good idea." I placed my wine on the table and pressed forward to look at Gwynne's list of ideas.

"I was thinking earth tones for your kitchen," she said, pointing at a card with several different shades of terra cotta paint chips. "Something like this."

I looked at the chips and nodded. "What about the one above it? The lighter one."

"Well, your kitchen gets a lot of natural sunlight because of those giant windows, so I thought the darker shade would be a nice contrast. It would give it a more earthy feel."

"She likes earthy," Ken said.

"Okay. Whatever you think," I said.

"Really?" Gwynne was surprised.

I shrugged. "You're the expert. Ken wants formal for the library, though. Something masculine."

"I've got ideas for that too," Gwynne promised, pulling out a *New Homes* magazine. She flipped to a page and pointed. "What do you think of this? Dark green walls, burgundy, leather wing back chairs, heavy drapes, and thick wood furniture. Maybe some French provincial thrown in."

"I have no idea," I admitted, shaking my head. "You look at this, Ken. It's your study."

Ken glanced over my shoulder. "I like it. Any wainscoting?"

"We can."

"Would it be excessive?"

Gwynne studied a picture she'd taken of our library. "No, it would be a nice touch in fact. Is that how you want to go?"

I shrugged again. Ken nodded.

"Master bedroom?" Gwynne asked. Amber looked away but I was the only one who caught it.

"What we discussed on the phone," I said, evasively.

Gwynne checked her notes. "Beige walls, white trim, lacy sheers, the antique desk from the library to be brought up and placed under the window for the fax machine--"

"*Fax machine?*" Ken shrieked. "No way, Meagan. You are not putting a fax machine in our bedroom."

"But business--"

"No. The fax can go in the library. You'll have an office uptown, there's the *Natural Beauty* offices, your cell phone, your damn computer-- how many lines of communication do you need?"

"Several."

"No. I'm putting my foot down."

"*You're what?*" I burst out laughing and Amber smirked.

"If you and Ted are going into book publishing it's not going to be as hectic as it was."

"What do you mean?"

"I mean things will get quieter. I doubt you're gonna have some big book emergency at two in the morning."

"True," I admitted, slowly. Then I laughed again. "Big foot, Ken."

He smirked. "Are you saying the fax can go in the library?"

"Yes, it can go in the library."

Gwynne changed her notes. "Guest bedrooms as we discussed on the phone?"

"Yes." I thought of something else. Something I'd wanted to ask her about. "Is it possible to rip out the tub in the master bathroom?"

"Why?" Ken asked.

"It's a big bathroom. I think I want a Jacuzzi."

"You think?" He grinned.

"Okay, I know I want one. Black."

"We can do that," Gwynne said. "But then we should change the toilet and sink to black ones too, and that project might not be finished before you return."

"Hire more contractors."

"How many?"

"As many as it takes."

"Spare no expense?"

"No."

"Meagan!" Ken's head snapped to look at me.

"What? I'll pay for it."

"No, I'll pay for it, but geez, why don't you just ask her to dig a hole for a swimming pool too?"

"I can't swim."

Amber chuckled. "Is that the only reason?"

"And Sammy. It would scare me to think he could be crawling around someday and fall in."

"So no pool." Gwynne smiled.

"No. Hey wait! What about a playroom?"

"Planning a family already?" Gwynne looked downright pleased.

"For Sammy."

"You wanna build a playroom for your *nephew*?"

"He's gonna be my godson. And not build one; just turn one of the guest rooms into one." I looked at Ken. "Would that be okay with you?"

"Why not? There certainly are enough guest rooms."

"Jenna will shit," Amber said, smiling.

I thought of the surprise I'd gotten yesterday and grinned. "No, she's gonna shit tomorrow morning when the pet store drops off Sammy's new puppy."

Amber's hands shot to her face. "You didn't!"

Ken only shook his head. "They have a new baby to worry about and you buy them a puppy?"

"It's for Sammy," I defended.

"He's two weeks old. You couldn't have waited?"

I laughed. "Josh is gonna kill me. It's a golden lab and when Jenna takes one look at it she won't be able to give it up."

"Honey, that's very sweet but you're only giving her more work."

"Should I cancel it?"

"Maybe."

The grin came again. "But I just can't. If it's too much for her we'll take it, okay?"

"You have a plan for everything, don't you? And you picked a lab on purpose."

"Why do you say that?" I asked innocently.

"Because you know it's my favorite dog and you were preparing yourself in case Jenna says she doesn't want it. Admit it."

"Okay, I admit it. But she *will* want it."

"You're pissing your brother off, you know," Amber said.

"I am?"

She nodded. "Gwynne and I were over there the other day and he was bitching about all the things you've been buying Sammy."

"Why? So what if I buy him things?"

"I think it makes him feel bad," she said. "Because you have more money than he does."

"Oh."

"Maybe you should stop, Meagan," Ken suggested.

"Well, I never wanted to make anyone feel bad. I better cancel the pony."

"*Pony?*" Ken shrieked.

I broke out laughing and Amber grinned. "You can't blame him for believing you, Meagan. Who knows what you'll do next?"

Ken stretched his arms above his head and yawned. "We're done here, right?"

Gwynne nodded. "Just tell me what kind of playroom and where."

"Last bedroom," I said. "And surprise us. Something cute."

"That's the best you can do?" Ken questioned. "What about a jungle motif?"

"Sure, that sounds good. But nothing tacky and nothing loud. Simple but fun."

"Okay. So I guess we'll see you in a couple of weeks then."

We rose from the couches and Amber and Gwynne walked us to the door. Halfway through it, I turned back.

"Sorry again about the imposition."

"I told you, it wasn't one," Gwynne said.

Nodding, I followed Ken outside. It could have gone worse, I supposed. It hadn't been easy sitting in Amber's home, but we'd gotten through it and a part of me was glad we'd gone after all.

Gran and Rosalie had done it. Maybe Amber and I could, too.

On Monday, we left for our honeymoon. Ted and I hadn't been pleased with the buildings we'd looked at and it was just one of the things that weighed on my mind as Ken and I toured the south of France and tanned ourselves in the French sun. The other thing was Gwynne. I thought I'd been fine with the idea of her decorating the house in our absence but I wasn't. Gwynne didn't like me any more than I liked her and it made me uncomfortable to picture her wandering the rooms of my home.

In Ireland the thought still disturbed me. "Relax," Ken pleaded, as we sat in a quaint little pub in Dublin with Seamus who had challenged us to a Guinness-drinking contest. Ken had stoutly refused --his body was his temple-- but I could never decline a challenge. Particularly one I had little chance of winning.

"I just don't know how comfortable I am with her being there." I sipped my Blond in the Black Skirt and watched Seamus down his like water. "The woman hates me, Ken."

"She doesn't hate you. She loves Amber. There's a difference." My husband had a way of twisting the facts to suit him. "If you want we can call and check on things."

"And have her think I don't trust her? No way." I wouldn't give Gwynne the satisfaction.

"I'm drinking you under the table, Meggie Pie," Seamus said. Big surprise.

Hard drinking had left my forty-three year old uncle looking at least five years older, but he was still quite attractive. With his curly black hair, dark eyes that always held a glint of mystery or amusement, square jaw and muscular face; he was by far the handsomest man in the pub. He wore a beige wool turtleneck, black jeans, and scuffed black loafers that gave him the overall appearance of an overly muscled university professor. All he needed was a pipe and a pair of wire-rimmed glasses. His arms were massive for a man who stood no taller than 5'7. Broad shoulders and a thick Irish neck. He grinned daringly and I felt the flame of ambition dance behind my eyes.

"How about we up the challenge, Seamus?" I suggested.

Ken groaned and shook his head. "Oh no, here it comes."

"Here what comes?" Seamus asked, blowing a long gray plume of smoke above my head. He crunched his cigarette in the ashtray.

Ken wrapped his arm around the back of my chair. "My wife," he explained, "has a real problem losing. She doesn't do it well."

"Dat, I know."

"So, she's going to raise the challenge to such an impossible height that neither of you will be able to reach it."

Seamus squinted at me. "Is dat so?"

I grinned. "What do you say, Seamus? Two shots of whiskey after every pint. The first person to puke or pass out has to make the next visit."

Seamus slammed the table with a heavy fist and roared with laughter. "You like airplanes, don't you Meggie?" His eyes flashed a fire to match my own. "Have you ever even tried Irish whiskey?"

People around us were listening in, amused by the challenge the skinny foreigner was making on her hard-drinking uncle.

"I can hold my own," I said confidently. "How 'bout it, Seamus? I'm here for a *craic*, isn't that how you say it? We'll just have to make our own party since my husband here is being a big *girl.*"

Again Seamus howled with laughter. He was a man's man and didn't have to tell me he thought my pretty husband was delicate.

Ken gave a wicked grin. "Okay little miss tough stuff," he said, rolling up his sleeves and twisting his watch so that it faced down on his wrist. "Count me in."

"You're going to drink?" I laughed. Ken never had more than a glass of wine or champagne at a party.

"I think I can at least beat you," he said.

"Oh, you're on, pretty boy."

Seamus clapped his hands and rubbed them together with eager glee. "Three pints," he yelled, turning in his chair. "And six shots of Powers. Me lovely niece here thinks she and her yuppie husband can drink an old Irishman under the table."

Seamus said this all so good-naturedly that even Ken joined in the laughter of the other men in the room. A few of the woman made the sign of the cross.

"Ah, Seamus. Go easy on the girl," a smiling woman with graying hair said in the thickest brogue I'd ever heard. "If she's never had Powers before you're gonna be spending the night holding the wee one's hair back."

"Not me, Fay," Seamus insisted. He pointed at Ken. "His wife, his problem."

Ken chuckled. "As long as I don't have to carry her home."

"What's the deal with the accent, Seamus?" I said suddenly. I'd been listening to my uncle talk for two days and the accent seemed to grow thicker every time he opened his mouth. It amused me so much I couldn't resist teasing him about it. "You've been back here a few years and suddenly you sound like the leprechaun on the Lucky Charms commercials."

"Leprechaun!" Seamus's eyes widened. I'd startled him. Maybe even embarrassed him. "I'll have you know I don't talk any different den I ever did. It's yer mother who's changed the way she talks. Yer mother and yer aunt Celia." He glanced around the bar and his voice grew louder because he wanted everyone to hear this. "Two sisters I 'ave, and because they've married fairly well they think they can forget where they come from."

"Seamus." I'd started something I was about to regret.

"They forget their grandfather was nothing more than a potato farmer in this country. And their own father, me beautiful da, God rest the poor man's tired soul, moved his family out of Ireland because he wanted a better life for them. Well, they got that didn't they, Meggie Pie? Da did right by me sisters and all they can do for his memory is hide their lower class brogue. Well, not me girl. I am the son of my father and I speak the way he did. I--"

"Seamus."

"Am a country lad at heart. Of this country. *My* country."

"*Seamus!*"

He seemed to snap to attention. "What is it then?"

"I've heard this story a million times. Potato farmers. A famine you are far too young to have even been a part of. Dirt poor beginnings. Blah, blah, blah. Get over it now."

My uncle respected me because I was the only person who dared speak to him this way. The only one who wasn't afraid of him.

"You make me sorry I even tried joking around with you."

Seamus's eyes softened and he patted my hand affectionately. "Drink yer whiskey, Meggie. Even yer pantywaist husband is beating you now."

Ken smirked. "Keep it up, Seamus, and I'm gonna have to take you outside."

"What for boy? To show me the roses in bloom?"

The next morning at breakfast Ken and I looked like we'd spent the previous evening in hell. Seamus almost had to carry us home. Bright-eyed and smiling, he spread some sort of jam on his toast and watched our efforts to eat with amused Irish eyes. Suddenly I caught on the expression, *when Irish eyes are smiling*, and wanted to reach across the table and throttle him.

"Teach you to mess with a true Irish," he said, when I glared at him from above the rim of my coffee cup. My throat was so dry I could barely swallow. Ken only shook his aching head.

"Oh God," he complained, rubbing his tired eyes. "I hate to get on an airplane feeling like this."

Seamus' grin widened into a full-out sneer and I knew exactly how my husband felt. I wished we hadn't decided to cut our trip short after the south of France turned out to be a tremendous bore. We had changed our flight schedule and arrived in Ireland earlier than planned, reservations already made for a flight home in three days time.

It was now the third day and I could think of nothing but wanting to head back upstairs to the lovely guest room with the soft flannel blankets on the bed and the view from the window that depicted a distant meadow, rolling hills, and a flower field that seemed to stretch on forever, an ancient unused stone well situated in the center of it. My uncle's property was Ireland at its most magical; paradise. Not bad for an alcoholic who changed jobs every three months. Somehow, he managed. Seamus O'Reilly was the person who taught me survival.

With kisses and hugs, we departed his lovely cottage and didn't arrive home until three a.m. the next day. There were flight delays, an unexpected layover in some part of the world I couldn't remember, and by the time Ken and I reached our new home we were ready to crash for the next six months.

"Nice job," Ken joked, as we sleepily stumbled through the dark house, noticing nothing in our haste to find the master bedroom. I managed a weak laugh then fell into bed beside him, curling my body to his, and succumbing to a deep sleep before my head hit the pillow.

Hours later we awoke and made love, slowly, tenderly. The way it always was between us. Each touch a gentle whisper. My husband liked to take his time with me, and it was sweet, but I didn't know how to tell him that sometimes I just wanted to fuck. It didn't always have to be flowers and candlelight. Sometimes wild and crazy was fun too.

He never would have agreed. Not for Ken, the outdoor adventures. Not for Ken the cries of, "Fuck me now!" or, "Oh Christ, I'm gonna come!" That would have paralyzed him with fear. He hated vulgarities. He was all about soft murmurings and declarations of love and, in the end, laughter.

Panting and grinning, he fell on top of me and I bit my lower lip in an effort to hide my frustration. It was good. As good as it ever was. But Ken was definitely going to have to loosen up or I knew I would not enjoy having sex with him for long. I needed diversity, and if Ken turned out to be a chronic missionary man, I was not going to be pleased.

"Where are you going?" he asked when I rolled from the bed and pushed my arms through the sleeves of his blue button down shirt. The smell of his cologne lingered on the collar and I folded the shirt in front of me, wrapping myself in his warmth and ignoring the buttons.

I yawned and stretched. "I'm gonna go down and see if there's anything in the fridge. Maybe Gwynne left some bottled water or something." I was really hoping for food. Leftover Chinese, a big fat sub, anything to fill the empty space in my stomach.

Barefoot, I padded downstairs, around the hallway bend, and into the brightly lit kitchen that Gwynne had indeed decorated in earth tones and creams, to match the terra cotta ceramic tiles on the floor. Maybe the house was more Spanish than Californian, I thought. Either way it was beautiful, and grudgingly, I admitted to myself that Gwynne had done an excellent job.

Copper pots and pans hung from a low beam above a small island in the center of the room that was still covered with an old sheet. To protect it from paint splatters, I thought. There was a small table in the breakfast nook with four wooden chairs around it; French doors opening to a small solarium that would soon house white wicker furniture and many plants; stainless steel appliances in the cooking area, very shiny and clean; and to the left of me a vase of fresh flowers on the counter top that seemed strangely out of place. They weren't a gift from Ken because he hadn't left my side since we'd stepped off the plane. The fridge loomed before me like a dream.

"Please, let there be food in here," I muttered, swinging back the door and peering inside. Pizza. Jackpot! I almost giggled with greedy glee. There was also a can of pop, two large bottles of Evian, and a plastic baggy filled with carrots and celery sticks, which meant there had also been wings here. I grinned. If Gwynne were there I would have kissed her.

Reaching for one of the bottles of water, I cracked open the cap and, finding no glasses, took a healthy sip straight from the bottle.

"I remember when your first instinct was to reach for a cigarette," a bitter voice said from behind me.

I choked. The bottle slipped from my fingers and bounced off the floor, spilling its contents across the tiles.

"*Amber*." I whirled around to face her. It was the second time in as many weeks she'd sneaked up behind me in a kitchen. "What are you doing here?" *In my home,* I'd wanted to add.

"Apparently, witnessing your afterglow," she shot. Her eyes were narrow and her voice a low jealous growl but she recovered quickly while I strained to maintain my composure. I *knew* having Gwynne do the house was a bad idea. Amber's eyes never left my face.

"I came to help Gwynne finish the study," she explained, folding her arms across her chest. "The real question is: What are *you* doing here? You weren't supposed to be back for another two days."

Was she challenging me? If she was, it was a challenge I refused to rise to.

"We came home early," I muttered, blushing and grabbing a towel from the counter to wipe up the spilled water.

Amber watched me place the bottle on the island that separated us. "Obviously," she said under her breath.

My back stiffened. Was she forgetting whose house we were in? What nerve!

"*Honey?*"

Ken's call came from the hallway a few feet away and I felt a cold rush of panic wash over me. My husband liked to stroll around naked in the morning.

"You said you were coming back to bed," he said, rounding the corner near the entrance to the kitchen. Ken needed little time to recover between lovemaking sessions and I could tell by the groan in his voice that he wasn't done with me yet, and in exactly two seconds Amber was going to be greeted with the sight of his second erection of the day.

"Ken don't--" I began. I ripped the sheet off the island, again spilling the water all over the floor, and darted for the doorway as he came through it, falling to my knees in front of him and wrapping the sheet around his waist like a lunatic.

His eyes flashed surprise as he looked down at me, frantically twisting the sheet around his lower body like a cotton vice.

"What are you doing?" he asked, laughing. Then his head popped up and I saw the red spread across his cheeks.

"We have company," I whispered.

"Oh." He didn't look at me. "I'll go get dressed." And calmly he strode from the room as if nothing had happened. His calmness annoyed me. Perhaps a perverse part of him was glad Amber knew what we'd been doing. How could it not remind her that I was *his* wife?

My head fell between my shoulders and I stood up. Turned to face Amber. "I'm so sorry," I said. Amber looked at me then her eyes quickly darted away. "We got in really late --or early I should say--"

"Meagan." She tried to interject, her eyes still avoiding my gaze, and in my nervousness I continued to ramble.

"I didn't expect that anyone would be in the house this early. I mean, what time is it? Seven?"

Amber stared at her boots. "It's after ten."

"Really?"

"Listen, your--"

Again, I cut her off. "I'm sorry, really. The last thing I'd want is for you to see what you just did. I know I wouldn't want to see if you and Gwynne--"

"*Meagan!*" Her voice was loud and sharp. The same frustrated tone I'd taken with Seamus only days earlier. It startled me.

"Why are you yelling?"

Again her eyes darted away. "Your shirt is wide open," she whispered.

I looked down and my cheeks flushed. I may as well have been naked for what little the shirt covered. I buttoned it quickly, closing myself off as my face continued to flame. My fingers shook on the buttons. Was it wrong I found myself wanting her just then? Probably. It was probably a little sick too. I tried to shrug off my humiliation.

"Well," I said nervously. "I guess it's nothing you haven't seen before." I couldn't believe I just said that.

Amber's eyes met mine and I almost stumbled under the weight of her stare. "No," she said, strangely. "It's nothing I haven't seen before."

I looked away just as Gwynne entered the kitchen, her arms filled with books, swatches of fabric, and a tin of coffee.

"What's going on?" she asked suspiciously. Her eyes took in the odd scene. Roved over Amber's cold stare, my flushed face, my bare legs that had taken on a healthy tan in the French sun.

Neither of us answered. Ken appeared in the doorway behind her wearing faded jeans and a black t-shirt. The look was pure Amber. Only Ken was all sandy-haired and smiles, like he belonged in the bar scene of a beer commercial, playing pool, surrounded by several grinning girls. In fact, everyone in this room was attractive, I noticed. Ken with his boyish face and puppy dog eyes. Amber with her thin body and flawless white skin. Me with my tousled hair and long bare legs. And Gwynne. Gwynne with her shiny black hair, ocean blue eyes, and curves like I'd never seen. The woman was absolutely stunning and the fact that she knew it only added to my misery.

I stared at the faces before me. Were Amber and I really this shallow? Ken and Gwynne this superficial? We were four shades of loveliness: the healer, the artist, the corporate runaway, and the beautifier. And I couldn't have disliked us more.

Ken tossed me his heavy flannel robe, which I wrapped around my body with a scowl that no one saw.

"I'm sorry, Amber," he said easily. He turned to Gwynne and smiled. "We got home early this morning," he told her. Was that a glint of laughter in his eyes? "*Very* early, and I guess we weren't thinking, strolling around the house the way we were." He shrugged and Gwynne caught on quickly, a happy sneer cracking the corners of her red mouth.

"Oh," she giggled. "Did we interrupt something?"

Her eyebrows arched like she wanted details and I was determined she wasn't going to get them. The bitch couldn't have been happier that Amber had seen what she had.

Ken gave another shrug and opened his mouth to spill the tale while Amber shot Gwynne a look as if she were thinking the same thing I was.

"Hand me that towel, Ken," I said before he could utter a word. He did as I asked but I noticed that he and Gwynne shared a pleased look first, like the incident had somehow solidified their relationships with Amber and me. My mind burned with rage and I fought the urge to grab Amber and kiss her, just to say, "Solidify this, you jerks."

Instead, I took a deep breath and groped for as much dignity as I could muster. "Listen," I said sweetly. "Don't go anywhere. I'm gonna run upstairs and get dressed and when I come down we'll all go out for brunch. Our treat." I gave my husband a warning look, which he guiltily avoided, and turned my attention to Gwynne. "We need to go over the expenses anyway, right?"

Gwynne nodded, a satisfied grin on her pretty little face. I wanted to wipe it off with a scouring pad.

I sighed and headed back upstairs. My first day home couldn't have started any worse.

Chapter 27

I was throwing up again. For the fifth time in one week, I was hunched over the toilet in the private bathroom adjacent to my office in the *Natural Beauty* building and I was throwing up. Ted had said there was a flu bug going around but the illness did not match my symptoms. If I had the flu, why did it keep going away suddenly only to return again a day or two later? Why did I feel weak and tired one minute only to feel vibrant and content the next? Something was going on but I refused to consider what that something might be. If I had caught some dreaded disease, I didn't want to know it.

The vomiting stopped and, clumsily, I reached for a toothbrush and toothpaste. I brushed my teeth vigorously, gargled with mouthwash, and felt better already. Then I went back to my desk and resumed my work. There was a short rap at the door.

"It's open," I called out.

The door swung back on its hinges and a blond head poked inside. "You busy?"

"Amber." Smiling, I rose from my desk. "No, come in. This is a surprise. I haven't seen you in weeks."

Amber stepped inside, nodding at the new plaque on the door. "Up to publisher now I see."

"Yeah. Needless to say, Elaine is thrilled. This used to be her office, but I kicked her down the hall to my old one. What brings you by?"

Amber closed the door behind her and followed me to my desk, choosing one of the chairs across from me. She tilted her head. "Are you okay? You look a little pale."

"I'm okay. Overworked I guess."

"What else is new?"

"Ken bitches that I'm never home."

"I'm sure he has every right to. That's part of the reason I'm here," she said.

"To tell me to go home?"

"No." She gave a throaty little chuckle. "I'm here because you're a workaholic."

I twisted a pen in my fingers. "I'm not sure I understand."

"Did you and Ted find a building yet?"

We'd been searching for several months. I groaned. "Would you believe, just last week?"

"So Markham-Summers is a go then?"

"Slowly, but yes. The building needs to pass inspection and it will need to be remodeled. It seems there are a hundred things to do."

Amber nodded appreciatively. "I want to leave Hector," she said.

"Okay."

"And I want you to be my publisher."

It wasn't surprising but that didn't stop my eyebrows from shooting up. "Does Gwynne know?"

"Not yet. I wanted to see what you'd say first. I'm still under contract with Hector for one more book but I want to break it. I want *you* to be my publisher because I know no one will work harder."

"Thank you, but we haven't signed any clients yet."

"So let me be your first."

The words made me laugh and I couldn't fight the image that popped into my head. "You like being my first for things, don't you?"

She grinned. "Yes."

"Are you sure this is what you want?"

"Positive."

"It could be uncomfortable," I warned.

"I don't think so."

"Okay." I carelessly tossed the pen on my desk and leaned back in my chair. "I'll be your publisher if you want me, but don't leave Hector just yet. Ted and I have a lot of things to sort out before we get started so for right now you're safer where you are. I don't think you should break any contracts until we're ready to get running."

"All right, but will you help me with that? I want out but I don't want to get sued either."

"I'll help you. I know a lawyer who's a genius with publishing law. You have a copy of your contract, right?"

"Yes."

"Good. Hang on to it. When we're ready to get down to business I'll put you in touch with him and he can look over your contract. If there's a loophole, he'll find it. Worst case scenario, we might have to buy your way out."

"How much?" she asked nervously.

I chuckled. "Well Cyrus Junior isn't too bright so probably not a whole lot."

"Your *whole lot* and my *whole lot* can be two very different things."

"No, I'd take care of that." I gave her a sly grin. "We'll just take it out of your first advance."

"Are you gonna give me big advances, Meagan?" she teased.

Was she saying what I thought she was saying? "We are discussing business, right?" I asked, slowly.

She grinned. "Sure. What did you think?"

"I never know what to think of you, Amber. You've always been such a flirt."

"You're married," she pointed out.

Yes, I was married. And I was having a hard time coming to grips with it, too. I loved my husband but there was something about forever with him that terrified me. Forever was one hell of a long time. It was going to feel even longer now that Amber was going to be my client as well as a friend. Nothing was ever simple.

"And you're living with someone," I agreed. "So yes, I guess we're discussing business. As for advances, well if you turn out books that have the potential to reach the heights *Butterflies* did, we're looking at some pretty decent advances I'm sure. How's, *Gemstones* been doing?"

"Okay." She shrugged. "But I don't think Hector's giving it enough push. He's counting on *Butterflies* to carry it and it's pissing me off."

"That's too bad," I said, sincerely. "Because *Gemstones* is a better book."

Amber laughed. "You only say that because it isn't about you."

"No, I really like it. You have a wonderful talent, Amber. It's a shame to see someone like Hector screwing with that."

"And that's why I come to you. I can write, you can sell – we complement each other."

Her words stabbed me in the heart. "Yes."

"Oh shit!"

"*What*?"

"Are you gonna start with that 'yes' shit again?"

"What is your problem with that?"

"I don't know. It just really bugs me."

"Yes."

The laughter burst out of her. "Shut up, Meagan."

"That's Mrs. Summers to you."

"What?"

"Mm-hmm. Professional relationship. You can't call me by my first name anymore."

"Screw you. Are you gonna call me 'Miss Reed'?"

"No. I don't have to show you that kind of respect."

"I hope you're joking."

"And if I'm not?"

"You better be."

"I am."

"So I'm allowed to call you Meagan?"

"I suppose it's better than 'cunt.'"

"Quit beating a dead horse."

"Do you take this attitude with all your publishers?"

"You're not my publisher --yet."

"Good point."

"But you will be?" she asked.

"No."

"What are you talking about? You just said you would."

I smirked. "You don't like it when I say yes."

"Smart ass."

"Yes."

"Shut up!" She tried to make her voice stern, but she was laughing. "You make me crazy, Meagan. What are you doing for lunch?"

"Excuse me?" The question startled me.

"If you're not doing anything, why don't we grab Jenna and go out for lunch? It'll be like old times."

"Amber, I'm not sure that's--"

She caught the trepidation in my tone and nodded. "Right. I wasn't thinking. Who needs more problems?"

"Problems?" Her words set off warning bells in my head. "Is everything all right, Amber? Gwynne's not--"

"No, she's not hitting me," Amber barked. "I told you she doesn't do that so why don't you just mind your own fucking business, Meagan!"

"Whoa." I raised my hands in the air like she'd aimed a gun at me. "Where did that come from?"

"Do I get involved in your marriage?" she demanded, putting her boots on my desk.

"Get your feet down."

"Christ, you're so fucking anal." Her boots dropped to the floor.

"Fine, then get up and do a goddamn dance on the top of my desk. What do you want from me? You come in here asking me to be your publisher and, against my better judgment, I agree--"

"Against your better judgment?" Her tone was sarcastic and her stare deadly. "Then don't fucking do it!"

"I want to do it but if we're gonna fight all the time, how can we have a professional relationship? I don't even know *why* we're suddenly fighting. Maybe you can explain it to me."

"You just --you really piss me off."

"Because I asked if you're okay?"

"Yes. Did I say I wasn't okay?"

"You said you were having problems. Excuse me for being concerned."

She rose from her chair. "Fine. Thank you for your *concern.* I'm just gonna go now."

She turned toward the door but I rounded the desk and stopped her. "Let's work this out first, okay?"

"What's to work out? You'll be my publisher; I'll be your client. End of story."

"Why are you mad at me?"

"I'm not." She looked at the floor and let out a long sigh. "I'm not mad at you," she said more softly.

"Then why the attitude? Because of lunch?"

She looked so pretty and so angry and I found myself desperate to make things better. It wouldn't be wrong to hug her, would it? I'd hug Jenna if she were upset.

"What if it was because of lunch?" she asked softly.

"I don't know," I responded, honestly. "It isn't because I don't want to be around you. It's just --Amber, we can't go back."

"To lunch? Does that mean we're going to fall into bed together? We both have other lives now, Meagan. It's not a big deal."

"Maybe not, but how do you think it would make Ken and Gwynne feel? It's one thing if we're all together, but alone?"

"We wouldn't be alone. Jenna would be there." She pushed her fingers through her pretty hair. "Just forget I mentioned it. The last thing I want is to start making you uncomfortable again."

Cautiously, I extended my arms to her. "Come here."

She just looked at me. "What?"

"I don't want to fight with you," I said, stepping closer and wrapping my arms around her neck.

"Meagan, you shouldn't be touching me," she said uneasily.

"I'm not *touching* you."

"It's inappropriate."

"Okay." I let go. "I just wanted to hug you the same way I would if Jenna was mad at me."

The sigh came again and her eyes met mine. "Hug me."

"No, you were probably right."

"I wasn't," she said, yanking me into a hug of her own. "I'm sorry, Meagan. I know you're trying to handle this the best way you know how."

"You don't make it easy," I said, laughing and releasing her. The spark was still there and I thought she'd noticed it too.

"I better get going," she said.

"And we're okay?"

She nodded. "We're okay. Goodbye, Meagan."

"Wait." My feet sprang into action and I grabbed her wrist. "I want to have lunch with you."

"You're not afraid I'll throw you on the table in a fit of passion?"

"Don't be so sarcastic. I'll call Jenna." The smirk came again and I released her wrist. "She'll make sure you don't attack me."

"Very funny."

"Should I call her?"

Amber shrugged. "Go ahead."

"Drop the attitude, Amber. Do you want to have lunch with me or not?"

Thirty minutes later, Jenna met us at the diner around the corner. My mother had taken Sammy for the day.

"This is so cool," she said, plopping herself down in the booth beside Amber. "All that's missing is Danny."

"How's your sister doing?" Amber asked.

I signaled the waitress for a cup of coffee. "She's okay. Still seeing Mark. Still calling me for money."

"She dented your cat," Jenna said. "That gross one you bought from Zeppo."

"*Janie?*" The word sprang out of my mouth before I could stop it and Amber's head snapped up to look at me.

"I knew it," Jenna blasted. "You bought that disgusting thing only to remind yourself of the horror."

"Did not."

"Then why do you have a mangled sculpture named Janie?"

"What did Danny do to it?"

"She dropped it. You should get rid of it anyway; it's morbid."

"No. And what was she doing picking it up?"

"Cleaning, I imagine."

"Danny doesn't clean."

"Well maybe she was having sex with Mark on the coffee table. What do I know?"

"Thank you. That's exactly the image I want in my head."

Amber picked up a menu and smirked. "Should we order?"

"Yeah, I'm starving."

"*You* are?" Jenna questioned disbelievingly.

"I do get hungry, you know," I said. "In fact, I've been terribly hungry lately. I've gained five pounds."

"I thought you looked fat," Amber joked.

"I'm gonna be. Suddenly I'm addicted to junk food. Chips, ice cream, chocolate bars. If I keep it up, I'm gonna look like Large Marge."

"Large Marge," Amber repeated, chuckling. "So what do you want to eat?"

Jenna glanced at the menu. "I think just a salad."

"Yeah," Amber agreed. "That sounds good."

The waitress came and Amber and Jenna ordered their salads. I ordered a chicken fajita, French fries with gravy, and a vanilla milkshake.

"I guess you *are* hungry," Jenna said.

"I told you, I'm starving. What does that woman have?" I asked, pointing at a woman at the counter who was eating some sort of pie.

Amber looked over. "Looks like lemon meringue."

"Oh, I gotta have that too."

Jenna and Amber stared in fascination as I signaled the waitress again and told her I wanted a piece of that pie. Now.

"You guys want some?" I asked, diving in.

They shook their heads and watched me devour the pie.

"It's all the working," I defended. "In London we lived on takeout those first few weeks. All the women gained at least five pounds. Then it dwindles off and you go back to normal."

"And you ate like this?" Amber asked.

"A little less. English food isn't exactly thrilling."

The food arrived and I ate like I was ravenous. I offered some to Jenna and Amber but they refused. The milkshake tasted good. The French fries smothered in gravy tasted good. And a wonderful thought occurred to me: Wouldn't they taste even better together?

I dunked a French fry into my milkshake and popped it in my mouth. Amber dropped her fork. "My God, what are you doing?" she asked.

"It's really good. Try it." I offered her a French fry sopping with gravy and vanilla milkshake and she shook her head like I was trying to feed her poison.

"No, thank you."

"Jenna?" I offered her the fry.

"I think I'll pass, Meagan."

"*You* dunk Oreos in peanut butter," I pointed out.

"I was pregnant."

My head snapped up to look at her and a flutter of nausea overtook me. *No way!* I was on the pill. That's not why I'd been sick. "What are you insinuating?" I barked.

Jenna wiped her mouth with a napkin. "Nothing. You mentioned the Oreos and I--" She stopped speaking and looked at me. Amber looked at me.

"Stop that!" I commanded. "I'm not pregnant. I'm on the pill and I'm fanatical about taking it."

"Okay," Jenna soothed, pushing away her plate. "You just have strange eating habits."

"Yes, and I always have."

"And you're not pregnant."

"No, so stop saying that word at me."

"All right," Amber said calmly. "No one at this table is pregnant."

Jenna giggled behind her hands. "Least of all you."

I laughed. "Sorry."

"Why is that so funny?" Amber demanded. "I could get pregnant."

"Yeah, with a turkey baster."

"Jenna!" I couldn't stop laughing. Jenna was not a sarcastic person and I couldn't figure out where this was coming from. She continued to giggle.

"So this is what it feels like to be you, huh Meagan? No wonder you can't control your mouth. You really amuse yourself, don't you?"

"*Me?* You're the one saying these things."

"Well, I'm not amused," Amber complained. "I can be just as maternal as anyone else."

"I should think so," I managed. "You've certainly had Zeppo at your tit long enough."

"Once again, *very funny.*"

"It's a compliment," I defended, pushing away my milkshake. At last I was full. "Zeppo takes more parenting than anyone. He cries, pouts --Christ, sometimes he even gurgles. It's a wonder you don't have to change his diapers."

Amber tried to look offended but she broke out laughing. "So what you're saying is that you believe I'd be a good mother?"

"Oh, definitely. With your patience? No doubt about it."

"Thank you."

"Gwynne on the other hand--"

"Meagan." Jenna shot me a warning look.

"Is none of my business," I finished.

"That one must have killed you," Amber teased.

I grinned. "It wasn't easy."

Amber sighed. "It never is."

"Huh?"

"Nothing."

"Okay." I glanced at my watch. 1:45 p.m. "Shit, I gotta go. I have a two o'clock meeting."

"So I'll call you about what we discussed?" Amber asked.

"Yeah, but I can't promise anything too soon."

She shrugged. "No problem. As long as I know you'll back me up when the time comes."

My gaze met hers and I smiled. "Don't you know? I'll always back you up." And with that, I strolled out of the diner, leaving the two women to stare after me.

Chapter 28

Pregnant. I pushed the word around my mouth and a wave of nausea flipped me. It couldn't be. *I was on the pill!* I took them at precisely the same time every day. I even took the green reminder pills my doctor told me were useless.

Hurriedly, I rushed to my datebook and frantically whipped through the pages. I had always kept track of my menstrual cycle and was shocked to discover there weren't any recent entries. In fact, there hadn't been an entry in—

"Two months!" I screeched. "Oh my God."

Ken waved a home pregnancy test at me. "Or we could go down to the office and I could examine you thoroughly."

"N-No. I'll --I'll take the test."

"First," he said. "And then we'll go to the doctor to have it verified. You have to stop taking your pill. Did you take it yet today?" Ken was far calmer than I was. He was downright pleased.

"No –I --I didn't." I couldn't stop the stutter in my mouth.

"That's good, honey." Tenderly, he rubbed my back. "Go take the test."

I took the test. We waited. Ken went into the bathroom to check the results while I sat on the bed nervously chewing a thumbnail. I didn't need a test to tell me I was pregnant. My period was clockwork. I had missed only one in my life and even then, I hadn't really missed it, it had just come late. Why I'd failed to notice that I'd just missed two now was beyond me, but once I realized it, there was no doubt in my mind why I'd been throwing up.

Ken returned from the bathroom and his grin widened into a full on smile. It forced his cheeks upward, lit up his eyes, and I heard the happy scream amplify through my head like the screeching of guitars at a rock concert.

"We're gonna have a baby!"

The vomit rose to the back of my throat and I darted for the bathroom.

A baby. I was going to have a baby. No matter how many times I said it to myself, I still couldn't believe it was true. Ken was as giddy as a schoolboy and his first order of business was to set me up with an appointment with the best OBGYN in the city. We agreed not to tell anyone until we were sure everything was fine. Everything was. I was two months along and as healthy as any doctor hoped their pregnant patient would be.

The news excited Ken. He wanted to scream it from the rooftops and I wanted to pretend it wasn't happening. It wasn't that I didn't want children; I just didn't have time for one. I was starting a new business, a new marriage, a new role as an aunt, and now I had one more thing to deal with and I wasn't prepared.

Then there was Amber. How would I tell Amber? My current life was the very reason she'd always stayed away from bisexuals. Eventually they'll want to marry and have children, she'd always said. I was her prediction come to life and the thought disgusted me. Ken pleaded with me to let him tell our families and, reluctantly, I agreed.

"But no friends yet," I'd said, thinking of Amber.

"No friends," Ken agreed. Then he went about happily calling his parents to tell them the news, and calling my family to invite them over for dinner.

"We have a surprise," Ken said later that evening, grinning around his dessert. I was amazed he'd been able to hold out until the end of the meal.

"What is it?" my mother asked nervously.

Ken grinned at me and took my hand. "We're gonna have a baby!" he yelled.

"Get out!" Danny was instantly on her feet. Mom burst into tears of joy and Dad smiled. Josh and Mark laughed and Jenna tilted her head at me, gauging my face for a reaction. I gave a weak smile.

"I'm only two months along," I said. "So we'd like to keep it quiet for now. Everything is fine but we'd rather not share the news with too many people until we get used to the idea ourselves."

"Used to it?" my mother squeaked. "Aren't you happy?"

"I'm --shocked," I said honestly. "But I'm not upset if

that's what you mean. I'm --I'm gonna be a mother."

"Well that is the point of pregnancy," Josh joked. "Congratulations."

"Yes," my father boomed. "We should celebrate!"

And they did. The rest of the evening my family told embarrassing Meagan stories and happily drank the three bottles of champagne Ken had had the presence of mind to buy. For me, he'd purchased sparkling cider and everyone laughed as I drank the non-alcoholic beverage with a wince. Jenna eyed me curiously for the rest of the evening and as the gang was leaving she pulled me into a hug and whispered, "The shock passes. But I do know what else concerns you."

My tone matched hers. "If she didn't hate me before, Jenna, she certainly will now."

Jenna kissed my cheek. "We'll talk later, okay? Take tomorrow off work and come by."

"Okay."

Jenna was as understanding a person as I'd ever known. Only to her did I share my fears. Only to her did I admit how unprepared I felt, how *unmaternal*. Over raspberry tea in her kitchen I poured out my soul and not once did she flinch or look at me like I was a despicable person.

"It happens, Meagan," she soothed. "It's pregnancy jitters. In my first months I was terrified I'd be the worst mother in the world."

"But you're a wonderful mother," I said.

"And you will be too. Josh and I weren't ready, but it happened and now we couldn't be happier. You know the love you feel for Sammy? Multiply that by a million and that's the love you'll feel for your own baby."

"Zoe," I said.

Jenna laughed. "See, how could you be a bad mother when you've already chosen a name? What if it's a boy?"

"It won't be."

"Why?"

"Call it a hunch. It's gonna be a girl and I'm gonna name her Zoe. It's derived from greek and it means 'life.' I looked it up in one of those baby books."

"It's pretty," Jenna agreed. "When are you going to tell your friends?"

"My friends, Jenna? You mean Amber."

"Yes."

"I was thinking somewhere in between 'Oww I'm having a contraction' and 'Oh look, Zoe got accepted to Yale.' What do you think?"

"I think you should come up with a better plan," she said, giggling. "How are you going to manage dinner tonight?"

I frowned. "What do you mean?"

"Ken didn't tell you? Gwynne called and asked if Josh and I would like to go out for dinner at some Mexican place tonight. She said Ken had already agreed and you guys were coming. We got a sitter and everything."

My head shook in disbelief. "I can't believe he would *do that!*"

"Can you handle it?"

"I don't know."

"Meagan?" Jenna frowned uneasily at the cup in her hands. "You're still in love with her, aren't you? And I don't mean the love you feel because you once loved someone, I mean truly, deeply in love."

"It won't go away," I whispered. "I try driving it away but it won't leave me alone and it kills me to have to look at her."

"And Ken?"

"I love Ken. He's my husband and he's been there for me since the day I met him. Now we're having a baby and I want it Jenna, I really do, but sometimes I just feel so awful inside, like it's all going the wrong way."

"Are you saying you want out of your marriage?"

"That was a pretty big leap."

"Was it?" Her pale blue eyes searched my face and I thought she could see through me. Could she see how hard it was for me to make love to my husband anymore? How I had to force myself and pretend I was enjoying it when really I wanted to scream, "Get off me, Missionary Man!" I loved Ken, and I tried convincing myself my passion for him would return when the morning sickness ended but I was very afraid I was wrong. I could get passionate enough if I thought about Amber and the reality of that terrified me. I was supposed to want my husband --my sweet, kind husband with the handsome boyish face and the taut masculine body. And I wanted so desperately to want him again.

"Meagan?"

"Hmm?" Groggily, I came back to the present.

Jenna sighed. "Nothing."

I stared down at my tea. "Thank you." Jenna's 'nothing' meant she was going to let it drop, and I was grateful.

So what are you going to do about dinner?" She pressed.

I shrugged. "Go, I guess. What choice do I have? If I don't go, Amber will think it's because of her."

"It would be."

"Yeah, so I don't see how I have any other choice. Besides, Gwynne will be there and Amber forgets me easily enough when she's around." I sighed. "At least one of us has moved on."

Chapter 29

The Mexican restaurant was a tacky place with sombreros on the walls and large round tables that looked like they might crack under the weight of the trays of food on top of them.

"Who picked this place?" I complained, as our group of six was guided to a table in the center of the room by a squat man with beady eyes and a perverted leer.

"I did," Gwynne admitted. "It's not much to look at but the food is good."

The food was nothing my weak stomach could handle. There wasn't one item on the menu that would agree with it and Gwynne took it upon herself to order the "party platter", a giant assortment of food with enough entrees to feed a starving nation.

You are a starving nation, I thought, and allowed myself a small snicker. Ken eyed me curiously. I shrugged.

At the table, Ken sat to my left and Jenna to my right. Josh sat beside Jenna, Amber sat on the other side of him, and Gwynne sat between Amber and Ken. Absentmindedly, I thought Gwynne was in my spot.

I didn't feel well. The nausea had been fluttering in and out all day and the smell of the restaurant was making me sick.

"How's Sammy doing?" Amber asked over salads.

"Great," Jenna said. "Danny's watching him tonight."

"*Danny?*" I demanded, thinking my sister too irresponsible. "That's your sitter? You should have asked me."

"You're here," Josh pointed out. "Danny's fine. She's good with him. *She* doesn't buy people puppies."

"Are you still on that?" I groaned.

"Do you know how hard that dog was to housebreak?"

"Speaking of the dog," I said. "What the hell kind of a name is Chuck for a dog?"

Jenna giggled. "He threw up a lot the first week. Josh kept

calling him upchuck and it just sort of stuck."

"Are you telling me I bought Sammy a sick puppy?"

"No, we just had to find the right food. Look how big he is now. Chuck's great."

"I'm glad you like him," Ken said. "Because if you didn't, I was going to end up stuck with him."

"And you would have loved him," I defended. "We just might--"

"No."

"What?"

Ken sighed. "You're going to say we're getting a dog and we're not."

I laughed. "That foot of yours just keeps getting bigger, doesn't it?"

"Eat your salad, Meagan."

"Why are you so bossy?"

"If I wasn't you'd be running a business from our bedroom with a dog in your lap, a phone to your ear, and Ted hiding in the closet." The whole table broke out laughing.

"That's my sister," Josh said. "The originator of the saying, 'it's my way or the highway.'"

"You are so full of it. I just have shit to do and only so many hours in which to do it."

"And if you don't slow down you're gonna be dead before you're fifty."

"Or I'll be in the loony bin with Jenna's uncle Steve."

"Stop saying that," Jenna reprimanded. "My uncle Steve is not insane."

"Lobotomy--"

"And he didn't have a lobotomy either."

"Just an anal probe from the aliens, right?"

"I never should have told you that."

"I should think not; I was a complete stranger. Besides, I only tease because I love Lobotomy Joe. He's cute."

"One of these days I'm gonna tell him you call him that."

"Tell him." I shrugged. "Tell him I believe in fairies too."

"You _what_?" Gwynne shrieked.

Amber laughed. "She believes in fairies."

"You're putting me on, right?"

"No." Ken shook his head. "My wife believes in the wee

folk. She's a bit delusional, I'm afraid."

"Am not. *You* believe in God."

"So?"

"So have you ever seen Him? If He can be invisible and still be believed in by billions of people so can fairies. At least there's a sense of romance to it. What has God ever done for you?"

"Meagan!" Josh threw down his napkin. "I swear sometimes I think you're the anti-christ."

"Oh come on. I'm only pointing out the obvious. I believe in God; I just don't think He does much these days. In fact, He hasn't done much since He led his Jews out of Israel, wrote His little commandments and moved on."

"His *little commandments*?" Josh demanded. "You're one hell of a Catholic, Meagan."

"Are we going to argue religion?"

"No wonder Celia calls you corrupt."

"Celia is a prime example of what religion *doesn't* do," I said. "She spends half her life on her knees but she's still ugly and filled with hate."

"And I suppose there's nothing wrong with Seamus, right?"

"Not anything other than drinking too much. Seamus is ten times the person Celia will ever be. Ask Ken."

Ken smiled. "Seamus is a great guy."

"Are you still really close to your uncle?" Amber asked.

"Yeah. Seamus is my other father."

"Dad's not enough?"

My head snapped to my brother. "What is your problem tonight?"

"No problem," Josh said, shrugging.

"Then relax."

The salads were cleared away and Ken frowned at my untouched plate. I couldn't eat. I felt too nauseated. When the entrees arrived I felt even sicker. Thought a piece of bread would make me feel better but it stuck in my throat and I couldn't finish it. Ken filled my plate with food and I stared down at it in disgust. It looked greasy and meaty and spicy and the smell alone was making me green.

The others at the table ate and commented on how good the food was while I remained silent and only sipped my water.

They talked. I stared at my plate.

"Well, look who suddenly got quiet," Josh teased. "What's the matter motor-mouth? Run out of smart ass remarks?"

"Yes."

Ken gave me a quizzical look. "Are you okay, honey?"

"Ken, I think I'm gonna be sick."

I darted from the table and ran for the ladies room, Jenna quick on my heels.

"Oh God," I groaned, head over the toilet.

Jenna held back my hair and giggled. "Well, you're calling Him now, aren't you?"

"Shut up," I muttered, even though I was laughing. I gagged but didn't throw up.

Amber appeared in the bathroom and approached the stall Jenna and I were in. "Meagan, are you okay?" she asked, giving a small rap on the stall door.

"She'll be alright," Jenna promised.

New footsteps entered the bathroom. Gwynne. She didn't ask about my health. Instead she said, "Your food is getting cold, Amber."

I heard Amber give an irritated sigh. "I just left it two seconds ago, Gwynne."

Her tone was sarcastic and it made me laugh. My head was in the toilet, but I laughed.

"Shh," Jenna whispered. "Gwynne will go nuts if she thinks you're laughing at her." But I couldn't stop and Jenna started coughing to try to muffle the sound. Gwynne heard me anyway.

"What is she laughing at?" she demanded.

"Like *I* know?" Amber said.

She knew. Amber knew me and she knew why I was laughing. Slowly, I stood up and we stepped out of the stall.

"What were you laughing at?" Gwynne barked, her eyes like fire on my face.

"I told her a joke," Jenna said.

"What joke?"

Jenna was stuck. She never lied so she wasn't very good at it.

"I was laughing at you," I admitted. "Or more precisely, what Amber said to you."

"Oh really?" Gwynne folded her arms in front of her huge chest.

"Yes, really. So what?"

"You push your luck with me, Meagan. I try to be nice but there's no denying I can't stand you."

"Well why the hell did you invite us here? Do you think *I* wanted to come? You did a good job on the house and I'm grateful for it, but that doesn't mean I'll put up with your shit, either."

"Do you two always have to fight?" Jenna complained.

"No, because this is the last of it."

"But Sammy's baptism--"

"We'll be there, Jenna," I assured. "And we'll all act civilized, and I'm sure we'll be thrust together after that as well but there won't be any more evenings out like this."

"We can deal with it, Meagan," Jenna pleaded. "We're all friends."

"No Jenna, *you're* everyone's friend."

"And you're no one's," Gwynne barked. "And if you think you're going to be Amber's publisher, you can just think again."

"That's my decision, Gwynne," Amber said. "If I want to be a Markham-Summers' client I'll be one, assuming they want me. We've discussed this. I'm not happy with Hector and I trust Meagan."

"You trust *her*? After what she did to you?"

"That has nothing to do with business. You don't have to like it, but Meagan is the best at what she does."

"She's a first time book publisher! Or *will* be if she ever gets around to starting the damn business. Hector was *raised* with it."

"And he sucks," I said. "If Amber wants me to be her publisher, she'll have me, and I guarantee you no one will push her books harder than I will. Don't let your jealousy mar her success."

"Jealous? Of *you*?" Gwynne gave a mocking laugh. "What I'm doing is protecting her from you!"

"Gwynne, that's silly," Jenna said. "I'm sorry, but it just is. Meagan would never do anything to harm Amber professionally. She wouldn't harm her at all."

"What does Ken think of this?" Gwynne snapped.

I shrugged. "Ask him yourself. *Ken* understands the

difference between business and personal matters. He knows the situation and he knows I'll take Amber right to the top if that's where she wants to be."

"Oh, you'll take her to the top, huh? *You* will?"

"I've done it twice for *Natural Beauty*. I'm sure I can do it for a talented author. It's not really any of your business anyway. I don't know your relationship but I'm fairly certain Amber doesn't tell you how to run your decorating business."

"I don't," Amber said. "And you won't tell me how to run mine. I trust Meagan. End of story."

Gwynne threw up her arms. "Fine, but when she screws you over, don't come crying to me."

"I won't because that won't happen."

A thin waitress entered the bathroom. "Excuse me, but there are two gentlemen at a table wondering when you ladies are coming back."

Jenna giggled. "We're on our way."

"Okay."

The waitress left and we followed her out. Back at the table Ken and Josh looked nervous.

"Are you okay, honey?" Ken asked, wrapping his arm around the back of my chair.

I leaned into him, suddenly very tired. "I'm alright, but I'd like to go home now, if you don't mind."

Jenna rose from her chair again. "I'll go with you."

Josh's head popped up. "What?"

"Why don't you and Ken go for a drink or something?" she suggested sweetly. "We're gonna do the girl thing tonight."

"Meagan?" Ken's eyes questioned me.

"Do you mind, Ken?" My tone was as sweet as Jenna's because I thought I'd rather be with her right now than anyone else.

"No. If that's what you want. Come on Josh, we'll go play pool somewhere."

The two men rose to leave. Ken kissed me goodbye and I watched him depart.

Jenna clapped her hands together. "Your place or mine?"

"Neither." Something else sounded better.

"Huh?"

I grinned. "Wanna take a trip in the way-back machine?"

Jenna's grin matched mine. "Danny's?"

"Why not? She's got Sammy tonight and I still have the keys. What do you say?"

"Alright, but are you gonna freak out if it's a mess?"

"It's her apartment."

"Yeah, with your belongings in it."

"I won't freak out. Let's go."

Jenna and I managed a quick goodbye to Amber. Jenna said goodbye to Gwynne and we left the restaurant to go downtown and back to our past together.

Chapter 30

The backyard was filled with people. It was a large yard with an opening leading into a small forest at the back of the house. Josh and Jenna had been planning this party for weeks. Forty-five guests to celebrate Sammy's christening. I held him in my arms and stared down at my beautiful godson the same way I had hours before at the font when the priest poured holy water on his head and he cried against my chest. Jenna's cousin Charles was the godfather and we'd stood at the font together, proudly taking on our guardianship responsibilities.

It was a symbolic responsibility. Jenna didn't believe in the purpose of Catholic baptism but she went along for Josh and our parents, who'd insisted that no Summers child would walk through life without being recognized by the church and by God. I thought God had recognized Sammy enough to create him, but that was just my humble opinion.

There had been a short service, which I hadn't really paid attention to, and then it was back to Josh and Jenna's lovely Victorian to celebrate. Sammy was six months old. I was pregnant. I thought I had taken the news well. Of course, I'd been taking it for a few weeks now. Ken was still thrilled. From across the lawn I saw his loving eyes take in the picture of me holding Sammy under the giant oak beside the corner of the house. I had distanced us from the party. No one seemed to mind. It was what I did these days, distance. I rocked Sammy in my arms until he fell asleep against my breast with his fist tightly wrapped around my pinkie. I smiled at the chubby digits and pressed them to my lips as Jenna appeared beside us.

"Maybe I should put him down for his nap," she said, extending her arms and beaming at us. She always looked radiant.

I rose from the wicker chair. "I'll do it."

"Are you sure?"

Nodding, I carried Sammy through the back door that Josh had finally shaved so it wouldn't stick, and into the empty house. I crossed through the kitchen, the dining room, rounded the corner and climbed the stairs to the second level. I thought I heard voices. Whispers. Sammy's pacifier slipped from his mouth, I caught it, and he gave a little gurgle as we rounded the corner at the top of the landing. I slid the pacifier back in place between his lips.

"Better, buddy?" I whispered.

I smiled down at him. Looked up and the smile froze on my face. Not five feet away stood Gwynne and Amber, kissing. They were near the door to the bathroom and Gwynne had Amber pressed up against the striped paper that lined the hallway walls. Her hand was moving up Amber's shirt. Amber pushed it down but continued to kiss her. The sound of their breathing filled my head as my own breathing seemed to stop. I wanted to run from the hallway and rescue my eyes from the awful thing they were witnessing but my feet refused to move and my stare took all of it in. Sammy's hand twisted around the front of my shirt and a little cry escaped his lips. Amber's head snapped away from Gwynne's. Her cheeks flushed when she looked at me. Gwynne remained impassive.

"I'm sorry," I said, wondering how I was able to speak without air. The air had completely fled the room, or perhaps, I was the only person it had fled. "I didn't mean to--" I nodded down at Sammy. "I was just putting him down for his nap."

They didn't say anything. Gwynne managed an evil smile and Amber bounced nervously against the wall.

"I'm sorry," I said again, and scooted past them down to the second door and into Sammy's room with the white crib and the white dressing table and the Sesame Street decals on the powder blue walls. It was such a pretty room. Soothing. The perfect room for a baby I thought, while my heart continued to pound like it would force its way right out of my chest.

I placed Sammy in his crib. Turned the dial on the mobile above his head and the tiny figures began dancing to the sound of a quiet nursery song that whispered out of the small yellow speaker. He looked up at me and his eyes softly closed. I rested my hand on his little chest and felt him breathing.

"You're so beautiful, Sam," I soothed. "Soon you'll have a little cousin to play with and we're all going to be very happy." The words sounded fake, even to me.

Sighing, I folded my arms across the top of the crib and rested my chin on the back of my hands, watching him sleep. A shadow appeared in the doorway.

"Hey," Amber whispered.

I glanced up. "Hi."

She crossed the room to stand beside me and smiled down at Sammy. "He's really something, isn't he?"

"Yes."

"Gwynne's downstairs. I'm sorry, Meagan."

"For what?"

"For what you saw out there. We shouldn't have been doing that. It was inappropriate and of all people, you of course, had to be the one to come upon us. I wasn't trying to hurt you."

I shrugged. "I'm not hurt, Amber. I'm married."

She glanced at my wedding ring. "Yeah, you certainly are that."

"So there's nothing to be sorry for. I've moved on, you've moved on --whatever. If you don't mind, I'd like to spend a few minutes with my godson."

"Okay." She turned toward the door. Stopped. "Hey Meagan?"

"Mm-hmm?"

"You looked great up there today."

"Thank you."

"I just thought --I just wanted to tell you that."

She left and I turned my attention back to Sammy. "I think that's it Sam," I whispered. "Don't make me come to anymore of these parties, okay?" He gave a little moan and smiled around his pacifier, still sleeping. I chuckled quietly. "Yeah, you know what I'm saying. Thank God you don't turn one for another five and a half months. That gives me plenty of time to recover before I have to do this again, right?" Another little moan and I stroked his cheek. "Okay, I'll let you sleep."

I grabbed his baby monitor from the dresser and carried it back outside. Most of the guests had left and we were down to a decidedly small group; immediate family, Amber and Gwynne, and a few of Josh's friends from the office. Amber glanced at me when I stepped onto the patio and I averted my eyes. Ken and Gwynne were talking by the rose bushes in the corner of the yard. He smiled at me. Gave a little wave. I pressed the monitor to my ear, heard nothing, and shook it. I checked the dial on the side and found it was set to *low.* I cranked it to *high*, patted Jenna on the shoulder, and handed her the box.

"Are you okay?" she whispered.

"Why wouldn't I be?"

"Come on, Meagan," Danny said. She was leaning against one of the picnic tables drinking a Coor's Light. "We know what you saw. I can't believe they were even doing that."

My eyes narrowed on her face. "I'm married, Danielle."

"So that exempts you from pain?"

"Yes." I stalked away from them and felt Amber's eyes on my back as I made my way back to the chair under the oak and sat beside my father. He took my hand and squeezed it in his.

"How about we go for a walk?" he asked, waving a tree branch from the top of his brown head.

"Where?"

"In the woods. Where else?" He stood and pulled me to my feet, then drew me into a paternal embrace. "Did I ever tell you how proud I am of you?"

Why was he saying that? I was no one to be proud of. I was making a mess of my life. In the past month I had done nothing but draw away from the people who loved me while I tried to come to terms with my existence and kept turning up empty. I wanted more than I had. More for me, and more for my baby. I wanted to cry. It seemed everything these days made me want to cry. I wasn't sure if that was because my hormones were out of whack or because I was already failing at my marriage. Ken was trying. I was trying. But I couldn't shake the feeling that it just wasn't right anymore. I wasn't sure it had ever been right to begin with.

"Do you mind if I go by myself, Dad?" I asked, feeling the weight of his words in my heart.

"Are you sure?"

I nodded. "I think the quiet will do me good."

My father agreed and I went over to my husband and whispered that I was going for a walk. "Do you want me to come?" he asked.

I shook my head, kissed his cheek, and headed toward the path leading into the woods. I felt him watch me leave, like he knew I was beyond his reach and he didn't know how to change it. Then I heard Josh announcing a volleyball game and calling for Ken to be on his team.

"I'm in a suit," I heard Ken say.

"So? I'll give you something to change into."

"Alright." Ken couldn't resist a good game of anything.

Their voices got quieter as I moved through the woods toward the small pond I knew was at the end of the trail. There were large rocks in front of it where I could sit and watch the wind make tiny ripples in the brownish-green water. I had never been much of a nature person but Jenna had taken me to the pond a few times and I found myself comfortable there, peaceful.

I moved along the trail. Took off my shoes and made the rest of the way barefoot. Within minutes I was standing in front of the murky water selecting my rock. There was a flat one nearest the water's edge with two tall rocks on either side of it, like walls. That was the place for me. Secluded. Nestled into nature where I could be alone with my thoughts.

Throwing my shoes on the patch of grass beside me, I sat down in the semi-hidden pit, and leaned back against the sun-warmed block of stone. Closed my eyes. The wind caressed my hair and the smell of flowers breezed in from the small wildflower field nearby. Josh and Jenna had access to the most lovely stretch of earth. I wondered what it was like to be as content as they were and thought I might never truly know such peace.

I plucked a tall weed from between the rocks and twisted it in my fingers. Enjoyed the silence. Sometimes being alone was all a person needed. Just those hushed moments when the world dropped away and you could wrap yourself in the solitude of a quieted heart.

My heart was a trap. Once I was locked inside it, escaping its chains was no easier than hiding your soul in your mouth. The mouth would eventually spit out the soul but the heart chains, oh, they only tightened their hold and the more you struggled the harder they squeezed until you felt like an anaconda was wrapping around your insides, crushing away your hope of ever breathing again.

That was what was happening to me --I wasn't breathing

anymore. I was taking in air, expelling air, but the action was no more real than it was for a person on a respirator. Something was causing the function, but it wasn't me. It was my invisible respirator pumping the oxygen into my lungs by mere force of survival. I wasn't breathing. I was merely allowing myself to have air.

"Cause I'm fucked," I whispered.

"No, I don't think so." The familiar voice came from behind and I sighed. Was I destined to always have her creeping up behind me?

"You're worse than Jenna," I said, without turning to look at her. "She's always creeping up on me too."

"Maybe that's because you spend too much time alone," Amber said.

"I like being alone."

She sat down beside me. "Why?"

"It's comfortable. Shouldn't you be at the party?"

"They're playing volleyball. Everyone else is gone."

I tossed my weed in the pond. "You're going to get us in trouble with Ken and Gwynne."

"Why?"

"Is that your question of the day?"

"We're allowed to be friends."

"Are we? I doubt Gwynne would agree."

I glanced down at my stomach. Three months along and waiting for it to grow. Sometimes I thought I felt it growing. Other times I believed Ken when he told me it was just my imagination. How *could* I feel it when my stomach was as narrow and flat as it had always been? The only indication of my pregnancy at all was the morning sickness that, lately, had been easing. Absentmindedly, I rubbed my belly. *It's okay Zoe, we're doing just fine. I'll keep taking in the air and you keep growing.*

"Why did you say you're fucked?"

"Because I am."

She shook her head. "I don't understand you, Meagan. You have a great husband, money, a beautiful home, a family that loves you -- what does it take to make you happy?"

I watched the water rippling toward us. Knew the change would have to come about soon. "The things I can't have, I guess."

"Like?"

"I don't know, Amber," I said exasperatedly. She was always so full of questions. "Just leave me alone. Why can't anyone ever just leave me alone?"

"Because you're not a universe unto yourself."

"Excuse me?"

"You're not the only person in the world, Meagan."

"I'm well aware of that," I snapped.

"I didn't mean it like that. I just meant that you don't have to be alone --you choose to be. You close everyone off and you hide out in that place inside of you until it makes you lonely and sad."

I looked at her. "What do you honestly know about it, Amber? You knew me for what, ten minutes once? Hardly long enough to sit here examining my soul."

She was unaffected by my sarcastic words. "I know you better than anyone else in this world and you know it. Run from it if you want, Meagan, but you can't escape it. Neither of us can."

"I'm not trying to escape it," I said quietly.

An image of my husband's smiling face came to mind and I felt fresh tears welling behind my eyes. How would I tell him I couldn't be married to him anymore? How would I tell him our whole lives were a lie? I knew now that I *was* going to do it; I just didn't know how.

"So what are you doing sitting out here when there's a party going on back there?" Amber asked.

"I could ask you the same thing."

"I followed you."

"Why?"

She stared out over the pond. "I don't know."

"I hope you have a better line than that prepared for when Gwynne asks you the same question." My eyes followed hers to the water. "Jenna comes here to meditate. Do you think anyone can be as peaceful as she is?"

"I think it would be an effort."

I picked another weed. "What isn't?"

"Is it always such a struggle, Meagan?"

"What?"

"Being you."

I laughed. "Sometimes. But sometimes it's good. For the most part I like myself--"

"Good."

"--I'm just not often inspired, I suppose. Jenna could marvel at a sunset forever. I'd simply see the sun going down and think, *big deal, it's coming back tomorrow*. I guess I'm not easily fascinated. What about you?"

She shrugged. "Some things bore me and others never stop fascinating me."

"Like?"

"I'm not sure, really. I just know it when it comes along. Things that are intangible --that fascinates me because I can never figure out why."

"Not everything needs a reason."

"I guess not. I just want all the answers, you know? I want an explanation."

"For what?"

"For everything." She plucked a weed from between the rocks and stared down at it. "Why do we always have these strange conversations?"

I smiled. "I didn't know we always conversed."

"I miss that sometimes." She threw the weed in the pond and it immediately floated up to mine.

I shook my head despairingly. "Freaking symbolism."

She looked at me. "What?"

"The weeds." I indicated the water and she smiled at the two weeds drifting upon the ripples like they were clinging to each other. "Things are changing," I whispered.

"What do you mean?"

"There's a lot you don't know but it will all come together soon."

"I don't understand," she said, watching me haul my shoes from the grass.

I turned to leave. "You will, soon enough. The world is about to crash out of control but at the end, I think there will be clarity. It's gonna come together, Amber. I don't know if it will matter to you one way or the other when it does, but you *will* know about it. You'll just have to trust me."

"Meagan, wait," she called after me. "Don't walk away on words like that. Tell me what you mean."

But I was already gone.

Chapter 31

Ken was crying. We were in his study and his face was pressed into his hands and he was crying.

I was crying. We were a new couple with a baby on the way and I was ending it all. I was keeping the baby, because I wanted her, but I was walking away from my marriage of six months. I just couldn't live with the lie anymore.

"This is because of Amber, isn't it?" Ken accused. "You want out of our marriage because you've been cheating on me with her the whole time!"

"No," I said quietly. "I would never do that."

I loved Amber, but I had never cheated on my husband. I wanted Amber, but most importantly, I wanted to be true to myself and to my Zoe and that meant leaving her father.

The guilt crushed me. *I'm sorry baby*, I thought, rubbing my stomach. *I'm sorry you won't be able to live with your daddy.*

"I don't believe you," Ken yelled. "You've been sleeping with her. I'm not stupid, Meagan. Don't you think I've noticed the way you freeze up every time I touch you? Why is that? Because making love to me would be cheating on *her*?"

"I don't cheat!" I yelled back. "I've been completely faithful to you and if you think so little of me maybe you don't deserve to be Zoe's father."

"What are you saying? Are you gonna run away with her, Meagan? You think you can? No one is taking my baby! I'm her father!" He started pacing the office in a rage. "I'll sue for custody," he warned. "I'll drag your past into court. I'll tell them about your history of abandonment, your lesbian affair, your years of therapy –by the time I'm done you'll be just another unfit mother and the courts won't think twice about handing me custody."

My mouth dropped open in horror. This wasn't the man I had married, the man I'd loved. It wasn't the same man who'd tried to rescue me from myself and make my nightmares bearable. This man was a monster!

"Fuck you!" I screamed, running at him and pummeling him with my fists. He yanked my arms above my head and I struggled against him.

"Do you want me to add assault to the list?" he growled, pressing my back against a row of bookcases.

I settled down.

We slept in separate bedrooms that night. The next morning Ken left for work and I got up and wandered the rooms of the lovely home we'd shared, taking it all in for the last time. I would leave this place today. I did not expect Ken to leave the house he'd made his home and I wouldn't have been able to live in it even if I'd wanted to, not after what its walls had witnessed. The house would serve only as a reminder of my failed marriage and the fantasy world I had tried to sustain but could not. It would infect me with its echoes of the time spent within it. The laughter, the forced joy, creeping into my bloodstream like a virus I had not built up immunity against.

The quiet settled into my bones. For once, the phone did not ring. The world had cast me aside, like it knew what I had done and, tearfully, I went upstairs to pack a bag. I didn't know where I was going, only that I had to leave, and I vowed that I would call Ken as soon as I reached a destination, perhaps some quiet motel on the outskirts of the city where I could be alone for awhile.

By late evening Ken had still not returned from work. I grabbed my bag, my passport just in case, and the five thousand dollars cash I'd withdrawn from the bank the day before. I thought the cash might come in handy in case I decided I wanted to disappear for awhile. I didn't want to use credit cards because that would leave a paper trail and I was thinking like a fugitive now.

For hours I drove. I circled the city several times. I went uptown, downtown, across the Bank Street Bridge and into the east side, passing several dingy motels. I thought I might check into one but realized there was something I had to do first. I had to talk to Amber. I had to tell her what I'd done. I had to go to her, tell her I loved her, and that I was pregnant and leaving Ken. I didn't expect her to take me back; I only wanted her to know. If she chose to remain with Gwynne I would know I'd made the right decision nonetheless. My marriage was a sham. It was the pregnancy that truly helped me realize that. Once I accepted the idea I was going to be a mother, I became suddenly aware of how quickly life could change. I didn't want to go through the rest of my life without ever being with Amber again.

I couldn't stop loving her but I *could* stop flinching because I wasn't afraid anymore, and I was going to ask her the biggest question one person could ever ask another: *Will you come back to me and help me raise my baby?*

I feared the answer would be no, and with that fear in mind I made a u-turn at the next light, drove fifteen minutes longer and steered my car onto Chestnut Avenue. There wasn't anything good on the radio and I needed music. I clumsily sifted through the CDs in the glove compartment and pulled out The Cranberries.

With one hand on the wheel and one on the CD, I popped open the case, jammed the CD in the stereo, and scanned the disc until I came upon a song that sounded right. The music comforted me as I neared a streetlight three blocks from Amber's building. The light turned yellow. I pressed the accelerator hard and cruised toward it.

I didn't see the truck barreling toward me.

PART III

Chapter 32

Sirens screamed in the distance. The street was a mass of commotion, traffic backed up for blocks, police pushing away curious spectators who gathered around the area, peering over the barricades at me, a bloody mangled mess, half on a stretcher and half pinned under a steering wheel rescue workers were cutting away with some sort of hacksaw.

I was more concerned with Zoe. I didn't know where she had gone but I had seen her spirit float away from the scene of the crash, led upward above the street lights by a brilliant man with black hair and eyes, and when I begged her not to go, the man turned and smiled at me like the two of them shared a secret that I was not allowed to be a part of. Together they disappeared behind the fog above the clouds.

I'd followed as far as I could, pulling myself from the lifeless body the paramedics were trying to remove from the crumpled car, and stretching myself across the sky until I reached an invisible barrier and could press no farther.

Zoe. I was going to name her Zoe because the name meant *life*. Now she would have none.

The paramedics continued to work on me.

"Grab her legs," someone yelled as the steering wheel gave way.

"I have a heartbeat here."

The men hauled my body onto a stretcher and speedily wheeled me toward the back of an awaiting ambulance.

"Goddamnit," one of the paramedics yelled. "She's hemorrhaging, Chuck."

The ambulance doors slammed shut, leaving me outside on the street while my body was whisked to the hospital.

"She's lost the baby," a voice in the corridor said. "I'm sorry, Ken."

Mom cried. Her heels clicked against the hallway floor outside my hospital room as she paced. "Will she wake up, Ken? Will she?"

"The doctors don't know yet," Ken whispered.

"Oh dear God! Oh God! Where is my husband? Where are Josh and Jenna and Danielle?"

"They're on their way. Jenna had to find a sitter for Sammy and Danielle is hunting down Amber."

I listened to their words from a detached place above the corridor, watching them.

"What do you mean Danielle is hunting down Amber?" my mother shrieked. "You are Meagan's husband, Ken. That woman has no place here."

My beautiful husband shook his head. "It's complicated Joan," he offered, quietly. "Meagan wanted a divorce."

"What?"

"She told me yesterday. I begged her to reconsider. 'If not for us, for the baby' I said. But Meagan said--" Ken choked on a sob and my heart ached for him. "She said I would always be the baby's father. We argued. I accused her of cheating on me with Amber and she said if I really believed she'd do that, then maybe I didn't deserve to be the baby's father."

"Oh, Jesus."

"I got angry, Joan. When she said that it scared me and I blurted out that I'd sue her for custody. But I didn't mean it, I swear." My husband shook his head. "She tried for me, Joan, she really did, but you see, I was never the one." Ken left out a few of the more hurtful details, I noticed, probably for the best.

"So I suppose you'll divorce her now," my mother accused. "Now that she's lying there in that bed and I have only your word to go on. How very convenient, Ken."

Oh, Mom.

"No," Ken said. "When Meagan wakes up she can decide for herself what she wants. Now that she's lost the baby there's really nothing keeping her to me, is there?" The pain was in his voice and I hurt for him.

Five people rushed out of the elevator doors at the end of the hall.

"Joan!" Dad raced over to my mother. "Joan, what happened?"

"Oh Patrick." Mom fell into his extended arms. "It was an accident. The police haven't put all the pieces together yet but they know she was speeding and may have run a red light."

Yellow. The light was *yellow,* and I'd had plenty of time to get through it. That truck just appeared out of nowhere. It slammed into me, spinning me once and sending me hurdling into a telephone pole.

"I've been here an hour," Mom cried. "Ken told me not to take Chestnut but I did. There were police everywhere and Meagan's car was crumpled around a telephone pole and a tow truck was trying to pry it free but it wouldn't budge. It was--it was--"

"Joan, you shouldn't have."

"I had to see! It was wrapped around the pole too tightly, Patrick. You couldn't even tell what kind of car it was." Mom was hysterical. "My windows were open and as I waited for an officer to wave me through the detour I could hear the tow truck drivers talking. 'That woman they pulled out of here,' one of them said, 'no way she's gonna make it. Blood everywhere. Never knew a person could bleed so much.' He was shaking his head. 'Young too,' he told his partner. 'Always a shame when they kill themselves off so young.'"

Mom sobbed. Dad held her in his arms and I floated away, over their heads and along the tiled ceiling, floating, floating, until I reached the other four figures and opened my ears to their conversation.

"How long will she be unconscious?" Josh asked Ken, squeezing Jenna to his chest as she cried.

Work a little magic for me Jenna, I thought. *Call up your high priestess and tell her your best friend needs help.*

"We don't know yet. Days, weeks." Ken pulled my brother aside. "Josh, this could go on indefinitely," he whispered.

Jenna, Amber, and Danielle were huddled by the nurses' station, crying into each other's arms.

"Can I see her?" Amber asked Ken, wiping her eyes with the underside of her thumb. I admired her courage while at the same time admiring my husband for the way he hid his pain. It tore his heart to have to look at her, I knew.

"*I'm* not your obstacle," he said, somewhat snappishly. "She is." And he pointed at my mother who stood outside the door to my room like a palace guard. Amber nodded and I followed her.

"Where do you think you're going?" my mother demanded.

Ken appeared at Amber's side. "Let her through, Joan," he commanded.

"Ken, need I remind you that is *your* wife lying in there?"

"You needn't remind me of anything!" he growled, grabbing Amber's arm. "Now please, let us through."

Ken guided Amber into the room, pulled a chair up to the bed, and deposited her into it. "You have fifteen minutes," he said without looking at her. He closed the door behind him as he left, a better man than anyone knew.

I stood at the other side of the bed, watching, curious to know what Amber would say to the unconscious form before her.

"Oh Meagan," she cried, pressing my hand to her forehead. Ken had lovingly washed the blood from my face and Dr. Lambert had stitched the gash above my eyebrow, but he hadn't bandaged it and the end of the thread now poked out grotesquely like an antenna above my eye. Amber moved to touch it, then drew back her hand, and instead kissed the inside of my wrist.

"Don't die, Meagan," she whispered. "Please don't die."

Then she did the strangest thing. Leaning over the bed, she stole a glance at the closed door, kissed my immovable lips, and pushed back my eyelids with her fingers, peering into the dead hazel space. "I know you're in there," she said, her eyes searching mine, "so I want you to listen to me. You have to come back. There's too much unresolved stuff between us for it to end like this. Okay, Meagan? Okay?" She removed her hand and the eyes fell closed. She started crying.

"Why didn't you tell me about the baby?" she whispered.

My heart twisted at the mention of my Zoe. Zoe, who had floated away to a place I couldn't follow, with a man I didn't know.

"Did you think I wouldn't understand? Damn it, Meagan. Wake up because I need to hear your answers. I need to know why you said those cryptic words to me last week, that it all would all come together soon. What in God's name were you planning? Because I know you Meagan, you always have a plan. *Please,* wake up."

Ken poked his head in the door. "Her family wants to see

her now, Amber," he said. I felt like I was watching my own funeral.

Amber nodded and brushed my forehead with a kiss. "I'll be back," she whispered, while Ken fiddled with the beeping machine at my side and pretended not to be listening. I watched Amber leave.

Ken took my hand. "I thought if anyone could snap you out of this before it went too far it would be her. That's why I let her in here, you know." He stroked my cheek. "It kills me to see you lying here like this. Zoe's gone. I'm sure you know that though, maybe you're even with her now. Yes, I think I will believe that the two of you are together because it comforts me to do so. What does she look like Meagan? Is she pretty?"

I don't know. I think she was.

"I'll bet she looks like you. I'll bet she has those same hazel eyes, or will if the blue goes away, and I bet she'll have your pretty brown-auburn hair."

Please stop, Ken. I can't bear to hear it.

"Zoe." Ken's face changed. His eyes flashed anger and he groped my wrist. "You were going to raise her with Amber, weren't you?" he accused. "I know that was the plan. You wanted a divorce and you were going to raise my baby with *her*. Why?" A solitary tear rolled down his face. "Haven't I been a good husband? I would have given her the world, would have been the most devoted husband and father there ever was."

I know. I moved beside him and even though he couldn't hear me talking, I said, *You're a good man, Ken. I never should have married you.*

"We never should have married," he said suddenly, as if he'd somehow heard me. "I knew I wasn't the one. To your credit, you never lied to me about that. I just thought that the love you did feel for me would somehow be enough. I wanted so badly for us to be that happy couple I imagined on our wedding day. I wanted the white picket fence, the kids playing in the yard, and I wanted those things with you." He shook his head. "I was never the one."

"Ken." Dr. Lambert was at the door. "I don't mean to disturb you, son, but the police are here. They've cleaned out your wife's car and need to turn over possession of her belongings."

Ken was holding my wrist, checking for a pulse no doubt, even though the machine beside the bed blipped away its constant diagnosis that I was still alive. "I'll be right there."

"Okay son, take your time." Such a kind old man.

"I'm going to send your family in, Meagan. In case you wake up."

There was no waking up for Zoe and my heart ached for the child I would never have.

My family gathered around me. Mom, Dad, Josh, Jenna, Danielle. Amber was out in the corridor with Ken and Mom was pinning an image of a saint to my bed sheets.

There are no saints here, Mom, I thought. And I wanted someone to tear away the image because the sight of it beside me bothered me. Being a ghost had been interesting at first, but as the hours passed and I sat, perched high above my family like some wingless bird, listening to them talk as if I were already dead, I grew impatient and distressed.

"Where was she rushing off to?" Josh asked.

Amber. I saw the word form in Jenna's mind and flew down beside her. What was this? I could see her thoughts. I touched her shoulder and she jumped, looking around the room as if she sensed something no one else could. A sentence formed in her mind. *Meagan, is that you?*

I was stunned. *You felt me Jenna?*

If my sister-in-law felt me, she could not hear me. But I could read the conversation that went on in her head as if it were being written for me on clean white paper.

You're in this room aren't you, Meagan? I wish I could hear you talking but I haven't developed my inner ear yet. It's a process, you understand. Listen to me, Meagan. You can't die. Josh needs his sister, so does Danielle. Sammy needs his auntie Meg and I need you. You're the only person who understands me, who doesn't think I'm strange for the things I believe or the way in which I view the world. Amber needs you. You may not know it but she does. As for Ken, well, you'll have plenty of time to work that out. I'm sorry about the baby, Meagan. I really am.

I floated away, closing my mind to her thoughts, and once again perched in my corner where I could mourn the child Jenna had been the only one kind enough to offer condolences for.

"She's not going to wake up, is she?" Danielle cried.

The room shifted, growing smaller, and their voices got quieter.

Something's happening, I called out. I was shrinking, melting away, and the darkness was surrounding me.

I can't see you anymore.

Meagan?

Jenna! Jenna I'm disappearing. I'm scared. Oh God, I'm so scared. What's happening?

Darkness.

Chapter 33

I was blind. Alone. Perhaps dead.

And then there was Victor.

"It's best if you just imagine this as a dream," he said, as a new world began to take form around me.

I surveyed my surroundings with interest. "But it's not a dream, is it?"

"No."

A green ground appeared below me and I floated down to stand on it. Victor hovered in the air beside me. "What is this place? And how do I know your name?"

"You have given me this name, Meagan," he said, smiling so brightly a light seemed to emanate from behind his teeth. "I cannot readily explain this place because your human language has no words for it. We call it simply, the Realm, and I have been sent to be your guide."

"Human language. Then I am still alive."

"Comatose, on a bed at St. Jude's University Hospital."

"For how long?"

"Entirely up to you."

"Then I'd like to go back now."

Victor chuckled soundlessly, only giving off a vibration that I recognized as laughter. "You can't go back yet," he said, speaking to my heart instead of my ears. "Your decision will have to be an educated one. First you must see the wonders we have here and what you will be giving up down there. You will inhabit the two worlds simultaneously until you have gleaned from this experience all that you can, and only then will you be allowed your choice. Some people pick it up quickly; others have been known to linger between the worlds for years."

"No." I shook my ethereal head. "I can't stay here for years."

"Time is an illusion, Meagan. What's your rush?"

"There's something I have to do, an amends I have to make, and I'm afraid it can't wait."

"All things in their own time."

"But Victor, you just finished telling me that time is an illusion."

"It is. *Here*. Down there it moves as it always has, with or without you."

"Then let's get on with this," I snapped. "I have no patience for astral games."

Victor sighed and the universe expanded. "Very well."

The lilacs were in season, perfuming the air with a purple I could smell. They swayed in the breeze that caressed my skin as we walked. Birds chirped in the trees above. Nature stretched across the periphery, Mother Gaia in her most pleasing disguise, as Victor led me through this astral enchantment he called, the Summerlands.

"Is it always like this?" I asked, noting the black panther curled around Victor's feet, waiting to be stroked.

"Pretty much. This is the place where departed souls come first because it is a part of the Realm closest to what they can recognize as beauty. Other parts are just as beautiful but not in such an obvious way. They are lovely, in and of themselves, but in ways beyond human reasoning."

The landscape stretched before me, a vision of silent loveliness. "I think it would be lonely here," I mused. "The quiet could drive you insane."

"There is never loneliness in the Realm," Victor answered. "And sanity is a human word that describes only what is understandable to human minds. Insanity means only that what is perceived is actually beyond the scope of the average human mind's comprehension. Genius is often mistaken for insanity in your world, is it not?"

"I suppose. Still, I would rather not stay in this place for long. It is beautiful but isolating. I need more if I am to stay in the Realm."

"And so you shall see more; but one step at a time. Take in the beauty of this place, Meagan. The word *Gaia* forms in your head but you fight her, not wanting to believe."

"Because Gaia is the earth, and this Victor," I waved my arm about me, "is not the earth."

"In the Realm, Gaia is beauty. Gaia is the wondrous parts of the universe represented by what you call *nature.* She is inviting and ever-present. Call to her only once and you shall be surrounded by such beauty, brought here from whatever section of the Realm you were previously in for a period of quiet contemplation and consolidation. *Meditation* is the word you would use, I think. But I must leave you now. Talk to Gaia and open your heart to her answers."

There were voices coming up from below. I could hear their muffled sounds but could not make out the words. A vibration of anger.

"Wait, Victor," I called. "What is that noise?"

"Ignore it, Meagan. Open yourself to the beating heart that is Summerlands."

The voices grew louder, filling my head with their negative energies. "I can't shut it out Victor. It's too distracting. Let me go down and look. Please Victor, I have to know what's going on down there."

"Is it more important than the voice of deity?"

I thought. "Yes, Victor. For now, it is."

"Very well, then."

"She was confused, was she?" Gwynne's tone was sarcastic and filled with hate as she paced the hospital room. "What the fuck is wrong with you, Amber? Look at that woman! It's the same woman who underhandedly takes over magazines, steals from old ladies…"

"She's never stolen a thing and you know it. She was protecting Jenna."

This was the argument I'd been hearing from the Realm and I settled in to watch.

"She terrifies Jenna! She's a fucking force of destruction. She marries a man she probably doesn't even love, then *murders* her baby…"

My heart ripped open at the mention of Zoe and Amber shot to her feet. "Don't you ever say anything like that again! What if she's listening?" Her eyes cast a fearful glance at my sleeping form.

"I hope she *is* listening," Gwynne barked. She leaned over the bed and pushed her face into mine. "Do you hear me in there?" she demanded, her eyes as cold and blue as an ocean. "I hope you do. I hope you know what a murdering, selfish bitch you are!"

"Gwynne!"

Gwynne whirled around at the sound of Amber's yell. "Are you coming home or not?"

"No."

"I don't believe this," Gwynne yelled. "I'm losing you to a fucking vegetable? She doesn't even want you Amber."

I do! Oh Christ, Amber I really do.

"I don't care, Gwynne. I won't leave her."

Gwynne was becoming angrier by the second. "The woman is a fucking maniac! She's insane, Amber. Her own brother calls her the antichrist and she doesn't even deny the fact that she'll be living in a padded room someday."

"She was joking." Amber moved to the side of the bed and smiled down at me. "She's not insane. She's just --wonderfully nutty. She's eccentric, maybe even neurotic, but she's levelheaded enough to always get the job done and she'll do anything for the people she cares about."

Amber's words touched my soul. She was taking a big risk talking about me like that and Gwynne was ready to snap.

"Amber, I will fucking dump your ass," Gwynne growled.

"I know," Amber said.

"Did you hear what I just said?"

"Yes." The word was a quiet acceptance and it startled me. Amber was *being me.*

Gwynne jumped in front of her. "What's that? Are you fucking *talking* like her now? Is that what you want? To turn into some fucked up lunatic coma case with a dead baby? She's half dead herself!"

Amber's voice was soft, her eyes kind, as she turned to Gwynne and spoke the words I so desperately needed to hear. "I'm sorry, Gwynne," she whispered. "I love her."

Gwynne's hand shot out and struck Amber in the face. I darted to her side. Amber rubbed her cheek and said, "I guess I deserved that."

No! I crouched before her. *No one deserves to be hit and if I ever wake up she'll pay for that. I swear to you, she will pay.*

"I never meant to hurt you, Gwynne. I'm sorry."

"You're not sorry," Gwynne scoffed. "Ever since that bitch came back from London all you've done is try to find some way or another to see her."

Again came the quiet "yes", and I smiled.

Gwynne grabbed Amber's arm. "You've been fucking her, haven't you?"

"No." Amber gently released herself from Gwynne's grip. "Meagan wouldn't do that."

"But you would, right? Just tell me this: If she had come on to you, would you have stopped her?"

Amber stared down at her boots. "No." Again, I smiled. "But she never came on to me, Gwynne. The truth is, you're probably right; she probably *doesn't* want me."

"But still you'd throw us away!"

"Because you should be with someone who can be completely devoted to you. I can't be that person. I'm sorry, but I still love *her.*"

"That's fine." Gwynne stalked toward the door. "Sit around with your bunch of broccoli, Amber. I hope you and the brain-dead corpse over there have a very happy life together. Honestly, I hope she fucking dies."

Gwynne marched out and Amber sat at the side of my bed with a small sigh. She would be alone now and I worried what would become of her. What if I never woke up? Would she be alone forever? It was too horrible to think about and a small part of me wished she hadn't thrown Gwynne away. Gwynne was right; I was a corpse now, and it scared me that Amber had chosen the dead over the living.

"I'm sorry if you heard any of that," Amber whispered, brushing the hair from my eyes. "Gwynne's just hurt, and she's mad. You didn't kill your baby, Meagan. It was an accident. You would have made a wonderful mother and, who knows maybe someday you still will."

My heart ached. It wouldn't be Zoe.

"Ken's been really good about letting me in here to see you. Your mother's been a bit of a hassle but we won't talk about that. Jenna's taking care of it."

I wondered how Jenna was doing that.

Amber shifted position and rested her head on my stomach. "I love you so much. I wish I had told you that before. Sometimes I wonder what would have happened if I'd followed you to London. I wanted to. I thought maybe we could have lived there together and it wouldn't have mattered because we'd be so far from everyone you couldn't possibly be afraid. I even booked a flight once. Then I chickened out and cancelled it because I thought you'd reject me and I couldn't deal with you rejecting me again."

I moved to the side of the bed and lovingly stroked her hair.

"You wouldn't have married Ken," she went on. "I wouldn't have gotten involved with Gwynne and we would have been together. When you came back I wanted to plead with you not to get married. I wanted to tell you how I'd never stopped loving you but again, I couldn't. Seeing the moonstone on my chain didn't make you change your mind so I knew nothing else would.

"I don't want you to die, Meagan." Silently, the tears rolled down her cheeks. "Please, I couldn't take it if you died. I want you to wake up and I want to see your face when I tell you that I love you. Because I *will* tell you, Meagan. I won't chicken out this time. Maybe you won't love me back but I have to tell you.

"Those things Gwynne said about you; they only make you more special to me. I love that you would take down anyone who hurt the people you love. I love how faithful you are to your friends and family. I love the way you look out for Danny, and I love the way you take care of anyone who screws with Jenna. It's not insane; it's passionate. You throw yourself so wholly into your mission that I can't help being a little bit in awe of you. It's like there's nothing you can't accomplish. Gwynne says you're a force of destruction but she's wrong; you're just a force. A strong, beautiful force and I love watching you in action. I hated that phone of yours when we were together but God how I loved listening to you talk on it. You were always so in control. People would call you with problems and you'd tell them how to fix them and I'd think, she's so fucking incredible. Look at the way she puts them all at ease.

"Oh, you're neurotic, Meagan." She gave a small laugh. "I do know that. You're impulsive and you're stubborn, but those are the things that make you great at what you do. So you're gonna wake up, okay? You don't have a choice. Do you think you can sleep forever? *My* Meagan rarely sleeps at all. You've had your rest now. In the past week you've gotten plenty of sleep. It's time to wake up. Okay, Meagan? Wake up now. Please, just--"

Her words trailed off and she coiled her body to mine, resting her head on my stomach, breathing air on me that I could not feel, and I moved closer, wishing I could tell her everything would be okay. She didn't know I loved her. That was the hardest part. I could die tomorrow and she would never know.

"That's not true," Victor said, suddenly appearing beside me. He was wearing white pants and a white shirt, and he glowed just as vibrantly as the first time I'd ever seen him. "You know who will tell her."

I smiled. "Jenna?"

"Yes. She would not let you die without sharing your truth. She will tell Amber. I don't know when, but she will."

"You're here to take me away now, aren't you?"

"Yes."

I glanced at Amber. "Will she be okay?"

"She'll be fine. Let us go back to the Summerlands, Meagan."

Glumly, I nodded and followed Victor away. We floated upward, but the floating stopped at the ceiling and Victor told me to use my thoughts. I closed my eyes, pictured the Summerlands, and opened them again to find we were there.

Silently, we journeyed through the forest and I wondered how such miracles were possible. Was there a name for the way we could pop from one place to another?

"Transmigration." Victor said.

"What?"

"You were wondering what it's called when we skip realms. Transmigration. You wonder so many things, Meagan; I am always amused by what I find in your thoughts."

"My thoughts, yes. How is it, Victor, that I am sometimes able to read Jenna's thoughts? She was in here yesterday with Sammy and I read things in her head. Sammy was crawling on top of me and Jenna was thinking: *Oh Sammy, don't crawl on Auntie Meg. I guess she can't feel you, though. Poor Meagan. You kiss her cheek and I think maybe the kiss of my beautiful son will wake her like some modern day sleeping beauty, but I guess she's not ready yet.* And there were pictures in her head, Victor. Pictures of me, in my old apartment. And her pictures frightened me because I looked sick. Sammy was sitting in my lap and I looked sick. Jenna was smiling in her head. Saying things like, *when you're ready, Meagan. When you're ready.* How is it that I was able to see these things?"

"Jenna is open," Victor said. "A special person. An old soul, one might say. She knows thing others do not. So much wisdom floating around in that pretty blond head of hers. Few people will ever be so wise during their earthly journeys."

"Am I an old soul, Victor?"

"You may be somewhere in between --I do not know."

"Why? Why do you know so much about everyone else but so little about me?"

"Know thyself."

"Explain."

He sighed. "In the simplest of terms, I know Jenna because she knows herself. I know the others only in the same way you know them: as living humans. You do not know yourself; therefore I do not know you. When *you* know you, then so shall I. No sooner, I'm afraid."

"Some help you are."

"I am only your guide, Meagan. Nothing more."

"Victor?"

"Yes, Meagan."

"Transmigration--"

"Yes, it is possible."

"To leave the hospital?" I asked. "It is possible? To follow them when they go home? To float above their rooms and watch over them? These things are possible, Victor?"

"Yes, but you have more important matters to attend to. Let us not forget that you are in a battle for your life, Meagan. You can't lose sight of that. You are here to decide whether you will live or die. *That* is what concerns you; the fate of your soul."

I sighed. "When I first got here Victor, when it was all darkness and empty space, you came and you told me I had an *educated* decision to make. You said I would see all, but so far you lead me through the Realm and you allow me to hear snatches of conversation below, but that is not enough. How can my decision be an educated one, a *fair* one, if I am limited to seeing only what you want me to see?"

"Meagan, I--"

"Take me down there, Victor. Let me see how their lives

go on without me. Let me see with my own two astral eyes and hear with my own ethereal ears the things they say and do. I'm lonely, Victor. There is only you and there is only me--"

"You'll meet others."

"So, until I do --Victor, please."

Victor stretched his arms like Christ, extending himself across the purple that was now my sky. "For short periods of time, Meagan. Unless you want to linger between the worlds forever; it is entirely up to you. Watching them live will only be beneficial if you *use* the information you glean from the experience. You cannot go down there just to be nosey. It's an invasion of their privacy."

"Privacy?" I raged. "You're talking to me about privacy? When I have none? Look what they do to my body, Victor. Always touching and fussing and sticking needles in my veins for God knows what reason. Then there's my mother, who pins those ridiculous saints around my bed, lighting candles, and dressing me up in clothes I've become too thin to wear, stripping me naked like some anorexic Barbie placed there for her amusement. Jenna with her incense. Ken with his little white flashlight in my eyes. Sammy jumping on me like I'm a trampoline. Danielle moving my arms and legs about, twisting me into poses when she thinks no one's watching. Dad laying a book on my stomach as if I were a coffee table while he watches a football game on the TV I hate to have to hear. Amber talking, always talking, like she's afraid if she stops I'll die. No, do not speak to me of privacy, Victor. You anger me when you do so."

"Who do you want to see first?"

"You'll take me?"

"You argue your case very well, Meagan. I understand your logic."

"I want to see it all, Victor. I want to see what Ken does when he's back in our lovely home with the four bedrooms and the pretty backyard and the solarium in the kitchen. I want to watch Jenna making her incense and Josh reading to Sammy. Finally, Victor, I want to crawl into Amber's bed and lay beside her, breathing in the skin I cannot smell and kissing the lips I cannot feel against my own. I want to wrap myself up in her and watch her sleep. If I could, I would want to creep into her head and see her dreams, the pictures she makes behind those beautiful emerald eyes. I would crawl into her skin and feel what she feels. I would wrap myself in the warmth that is Amber. Can you understand that, Victor? The things I've never told her, I would tell. She's the poet, but I would whisper to her of love and devotion, and of the completeness of my soul I only seem to feel in *her* presence. I would pour out my shame, Victor, telling her all the reasons I was cruel and unjust in my abandonment of her. And the fears, Victor, I would tell her about the fears loving her brought out in me. How I was afraid I could never be enough, could never be--"

"Gay?"

"If you know me, Victor, then you know I don't believe in that word. Being with Amber made me no more gay than being with Ken made me straight. I love who I love, regardless of gender."

"Tell me something, Meagan. You say you love this Amber, and by your truth, you swear it--"

"I do."

"Why then did you insist on denying her the only thing she'd ever asked of you? I see your thoughts, and your thoughts tell me that all Amber ever wanted was to hear you say that word. Why not give it to her then?"

"Because it would have been a lie."

"A lie to spare her heart or a truth to break her spirit? You make your decisions, Meagan, on what you believe is the side of right but you do not consider the consequences. The baseball team Ken coaches, the children are mentally challenged, correct?"

"Yes."

"Would you call one of those children retarded?"

"I'm not a monster, Victor."

"But it is the truth, is it not? The children are retarded, yet you hold your tongue. You hold it because the truth would inflict injury and the lie, dressed up in a pretty PC term like "challenged" maintains your sense of honor. I see no harm in that. I see no harm in a lie that is for the greater good. You may believe in a soul's capacity to love beyond human conditions like race and gender, Meagan, but Amber needs labels. She needs words for what she is—for what she believes you are. If you went back, could you give her that?"

"Give her the lie, you mean."

"Yes. Do you love her enough to lie to her?"

"I promised her truth."

"But your truth destroys her. Can you not understand how that one truth of yours makes who Amber is as a person a lie? You say there's no such thing as gay or straight but Amber cannot feel physical love for a man, so when you say such things you turn her into fiction."

"I think I understand," I said, nodding. "What you're saying is, truth is relative. I know this, Victor, *intellectually.* My mind understands how one person's truth can be another person's lie --but my spirit wants to insist I'm right."

"I did not say you were wrong, Meagan. If you could see your spirit right now, without the intrusion of your conscious mind that links your appearance to what your external body looks like, you would see that you are sexless, asexual. The spirit is without gender and it is that part of you that loves Amber. Evolutionally, your spirit has surpassed Amber's, and that is the reason you abhor labels, you know better. Amber, on the other hand, is somewhat like a newborn. She is very grounded to the physical world, and therefore, needs physical world words to describe her. Had she been born attracted to men she would insist attraction to women was impossible for her. She knows bisexuality exists but she doesn't see it the same way you do. She pities bisexuals, thinks they're confused --and some of them are-- it's the others she can't understand, the ones like you who have evolved to a point where spirit is the love and not the body."

"But I've explained this to her, Victor. In almost the exact same way you have explained it to me."

"Yes. And you told her that you were not even *bisexual* because it was only her, and that you loved the spirit her body houses. She can't understand that, Meagan. To her, love and sexuality go hand in hand. She loves you with her spirit but she does not know it; she thinks it is her heart, and her heart tells her its own lie: that she would not love you if you were a man. That is why she cannot understand your talk of these universal truths of the spirit. So I ask you again: Can you give her your lie? If you cannot then you'd do just as well to stay here because, in this case, the truth is no longer the right thing."

Plagued with riddles, I felt. Live, die, tell the truth, lie. Where was my peace? People always thought being in a coma was somewhat like enjoying a long and restful sleep. That's why they were always begging you to wake up. I knew differently. My mind was never at rest. In some ways it was like being in the middle of a waking nightmare. There was no sleep in the Realm, but I never felt tired, and aimlessly I wandered from place to place in search of the clues that would help me decide my destiny.

As promised, Victor showed me all, helping me unravel one mystery at a time and even allowing me to transmigrate to places within the earth plane, almost whenever I wanted. In the isolating world that was my journey, Victor became my only companion. He taught me humility, how to question myself even when I felt most certain in the things I knew. "A wise soul is the one who always questions, Meagan. The universe is full of contradictions." He taught me empathy. "Feel what they feel, Meagan." And often I found myself weeping at the love and fear I felt in their hearts. They thought I would never wake up and I mourned for them because I knew that was a possibility. There were wonders in the Realm yet to be seen, greater mysteries to uncover, and I threw myself into my mission whole-heartedly.

"You do not resist me anymore," Victor said one day. We were in the realm of winter and frost but I felt no cold.

"No. When I resist I only slow down my progress, correct?" I was starting to talk like him.

"Correct."

And onward we went. Through the barren lands and the desserts, through space and the darkness therein. We moved through time as if it did not exist, going backward, forward, even sideways sometimes into what Victor called, *the parallel universe.*

"There will be times, Meagan," he said, "when I will have to leave you. Fear not for it is completely necessary. Some things you must uncover on your own. Can you understand this?"

I nodded. "Yes." But I did not want to be left alone. I wanted to meet others or go home.

"You will, Meagan," Victor assured, reading my thoughts again. "All things in their own time."

I took him at his word. What else could I do? If I could not believe in Victor, who, then, could I believe in? There was no one else.

Chapter 34

On day eleven of my sleep, Victor left me to my own devices. "I'll return, Meagan," he'd said, minutes before I'd watched him vanish into thin air. Transmigration was easy for Victor. He was an experienced spirit who could transmigrate as easily as I could walk. For me, transmigration was a source of discomfort. I felt like my spirit was constantly being snapped in one direction or another and it always took a few moments to recover from the experience.

I had inhabited the Realm for a lifetime it seemed, but I still recognized time on a human scale. I could not coil myself around the idea that, in this place, there was no true time for I had watched it come at me from all sides. Time did exist; it simply wasn't linear. More like a helical force that engulfed me, caressed me with memories and fragments of an altered reality within the Realm, and pleaded with me to abandon my human form forever. Sometimes I thought I might.

"I'll return, Meagan," Victor had said. "And remember, there is nothing to fear in the Realm except perhaps what your own mind can create."

His words were like a warning of foreboding. I may not have known what the Realm was capable of but I knew the kinds of horrors my own mind could create. I sat on the icy riverbank in the land of frost and shivered at a coldness I knew did not really exist. The Realm was devoid of temperature, for without a physical body one could not feel such things anyway. I could feel Victor when he touched me but only because it was a blending of astral matter --mine and his.

I thought of darkness and it surrounded me. I was blind again, like in those first fearful moments before Victor, and stumbling through the blackness of my own wayward consciousness, terrified by what I might find. *Death.*

No, do not think that word, I reprimanded. Do not think of zombies rising from their shallow graves and incubi baring their razor teeth. Do not think of screams filling the night and goblins rattling around the Underworld in search of blood. Do not think these things or they might appear. Do not think of spiritual sacrifice -- the disenchantment of your own corruption. Do not think of horrible beasts gnawing on half-chewed faces. Do not think it!

Gaia. I forced the word to the forefront of my mind. *Nature. Beauty.* "Summerlands," I said aloud. "Gaia." I squeezed my eyes, half in terror, half in prayer. "Please, Gaia now!"

When I opened my eyes I was back in the lovely forest I had grown to adore. Greenery surrounded me. A carpet of soft dirt and grass underfoot. Sweet-smelling foliage. Astral birds and glimpses of fair-skinned, pointy-eared tree fairies humming along to the harmonies of nature. This must have been my idea of heaven, I assumed, because Gran's fairies were as elusive as she'd promised they would be.

The forest creatures gathered around me and I felt like Snow White, or perhaps Saint Francis of Assisi. A snake slithered around my feet but I had no fear of it. Its warm body twisted around my ankles like it was embracing me. I offered an olive branch and the serpent swallowed it whole, symbolically bonding us to the collective spirit of this place. It slithered away, a singular tail rustling the leaves on the ground as it curved a trail of its own design across the endless terrain.

"May I join you?" a soft, masculine voice questioned from behind.

Startled by the sound, I fell off the log I was sitting on and the man helped me to my feet. He was the most beautiful man I'd ever seen. Dark, hooded lids. Olive skin. Something familiar about his face, so exotically handsome. Like a Mediterranean god. A sudden euphoria filled my head.

"I'm sorry if I stare at you," I said, not feeling like I could look away.

The man shrugged his massive shoulders. "It happens."

His shirt looked like black silk. Everything about him looked silken in fact; his clothes, his hands. He seemed to gleam with an unknown shine and his mere presence was like a chemical flowing through my body, like a drug I had once tried but couldn't readily recall. Ecstasy? No, I had never experimented with that, but it was the word that came to mind. I had experimented with acid when I was sixteen but had failed to hallucinate. My friends had tripped, seeing trails, bugs, and distorted images in each other's faces. I'd seen nothing. I'd only felt a harmonious joy as I sat cross-legged on the floor, quiet as Buddha, and felt myself flow through what seemed like a transcendental state. Altered consciousness. I had rather enjoyed the experience.

Yes, I thought now, looking at this man is like that, like reaching a false state of enlightenment.

His serene expression cracked like I had hurt his feelings. "Why false?" he asked. And I thought, *A mind reader like Victor. I must be careful.*

A smile formed behind his black eyes and I felt my reserve evaporate like condensation on a window after the sun comes out. I saw the life dance behind his eyes, a masquerade ball I could attend if I wanted, and I thought, *If you lead me somewhere, I will follow.*

The man laughed; a throaty vibration that tickled my ears. "That was her thought too. I didn't take her from you. She wanted to go."

"*Zoe!*" The word came out of my mouth like a shard of glass, slicing my tongue with its sharpness, and I staggered away from him. The illusion was broken. I tripped on a tree root, fell, and glared up at him. "It was you that night on the street," I accused. "You took her. You took her and you wouldn't let me through." A sob choked me. "You took my baby!"

He shook his head, patiently. "No, Meagan. She wasn't yours."

"She was!"

"No." His voice was stern but kind. "She had not yet been born. She was still spirit and spirit always has a choice. She chose to leave you."

"You're lying. I don't believe you."

The man stood and reached for my hand. I yanked it away and he frowned. "Has Victor not told you that it is impossible for a lie to exist in the Realm? If I wanted to lie I could not, for this is a place of truth and the truth would destroy the lie almost immediately." He smiled sweetly and I thought I might believe him. "Sit with me, Meagan," he said, taking my elbow and guiding me back to the log. "We can discuss many things. I am Quin."

"I didn't name you that," I said, self-righteously.

He chuckled. "No, I have always been Quin. You name only your guide. For instance, the one you call Zoe calls me Thomas."

"Then you are --her guide?" I wanted to say *my daughter* but sensed he would correct me.

"Temporarily," he said. "Even three months in the womb can make one forget certain things. Once she remembers everything she will no longer need me and perhaps will go on to be someone else's guide."

My fingers twisted around a pretty white daisy. "Why did she leave me, Quin?" I wanted to believe whatever he would say.

"Her death was inevitable. She could not have survived the crash, especially if you don't survive it."

"But you said she chose to leave me."

Quin nodded. "Yes, on the street. She asked me to take her away because she didn't want to have an ending with you if there would be no beginning. Do you understand this?"

I chuckled down at the flower in my hand. "Yes, backward logic I understand. It comes up often for me." Then another thought. "She's quite like me, isn't she Quin?"

Patting my knee, his smile glowed. "More than you could imagine. She is willful and determined, somewhat of a handful, but she soaks up information like a sponge that has no absorption limit." That pleased me. I smiled back. "On earth she would have been a miniature version of you, taking only from your husband his interest in healing."

"She would have been a doctor?" I asked proudly, thinking I couldn't wait to tell Ken. If I went back, that was.

"A neurosurgeon," Quin said. "But even if you remember that your husband will not believe you. How could he? He is a man of science and this--" He waved his arm about us, "has no scientific explanation as of yet."

I studied his brilliant face. "I know why Zoe went with you," I said, reasonably. "You're very seductive to look at."

"I don't try to be. That is my spirit."

"I would go with you, I think, if I was sure I wanted to die. If I knew I would be with my daughter who you tell me is not my daughter." My eyes met his hooded gaze. "I think you are probably the most beautiful man I've ever seen, and yet you are not a man at all."

"No, I am spirit. I assume this form because it is the one you would most readily accept. That is why Victor is your guide instead of me. I would beguile you, I'm afraid, coerce you into joining us."

His words startled me and I shot to my feet. Angrily, I paced the ground before him. "Then you admit seduction exists in the Realm," I accused, feeling somewhat betrayed by the easy way in which he spoke of entrapping me. "You assume a pleasing form because that is how someone might follow you. That's trickery, Quin."

"No." Quin stood before me and pressed my hand over the spot where his heart would be. "Not trickery, Meagan. Trickery would be a lie. Seduction, yes. But only because beauty is its own truth and comes in many forms."

I pulled my hand from his heart. "But you can shape shift." I was catching on to the way things worked here. "There is a sort of shamanism at play in this place and you could shape shift, thereby turning into something I would willingly follow across the universe." My mind thought of Amber and I drove away the picture. "You could trick me into going wherever you wanted."

Quin searched my eyes. Formalities did not last long in the Realm and he spoke his truth. "I suppose anything is possible, but what you are talking about is against the laws of love. And I am love, Meagan. Can you not see that? I could never keep such a deception going for long. It is true, I know what could keep you here, but to do that would be dishonest."

I found myself even more angered by these last words. It frightened me to think he could peer into my soul and use what he found there against me. "I think we're done talking now," I said, dismissively.

Quin gave a sad nod. "I will go, Meagan, if that is what you truly desire."

"It is."

"Very well. I'm sure we will meet again."

The illusion of the sun began setting in the distance and I sat on my log and watched it go down in a shade of pale orange. It descended slowly behind the mountains in the distance like a giant orange ball someone had finally let go of. It crept downward, easing its way behind the snow-capped peaks where I knew the frost fairies lived for Victor had taken me there and I had seen them with my own eyes, like shimmering speckles of diamonds glittering against the icy backdrop. Tiny pixie faces. Wingless little beings frolicking in the snow. I wished I could tell someone that Gran had been right, but there was no one to tell.

"You can tell me," a tender voice whispered. Familiar. I jumped. There was no one around.

"Who's there?" I called. A lone figure appeared behind some trees in the near distance. Another surprise guest. "I know that's you, Quin," I said, knowing nothing of the sort.

A light emanated from the woods. It began moving toward me, and I watched in stunned silence as it took on its form. "I know what you're doing, Quin," I shouted. "So you can just stop it."

The body took shape. The crop of blond hair appeared on the head and the emerald eyes formed and shone as brilliant as real jewels, illuminating the darkness that had fallen over Gaia like a witch's cloak. The arms stretched down the sides of the body. The legs, long and thin. Taut stomach. Small breasts. Smiling, radiant face. Dead beauty.

"Stop it!" I yelled. "You're not her!"

"Meagan." It was Amber's voice that filled my ears and I covered them quickly to block out the feminine little whisper.

"You're not her!"

"I died for you, Meagan." Her arms stretched out to wrap me in an embrace and I stumbled away from her.

"No. Amber wouldn't do that. She wouldn't die for *anyone.*"

The false Amber reached for me again. "Don't be afraid. I did it so we could be together. You died, Meagan. You died three days ago and I couldn't bear the thought that I would never see you again." Her fingers stroked my face and she glanced around the dark forest. "It's not so bad here. At least we're together again -- and we can find Zoe."

I stared into her face and tried to recall if I'd heard anyone on the earth plane tell her my daughter's name. My heart filled with longing for her and I fought the urge to touch her. She was so real. So *Amber.*

Taking my hand, she kissed the inside of my wrist. Amber *would* do that. She would try to ease me into her presence. Handle me carefully so as not to frighten me. "I missed you so much," she whispered.

My heart ached. "Don't," I begged. "Please, let go of me."

"Meagan, I died to be with you."

"Stop saying that!" I staggered away from her and her face crumbled in pain. The same wounded look she had given me that night on the street.

"You would turn your back on me even in death? How could you?" Tears filled her eyes as she moved closer. "I thought you loved me."

I was losing my mind and it was happening very quickly. I fell to my knees before her, wrapped my arms around her waist that seemed alarmingly real, and pressed my cheek against her stomach. "You didn't do this," I sobbed. "Tell me you didn't do this!"

She cradled my head. "I did, Meagan."

No. It was a lie. Amber couldn't --wouldn't. She was too filled with life to die. I felt myself letting go of her waist and sinking to the ground. I bent forward, pressing my forehead to the cool dirt and willed myself not to look up at her, lest I lose myself to the illusion. It was a lie. The biggest lie. I ground my forehead from side to side as if rubbing the truth directly into my third eye. "Please," I begged of the chunks of earth I squeezed between my fingers. "Please, make it stop. It isn't her. It's only Quin trying to trick me."

Quin. I grasped onto the word like a lifeboat in a dark ocean. Victor had said the only frightening thing I could encounter in the Realm was what my own mind could create. That was the answer. Quin had plucked the image of Amber from my mind in the one second it had appeared there and he had shapeshifted into her to show me what he was capable of doing. I squeezed my eyes and pictured his beautiful face. *Quin. I see only Quin.*

Hands on my arms. "Very good, Meagan," Quinn said, lifting me to my feet. "You learn quickly. A good sign. Now do you believe a lie cannot exist in the Realm?"

I shook off his aid and angrily wiped the astral dirt from my forehead. "You're very cruel! Why would you want to make me believe we were dead? That she had killed herself because of me?"

Quin shrugged. "So you could prove that you would not believe it."

"Well, I almost did."

No. You may have wanted to, but your truth saw through the lie. It would not let you believe. That is the real wonder of the Realm, Meagan, to be able to discern truth from illusion. You have seen anything is possible but you have also seen it can be illusory. Think of the Realm as liquid. Illusion is liquid. It can be poured into a tall glass, a small cup --any viable container--but it is always liquid. Astral substance can be shaped but can never be altered. That is what you have learned. I'm only sorry it had to be such a harsh lesson."

I mulled over Quin's words. Indeed it *had* been a harsh lesson, but wasn't I glad I had learned it? In the Realm, the more you knew, the better off you were. I was aware of how much of it was illusion, of course, but I had never known its full capabilities or what the other guides could achieve. I had known only Victor. What he had shown me and the things he had told me. He never told me about the shape shifting; that had been left to Quin, perhaps because I might never trust Victor again if he had done such a thing. I wasn't sure I trusted Quin.

Days passed down on the earth plane but I continued to draw away from it. I was always aware of what was going on but it concerned me less and less. I didn't care what they did to my body anymore because that wasn't really me. I didn't care that the face was becoming alarmingly thin, the eye sockets bulging like lidded superballs. My physical body continued to waste away with each moment I remained asleep, the bones becoming visible under the skin of the hands, the stomach sinking under the narrow ribcage. I was becoming an anorexic's vision of loveliness, a skeleton, and I couldn't have cared less.

The experience with Quin helped. Zoe had been a part of my indecision from the beginning and I realized Quin had been forced to come, if only to tell me the truth that I would not be with her no matter what I decided. She had never really been mine. I was trying to accept that while at the same time clinging to the idea that my daughter would have grown up to become a neurosurgeon, which meant I would have made a good mother despite my shortcomings --something I desperately needed to believe.

Ken came every day. Loyal to the end even after all I had put him through. I continued to love him in my passionless, platonic kind of way. Amber came daily. As did my mother and Jenna. Josh, Danielle and my father were less generous with their visits, only showing up on weekends and then hitting the doctors and nurses on staff with an endless litany of questions about my condition. I understood their reluctance. They had lives to live and my situation didn't seem to be improving.

It was Amber who baffled me. She spent more time with my sleeping form than anyone, arriving at the beginning of visiting hours and often not leaving until well after the end. Each day she came and pulled the blue vinyl chair with the wooden arms and legs up to my bed and wrote her poetry, staring out the window as if my sterile room had become her office and the scenery outside her inspiration. Sometimes she read to me as she wrote, questioning out loud whether I thought such-and-such a verse was good enough to add to her ever-expanding manuscript. She was fanatical about her work. I had always known that. Admired it even when Jenna and I would sit in the Cauldron watching her test out her latest efforts on the eager live audience. I had loved her then without knowing it.

Amber was a true soul. She never wavered in her beliefs and lived each day as if it could be her last. Every second counted. Every word held the weight of importance, even silly words, for it all mattered somehow. She wasn't afraid, like I often was, or spiritual like Jenna: Amber was *alive,* and it was all she needed to get by. A heartbeat and a pen. How I admired her vibrancy.

In my room I learned that Gwynne had indeed moved out. I had listened to Amber relay this news to Jenna as dispassionately as if she were describing a change in the weather. She scribbled in her notebook and shrugged, like the fact that she had given up a chance at happiness meant nothing. She was risking her world on the off chance I might actually wake up, never really knowing if I would go back to my husband when I did. It tore me up.

"How can you love me so much?" I often whispered near her ear. "When I have never truly been deserving of it?"

How could Ken? What deity had seen fit to give me the love of two such wonderful people when I had hurt them both? It was guilt-inducing. Maddening. And there were times when it made me want to die. Spare everyone the trouble that came with loving me, I thought. But Victor told me that was not a good enough reason. He could argue a case for life as well as he could for death.

Twenty-one days I had been unconscious; twenty-one days of journeying the Realm and talking to Victor and watching my loved ones as they roamed in and out of this room with worried expressions and tired eyes. It was only by the look of fear on their faces that I realized how worrisome my unending sleep really was for them. I had options, they did not. Their only choice was to wait. Wait for me to wake up or wait for me to die, and I sometimes wondered which one they hoped it would be. Their faces said anything would be easier than this. The waiting was more destructive, maybe, than whatever else they could imagine.

"What if she doesn't wake up, Jenna?" Amber asked one day after a particularly trying discussion with Ken in which he had suggested she go home and leave my care to him. Amber had refused and Ken had left the hospital angrier than I had ever seen him. He blamed Amber for my failure to awaken. Somehow he'd convinced himself that I refused to come out of my coma because she was there and I didn't want to face her. It surprised me, as he had been the one to encourage her visits. Now he thought my sleep was her fault and I wished he could have known that he was the one I had trouble facing.

I dreaded Ken's visits. His fussing. His *love.* I wanted his hate and the wrath I deserved but he staunchly refused to give me those things.

"She'll wake up," Jenna assured, placing Sammy in his stroller.

"How do you know that?" Amber pleaded. Her eyes looked desperate these days. There was a new fear behind them and it broke my heart. It seemed everything I did caused someone pain, even when I did nothing but sleep.

Jenna's eyes darted to the open door and Amber's followed, curiously. "I'm gonna tell you something," Jenna whispered, peeking into the hall and closing the door. Light flowed in from the crack along the bottom and she stepped into the center of the shadow it made on the floor. "Do you know what they found in Meagan's car after the accident?"

Amber shook her head. "No one tells me anything."

"We'll, I'll tell you." Her pale blue eyes swept the room

like a CIA agent in search of hidden microphones. Satisfied that they were quite alone, she continued. "First I have to tell you that I only just found out all of this myself."

Amber nodded anxiously and twisted in her seat to get a better view of Jenna's solemn expression.

Jenna took a breath. "When the cops cleaned out Meagan's car they found a black bag in her trunk, filled with clothes, her passport, and five thousand dollars in cash."

Jenna's words lingered in the air for a moment while Amber digested this information then let out a short gasp, glancing in my direction. "She was running away? But why, Jenna? She was married. Pregnant."

Jenna pulled a chair from the wall and placed it so that she and Amber were knee to knee. "I think she wanted to run away but couldn't bring herself to do it."

"I don't understand."

"Josh thinks she was planning on hiding out with Seamus. Seamus would have helped her disappear if that's what she wanted. They have that strange sort of relationship. She even bailed him out of jail once after he assaulted a bartender with a broken beer bottle when he found out the man was sleeping with his girlfriend. I remember that because Meagan hired him the best attorneys and went to court as a character witness. She was so convincing up on that stand --well you know Meagan when she wants to sell you something --that Seamus ended up getting off with a month of community service. Even the judge was impressed. He told her she should have saved her money and argued her uncle's case herself."

Amber crossed her legs under her and chuckled. "Sounds like Meagan. Do you know she once convinced me there are unicorns in Africa? Can you imagine? We'd had a few drinks and by the time she was done I completely believed her. She actually had me wanting to go on safari just to see them for myself. I could have killed her when she broke out laughing, howling about what an easy sell I was. I felt like such an idiot. Unicorns!"

Amber was smiling and I laughed at the memory. Even I didn't know why I'd done it --it just seemed funny at the time. And Amber really had been ready to catch the next flight out. She was so enthralled with the idea of there actually being multi-colored unicorns that I'd felt a little guilty when I had to tell her unicorns did not exist. Of course she had known that, but I'd convinced her otherwise.

"Anyway," Jenna went on. A peek at her thoughts said she wondered if I might have been able to convince her of the same thing. "Seamus is the black sheep of the family, big time. And you know Meagan, there's nothing she loves more than an underdog to protect. Seamus treats her like gold and because of that she ignores his alcoholism."

Amber knew all about Seamus and I didn't understand why she didn't stop Jenna from telling her what she already knew. She was so focused on Jenna's words, mesmerized by the tale Jenna so obviously relished finally being able to tell. Then I thought perhaps she wasn't listening at all, only pretending to listen while her mind ventured into places Jenna could not understand because Amber knew her own secrets about me, like the real reason I would protect Seamus with my life --he was blood. That was it. There was no greater reason, no mystery about our relationship like everyone thought. Seamus was my blood and only Amber knew how important that really was to me. I was tribal by nature, and the only people who really knew it were Seamus and Amber.

"There's more, Amber," Jenna said, when Amber began looking like she might lapse into a coma of her own. Jenna went to peek out the door again then resumed her seat across from Amber.

That's right Jenna, I thought. Make the most of this. And I couldn't help laughing. Her mind said she wasn't sure she should be telling any of this but, oh how she wanted to!

"What more?" Amber was getting impatient. Fiddling with her bootlace and rocking a little in her seat.

"A divorce."

"No!"

Jenna nodded emphatically. "Ken told Josh everything. I guess he sort of broke down. Apparently the day before the crash Meagan told Ken she wanted a divorce. She knew she was living a lie and she couldn't deal with it anymore. You know how Meagan gets. She creates a fantasy world and then when it can't meet up to her expectations, she flees."

Hey!

Amber was flabbergasted. "But the baby," she whispered, as if mentioning my Zoe would kill me. "Was she planning on raising it herself?"

Jenna gave a conspiratorial grin. "Or with someone else."

Finally, she'd gotten Amber's attention. "*Me?*" Amber jumped to her feet and immediately began pacing the tiled floor in front of my bed. "Jenna, you must be mistaken. Meagan has never given any indication that she wanted me back, let alone wanting me to help raise her child. What makes you think she could be a lesbian parent when she couldn't even be a lesbian?"

Hey! Hey now!

Their words were getting a bit sharp for my sensitive ears. Lapse into a coma and the truth comes out, whether you are prepared to hear it or not.

Sammy fussed and Jenna popped a soother in his mouth. He went back to sleep. "It's just a theory, Amber," she said. "But think about where the accident took place."

"Three blocks from my building."

"Exactly. What would she be doing downtown? The only people who live there anymore are you and Danielle --and that's not the direction she was heading. My guess is she was coming straight for you."

"But Gwynne--"

Jenna waved away Amber's words. "By that point Meagan wouldn't have cared whether or not Gwynne was home." How well she knew me. "You know how she is when she puts something in her head, she just goes for it. She's impulsive sometimes. Doesn't think of the consequences. Had she been a different way, the two of you never would have gotten together in the first place."

Amber was silent for a moment, thinking. She moved to the side of my bed and tenderly tucked a wayward strand of hair behind my ear. "I would have done it, you know," she whispered. "I would have welcomed you back in an instant and helped you raise the baby. Nothing in the world could have prevented me from doing so."

I smiled, remembering the dedication in her book. Fire purifies, forgiveness heals, but Amber, the journey had yet to begin.

Jenna placed a hand on Amber's shoulder. "Maybe I shouldn't have told you all of that. I just thought you needed to know. That she would have wanted you to know. But now I think I've only made your struggle harder."

Amber pressed her face into her hands. "If she dies,

Jenna--"

"She won't."

"But the possibility is there. What will I do then? I already lost her once. I don't think I can do it again."

Jenna took Amber's hands. "What will you do if she stays in a coma the rest of her life, Amber? Will you sit here and wait until five years from now, fifteen years from now, until she expires and you realize you've done nothing with your life but wait for someone who wasn't quite alive to finally die? Where is the limit on your waiting?"

"Where's the limit on *yours?*" Amber countered. "On Ken's? Why should mine be any different? Because she isn't my sister-in-law? Isn't my wife? I won't give up on her, Jenna. Not as long as that machine keeps beeping the diagnosis of her *life.* I'll stay as long as it takes. I won't budge until she either dies or opens her eyes. You shouldn't expect me to."

Jenna wrapped her arms around Amber's shoulders and gave her a sympathetic hug. "I'm sorry. I didn't mean to offend you. You have just as much right to be here as anyone else and if we were to ask Meagan, probably *more* than anyone else. I just worry that you'll throw your life away. I can handle the wait, Amber. I have Josh and Sammy. But you, I worry for what will happen to you."

"Don't worry for me, Jenna," Amber said. She brushed a kiss across my forehead. "Worry for her."

Chapter 35

"Hi. I'm Beth."

Ken stood with his back to the door, ignoring the tall girl with the long red hair and hazel eyes who suddenly appeared in my room. She had an earthy quality, a cuteness. Wearing a long floral print skirt that grazed her ankles and a matching knitted cardigan that exposed a tiny waist as she raised her arms to adjust the barrette at the top of her head, she gave a sweet smile. Ken was being rude. Why?

Suddenly, the girl's eyes met mine and she waved her hand in front of my face. "He-*lo*?"

"*Me?*" My mouth dropped open. "You can see me?"

The girl giggled. "Of course, silly. You're Meagan, right?" I nodded dumbly. "I'm Beth," she said again. "Nineteen-year-old coma victim across the hall. Wanna go for a float?"

"A what?" I couldn't believe she was actually talking to me. She was so *thick*, like a real person. Not airy-looking like I was.

"A float," Beth repeated. "That's what I call going for a walk because my feet never quite touch the ground. You know, the whole spirit defying gravity thing. We can check out the grounds or something. There's some pretty cool flowers out by the entrance. Daisies, I think. 'Course I couldn't tell a dandelion from a carnation, you know? Any way, you wanna?"

She spoke really fast, like she was on speed. Ken had gone into the small private bathroom to wash his hands before he began his usual process of inspecting me for bedsores. So far I'd been lucky. Must have been the rubbing alcohol the nurses continually doused me with.

"Sure, we can go for a --float." I shrugged, admiring the energy I felt coming off this girl.

"Cool." Beth smiled and I felt a hundred times older than the eight years that separated us. She had a fresh-faced quality, not a line or crinkle on her perfectly smooth face and I thought of my sister Danielle, while at the same time pitying Beth, that she should end up in the same place as me.

"How long you been sleepin'?" she asked, as we floated out of the room and down the corridor to the front doors. We were like old pals and we'd barely said two words to each other.

I sighed. "Twenty-six human days and counting. You?"

"Five months. I haven't been able to make up my mind but I think I've reached a decision now. I don't think my family really needs me anymore. Like they ever did." She shook her head despairingly. "I'm more of a burden to them now than anything, you know?" We reached the outside. "Wanna sit on the front steps and watch the visitors go in?"

"Sure." Three people passed through us, one a large man who was hungry for a taco, and I cringed.

"I hate that," I told Beth, after the people had entered the building. "Usually I stick to floating along the ceiling just to avoid that awful feeling of people going through you as if you don't exist."

"To them we don't," Beth replied, sagely. "I kinda like it though. They go through and for a second I remember what it's like to be real. I like the vibes; though taco man I could have done without. Dora talks a lot about vibes. She's the one who told me I should come talk to you."

I watched the wind whip through the short blades of grass on the front lawn, calling them to attention like a general.

"I don't know a Dora," I said. "What does she look like?"

Beth scratched her arm. "Short with really round blue eyes and crow's feet. She looks like my aunt Beth --my namesake. Or am I hers? Whatever."

Another gust of wind blew through the tiny garden along the base of the building, knocking the head off a pink tulip. It fell at my feet. "Doesn't ring a bell," I said, noting the way the leaves of the flower head fluttered in the wind like a grounded butterfly. I sighed.

"Oh." Beth smacked her forehead with her palm and I

could swear it made a sound. "Quin. Dora says you'd know her as Quin. Even shape shifted into him so I could see, and let me tell you, that man is fucking hot."

My mind drew a picture of Quin's exotic face and I laughed. We'd talked several times and I still wasn't sure I liked him, but he seemed honest. "I'm sure he'd love to hear that," I said. "I suspect he has a giant ego for a spirit."

"You know who else is really hot?" Beth went on as if I hadn't spoken. "Your husband."

"Ken?"

"Do you have another? Seriously though, when I first came here, after I swallowed all those pills, you know? Well, they put me in with this little ten-year-old with a broken leg, God knows why, as if she'd want to share her room with a suicide case. Anyway, she was there for three days and your husband came everyday to check on her, and I'd think, damn that guy is hot. Dora told me to leave him alone because eventually I'd meet his wife and then I'd feel guilty about wanting to screw him." Beth shrugged. I was stunned by her candor. "Not like I could have anyway. I mean, *hello*, I'm dead here. Or close enough, anyway."

She fiddled with her barrette again and my eye caught the two long scars along her wrists. Apparently, the pills hadn't been Beth's first attempt at suicide and I wondered what could hurt her so much that she would be so desperate to die. Especially considering that she seemed so full of life. I didn't ask, assuming she would volunteer the information if she wanted me to know. Until then, it was none of my business.

"Do you think you'll go, Meagan?" she asked, flitting around the passersby like a bee that didn't know which one to sting. "I probably will. I've never had many friends so maybe I'll meet some there. Sure beats this shithole planet, you know?"

I crossed my legs under me, wondering why I did such things, why people like Beth and I adopted any mannerisms at all because they weren't real, only more illusion. "I don't know," I said. "I kind of like it here."

"But the Realm," Beth gushed, "is incredible."

"Yes," I agreed. "But there's some incredible stuff here too."

"Like?"

"Mostly the material, I suppose." I wasn't the slightest bit offended that she'd wanted to sleep with my husband, I realized. Who wouldn't? Besides, I liked Beth. She reminded me of what it felt like to be young. Then I remembered that I was never young, even when I was. I was always a worrier, always a worker from the day I turned eighteen and realized life was not going to hand me anything.

"*Material*," Beth encouraged when my words fell short.

"Right." I waved away the sudden sullenness that filled my head. "Money, cars, travel, family, sex."

"Yeah." Beth nodded agreeably. "Sex I'll miss. I wonder if there's some sort of astral equivalent for that. Invisible dildos or something."

I laughed. There was nothing I admired more than a straight-talker and Beth was certainly that.

"Look," she said suddenly, pointing across the narrow walkway leading to the building. "Here comes your lover."

"My what?" Peering in the direction of Beth's pointed finger I saw Amber coming up the path, little blue notebook in hand.

"No wonder you don't want to leave," Beth said, rolling her eyes at me as Amber approached. "A husband who looks like a Calvin Klein underwear model and a girlfriend who looks like *that*! Geez, if I were you I couldn't wait to get back to screwing them either."

The girl was over-sexed. Amber reached the bottom step and stopped to tie her always dangling bootlace, her hair falling forward in her face.

"Hang on, Beth," I said, watching Amber loop the string around her finger before pulling it through the other side. "You've got it wrong. I haven't been doing anything with Amber. I've barely been doing anything with my husband."

"Why not?" Beth joked. "Holding out for God?"

"It's a long, complicated story."

"Well don't bother telling it," Beth said. She hovered around Amber, stepped through her, and shuddered with pleasure. "Mmm, nice energy." I cringed. She made me think of a vampire sucking up Amber's vitality like blood.

When she stepped through her again with another small shudder of pleasure, my voice turned to ice. "Stop that."

"Why? She can't feel me."

"I don't care, you're violating her. I've never even passed through her. It's like stealing."

"*Stealing!*" Beth shot me a disapproving look, like I didn't know what I was missing.

"Listen," I said. "I want to tell you--"

She held up her hand. "I know. Dora told me everything about you. Car accident. Dead baby." Again I cringed. "A husband and an ex-girlfriend, each of whom want you. I just wanna know which one you're gonna go back to. The chick, right?" I didn't answer. "Yep," Beth said knowingly. "It's gonna be the chick."

Amber stepped into the building and Beth and I rose to follow. She walked fast and it was a bit of an effort to keep up with her.

"They're gonna run into each other you know," Beth said as we floated down the corridor behind Amber.

"Who is?" Amber wasn't watching where she was going.

"Duh. Your yummy husband and your dish on the side."

"I told you--"

"Yeah, you're not screwing her. So what? You wanna be and that's adultery of the heart. You don't have to actually cheat to be cheating, you know?"

I wish she'd give it up with the '*you knows*', but I *did* know, all too well. And just as Beth predicted Amber and Ken slammed into each other directly in front of my room like a hallway train wreck, scattering papers and Ken's clipboard across the floor.

"I'm sorry, Ken," Amber said, helping him retrieve the fallen objects.

He took them from her hands without looking at her. "No big deal. I was just leaving anyway." He glanced at her then looked away. "There's been no change."

"Wow," Beth said. "They're pretty stiff, huh? Like they don't know how to talk to each other but think they should. Yum and Yummier. You really have it made, don't you?"

  If only you knew, I thought. On the outside I guessed my situation might have looked pretty good, if you were the sort of person who believed you should have your cake and eat it too. But the problem with that was it was all icing, no substance. If one could enjoy such a situation it would be purely on a superficial level and that wasn't for me. I didn't want a doughnut hole; I wanted the entire doughnut. I wanted to be full.

  Ken headed down the hall and Amber stepped into the room, immediately pulling her favorite chair from the wall. She looked at my face and frowned.

  "Watch this," I said, nudging Beth. I knew exactly what Amber would do next. "This is so funny."

  "What is?"

  "In three seconds she's gonna go and grab a clean washcloth from the bathroom and wash that ridiculous makeup off my face. My mother puts it on me and Amber hates it. Probably because she knows I would never wear reds and pinks. She's gonna curse, then she'll wash it off." The makeup on my face made me laugh. I looked like a dead hooker. "Look at how silly I am," I told Beth. "You'd think your own mother would know you prefer earth tones to streetwalker reds."

  Amber went into the bathroom and Beth and I broke out laughing when she returned with a damp cloth muttering, "Goddamn, Joan," as she wiped the goo from my face. "Why does she do this to you?" Amber took care of me like we'd never broken up.

  "Aw," Beth said. "That's so sweet. All my visitors do is watch TV. You should come over and check them out sometime. A bunch of buck-toothed people with stiff red hair, watching something queer like *Friends* or some shit."

  "I like *Friends*," I said, laughing.

  Beth looked at me like I was the biggest loser in the world. "I'll disregard that last comment," she said, "'cause I like you."

  "Okay."

  Amber was back to scribbling in her notebook and Beth's eyes followed mine as I stared at her. Few things mattered when she was around and I realized I had the perfect psychological makeup to be a stalker.

"Well," Beth said, "I'm gonna float off now and leave you two lovebirds alone. I just thought we should meet, you know, in case we end up somewhere together. Now that I've met you though I doubt that will be happening. You may not know what you're going to do yet, but I do."

I squeezed her hand. "I guess you're pretty positive about what you want so I won't try to persuade you otherwise. If we don't meet again I just want to say it's been --an experience."

Beth laughed. "Yeah, meeting me is always an experience. Do me a favor, though?"

"What's that?"

"If you do decide to go back, sleep with that yummy husband of yours one last time. Consider it a personal favor."

I laughed. "We'll see."

"Aw, you're not gonna do it. You're going after the chick and we both know it." Beth pulled me into a hug. "Okay, the Realm awaits. A few goodbyes and I guess I'm outta here. See ya around, Meagan." She glanced at Amber. "Maybe not." And with a wry laugh, Beth floated out the door.

It didn't really sadden me that Beth had chosen death. For her, perhaps the Realm was the better of the two worlds. I only wished her time on earth could have been more fulfilling. She was just a child, I thought, and realized I had more blessings than I'd ever dreamed.

There were others in the hospital. I didn't know why I hadn't come across them sooner but after Beth, discarnate spirits began arriving one after another from their various rooms around the building. Beth, it seemed, had opened some sort of door for them, and they popped into my room whenever they felt like it, encouraging me to visit them in turn. Strange, but I grew to know each of them in ways that never would have been possible had we been conscious for it was unlikely I'd ever run across such a varied group of individuals in my regular life.

Mrs. Marten from ICU was the first to come after Beth. She'd survived two heart attacks, and now on her third, was scheduled for a double bypass within the next few days.

Then there was Todd Garrison, a thirty-seven-year-old biker with hair down his back and cold grey eyes that contradicted the gentle manner in which he spoke. He had driven his Harley Davidson into a parked car (an even dumber move than my yellow light incident) and now lingered at death's door with four cracked ribs and severe swelling of the brain.

Jacob Ebstein, nine years old, and by far my favorite. He was burned in a fire that destroyed his home after his cousin Benjamin convinced him to take up smoking in his bedroom closet. Jacob was going back. If only to beat the crap out of Benjamin.

Linda Hespeler. Thirty-two-year-old mother of three. Cancer. She was moving upward.

Carlo DeAngelo. Thick Italian accent. Seventy-two. Second stroke in eight months. Also moving upward.

Winston Bradley. Forty-one-year-old millionaire. Pretentious. Injured in a boating accident while sailing a tour of the world race. He was going home to his wife, his mistress, and his piles of money.

Everyone knew where they were going except Todd, Mrs. Marten and me. Todd had a pregnant girlfriend, a pierced and tattooed beauty name Jade who came daily, spilling her salty tears on his bed sheets and wondering out loud how she would raise their child alone. It broke Todd's heart. Mrs. Marten had little family-- a couple of dogs-- but a true zest for life. She was an active member on several charity boards and believed her purpose in life was to help others. She wasn't sure she had finished the job.

Suddenly the hospital was like a party for the undead dead and their guides. We walked, laughed, spied on each other's families when they came to visit, and all around reveled in our limbo until one by one people began deciding.

Winston was the first, telling Quin whom he had shared with Beth, that it wasn't his time yet and he wanted to go home. Quin nodded and we waved Winston goodbye with whispers of how he wasn't kind enough to inhabit the Realm anyway. Victor gave me hell for it. "You are no one's judge, Meagan," he scolded, while the others giggled behind their hands, grateful their guides hadn't been around to hear what they'd been saying.

Jacob followed Winston and I held him close as if he were my Zoe. "We probably won't remember each other if I go back too, Jacob," I said, holding back the urge to cry my invisible tears. "But I want you to know you've been very important to me."

Jacob gave me an extra squeeze and kissed my cheek. "You too, Meagan," he said. "You've been like my Mom in this place." My heart swelled. I had only known him a week but a week was the equivalent of a lifetime in the Realm.

One by one they left for their various destinations until the only ones left were Mrs. Marten, Todd, me, and our guides. We made a friendly but indecisive group. Victor had said we could help each other, that in fact that was the point of meeting, so I grabbed the opportunity and told Todd I thought he should go back.

"You have a girlfriend who loves you," I said, "and a chance to raise your baby. I don't have that chance anymore so I know how important it is. I think you should take it."

"What about you?" Todd asked, his steely gray eyes meeting mine as we sat in the waiting room like visitors.

"I don't know."

Mrs. Marten came barging into the room like a wildly excited spirit. "Meagan," she said, winded as if she even had breath to begin with, "you have to see this."

Todd and I exchanged a look. "See what?"

"What's going on in your room."

Sometimes we took turns watching over each other's families and her words alarmed me. Todd and I rose to follow her down the corridor. "They've been fighting," she said.

"Who?"

"Everyone. Your mother, Ken, Amber. Even the strange one with the incense and crystals."

"*Jenna was fighting?*" I couldn't believe my ears. Eight years I had known her and I'd never seen her argue with anyone. "Jenna," I said again. "You're sure?"

"Oh yes." Mrs. Marten's head bounced up and down like a basketball. "She was the worst one, telling your mother off and calling her a controlling bitch."

"No way!" I was stunned. The thought of Jenna cursing at anyone, let alone my mother, made me howl with laughter. Todd grinned like a giant devil and we floated into the room behind Mrs. Marten and directly into the battlefield.

"Jenna Summers," my mother huffed, "how dare you speak to me like that!" She was pacing back and forth and I suddenly realized where I'd learned the habit.

"I'm sorry Joan," Jenna responded, "but you should have more respect for Meagan than that. Why are you always trying to drive away the people she loves? She needs them here. You tell me to go home and put Sammy down for a nap. You tell Ken to go back to work, Danielle and Josh to stay away." That was news to me. "Now you're all flipped out about a ring you haven't even given a second thought to in seventeen years."

A ring? Amber sat quietly on the side of my bed and I moved beside her, peering at her neck. Gran's ring was gone from her chain.

"Shit," I said to Todd. "My mother took the ring from her."

"Not exactly," Mrs. Marten said smiling from beside my sleeping form. "Look." She indicated my left hand and there on the middle finger sat the silver moonstone, pressed obscenely against my wedding rings.

"That's what they've been fighting about," Mrs. Marten whispered. "Your mother came in and saw Amber slipping it on your finger. 'Where did you get that?' she demanded, but Amber ignored her and only pleaded with you to remember its symbolism, something about giving it to the one she loved."

I smiled. So Amber thought the ring was to be Sleeping Beauty's kiss of life? Her hand rested beside mine and I wished with all my might that I could touch it. The index finger moved.

"Hey!" I shouted. "Did you see that?"

"You moved your finger!" Todd exclaimed.

"Try again," Mrs. Marten encouraged.

Closing my eyes, I focused all my energies on moving my hand while the chaos continued around us. Nothing. I tried again. And again. I continued to try until I felt depleted and defeated.

"Maybe it was a muscle spasm," Todd offered sympathetically. The two seemed sad for me.

I nodded. "Yeah, I guess it must have been." I was disheartened but I was sure I'd made it move the first time and was determined to keep trying until I did it again. The fighter in me reemerged and I knew once that happened I would never give up.

"Take that ring off her finger," my mother demanded, for I had once been foolish enough to tell her a bit about the ring's meaning.

Amber shook her head. "I can't. It belongs to Meagan now and only she can remove it." God, she was brave.

"That's ridiculous!"

"But tradition, Joan," Jenna stressed, avoiding looking at Ken. Her mind said she didn't want to pick sides but had already chosen Amber's. "*Your* mother's tradition."

"I don't give a damn. Ken, do something."

My husband glanced at me then stared down at his feet. "No," he said quietly. "It's not my place." His eyes stayed on my face as he moved to the bed, slipped my wedding rings off my finger and squeezed them in his fist before placing them on the nightstand.

His eyes met Amber's and they seemed to say, "You win". He bowed his head and left the room. Only the moonstone remained on my finger now and Amber smiled down at it.

"You people are all insane," my mother huffed, then stalked from the room, no doubt in an effort to find my husband and chastise him for letting me go.

Jenna turned to Amber. "Now what?"

Amber shrugged. "Now I wait. I've given her back the ring, she knows what it means, so I wait, and pray she'll come back to me."

"That's it," Todd said, placing his hand on his hips. "If I have to go back, so do you. How could you not after this?"

"He's right," Mrs. Marten agreed. "I don't go in for this lesbianism stuff." Todd and I exchanged a look and laughed. "But anyone who loves that deeply deserves to be loved in return. Go back, Meagan, if only to tell her that her love has not been in vain."

The moonstone sparkled around my finger, the silver part of it glinting in the light, and I felt very close to reaching a decision. The time was almost at hand.

I took another few days of deliberating. One couldn't be too careful when deciding one's fate, especially when the decision was a matter of life and death.

Death was an appealing option, I'd give it that much. It was peaceful and seductive, a place where eternity stretched out before me like a wish I had once dreamed up before I learned how to survive. I had never been afraid of my own mortality. I had no illusions that I would live forever and death was just the beginning of a different journey, another spoke on the wheel of life. Dying didn't bother me; dying the wrong way did. Dying before I had had the chance to correct my mistakes, make amends with those my actions on earth affected, spread my love-- these were the reason my decision was such a hard one to make. I didn't think I could peacefully move upward without first getting the forgiveness I believed I needed.

Not that I had been such a horrible person ---just confused. Unsettled. But that can hurt people worse than any intended malice because no matter how badly they'd like to blame you, they feel they can't. You just didn't know any better. It was a convenient excuse I was tired of using.

For three days I journeyed the Realm on my own, thinking, weighing the pros and cons and feeling like Justice with the blindfold on her eyes and the uneven scales in her hand. Could I ever balance them? I had turned twenty-eight while I slept and wondered how I could have done so much, and yet, so little in my life. I had traveled the world, true, lived in another country; turned a little known magazine into an international success; married; almost had a baby, but what had I done of value? Whose life had I touched so profoundly that they were a better person simply for having known me? Everything I'd ever given had been on a superficial level. I gave money to charities instead of my precious time. Bought lavish Christmas presents for my family instead of telling them I loved them. Gave my husband my body instead of my heart, and then, when I could no longer do that, a divorce request.

To Amber I gave empty words, for even though my words were true there had been no action behind them. It was easy to tell someone you loved them; much harder to prove it, and I realized that I had proven nothing. I had lived my life in the shallowest way without ever knowing I was doing so because I wasn't living *consciously*. My life had been a fog of ambition and material success. I was no better than Winston the snob, except that I wanted to be. The question was: Could I be? Ironically, it was in the unconscious that I was learning how to be conscious, but could I carry this new knowledge with me?

On what would have been a third evening on the earth plane, I went back to the Summerlands, taking up position on my favorite log, and called out to Victor. Of all the places within the Realm, I would miss the Summerlands most.

Victor appeared beside me as if he had been there the whole time. "I see you've reached your decision, Meagan," he said. I nodded and he asked, "Are you sure this is what you want?"

"Yes, Victor. I love the Realm and those I've met here but it isn't my time yet. I've been doing a lot of thinking and I've realized that eternity is exactly that, forever. To me that means I will without question return here someday, so let it be forever *then*. I have only so many years on the earth plane and much to do. I want to make a difference before I come back here. I want to know that I have done my best down there so that when I return it will be with a clear conscience and a light heart."

Victor patted my knees affectionately. "A wise choice."

I looked at him strangely. "You mean you didn't want me here? I thought it was your job to convince me to stay."

"No," he laughed. "You don't understand the meaning of *guide,* do you? It means only that I show you. The rest is, and always was, up to you. Truthfully, I'm surprised it took you as long as it did to decide. You have much to live for, Meagan. And you're right; when you come back we'll all still be here. Well, I will be anyway. I'm through reincarnating. For me, the earth plane holds little of worth, for you, it is everything."

I grinned, remembering home. "Yes, I suppose it is. I'll miss you Victor." I felt like Dorothy kissing the Scarecrow goodbye.

Victor shrugged. "We'll meet again." And I rose to my feet, taking one last glance around my forest.

"Any parting words for me?" I joked. The Tin man had said, *Now I know I have a heart because it's breaking.*

Again Victor threw back his head and laughed. "Is that what I am to you, Meagan, a character in Oz? I suppose I should be thankful you didn't make me Glinda the Good Witch."

"Are those your parting words?" I asked.

Victor's ethereal face grew serious. "No."

"What then?" I asked impatiently. I'd made my decision and now I was itching to go.

Victor took my hand in his. "The path isn't going to be easy, Meagan," he said. "There will be challenges. You can handle them but you may find it difficult."

I shrugged. "Okay."

Victor's eyes widened. "Don't you want to know what they are?"

"No. I've made my decision and knowing what I'm up against might make me change my mind. I don't want to know the future Victor; that only takes the fun out of the present. I've spent the better part of my life preparing for what may happen tomorrow. This time, I'm only going to live for today. I've seen death and it's welcoming. Why worry about anything else?"

Victor smiled encouragingly. "Very well. Shall we go then?"

"Definitely."

The heavens began disappearing behind me, drifting away like clouds on a sunny afternoon. I struggled to take a small piece of it with me as I sank, tried to press a tiny bit of euphoria into my heart, but it eluded my fragile grasp. And I floated.

Down.

Down.

Until my mind stretched open and I could feel the rhythmic breathing of the body on the bed.

Inside it.

Easily, I had come back into it, the rib cage expanding as if making room for the sudden presence of my soul. The body swelling, taking me in. Welcoming me back like an estranged lover after months of sleeping alone in an empty bed.

A finger moved. A spasm in the hand. I felt it jerk upward, as if yanked by an invisible string, then fall back against the mattress with a soundless tap. Something different about the hand. Something missing and something else added.

Sound came next. The senses slowly coming back to my consciousness one at a time. Taste of medicine. Smell of familiar perfume. Another presence in the room. Someone breathing other than me. I could hear the air filtering in and out of the lungs like a whisper. A shuffling sound, like the pages of a worn novel blowing in the wind. A frustrated sigh and then the crinkling sound of a mistake being crumpled and tossed into the waste paper basket beside my bed. I smiled and struggled to open eyes that seemed weighted down by iron lids. Someone had sealed them shut with superglue. A frown creased my forehead. *Open*, I commanded, and the eyelashes fluttered once then separated, giving me a hazy view of the spinning room. I thought I had the worst hangover of my life.

Images came into blurry focus. A chair by the bed. Empty. A nightstand beside me with a half-eaten muffin on a plate and an unused fork. There was a jacket tossed over the metal foot board at the bottom of the bed; black leather, fashionably creased; familiar.

I tilted my head to the left. A woman at the window, turned away from me. Blond. Thin. If she shifted toward me I would see the sad green eyes and the thick black lashes. The heart-shaped lips with the perfectly straight toothpaste-ad teeth behind them. She stared out the window like a lonely child on a rainy day. Again I smiled. I sighed but she didn't hear it, probably didn't expect to hear it, and I turned my head even farther, pressing my cheek against the pillow to get a better look. There was only one way to get her attention but I hastened to scare her. How long had it been since I'd spoken, I wondered. Would my voice even work? Her hands pressed against the glass like she would push her way through it. I had to speak.

My throat felt like a dry canal. "What's the weather like?" I asked in a hoarse whisper. It hurt like hell.

Amber's back stiffened. "Meagan?" She whirled around so quickly I thought she would faint.

"Careful," I said hoarsely, as her hand groped the window sill in an effort to steady herself. I thought I sounded like Janis Joplin after a week of boozing --raspy and confused.

"*You're awake*," she cried, darting for the bed and nearly tripping over her own feet and the always-dangling bootlace. Brushing the bangs from my eyes she attacked my face with kisses. "I knew you'd wake up. I knew it!" Frantically, she stabbed the call button pinned to my sheets.

"Amber." God, it hurt to speak.

She was jumping up and down beside me, sobbing fat tears of joy. "Ken's down the hall," she rambled excitedly as the ancient call light above the door to my room flashed a blinking red shadow on the dark corridor floor outside. "I'll go get him. I'll--"

I grabbed her wrist with no more strength than a sickly infant. "Wait --I have to tell you first." Each word was like sandpaper rubbing against my larynx. "The accident--"

Amber smiled down at me. "I know, Meagan."

"No." I tried to squeeze her wrist but my grip refused to tighten. I had to tell her now, before anyone came in. Something was hurting my hand, poking me. An IV. I yanked it out.

"No, don't do that," Amber said nervously, her eyes casting a fearful glance at the empty doorway. The tape ripped away from the top of my hand and the needle fell to the mattress. Amber looked down at it like I had torn out my life supply. Perhaps I had. I didn't know. "Jesus," she said. "Where's the nurse?"

I ignored her worry. "Listen to me," I said, my voice coming in a bit stronger. "I wouldn't die. I refused because I had to tell you."

Amber looked at me like I wasn't making much sense. "Honey, I know," she said, her tone a worried strain. "Please, let me get Ken. We can talk later, after he's checked you out."

I groaned in frustration.

Amber panicked. "What? What is it?" Again she stabbed the call button.

My head rolled on the pillow. "You're making me -- crazy already. I love you, okay?" I saw her smile as an ache pressed into my forehead and I ground my palm against it, trying to focus my thoughts. "I always have. Coming to tell you. No air. Do you understand? And the party --for Sammy. Kissing Gwynne and I couldn't --I couldn't *breathe*."

Amber looked like she might cry. "Meagan, it's okay."

"No. It was never --okay. Not without you. And then the pond. And to build up the nerve to change it --and to tell you. And I was coming that night --to tell you. And something else. A very important question for you. And then the truck--" Another thought occurred to me. "The driver --is he okay?"

Amber's lips tightened. "Not a scratch."

"Good," I whispered. "That's good. So if I die now, it's okay. I told you. I --I just had to come back to tell you."

I closed my eyes and she shook me. "No, Meagan. You're not dying."

"It's okay," I muttered. "It's okay because I finally told you. I don't mind so much now. The first time --it was bad. The dying --it was hard." I opened my eyes, somewhat surprised to find that I was still in the room with her. "I am alive, right?"

Amber brushed her fingers through my hair. "Yes honey, you're alive."

"And you're not fake again?"

"Excuse me?"

I swallowed the lump that formed in my throat. "In the forest --you weren't real. Someone tricking me. You came and said you were dead and it was --*horrible!*" Tears sprang from my eyes and she pulled me into her arms. "It was horrible because you were dead!"

"It's okay. It's okay, Meagan. We're both very much alive."

She eased me back against the pillows just as Ken came rushing through the door, followed by two nurses. He raced to the side of the bed as Amber squealed, "She woke up, Ken. A few minutes ago. She's not making much sense, but she keeps talking and I've been pressing the call button and I could hear it buzzing down at the nurses' station but no one was coming. I wanted to come get you but I didn't want to leave her alone." Her eyes followed Ken's to the dangling tube at my side. "She ripped it out," she said quickly, as if she was sure she'd be blamed for this. "I think it was hurting her."

My husband shone his little white flashlight in my eyes, stinging them. "How do you feel, honey?" he asked kindly, while one of the nurses moved to re-attach the dangling IV. "Can you talk?"

Everyone's honey, I thought bitterly, and yanked my bruised hand from the nurse's grasp.

"Mrs. Summers we have to--"

"No. I don't want it."

Ken shook his head at the nurse. "It's okay, Hilda."

My mouth produced the tiniest bit of saliva and I swallowed it, wincing at the pain. "Could I have some tea?" I asked. "My throat really...hurts." It was getting easier to speak, but no less painful.

Lovingly, my husband tucked a wisp of hair behind my ear. "Ice chips, sweetie. We'll start you out on that, okay?" He was surprisingly calm for a man whose wife had just come out of a coma. Amber only stared and I thought Ken's peculiar reaction might have something to do with her. Had they discussed what Ken and I had been fighting about the day before the accident? If I learned anything while I was sleeping, I was drawing a blank.

A neurosurgeon. The thought came to me quickly and though I didn't know what it meant I burst into tears, startling both Amber and Ken, who grabbed my hands.

"He took our Zoe," I cried, feeling an unbearable shame in my heart. I wasn't sure what I was talking about, but Ken's face clouded over and the tears spilled down my cheeks. "I tried to go after him, I swear, but I couldn't stretch up that high. There was a block up there and he wouldn't let me through. The sky was all pink and I think it was raining, or maybe I was crying--" The words were coming out of me like shards of glass. "And I screamed at him to give her back but he wouldn't listen. I kept screaming but the man only smiled at me as he led her away. He was so beautiful. I wanted to go with them but the paramedics wouldn't let me. They were pounding on my chest and every pound pulled me down from the sky. They wouldn't stop. Wouldn't let me go to her."

Ken pulled me to him and I sobbed into his chest. "He took our baby. Oh God, why did he take our baby?"

"It's okay, honey," Ken soothed, his voice hoarse as he battled the sob that threatened to erupt in his throat. "We lost her." He rocked me back and forth in his arms. "She died, honey. I'm sorry. She died."

It seemed everyone in the room was crying now, even the nurses who witnessed death on a daily basis. Ken held me until my tears subsided, then lifted my chin and said, "I'm going to call your family, okay sweetie?" Amber's face was buried in her hands and Ken wiped the tears from my cheeks. "They need to know you've awakened." He kissed my cheek and the two nurses followed him out the door. I listened to their footsteps getting quieter as they moved down the corridor away from my room.

Amber sat on the side of my bed, silent.

"How long have I been out?" I asked, knowing she'd give me the truth.

Her eyes looked away. "A month."

"*A --month?*" It seemed impossible that someone could sleep that long but I knew comas could sometimes go on indefinitely. I'd been lucky, I supposed. I thought of Zoe then pushed away the image before it could make me cry again. Amber hadn't known about Zoe, I realized, unless someone had told her. I peered up at her through half-closed eyes. "You come every day, don't you?" I asked, taking in as much of her as my eyes would allow.

"Yes."

My stare fell to her neck and the chain that dangled from around it, weighted by a pendant instead of a ring. My heart broke. I had come back too late.

"What's wrong?" Amber asked, noticing my pained expression. "Does something hurt?"

Yes, I thought, *something hurts horribly.* And within seconds I was back to my old accusing self.

"Why are you here, Amber?" I demanded. Back from the dead and I handled pain in the same angry way.

"I --What do you mean?"

"I mean, what are you doing coming here every day when you've obviously given my grandmother's moonstone to Gwynne? Don't you know what that means?" I couldn't hide the hurt in my voice.

Amber laughed. "When I what?"

Did she think I was stupid? "I'm not blind, Amber," I hissed. "I can see that it's gone from your chain." I was getting stronger by the minute, or perhaps just angrier. "You gave the ring to Gwynne. Good. Fine. You did what you were supposed to do. You gave it to the one you love."

"Yes, I did give it to the one I love," Amber said softly.

She was grinning at me. The look made me even more irate. "But you are a *little* blind, Meagan." She lifted my hand into view and my eyes widened in surprise. "Tradition," she said, twisting the ring around my finger. My wedding rings were gone and only the moonstone glinted in the light. "Slip it on the finger of the one you love and only she can break the bond by removing it. Isn't that right?"

I nodded dumbly. "Are you sure Amber? Because once it begins there's no going back. I've already decided that. I'm not afraid anymore. The night of the accident I was --"

"Shh". She pressed her fingers to my lips. "Save your voice. I can see that every word hurts and you don't have to explain anything right now." She gave a sly grin. "I'll hit you with all that later."

I grinned back, grateful I didn't have to continue because I wasn't sure how much more talking my throat could handle. Only one matter remained.

"Gwynne?" I muttered.

Amber kissed my hand. "Long gone. Don't you know, Meagan? I've been waiting for you."

It was all I needed to hear.

Printed in Great Britain
by Amazon

20386351R00243